The Fated King
&
The Realm of Old

TO Judy

The Fated King

&

The Realm of Old

S. S. Snodgrass

gatekeeper press™

Columbus, Ohio

Published by Gatekeeper Press

Edited by Cassandra Byelene

Produced with the following font types:
Adobe Caslon Pro
Fertigo Pro Script
Kunstler Script

The editorial work for this book was overseen by Cassandra Byelene. Gatekeeper Press did not participate in and is not responsible for any aspect of its elements.

Library of Congress Control Number: 2020952327

ISBN (hardcover): 9781662908477
ISBN (paperback): 9781662908484
eISBN: 9781662908491

A special thank you to Olesya from OGsquad for the handmade crown used on the cover photo. A stylish crown fit for a king!

The sword used on the cover is © of iStock.

Dedicated to my mother.
A woman of many virtues.

Contents

Troublesome Times

The crack of a whip cast a shadow of terror over those who had gathered before their king in the midday sun. Cadoc cared not that it was winter as he watched his guards drag people from their homes. The soldiers tossed them into the cold snow before the King of Remette. All of the subjects who had been thrown before him bowed in fearful respect to their tyrant king. Glaring at them, Cadoc kept a snarl on his lips.

King Cadoc was a stout man; he being one of the few in his kingdom to have food in plenty. His cheeks held a red tint of fury which seemed never to leave his soul. The king clutched so angrily to the arms of his chair that the whites of his knuckles shone through his flabby skin. The only calm thing about his appearance was his well-combed hair which held flakes of gray within the predominant brown. His dark brown eyes were empty and heartless.

To his right sat a much smaller, second throne. Inside it his son, Prince Carter, twitched nervously. He looked much like his father in regard to the same deep tan that set to his skin and his hair of a matching color brown. However, Carter's eyes seemed to hold a softness that was not present in his father. The only other difference between the two was the round bulge that protruded from under the king's ribcage. The young prince was not plump, but rather in superb physical condition. He had the ability to appear even more imposing than his father, but he seemed too preoccupied with his fingernails as he chewed anxiously on them. To those who did not know him, it would seem that the prince was a mere recreation of his father. This could not be further from the truth. While Cadoc's entirety had been set to anger, Carter was set to kindness.

Both of the royals were dressed in majestic garments which bore the Remettian kingdom's colors of scarlet and gold. Their brows were crested with golden crowns that were encased with diamonds and rubies. Around the platform where they sat was an evenly placed arrangement of sixty-two guards. All those present in the garrison also bore the scarlet colors to signify their allegiance. Two of the soldiers stood on the platform; one on each side of the royal household. Twenty guardsmen were stationed behind the platform. Ten more aligned themselves across the road to the left side of the gathered peasants, and likewise stood ten on the right side of the crowd. The remaining twenty faced their king from behind the cowering people. As was the design of this arrangement, all who were present were trapped inside an impenetrable wall of soldiers. The serfs who had gathered shook in fear as they shot quick glances up at the man whom they knew to be the designer of their temporary prison, the king's personal advisor.

To the king's left stood the figure of a man who towered over even the height of the thrones. The man was not only tall, but strong. Much to many a young maiden's delight, Sir Roland the Advisor's muscular outline could easily be seen through his tight-fitted shirt. His skin was paler than that of the king and his son. The advisor's hair was kept short and his face clean-shaven. Even so, waves, which had been combed into control, could be seen in his blonde hair. His cold, blue eyes seemed to pierce through the peasants of the crowd as he judged them. He stood out amongst the rest not only because of his massive physique, but also for his apparel. Sir Roland wore all black as opposed to the overly present scarlet. A silver crest of a shield with two axes and a longsword running through it was pinned to his chest. This, in itself, was a message. It was his crest from before he had been appointed as the king's advisor. His old sigil as the Lord of Morer.

Sir Roland had been well respected throughout the land due to his success in the last Great War, which had taken place some years ago between the countries of Remette and Poniere. The man personally butchered thousands of the enemy's soldiers. When the king realized his talent and bestowed upon him a personal squadron in his army, Roland defeated platoon after platoon of the Ponierian forces. He ruthlessly ripped apart towns, never ceasing in his efforts to destroy his enemy.

After the war had ended, Roland returned to his manor in Morer. The king found the way that the nobleman ran his estate extremely pleasing. At his son's suggestion, Cadoc took the war hero into his inner courts and Sir Roland instantly became his right-hand man. The people of Remette knew why King Cadoc had favored him so much. If the king were to request something of him, Roland never disobeyed. Should he be instructed to destroy this town, as he had those of Poniere, he would not hesitate to do so. For this reason, the people were more afraid of him than of their king. Cadoc may wish to hurt them, but it would be Roland who would inflict the punishment.

The king's voice interrupted the unnatural silence as he spoke out in a cold, gravelly voice, "There is no member of this town who is not indebted to me. There is also no member of this town who has paid those debts in full during this past collection season!"

The villagers shuddered under the accusation. They were unable to pay because the king had utterly pilfered their lands. Most of them were starving at that very minute. Still, none dared to look up from the ground, shivering more from fear than the cold. Seeing their understanding, Cadoc continued with an unyielding tone. "All those indebted shall receive a lash for each shekel owed to their king."

The crowd looked up in horror as the first seven men were dragged to the front of the crowd. Roland calmly unrolled the scroll he had been holding behind his back. In a clear voice that was deep and demanding he called out, one by one, the crimes of those before him. "Ian Muldrow of Krepthor, thirty-five shekels."

And so, the first man received thirty-five lashes. Screams came from him and the members of his family who were wrought with pain over his afflictions.

As the king's men tore into the backs of his people, steam could be seen rising in the cold air from their wounds. When each set of men had received their lashes, they were dragged to the side. They were left too weak to move on their own. Their blood stained the white of the snow, leaving a putrid smell clinging to the crisp winter air. In unison, the collectors then moved on to the next seven victims.

This vicious cycle lasted throughout most of the day. The king's men seemingly enjoying themselves as they beat those who had not paid their dues. Sir Roland continued on his list, never showing any concern for those who were being tortured. The king snarled unmercifully down at them. The people's suffering did not seem to lessen his anger for their lack of payment. To those of the crowd, there was an overwhelming fear that the beatings taking place would not be the last punishment they would receive.

The longer Carter was made to watch, the more distraught the young prince became. Still, Prince Carter tried to hold his composure. He knew what would happen to him should he humiliate his father in front of the people. It wasn't until an elderly man, who had been relentlessly coughing all day, was brought up for his beating that Carter could take no more. He leaned over to his father as Roland read the man's debt.

"Please, Father. I beg you. He is just an old man. He looks as if he should be bedridden! Can we not forgive him of one late payment?"

The king growled back to his son in spite. "If I forgive one, I must forgive them all. He is to be treated the same as the rest."

"Father, please!" Carter begged of him as the whip was raised. The prince clutched to the arms of his throne in worry.

The king gripped his son's arm, squeezing it tightly until he felt pain. Carter winced, but tried to hide it from the public. If he let them know what was happening, his father would only do worse. The king whispered angrily as the whip came down on the old man. "All day you have been an embarrassment to me. Your nervous actions cause the people to see your rebellion against me. But now, you would try to undermine my authority by pardoning this man's offense in front of all these people? That is unacceptable." Carter gulped as his father finished, "We will continue this conversation when we get home. As for now, try to stop acting like your foolish self and more like a son of mine. Look to Sir Roland as an example. Him, I am pleased with."

The king gave Carter what was most likely a grin as he reset his gaze on the peasants before him. The prince wanted to rub the pain from his arm, but did not dare to do so. Instead, he left it where it had been and sat back into his throne to watch the old man be dragged to the side. A young woman, Carter could only presume to be his granddaughter, ran to tend to him. After looking over him for a while, she let out a heartbroken cry. It seemed that the old man had succumbed to his wounds, dying for his crimes against the king.

Still smiling, Cadoc turned to his son to see his expression. Carter was unable to hide the sorrow on his face. Seeing his father's gaze, the prince turned away. He spent the rest of his time there looking into the trees of a nearby forest. How quickly would he need to run to reach them, he wondered? Carter sighed lightly to himself. He would never reach them. No matter what he attempted to do.

Carter's daydreams were broken apart as he heard Roland shout. "My king!"

"Oof," Carter groaned as his advisor landed heavily on top of him, covering the prince's body with his own. "What's going on?"

"Are you alright?" Roland quickly inspected both the prince and his father. King Cadoc now faced the opposite direction. A quivering arrow was stuck into the wood where the king's head had been only moments ago.

"Yes, we are fine," the king growled. "Why are you still here and not chasing down that archer?"

"I apologize, my liege," Roland bowed. "I motioned for some men to search them out. I had hoped to remain here with you and Prince Carter in case of another attack."

The king clenched his jaw as he nodded in approval. Why should he send away his best fighter if there was a chance that there were more hidden archers?

"Very well," he said grudgingly.

"Then," the advisor replied with conviction, "shall we continue? We are nearly through the list. I expect to be done before sunset."

Cadoc had always liked how Roland thought; it was so similar to the thoughts he held himself. "Proceed."

The team did so, never ceasing until the last score had been settled. By the end of the day, thirteen people had died either by the king's punishments or from the bitter touch of the cold. Much to their dismay, the soldiers Roland had sent out were unable to find the would-be assassin who had targeted the king. After giving them a harsh rebuking, Cadoc entered a tent his men had set up for him nearby. It was there he spoke to his advisor. "These townspeople had to have known who it was that took the shot, yet none have come forward. I will burn this entire town for their treachery!"

"Father," Carter chimed in with a strained voice, "you can't mean that! They were just beaten to please you and now you will kill them? Those people did not try to harm you. Why harm them more?"

The king gritted his teeth as he walked up to his son. Grabbing him by his shirt, he pulled Carter's face inches from his own. His breath stunk of spirits as he hissed. "Is this all you are capable of doing?"

Cadoc threw Carter forcefully onto the ground, the prince letting out a cough as his lungs started working again. "All day you have done nothing but disobey me! You are a worthless, insolent child! Why must I be cursed with an heir like you?"

"My liege," Roland spoke from behind him calmly, "I should like to continue our conversation of the town's judgment, if that is alright? I simply want to have everything in order before you return to the castle this evening."

"Why can't you be more like Roland?" The king raised a hand of praise to his advisor. "He sees the importance of what I do."

"Indeed, I do, my liege." Roland bowed. Not once did he look to the prince, who was now trying to lift himself from the ground. "However, I must say that I also believe this town should remain."

"Impossible!" the king spat.

"Though it is meager, the town of Krepthor does have potential in the future. Especially since the Luxborne provenance to the north is acquiring so much trade with the Ponierians these days. I expect that this town shall become exceedingly profitable within a year. In turn, the peasants will be able to pay their debts to you, my king. Just know, I will support you fully on whichever decision you make."

"I see your point," the king thought, "but what of this assassin?"

"I will change the guard schedules. The attacker must have learned our routes as the rotating forces were an equal distance away from the village at the time of the attack. Once we change our tactics, we will be able to find this traitor easily. You do not have any more gatherings planned outside your castle until the spring, so your safety will be solidified for now. However, if I may advise it-"

"No," chuckled Cadoc as he stopped the advisor's plea. "One personal guard is enough. I cannot walk five feet in the castle from passing one guard to finding another, let alone to have one with me at all times. I shall not add more!"

"It will be as you wish, my liege. I simply want to be thorough."

"You always are," Cadoc said to him. "Shall we set off then? Since we have nothing more to do here?"

"I will alert the guards, Your Highness." Roland bowed one last time as he exited the king's tent.

Carter dusted himself off as he prepared to go home. He smirked a little when he found that the elbow of his sleeve had ripped from the fall. At least he had an excuse to throw away this itchy garment! Thinking of home, he began to wonder. What danger awaited him there? His father had been quite angry with him today. The prince peeked at the king, who did nothing but glare at him. He was a dead man.

The pair of royals did not speak to one another the entire time that their advisor was gone. The tension in the air was so thick it seemed hard to breathe. Carter only found relief as Roland returned, pulling his father's attention away from him. "All is prepared, my king. You may set out forthwith."

"You say that as if you are not coming with us?" Cadoc questioned him.

"Perceptive as always, my liege." Roland bowed in respect. "I had hoped to go to Morer tonight. You see, after learning of this village's inability to pay their debts to you, I felt that I must check in on Morer's functionality. If such a thing were to happen in a town of mine, though I have been away, I would also feel the need to bear lashes. For it would be I who had failed you, my king."

"Your dedication pleases me," Cadoc replied. "I will allow this trip of yours. How long do you believe it will take?"

"Thank you, Your Highness." Roland bowed again. "It should not take long. I should return to the castle before sunset tomorrow. In the meantime, I have instructed the guards to display extra precaution to ensure that you arrive safely."

"Of course, you have." The king drew in a breath. "I shall see you tomorrow then, Advisor. Let us hope I do not have any questions while you are gone."

"My liege," Roland grinned, "I fear to say, you do not need me at all. Over these many years, you have ruled this kingdom supremely on your own."

The king put a hand on his advisor's shoulder, leaving the prince behind without a glance. "This is why I favor you, Roland."

"Thank you, my king." The advisor bowed one last time as Cadoc swiftly strode through the tent's opening. Once Cadoc had left to enter his carriage, Roland turned to his dear friend, the prince. He pulled up Carter's sleeve and found a large bruise where the king had gripped earlier. Although Roland served the king, his true loyalty lay with the prince. The tough exterior he usually displayed faltered at the sight of the wound. For the first time that day, Roland let his emotions show. Sorrow could be heard in his voice as he asked, "Carter, are you alright?"

"I would be better if I had some pie, but I'll survive," the prince shrugged. "Maybe I'll have some when I get home. Apple pie would be perfect. It'd have to be freshly baked though, so it's still warm."

Pausing for effect the prince jested, "It's a shame you won't be coming back with us. You know I'd do just about anything for you, but when it comes to pie it is every man for himself."

The advisor grinned. Carter was tilting his head to one side as he held back a smile of his own. Roland said to him, "Only you would think of food at a time like this."

"What else do I have to look forward to? My best friend is leaving me. I have to return home with Father alone. Undoubtedly, he is going to chastise me for what happened here today. All I have is that apple pie."

"You must understand why I'm not going with you. You saw what happened here today! These people are suffering and need attention. I fear more will die through the night. I must see to them, don't you agree?"

Carter nodded softly in approval. "You're right, but what of the assassin? Will he try to kill you if you remain here?"

"I am not staying here. I am going to Morer for supplies. Besides, I honestly doubt Jasper would try to harm either you or I."

"That was Jasper!" Carter exclaimed. "I haven't seen him in ages!"

9

"Nor have I," chuckled the advisor. "We've stayed too long in the palace, perhaps."

"Roland," Carter asked of him, "why didn't you let him take the shot?"

"It would not have ended well," his advisor chided. "There will be a better opportunity to overthrow the king in the future. One that provides time for ample planning and does not risk your safety. Now, please go. Your father will begin to wonder what you are doing."

The prince turned still as stone. "Is it bad that I don't want to go?"

"No," Roland sighed sorrowfully. "I can only hope that what you have already undergone was punishment enough in his eyes. My advice to you would be to head straight to your chambers when you get back. Do not let him get you alone until I return. Do you understand me?"

"Yes," Carter nodded in dedication to the plan. "I will hide in my room!"

"Best of luck, sire."

"I'll be needing it!" Carter let out a nervous chuckle as he exited the tent.

Roland scratched his head in irritation as he also left the seclusion of the tent. It had been set up not far from the town's outer housings. When the advisor emerged, he was caught by the eyes of injured and wrathful villagers. He felt torn in his heart but walked about carefree all the same. Should the king know he felt shame in his actions, he too would be punished.

Reaching a line of horses, Roland untied one near the end. It was a large steed, black in color. A white stripe could be seen running down its face under the light of the moon. He led the steed from where it had been, walking it down the bloodied road in the middle of the town. Patting the horse's nose, he spoke to it as if it were his best friend. "Well, Hymir, did you have a good day?"

The horse responded by pulling at his clothes with its lips. After letting out a small chuckle, the advisor reached into his saddlebag and pulled out a small, burlap sack. As he drew on the strings, three apples could be seen. The horse's ears perked up as it awaited a treat. His master held one up to its mouth. "Here you are."

Looking down at the other two, Roland thought of who might need them most. All in the village seemed just as needy, but there was one couple he felt the most compassion for. He had watched them return home after the husband's beating was over. The wife was pregnant and near birth. In the chill of the air, she seemed to suffer more than her husband. Her complexion showed the truth of her condition. Sir Roland had seen the look too often before in the gloom of battlefields. It was not death from a sword he had feared while he fought his enemy, but disease and starvation. One could tell weeks before a man would die that his time had come just by his physical state. This was the face she bore. Her skin was pale; her cheekbones could easily be seen. She looked like a hollow doll. The only healthy-looking part of her was her extended belly.

As he tied the sack to a hook near their door, the advisor felt a sense of dread. He would need to give special orders on their behalf. If she did not receive proper nourishment soon, she would not only lose her child but also her life. Letting out a soft sigh, Roland jumped onto his horse's back.

With a click of the advisor's teeth and a kick of his heel, the horse sped into the night. The two traveled quickly through the woods. Roland saw the flicker of a fire in the distance. To that fire, he set a course.

When he reached the camp that he had seen from afar, Roland skidded his horse to a stop. All fourteen who sat around the flames pulled out their swords to kill him. The advisor paid little mind to them as he dismounted, stating calmly, "How foolish must you be to build a fire which can be seen and followed from the town where you made an attempt on your king's life but hours ago?"

"How foolish would we be if we let ourselves die in this bleatin' cold!" snarled a man whose cheeks were as red as his hair from the chill of the night.

"Why didn't you let me kill him?" came a cold reply from a brown-haired man, his green eyes showing extreme frustration towards the advisor.

"Should I have let you?" Roland asked with matching anger in his words. "How many times must you go off on your own? Why do you never listen to me?"

"Perhaps I do not find you trustworthy!" Jasper raised his voice against the advisor. The others of the group watched quietly as the two faced one another. "You who says he is one of us but protects the king day in and day out. You who sends his guards to kill us! Over all these years you have told me that you want the king dethroned. Yet, every opportunity we get, you tell us not to take. When I have a perfect shot, you save his life!"

"It was not a perfect shot," Roland stated, his hand traveling through his hair in a slow, meditative way. His voice was calm and quiet, everything about his stance struck fear into the men in front of him. He meant what he was about to say. "Should you have achieved your goal the way you had hoped, Carter's life may have been lost. The king was conducting torture upon an entire town when you tried to strike against him!"

"All the more reason to take him out," Jasper spat through a clenched jaw.

"This is all the more proof that you do not listen to me," the advisor replied sharply in order to quiet his pupil. Closing his eyes momentarily, he explained why Jasper's actions were ill-fated to the prince and to their goals. "Should you have so swiftly defeated the king today, the people would have been encouraged to revolt while the royal household was shaken. Carter would have become their main target as he is heir to the throne of his father. All that stands between the people and their freedom are those of the royal family. You know that."

"You could have protected Carter from the peasants," Jasper shrugged. "They are half-dead already. They couldn't have harmed him if they tried."

"You lack foresight," Roland tutted. "I said the people want the royal family dead. The peasants were not the only people in that town today, and they were not the ones who would have tried to harm the prince. There were soldiers surrounding the prince that would have endangered his life had control shifted from he and his father. The only thing that stops the king's men from turning on him is their fear of him. What is there to fear in a carcass?"

Jasper's shoulders sunk. He kept his eyes towards his shoes, unable to respond to the reproach of the advisor.

"You see, that is the reason I do not follow along with these pitiful schemes of yours. You set only to accomplish a goal, never thinking of the consequences." Roland looked at them disappointedly as he crossed his arms, his voice remaining balanced in an eerie calm. "What is the point of killing the king if our beloved prince will not take his crown? Our actions should be to help Carter, not ourselves. So, you will wait until I say we move. We will do so in a way that pleases our true king, or do you not wish to serve him?"

"We serve Carter," Jasper said through gritted teeth.

"Good," Roland replied as he climbed back onto his horse. "Now, put that fire out and pack your gear. You may stay with me in Morer tonight. In fact, you may remain there until spring if you'd like. There will be no use for you to sleep outdoors until then. The king will not be taking any further action outside of the castle this winter."

Those of the group hurriedly packed their things. All of them were excited to once again sleep inside a warm room. Besides the king's castles, Morer was the best place in the entire kingdom to travel to. They could only assume the rooms would be magnificent.

As they were traveling, Jasper spoke. "We had planned to go to Poniere soon. There is talk of a gathering of nobles just across the border from Luxborne. The riches we could gain would be more than enough to pay off the debt of the town that was brutalized today."

"I'm sorry, my friend," Roland sighed. "I know you hate when I tell you not to act, but if you did this, your movements would be too easy to track. The attack on the Ponierians would be traced to Remettians, and we would be at war once again. Surely you see that?"

Jasper let out a huff as he yielded. "Yes, I suppose I do."

They rode in silence the rest of the way, other than a few sighs and grumbles from the ruffians. The men would have rather rested in the cold and completed the journey in the light, but Sir Roland would not stop. The group carried on through the never-ending darkness of the night for hours on end.

They had to move slowly due to their impaired vision and the power of the winds as they howled around them. Finally reaching their destination, the group of men put their horses inside the manor's stables. Quietly, they crept into the dark house. The warmth that met them made the outlaws overjoyed. They could have slept in the lobby and been satisfied.

Roland was not as delighted. He had hoped to at least get some preparations done that night, but it seemed his staff was already asleep. Leading his men to the kitchens, he lifted a piece of bread from the table. "Get something to eat and follow me."

The outlaws did so, filling their hands with as much food as they could carry. It had been an eternity since they had eaten such delicious morsels. Roland led them to various rooms within his manor, distributing the men so that all would have a bed. They quickly devoured their small meals and lay down to sleep. Having provided for his guests, the lord of the manor set to his own room on the upper floor.

Lying on his bed, Sir Roland thought of all he had yet to do. Nevertheless, it felt good to be in his mansion once again. In the royal household he never felt at home. He always had to be on guard to seem as if he fit in with the king's other minions, when in fact, he found them all despicable. Being in this place, he was finally able to relax. It calmed him to feel his old sheets again and to hear the familiar sound of the walls creaking against the wind. This was where he belonged, not some stuffy castle where he had to come like a dog to the king's beckoning call.

Prince Carter's version of home life was massively different than Roland's. When he and his father had arrived at the king's winter castle, Cadoc had followed his heir as he tried to escape to his room. Bursting through the door of the prince's quarters, he threw Carter into the prince's study.

The suite Carter lived in was quite large, but the rooms within it were relatively small. His study was the quaintest of all. It was dimly lit, and the gray stone walls made the room seem colder than it was. The study's disheveled state only made the king grow angrier. Had he raised a bum? Strewn across the table were maps and charts of the country. Books laid open on chairs, the floor, and even partially stuffed back onto their shelves. The only portion of the room to remain intact was the wall of weapons which Carter kept. It was easy to tell they were all he seemed to be interested in during his time there. Each was polished and centered in its place. The collection contained swords, shields, spears, and other equipment.

"That old man received twenty-six lashes because he failed me once," the king said coldly as he picked up a whip from the prince's abounding collection of weapons. "You have failed me twice today. Once before the people and once before Sir Roland."

"I'm sorry, Father," Carter begged of him. "I'll do better! I promise!"

"You will do better," the king replied. A crack let out as he smacked the floor with his whip. He was simply testing it to ensure he could inflict damages properly. Cadoc gritted his teeth with pleasure as he snarled. "Perhaps it will teach you to honor your father, to receive fifty-two lashes."

"Father, please!" the prince quivered as a second crack went out. Cadoc's gaze was set against him without remorse. Knowing there was no escape, the prince withdrew his shirt and exposed a back that was already laced in scars. Carter sunk to his knees before his father.

His bare shoulders were given up as an offering of atonement for his behavior that day. All was silent for a moment. The king must have been planning on how he would continue their session. Carter shivered in fear as he knew no one would save him.

"See how easy it is to obey," came the king's unremorseful tone. "If only you would do what is expected of you, your life would be bliss. Can you see now, what you have done wrong?"

"Yes, Father. Twice I-" Carter gulped before continuing, "I showed remorse for those who didn't deserve it. I let my emotions cloud my judgment."

"What have I taught you of such emotions, boy?"

Carter hung his head in sorrow. "They are crippling to conviction."

"Yes," Cadoc egged him on.

"Emotions are for weak-willed men. I must not give in to them, lest I lose sight of my purpose."

"Were not your actions today based solely on emotion?"

"That is why I failed," Carter trembled, "because I am weak."

"Let us hope this helps you to become strong." Carter could hear the whip as it withdrew from the floor and whisked through the air. Cadoc spoke as it landed across the prince's back. "Since you understand your failure, you will only take half of the villager's punishment."

The prince held back a scream as he began counting. He had found it helped pass the time if he counted. That old man had been given twenty-six lashes, which meant he only had to endure thirteen. One down, twelve to go.

Crack! A second gash was left on him that seeped blood, his skin and muscle tearing from the force of the blow. Carter continued to wait as his punishment was set out. By the time the last stroke descended, the prince was huffing in pain. He was barely able to hold himself up because of his overwhelming exhaustion.

"Do not disappoint me again," his father growled as he left him kneeling there on the cold floors of his room. Carter felt a sense of peace now that the king was gone. The prince slowly laid down on his stomach, sleeping his pain away. One positive side to his father's constant brutality was the ability Carter had gained to sleep anywhere. And sleep well he would, never awakening until his advisor came to his aid.

Without the prince's knowledge, Roland had already been his saving grace that night. Even in his frustration, Cadoc knew all too well of the advisor's devotion to his son. Ever since they were children, Roland had stood by the young prince's side. Throughout their years of friendship, Roland had made excuses for the prince's behavior and had tried to take or at least lessen his punishments.

Cadoc could hardly forget one night that he visited the prince, only to find the young son of his highest-ranking general guarding Carter as he slept. After asking him what he was doing in the prince's chambers, the boy led King Cadoc outside so they would not awaken Carter. Roland then fell on his knees before the king. He begged to have Carter's punishments taken out upon himself instead, so his prince would not be harmed.

Cadoc found pleasure in Roland. He was bold enough to speak to his king in such a manner, yet did it in a way that was submissive to the king's authority. More so, he seemed to understand the lesson's meaning and did not fear taking pain to serve the crown. That night, Cadoc did no more than command the boy to teach Carter to be as strong and courageous as Roland had been.

Throughout his life, the boy had done his best to follow the king's order. Roland had taught Carter the means of combat, strategical advantage, and the management of others. Even when they had become men, the young lord dutifully cared for his prince.

While watching the two boys grow, Cadoc's greatest displeasure was to have Carter for a son and not Roland. When Carter suggested him for the role of court advisor, the king thought it absurd to have such a young man appointed to the position. In the end, he accepted with hopes that when his kingdom passed into the hands of his son, Roland would manage it to its full potential.

The king found only one flaw in Roland. His judgment always became clouded around Carter. For instance, when they were in Krepthor earlier. Cadoc could feel the advisor's gaze on him as he rebuked Carter for his plea to release the old man. And again, Roland had stepped in when Carter had been confronted on his statement of sparing the small town. There was no mistaking; both it and its people were worthless. The kingdom would most definitely be better off if the space were instead used as fields for crops or livestock. Roland had simply made up a better reason for why Carter might have seen things differently than his father, but he made it clear that it was the king's choice. That was just the devious cleverness he held, one of his traits which Cadoc favored most. In the end, the king had let the town remain for Carter's sake. Just as he had lessened his son's punishment, even though it was clear he had learned nothing. Cadoc was kind to Carter, not because he cared for him, but because Roland cared for him.

As he left Carter's chambers, the king knew Roland would be upset with him for his actions. Still, it had to be done! Carter was a man, yet continued to act like a child! Cadoc let out a sigh. Even though this would make him upset, Roland wouldn't act upon it. To the king, this was both a blessing and a curse. He appreciated the respect Roland showed by not speaking against his actions; but at the same time, he wished they could discuss why he felt the actions were necessary. Yet, Cadoc could not approach Roland with his explanation. Such an occurrence would make him appear vulnerable and full of regret, neither of which he was. The king put his thoughts aside. Only tomorrow would determine what would come of this.

The Call to Aid

Roland woke to muffled voices. Opening his eyes, he soaked in the sight of his room. The drapes and bed sheets were a deep burgundy color, everything else made of dark wood. Rubbing his eyes, he got up to change into a new shirt. After changing, he did a quick stretch and exited his room.

Upon seeing him, those of his house cheered in unison. "Good morning, Lord Roland!"

Roland allowed himself a small twitch of his lips, which amounted to a large smile in his case. He had missed that. "Good morning, everyone. Have any of my guests awoken yet?"

"They are in the dining room, eating," an elderly woman replied as she walked up to him. Roland leaned down to her outstretched hands. The woman patted his cheek lovingly before wrapping him in a hug. "My, you're all skin and bone. Let's get you something to eat! Have they been treating you well?"

"Yes, Belinda," Roland chuckled as she dragged him into the dining hall. "I am well taken care of. Now, if you don't mind, I was hoping to speak with George."

"So, that's why you're thin! Just as before, you never know when to eat if you're not told. I doubt you've slept well recently either by the state of those tired eyes." The woman plopped him into a chair at the head of the table. She proceeded to set for him a plate and prepare a drink. With one last pat on his shoulder, she told the king's advisor what would happen during the morning. "Now you eat all that up, and I'll fetch George. You can talk to him once you're done."

Roland wanted to retaliate, but Belinda had already left the room. He sulked momentarily, only to pick up his fork. On the other side of the table sat the fourteen outlaws, all with their jaws dropped at the sight of him being treated like a child. Remembering them, Roland cleared his throat. "I have a favor to ask of you."

"Can it wait 'till you're done eatin'?" chuckled the redheaded comedian.

"I was hoping to tell you before you died, Martin," Roland growled in return. He had a hard time accepting Martin's sort. The man came from a cluster of villages in the mountain ranges to the west. All from that region found themselves funny and quick-witted. They were easily distinguishable by their weak jests and speech patterns. They were a lively bunch, to say the least. Their speech was high-pitched and their words shortened to an almost incomprehensible degree. Martin was no exception with his slang versions of words. Still, Roland was always taken aback by the rhythm within their speech. It was almost like a song, albeit an irritating and brash one.

"Sorry," the redhead replied, bringing a piece of bread to his mouth before he could say anything else that might upset the advisor.

Between bites, Roland told them what he needed them to do. "I want to send supplies to the village of Krepthor, but neither my people nor I can be the ones to do so. If it became known that I aided them, my allegiance would be questioned. That is why I hoped you might deliver the supplies for me. The people must know of you by now. They trust you and will accept the supplies from your hands."

"It is the least we could do to repay your hospitality," Jasper replied.

"Good," Roland beamed as he feasted on his breakfast. "There is one house in particular near the end of the main street, a couple about to have their first child. I want you to give them extra attention. They seem to need a lot of care."

"I will do so," Jasper nodded.

"Would you be able to go today? There are many injured. I fear for their lives should they be left without treatment for too long a time."

"Yes, we can leave before midday."

"Wonderful. I will speak with George and get a few carts of supplies ready for you. Feel free to return here once you are done. As you well know, my home is yours."

"Thank you."

"Now, I must be going." Roland stood, his plate now cleaned and glass empty. "Good luck to you all!"

"Same to you," Jasper raised his glass to the now empty side of the room. He shook his head as he sipped at his drink. "He never slows down, that one. I don't even know how he can function with all he is doing, and yet he seems more capable than the rest of us."

"He's a wee bit freaky, ya ask me," Martin chuckled. "But who cares? We got rooms now, lads!"

All others in the room cheered. It was indeed a joyous day!

Outside in the main lobby, Roland found George. He instructed him to load carts with food, clothing, blankets, and medical supplies. All of which were to be purchased with his personal funds. The order was carried out immediately. Satisfied that his requests would be taken care of, Roland set out in a quickened pace towards the palace on his trusty steed.

When he left, George turned to Belinda and asked of her. "Did you tell him of your financial troubles? Here he is helping people he does not know, has he not also helped you?"

"I didn't want to worry him," Belinda replied earnestly. "These are my troubles; I'll deal with them."

Meanwhile, Roland raced as quickly as he could back to the castle gates and reached his destination near dusk. Cadoc's winter castle was made of gray stone. One of the main rivers that flowed through Remette encircled it. The constant flow of the water made its design far more dependent than a moat. There were only two entrances, one to the northwest and one to the southeast. Either way the fortress was approached, a drawbridge needed to be lowered to allow one to enter. This was how it had assumed the name, The Fortified City.

Scarlet flags of Remette flapped from the power of gusty winter winds as the guards opened the northern drawbridge for him. After entering, the advisor dismounted his horse in the castle's courtyard. Roland did not make it far before he was pulled aside by Queen Zisca. When he saw the tears on her face, he already knew what had happened. Carter must never have made it to his room.

"He…he did it again!" She sniffled softly, wiping at her tears. "He!"

"I'll tend to him," Roland reassured her. "It'll be alright. I'm sorry I wasn't here to stop it."

"You're here now. I am the one who should be sorry," the queen whimpered. "I've been here this whole time, and I cannot bring myself to dare do anything about it. So, thank you!"

"You're welcome," Roland replied as he walked away. "I'd let him rest today. You can see him tomorrow."

"Of course." The queen touched her nose with a handkerchief as she forced herself not to cry. With that, she departed. Roland went the opposite way to tend to the wellness of the prince.

First, he went to the prisons, but could not find the prince there. With a quickened pace, he made his way to Carter's chambers. After stepping inside, the advisor's stomach turned to lead. Blood stained the walls, floors, and papers within the prince's study. Carter's back was laced with cuts from the end of a whip, which lay bloodied beside him. Fighting the lump in his throat, Roland called out softly, "Carter?"

The figure gave no reply, remaining quiet as if dead. The advisor called louder as he closed the door behind him, "Sire?"

A loud snore replied to him, making Roland give a flicker of a smile. The advisor came to the prince's aid, slowly lifting him from the floor. Amidst the struggle, the prince's body slumped onto Sir Roland.

"Ugh," Carter groaned as his peace was broken by the searing pain stretching across his back.

"I'm sorry, sire," the advisor said softly. "I had tried to be gentle."

Roland could feel excessive amounts of heat coming off of the prince, his body trying harshly to repair itself. Holding him carefully so he did not bring him additional pain, Roland moved Carter to the bed. Fetching some medical supplies from the prince's study, the advisor began to treat the wounds which the king had inflicted.

Roland began by addressing the prince's aggressive body heat. After fetching some cool water, he placed a damp cloth on Carter's brow. Next, he dabbed at the prince's back with another wet cloth to wipe away the dried blood.

Groaning as he fully awoke, Carter saw his friend at his bedside. After noticing that Roland was caring for him, Carter could think of only one thing to say. "I'm sorry, I failed you."

"Nonsense," Roland spat as he finished prepping the prince's back for treatment.

Wincing at the stinging sensation he felt, Carter tried to make light of the situation. "No, you're right. I did great. I made it all the way back to my room!"

"Carter," Roland tutted as he applied a healing salve. The ointment making the prince's wounds feel almost instantly, if only marginally, better. "You mustn't think so lightly of these things. You should be thankful for the chill in the air this time of year. Had it been summer, these wounds would have borne a greater consequence."

"I know," sighed the prince in his despair. After letting out a sigh of his own, the advisor stood and poured a glass of spirits. Leaving it on the prince's nightstand, he went to the door.

"Once you feel well enough, try to get that into you. It'll numb the pain. I'm afraid this is all I can do for now," the advisor told his prince in sadness. "I must report to your father. I will be back as soon as I can."

"Go," Carter tried to chuckle, "maybe at least one of us can make him happy."

While Carter rested, Roland made his way to the king's side. He worried it might have angered Cadoc for him to have attended to Carter first, but it mattered not.

Roland bowed as he entered the palace vault. The advisor knew of all places, Cadoc would be there. The king spent most of his time in the vault counting and recounting his riches. A deep growl came from inside when Roland was noticed. "Ah, Advisor! Tell me, how is my son?"

"He is quite well, my king," Roland said, trying to keep his emotions in check.

"Did my actions worry you?" Cadoc asked. "Is that why you reported first to the prince and not your king?"

Roland had heard such questions before. Cadoc repeatedly brought up the fact that the advisor was more loyal to Carter than himself. Roland felt his answer could not show any regard for Carter but instead show that he was forced into such action. "I tell you truthfully; the queen approached me as I entered the castle courtyard. She beseeched me to attend to Carter in his chambers as I have done in the past. I simply did as was requested of me, so the queen would no longer appear so distraught."

All was quiet for a moment as Cadoc took in the new information. He nodded in reply. "You've done well. That woman, she can never keep her wits about her. No doubt she had waited all day near the courtyard, making me look like a fool!"

"Of this, I cannot be certain."

"I am," the king replied in a stale tone. Changing the subject back to Roland's endeavors he asked, "How went things in Morer?"

"Very well. The town seems to be in an orderly fashion."

"As was to be expected." Cadoc continued in his counting. The king mused to himself as he tallied coins and thoughts. As usual, Roland would not admit that it grieved him to see Carter in such a state. Still, the king knew Roland had been telling the truth about Zisca. He had seen her sobbing quietly in the courtyard earlier that same day. Simply looking from the corner of his eye, Cadoc could tell his advisor did not want to remain much longer in his presence. Perhaps a bit of distance would be best for the time being. "That will be all for now."

"Of course, my liege." Roland bowed as he left the room, traveling directly back to his prince's side.

Carter had pulled a pillow under his chin as he sulked in his wounds. Too long, he had taken these beatings. He was growing tired of this eerie game the king made him play. It was one thing for his life to be tarnished by his father's presence, but for his people to suffer also? To have witnessed that old man's death felt unbearable! As he laid there, the prince decided that he could not wait any longer to act. As his advisor entered his chambers, he stated his plight.

"Roland," Carter's tone was icy, "I will stand it no longer. We must get rid of him. We must do it now!"

The advisor quickly shut the door and locked it behind him. "You're angry. I understand, but you must be more careful with your actions!"

"Then tell me how to do it carefully, Advisor."

"Carter," Roland said in a quiet voice, "there are many things to take into consideration with something like this!"

The prince looked at him solemnly. "I have taken many things into consideration. Those people in that town who are suffering, for example."

"I have already attended to them."

"They are not the only ones!" Carter spat. Looking Roland in the eyes, he pleaded. "There must be a way."

"It would be risky, sire."

"I'll take the risk. Tell me how!"

The prince gave his advisor a moment, Roland remaining quiet for quite some time. His hand rummaged back and forth over his hair until, at long last, the advisor let out a sigh. "You must be patient. This castle is a fortress, as was its design. For this to work, the king must be in his summer palace to the east. It is larger than this one. His guards would be more spread out and easier to manage."

"But we could get him alone here just as well."

"He will expect such a move on your part, Carter. Any such action will likely lead to our deaths. Your father is a corrupt man. He lives each day looking for enemies. The one he focuses on most being you. For you to have any chance at success, you need to find him a new enemy to focus on. Someone he cannot trust."

"He doesn't trust anybody," Carter exclaimed in exasperation.

"No, but to make him hate that person more than he does you, that is the trick." Roland paused for a minute. "Now, not only will you need a distraction; you need a strategy. Before any action can be taken, all portions of the attack need to be thought out to the minutest detail. It is not only our lives we will be sacrificing, should we fail-"

"But those we love," Carter interrupted as he thought of his mother.

"It is hard to make such a huge change happen on your own," the advisor said as he approached the prince's bed. "It would be much easier if we had others within the palace to help us, but they are all loyal to the king. Perhaps if we could scrounge enough money to pay some of them off, they would aid us. Even then, the king would notice a depletion of his funds."

Roland laughed a bit to himself. "Perhaps Jasper's idea isn't so far-fetched after all."

"Jasper's idea?" Carter asked.

"I didn't have a chance to tell you," Roland replied. "I met with Jasper in Morer. He was going to cross into Poniere and attack a group of wealthy nobles that have gathered near Luxborne."

"Luxborne," Carter muttered to himself. He couldn't help but wonder if he might be able to speed up the timetables of the operation, but Roland was always one to plan. He had to review the details thoroughly to ensure that nothing went wrong. The advisor had already put his timetable to mind. Should the prince have other plans, he would have to do so by himself. "There's a town we could do without."

"Come now," Roland laughed. "It is one of our greatest trade centers!"

"Those Luxbornes think they are the best people on the planet."

"I would have to rank them pretty high myself," the advisor replied. "They are very prosperous."

"Sure," Carter scoffed, plopping his head onto his pillow. "If you ask me; I think you only approve of the one."

"May I offer you some advice, sire," Roland grinned mischievously as he loomed over the prince's bed.

"Do you think I too should swoon over the lovely Lady of Luxborne? I'd love to, but I wouldn't want to step on your toes, old friend."

"Actually, I was going to advise you not to jive at your caretaker when he has yet to finish treating your wounds."

Carter gave a gulp as he said simply, "Oh."

Roland smiled, tugging at a piece of bandaging between his hands. "I wonder how tight you can wrap these before they break?"

"I take it back!" Carter screeched.

"No need," chuckled the advisor. "It is no secret that Fae is a remarkable woman, but to say I swoon over her? I doubt that."

"True," Carter nodded. "You don't really swoon over anyone."

"Do you think you can stand?" Roland sighed. "It will help me wrap up these wounds."

Carter stood with a grimace. As the advisor set to work, the prince chugged down the alcohol that had been provided to him. "Why is it that you do not swoon?"

"Why is it that you have grown to enjoy that word so much?"

"What?" chuckled Carter as he leaned against his bedpost. "You have women flocking over you, yet you don't pay them any actual attention."

"Some would say I give them attention," grumbled the advisor.

"Not real attention. Name one woman you have courted," the prince smiled, only to find his advisor glaring at him. "Why not court Lady Luxborne? I'm sure she would accept; you being the king's right hand and all."

Roland huffed in irritation as he finished his work. "I pay women as much attention as I deem them worthy of, sire. Should I find a woman that I feel is worthy, I will gladly court her. I doubt I will meet such a woman any time soon."

As he was moved back into his bed, Carter sighed. "At least you get to choose your wife."

Roland hung his head a little. "Yes, I suppose that is a blessing."

Placing the pillow under his chin, Carter said quietly, "I'm actually quite tired now. Would you mind?"

"Not at all, sire," the advisor said as he made his way to the door. "Sleep well! I told your mother it would be best to wait to visit until tomorrow, so you will have no further distractions."

"Thank you, Roland," Carter said as he closed his eyes. The advisor shut his door gently. After he was in the safety of the hallway, Roland scratched his head nervously. How foolish for him to complain about finding a wife in front of Carter! As if the prince wasn't in enough pain!

to put his diplomacy and communication skills to the test. He didn't know these nobles, but that didn't matter to him. No matter who he chose for a wife, he would love her unconditionally for her aid in overthrowing his wretched father.

As he approached, Carter found the town puzzling. The gates were opened wide and inviting; no one even tried to stop him as he passed through. In his kingdom, his father kept everything under lock and key. More so, he could hear music and singing from inside the city. What a joyous sound, unlike the screams of his countrymen.

Everything inside the town was lined with purple and silver, the colors of Poniere. He stuck out boldly amongst those gathered, but the people did not seem to mind him. His face reddened as he wished he had taken his mother's advice to learn the Ponierian tongue. He had no idea what the people were saying! How was he supposed to ask for a bride when he didn't even know the word for it? How foolish he would appear to these nobles.

It was to his surprise, as he sat upon his horse nervously, that a well-dressed Ponierian man approached him. Carter couldn't help but think he looked very similar to the rest. All of the Ponierians seemed to hold a dark tan to their skin. They had dark eyes and either dark brown or raven black hair.

Carter was delighted when the man spoke to him in Remettian. "Good sir, have you come to join the festivities? I knew most of the nobles of Poniere were to come, but I must say I did not know a Remettian was coming. Did Norvell invite you? He is always inviting new people to my parties!"

The Ponierian laughed. "Not that I mind. The more, the merrier! Shall I have a servant take your horse for you? Come, let me show you inside!"

Carter was taken aback as he dismounted, a servant scurrying to take his horse for him. These people were so nice! Roland had always made them seem like the plague! Looking about him, Carter felt uncomfortable standing within the group of partygoers. Not only was he wearing the wrong color, but he towered over the people there. Though, his host did not seem to hold it against him. "Come, sir, follow me. I shall set you at the front of my table."

"That is very kind of you," Carter replied nervously.

"You are very welcome," the host said as he set the prince within a large group of people who gleamed with wealth. Between Carter and his host sat an older gentleman. His hair, long and gray, was draping over his shoulders. The golden crown that crested Carter's brow caught his attention.

"Who are you?" the old man asked in Remettian.

"My!" the host thought aloud. "I feel awful, having forgotten to ask!"

"I'm," Carter gulped under the pressure. Would these people hate him when they knew who he was? Just how far had his father's reputation spread? "Prince Carter of Remette."

At the time of the declaration, the host had been taking a swig of wine from his goblet. He couldn't help but spew it across the table as he heard the words. All others who were gathered turned their eyes to Carter, the sounds of happiness dying around them. He picked nervously at his fingers, trying not to look at them. Apparently, his father's reputation had spread pretty far.

"Prince Carter of Remette?" another man at the table exclaimed. "Why are you here? I mean, to what do we owe the pleasure?"

"I have," Carter closed his eyes as he let out a breath. This was harder than he had expected. With a lump in his throat, he spoke to the gathered nobles. "I have come in search of a bride."

The host dropped his goblet entirely out of his hand. Others in the room looked about at each other nervously. The elderly man to the prince's side stared at Carter as if he had committed a crime by the request. He spoke to the prince in a calm tone. "Did King Jessinias not set a plan with your father to give you a chance at marrying his eldest daughter Cida, heir to his kingdom?"

"I understand," Carter tried to reason with them. "You would not wish to betray your king by offering one of your daughters to me, because he has already made arrangements between me and his eldest. I tell you truthfully; the princess would not choose me over the Prince of Measul. Even if she did, I doubt she would make the choice in order to find happiness."

"I have heard what she thinks of Remettians," Carter added while looking about nervously, "and I'm afraid I cannot take a wife who will never love me. That is why I have come to you. I can only hope one of your daughters may find a way to accept me as I am."

The older man spoke again. "What is it that would make our daughters more worthy than others? Do you not have women in your kingdom you could choose from?"

Carter gave a nervous chuckle as he tried to come up with a decent reply. He needed funds; that was why he was there. More than that, he feared what his father would do if he took a wife of one of their noble families. He could destroy them and their entire provenance for their impudence. As for her qualities, Carter didn't really have a preference.

Seeing his inability to come up with an answer, the man continued. "Is it a woman of beauty you seek, or perhaps one of intelligence? Maybe one who could provide you with a monetary gain if you were to select her?"

"Those are all good things, I suppose," Carter replied uncertainly.

The old man laughed aloud, all others remaining quiet. "You do not seem to be very prepared for this, young prince. To come all this way without knowing what you are searching for."

"I-I know what I'm searching for!" Carter stammered. The old man appeared to be losing his humor. "And I have already told you! I wish for a wife who will truly care for me. These things you speak of are not of importance. I seek a loving woman, like my mother."

"And you feel that no woman in your kingdom could come to love you?" the old man asked, his eyes alight with curiosity.

"When they look at me, will they not only see a throne?" Carter replied honestly. "If I were to ask for the hand of one of my noblewomen, they would feel forced to accept. Not out of love, or even the hope of such a thing. To them, the marriage would be only duty. Perhaps a means to gain profit for their families. At least with a woman from your country, I can feel more assured that even if she were to pursue me for my worth, I think she would respect me. This is proven true by your behavior tonight. Respect, even if it comes from fear, is a powerful thing. Still, I will do my best to prove myself not to be the monster you must all think I am."

The old man smiled slightly at the prince's answer. "I have a daughter I think you might be interested in. She brings me nothing but happiness. I can only expect she would do the same for you. Though I will tell you, she is a bit reluctant to trust a Remettian. You see, our family suffered great losses to the hands of your men."

Carter hung his head. Was there one person in all the surrounding lands his family hadn't harmed?

The old man continued, "But such things are in the past! Tell you what, why don't you rest here for tonight? Surely there is an extra bed. I would like to know you better, so I may tell her of you when I return home. Should she agree to this, I will send word to you."

The prince's heart pounded in his chest. Was he about to get married, and to someone he didn't know? This man before him looked distinguished, but he seemed fairly aged. With only one question in mind, Carter spoke again. "Thank you for hearing me. I'm sure she is a wonderful girl, but may I ask . . . how old is she, exactly?"

The old man laughed again, Carter's face turning red. With a father as old as this, she had to be at least ten years older than him!

"She's nineteen."

"Oh," the prince breathed once again. She was young! "I've only just turned twenty-one."

"Yes, we know," the old man spoke for the group. Carter looked down timidly, causing the old man to proceed in his daughter's praise.

"I promise you; my daughter is beyond compare. Not only does she have a wonderful heart like you seek, but she contains all of the qualities I have told you. She is beautiful, intelligent, and of course, there is to be a plentiful dowry paid unto you for accepting her."

"She sounds exquisite," Carter smiled shyly. None of the other nobles had offered their daughters, so this old man's would have to do. All the prince could hope was that she was indeed as perfect as her father had made her out to be.

Throughout the night, Carter ate and drank with the old man, the two sharing stories as they got to know each other. The prince could hardly believe that such a prosperous man would have found favor in him so easily. By the time he was to take his leave, Carter had found assurance in the girl he had been promised. In fact, he feared her too glorious. If the king were to know about her, he would end up respecting her rather than hating her. So, the prince took action. How could his father respect someone who deliberately kept things from him in his court?

"Now that I am more aware of your daughter's tenseness towards Remettians, I fear she might become afraid over the thought of coming to my kingdom. My court is obviously full of people she will be skeptical of, not that I blame her. You must understand those who she would fear most are the ones with the highest rank in my country."

"Like that Beast of Morer," the old man grumbled loathingly.

Carter gave a silent apology to his friend in his mind as he recognized the derogatory title that the foreigners had given Roland during the last Great War. Roland's reputation seemed enough to make the Ponierians both nervous and wrathful. "Indeed. The Lord of Morer has a very high standing in my father's court. I can only presume that being in his presence might make your daughter feel uneasy. I do not want something like this to taint her judgment of me."

"What are you proposing?"

"If it were to make her feel more comfortable, should she choose to be wed to me, perhaps we would keep her identity hidden from the masses. Once she shares my title, she can rest assured that none of my country will oppose her."

"And none of my country will oppose you, so long as they do not know she is set to be wed to you," the old man nodded as he thought over the scheme. "Perhaps it would be better. This way, it is over before people know it has started."

"Right, and those other royals shall not be able to stand in the way of it because they will not know!"

"And should my daughter reject this proposal, no shame will befall either of our families."

"Agreed," Carter held out a hand, the old man grasping it heartily. "I await your word."

"You will have it before the winter is out!"

Unjust Imprisonment

Having completed his mission, Carter returned to his father's court. As soon as he dismounted his horse, guards surrounded him to take him prisoner. The prince was prepared for this. Knowing his old wounds had not yet healed, Carter couldn't help but wonder what his father might do to him this time.

"Release him," came a cold order from above. The guards did so, quivering as the advisor raced past them to his friend. When Roland reached him, he whispered in a low voice that no one else could hear. "Carter! Where have you been? Do you realize how reckless it was for you to go off on your own like that?"

"It was something I needed to do."

"I'll warn you; the king is not pleased."

"I doubt he is," Carter smiled nervously. "Let's not keep him waiting any longer."

With one last worried look, Roland walked Carter to the king's courtroom.

"Where is it you felt compelled to run off to?" growled his father from his throne. Carter found assurance in the fact that Roland stood directly beside him.

"I went to Poniere, Father," the prince said. He knew he would have to tell his father of the engagement sometime. Why not share that beating with this one? The man could only go so far.

"Poniere," the king spat. "Why did you go there? To lead back an army for Jessinias?"

"I attended a party," the prince groaned. His father always took things for the worst.

"Do we not have parties here?"

The prince let out a sigh. Once his father learned of his efforts to gain a wife, his beating would be horridly severe. For once in his life, Carter felt free to say what he wanted. In the end, the punishment would be the same. "Those are your parties, Father, and I find no joy in them. It must say quite a lot that I would need to leave your entire country to find a bit of relaxation."

Roland waved the guards out of the room. No one should hear the words coming from the prince's mouth. This was preposterous! Carter would undoubtedly get himself killed for behaving so foolishly.

From his throne, Cadoc roared in anger. "You despicable, ungrateful child! Why must I be cursed with your insolence?"

The king stood, making Roland look back and forth between the royals, wondering if he should dare to intervene. As the king stomped down the stairs of his platform to where Carter stood, the prince looked up with a smile. He did not seem worried but instead chuckled. "I know you plan to beat me, but you shouldn't yet."

Carter cocked his head playfully to the side. "Actually, you should be congratulating me."

"And why is that?" growled the king as he trudged closer still.

"Because, while I was at the party, I got engaged."

"What?" the king let out a shout that shook the very foundations of the castle's stone. His words then turned to the sound of pain-stricken pleading. "Tell me! Tell me this engagement is to Princess Cida of Poniere!"

A flash of hatred momentarily held to the advisor's face at the mention of the princess's name. It was quickly replaced with the ever-present look of worry for the prince's wellbeing. Carter chuckled again as he looked his father in the eye and said with a shrug, "Well, she's Ponierian, does that count?"

"You!" Cadoc's face was red with fury. Carter prepped to tease the king some more. He felt he might as well enjoy himself before he was crushed under his father's heel.

"Would you be angry to find that your heir was engaged to marry a simple noblewoman?" the prince grinned ear to ear. "A noble from a foreign land at that. What could I possibly gain from her?"

Cadoc looked at Roland, whose face was glued to the ground, eyes wide in terror. Curling his hands into fists the king ordered, "You will cancel this engagement immediately!"

"I'm afraid I can't, Father," Carter smiled happily. "You see, her family happens to live on the far side of Poniere. Her father was only in the area for the party. We departed at the same time in opposite ways. You'll never catch him now!"

"Roland!" the king shouted at the edge of his restraint. They had waited together for Carter to return. Roland had remained quiet in his presence, his depression more obvious after Cadoc had refused to let him go after the prince. Now that Carter had returned, all Cadoc wanted to do was beat him to the edge of life, but he wouldn't dare in front of the advisor.

"I'm afraid he is right, my liege," the advisor replied softly. "From what I have heard, this party took place on the far side of Luxborne. He is now not one, but two days ahead of us."

"Argh!" the king growled. Reaching a breaking point, Cadoc grabbed his son by the hair and pulled him to his eye-line. "Tell me all that you have done."

"I told you. I went to the party. I got engaged."

Carter's retort was met by a raise of the king's hand. Roland stammered in an effort to rescue the prince. "It's my fault, my king!"

"No!" spat Cadoc. "You did not run off to some grimy Ponierian pit and engage yourself to a filthy peasant!"

Roland sunk to his knees as he looked at the floor. "It was I who told Prince Carter of the party. I told him of who would be attending, as well as where to find it."

"What?" Cadoc asked as he dropped his son, who crashed onto the floor beside his advisor.

Carter clenched his teeth. Roland always did this, always taking his punishments for him! No longer! "He may have told me that there was a party across the border, but I came up with this plan by myself!"

"And why would you do that?" growled Cadoc.

"Well, I-" Carter had no words. He couldn't tell his father he was using this woman as a distraction to dethrone him!

"As she grows older, Princess Cida has shown little more than hatred toward our countrymen, my king," Roland lied for him, raw contempt lacing his words as he spoke. "She is surely at an age to be wed, but we have heard nothing from the Ponierians about an engagement."

Catching on to the story they were trying to feed the king, Carter added details. "Yeah! So, I went to Poniere as quickly as possible to attend this party full of nobles from all over Jessinias' kingdom. When I was there, I asked them about the princess. They all seemed to hate me themselves."

"Did you know of this?" Cadoc asked Roland directly.

"No!" Carter stated as Roland refuted his reply.

"There is no need for you to lie over this," Roland said rebukingly to Carter before bowing lower to the ground in front of Cadoc. "I'm afraid I have failed you, my liege. I approved of what the prince would do."

"No, he didn't!" Carter pleaded, but Cadoc raised an angry hand to hush him.

"It was I who even advised he take a different Ponierian as a wife if these nobles would inform him that Princess Cida persisted in rejecting him," Roland lied masterfully. "More so, I have kept this from you. Even knowing what Carter had been doing, I led you astray by not informing you of what was happening."

Carter was too afraid to speak as his friend once again saved him from his father, entering into the flames of persecution in the prince's stead. The king's reply was calm and quiet. "Why would you think to advise him in this way?"

"The amount of disdain I hold against Ponierians is no secret," said the advisor in an icy tone, "but if we are to remain at peace, we must show them that we mean them no harm. If Princess Cida rejected Carter as she seemingly has, would it not be better to solidify our standings with them through marriage to a Ponierian noble rather than a noble of these courts? To choose a woman who is already subjugated to Your Majesty would be a wasted effort. Whereas, this way, we can at least gain something from the woman."

Carter shuddered. Sometimes Roland sounded too much like his father!

"And you say, Princess Cida has rejected you? This is why you have chosen this noble?"

"Y-yes," Carter choked out, "but it's not set in stone."

The king growled with impatience. "What does that mean?"

"I have only met the father. It is now up to the daughter if she will accept me."

"And what will take place, should she also reject you?"

Carter gave a nervous chuckle. Why did his father seem so calm? Something wasn't right. "Well, I'd say this is my last chance. Of all the people at the party, only one man offered me his daughter."

Cadoc pulled his son from the floor, bringing their faces so close they were almost touching. "Then, for your sake, she had better accept you and she had better be a worthwhile woman. Should I find her unworthy to be here, I will ship her right back to Jessinias; whether it brings war or not!"

After throwing Carter back onto the ground, Cadoc glared down at the pair of friends. "Lest you have forgotten, I am still the leader of this country!"

"We were foolish to have acted the way we did, Your Majesty." Roland laid his face flat against the floor as he bowed.

Cadoc called out to the guards in the hall, "Take them to the dungeons! They are not to have anything but water and stale bread until I hear this woman's reply."

Carter's eyes grew wide as he bleated. "Father! That could be months!"

"Not to worry," the king retorted, returning to his throne without looking back at them. "You have a friend."

As they were led from the room, the king sat and spitefully said. "I'll be sure to visit."

The prince gulped as he and the advisor were dragged to their cells in the dungeons. That didn't sound good!

The guards bound both of them in shackles. For fear of him, they sealed away Roland first. He sighed lightly as he ducked to enter his cell. Carter was pushed into the one beside him. The prince did not seem as calm about the predicament as his advisor. Roland sat beside the bars of the prince's cell. Looking up at the ceiling in boredom as he listened to the prince fervently shake his chains, the advisor couldn't help but let out a small smile at the excessive rattling and exasperated grunts coming from his friend.

In a huff, Carter sat down beside him. "Why won't they take these off? We're already locked up!"

"Because they don't need to," Roland said simply. "What would you use your hands for in here?"

The prince looked side to side. What he saw in his cell was nothing more than iron bars, rock, and what appeared to be human feces. "Well . . . nothing, I suppose."

Roland smiled again as he leaned back against the wall of his cell. He closed his eyes as he chuckled, "Exactly."

"I must say," Carter said, showing his inability to remain quiet for more than a minute, "this isn't as bad as I thought it would be."

The advisor looked at the prince solemnly. "It's not over yet, sire."

"Right," Carter gulped.

Their first week in the dungeon of Cadoc's winter castle was uneventful and calm. By the seventh day, Carter's stomach had already started to long for its usual delicacies. The prince grew more restless the longer he was stuck there. To his despair, the guards would not even offer him reading material to pass the time. However, Carter was happy that his advisor had decided to be locked up with him.

Not once did Roland bring up what had happened. It was odd to the prince. He neither complained about what they had gone through nor asked Carter what had actually taken place. Carter did not bring it up either. Everything the advisor did was with a purpose; he would talk about it when he was ready. For the time being, Roland did as the king had commanded him. He was Carter's friend.

For the most part, he was quiet; but that was his normal demeanor. Roland had a way of working things out in his mind. He could solve a problem that had not yet occurred while in the middle of a separate task. The prince could only imagine what was going through the advisor's head. Especially now that he had all this time to himself.

It was comical to Carter; the longer the pair of them were imprisoned, the better Roland began to look. No longer having to deal with the stress he was accustomed to, he became better rested. Even though he was eating far less than usual, he seemed to remain healthy.

As time passed by, Roland would quiz the prince on the regulations and policies of Remette. Carter was learning more and more about his country every day. At some points, it felt shameful that Roland knew so much more than he did. The advisor also walked the prince through different tactical maneuvers and fighting methods, but Carter had a hard time because his hands were bound. So, the advisor instead taught him how to fight while shackled, whether your hands were shackled before you or behind you.

When the guards saw the two practicing how not only to disarm, but kill while shackled, they no longer got close to the cells of the prince and the advisor. Instead, they had maidservants bring the men their meals. The maids did not mind the additional task, but fought over shifts of attending to the dreamy pair of men who in any spare moment could be caught keeping up their physical wellbeing in workout competitions. It just so happened; they had a lot of spare moments.

After some time, Cadoc came to the dungeons. Roland bowed as soon as he saw him. The king spoke to his son, ignoring his advisor. "No word has arrived from this woman of yours, Carter. Am I to believe that the story you told me is even true? That this woman is real?"

"It will be weeks before we hear her reply. Her father hasn't even made it home yet."

"And who is he, exactly?" Cadoc snapped. "This father of hers? I have sent men to find out what they can about this proposal, and it does not seem to have taken place at all."

"They wouldn't find anything. Her father and I reached an agreement."

"What agreement?" Cadoc snarled.

"This engagement is to be kept secret. People are only to find out who the woman I am marrying is after we have exchanged vows. That's also why I cannot tell you who either she or her father is. They would rather no one knew."

"That's absurd!"

"Alas, those were the terms of the engagement," Carter shrugged.

"You expect me to believe this?" Cadoc spat. "Why would you agree to such terms?"

"Just as Princess Cida hates Remettians, this girl's father informed me his daughter is squeamish of us as well. For fear of our people, she wants to keep her identity from everyone else. Especially now, since she may still reject my proposal," the prince chuckled. "Apparently, they think we might kill them or something."

"Is this all you will tell me of this noble? That she is afraid of us and hates us? And you expect me to believe she wants to marry you!" Cadoc's face grew red with wrath. "What is the point of this engagement? It seems just to be a nuisance to me! You do this without my consent and you do it to intentionally cause me pain. You have ruined everything I have set up for you. This is why you keep her identity from me, so I cannot stop your foolish marriage!"

"I will tell you now; I think you will like her," Carter leaned against the cell bars. "I was lucky. Her father is an extremely wealthy man and he has promised to pay a plentifully rich dowry for me to take her as my bride."

"How great of a dowry?" Cadoc asked, his anger fading slightly at the thought of the booty to be had.

"Extremely, I'm sure," the prince smiled, "but only time will tell. She has yet to accept me."

"We shall see," King Cadoc snarled. Turning on his heel, he left them behind without a second glance.

"Isn't that crazy?" Carter chuckled as he turned to his advisor. "I try and save one old man from a beating, and I earn one myself. I get engaged to a woman he doesn't know and isn't sure exists, and all I get as a punishment is living down here for a while."

"Sire," Roland shot him a nervous glance as he replied, "you had best hope she accepts."

"Why do you say that?" Carter gulped. He didn't like that face.

"You need to be presentable, should she accept, because she will send messengers to meet you with her acceptance. More than that, you will need to remain presentable for your wedding." Roland ruffled his hair in agitation. "Should she reject you, there is no need for you to be presentable because you'll just be given one of our nobles instead. They cannot reject you."

"Oh." Carter was filled with dread. If this marriage fell through, that was when he would be punished. The girl's father had already seen him in a healthy condition. If the king wasn't punishing him now, it was only because the amount of pain he wanted to inflict on Carter would leave him deformed. "What about you? He hasn't harmed you either."

"He must not have decided what my punishment will be. Should all work out well with you and this Ponierian, my misjudgment will not seem as severe. If it doesn't, I suppose I will share your punishment."

The prince slouched a bit. Roland was sticking to his story. Listening to him speak, Carter almost believed he had been a part of it. "You are too kind to me, my friend."

"Nonsense," Roland tutted. "I live to serve you, sire, and I shall do so to my last breath."

Roland's words left an uneasy feeling in the prince's stomach. He knew the advisor meant it. It was as he waited, week after week, that Carter came to a decision. If that woman thought to reject him, he must change her mind. He had to marry her. Not for the plan or his future, but for his advisor's sake.

The Word of a Messenger

It was during one of the irritatingly repetitive days that fate would show itself to the prince. As Carter traced the stone wall of his cell in boredom, he asked the advisor, "How long has it been now?"

Roland chuckled. The prince asked the same question every day! "Your father has visited nine times, the last being four days ago. It has now been sixty-seven days."

"That's a long time!" Carter groaned as he flopped onto his stone bed.

"Indeed, it is, sire," the advisor said without a trace of care in his voice.

"You know," Carter thought aloud, "it scares me."

"That this woman would take so long to answer?" Roland guessed.

"That you seem so at home in this horrid environment," the prince said as he looked at his advisor. Roland's usually wavy hair had spun into curls over time. Both of their beards had now grown out and were scraggly. His face was one of little emotion, his eyes cold and uncaring. Adding in his massive figure and now tainted robes; the man seemed like a rogue who deserved to be in prison.

"Some would say I belong in this environment." Roland's reply held no remorse as if he believed the statement himself.

"I suppose it is dark and damp, and there aren't many people around. It's the perfect habitat for a hermit such as yourself," chuckled the prince in an effort to cheer him up. "Honestly though. You are too important to be wasting away. I only hope my father sees that too."

"That is what I hope for you as well, Carter." The advisor's expression was serious and sorrowful. The prince couldn't understand. For the past few weeks, every time the advisor had looked at him, he did so with that expression. What was going on in that head of his?

"Thanks," Carter smiled nervously in return. The pair were caught by surprise when the prison door flew open. A servant gasped for breath as he grabbed a guard's arm and pointed to Carter. The prince didn't know what to think. "What's going on?"

"They!" the servant panted. "They're coming!"

"They?" Roland asked as Carter stood frozen in panic.

"Convoy! Massive!" the servant responded as he forced the guard to release Carter. "Ponierians!"

After his shackles were finally taken off of him, Carter's limbs seemed light. He hadn't realized how accustomed he'd become to the darkness and loneliness of that place, as well as not having the freedom of movement. Prince Carter couldn't help but wonder what his father had in store for him. They had yet to hear the woman's reply, but if the convoy was as large as the servant had made it out to be, it could be assumed they bore good news. Regardless, his father was a plotter, quite like the advisor. The prince shuddered at the amount of time the king had to plan his punishment, and he was sure that Cadoc had utilized every day of Carter's long imprisonment to think of evil schemes. Even if the marriage proposal had been accepted, his father would not allow him to walk unscathed. What new restrictions would be imposed upon him when he was freed from the darkness of the dungeons? Carter pitied himself. How horrible was it for him to wish that he could remain in chains next to his advisor, rather than sitting on a throne beside his father?

"Come," said the servant, who had finally found his breath. "We must prepare you quickly!"

The prince looked back to his advisor, who gave him a nod of encouragement. The prince's mind filled with more questions. Why wasn't Roland being freed? Why was it only him?

Carter was taken to his room. When he arrived, he found that a bath was already drawn for him and clothes were laid out on his bed. Seeing his comfortable sheets, he was tempted for a moment just to lie down and sleep, but servants had remained in his room to ensure he did nothing but get prepared for the convoy that had been spotted in the distance.

After removing his shirt, the prince glanced at himself in a mirror. He was unrecognizable! His skin that usually held a tan was clammy and gray in color. His features were shrunken as if he were one of his starving serfs. With his hair and beard untrimmed, he seemed like a beggar.

In the mirror, he spotted a treasure behind him. A plate filled with the most luxurious of meats and cheeses! The prince thought for a moment. What if the Ponierians were coming to reject him, instead of to accept him as he had thought? This might be the last time he got to eat a decent meal. As his stomach growled, the decision was made. Carter left it up to his servants to work around him as he ate his fill. He savored each and every taste that entered his mouth. What bliss!

The servants did their best. Cleansing him from head to toe as quickly as possible. They trimmed and combed his hair as well as shaved off his overgrown beard. The prince's time in the prisons seemed to have aged him. Without the beard to cover his face, he was found to be thinned out. His eyes were noticeably tired as if he were on the edge of life. Now Carter understood why Roland had been looking to him so sorrowfully. Had he known he looked this awful, he would have been worried too!

"Are you ready, sire?" a servant asked, holding out a crown for Carter as another placed a golden hilted sword around his waist.

"Yes," Carter replied, placing his crown on his head. As the servants opened his chamber door, Carter's heart turned to lead. He had been worrying about so many things that he had forgotten to worry about the wedding. What if she was already with the convoy?

Did he have to get married now? The prince gulped as he made his way to the courtyard.

After finally arriving to greet his guests, Carter was surprised to see a Ponierian man already speaking to his father and mother. When the queen saw him, she left her place beside the king. After a quick inspection, she kissed Carter's cheek and hugged him. "My son."

It had been so long since Carter had been in contact with such affection. He could hardly imagine if this convoy hadn't come. With a smile, he hugged her tightly. "I love you, Mother."

"I love you too!" Pulling away, she held lovingly to his sunken cheeks. "Now, let's go introduce you."

"Of course," he grinned back. The queen led him to his father's side by the hand. When they arrived, she released him and instead took up the king's arm. Cadoc lightly patted her hand with his, the whole act of affection was faked for the sake of the guests. Carter tried not to grimace at the sight as he introduced himself to the man before his father. "Greetings, I am Prince Carter of Remette."

"You?" the Ponierian questioned in shock. With a disgruntled look, he quickly inspected the prince from head to toe. "My, what a pleasant surprise."

Carter smiled politely. This man thought he was ghastly looking too!

"I have come with news from My Lady."

"My Lady?" Carter asked, only to realize he was keeping her identity from his father. It all flooded back to him. The plan! Glimpsing at Cadoc from the corner of his eye, Carter could see it was working. The king acted as if it did not affect him, but the prince could tell it truly did! Cadoc loved to be in charge, but in this situation, he was left in the dark. With a grin, Carter continued. "What word do you have for me?"

With a bow, the man handed him a letter. Carter opened it nervously. Was it a rejection? Why did the old man feel he had to put it in a letter? Couldn't they just tell him yes or no? Why send so many people if they were going to make him read a letter? His breath caught in his throat as he read the first line aloud. "My Dearest Prince."

Carter quickly looked up with a reddened face. Never in his life had anyone called him that! All who were gathered looked at him eagerly to read the rest of the letter aloud. After clearing his throat, the little prince declared. "I-I'll be right back!"

"Carter," called Cadoc as the prince ran back into the safety of the castle. With a sigh, the king turned to his guest. "I apologize. He's like this sometimes."

"It's alright," smiled the messenger. "I heard that it took My Lady multiple attempts to even write that letter."

"Really?" the queen asked excitedly.

"Indeed." The man bowed to her. "After writing the final version, she instructed me to provide these to you."

At the snap of his fingers, all the servants of the caravan immediately began to unload gold and other rare items from the carriages. They bowed with their gifts before the king. Cadoc's smile grew wide as he looked down at the treasures before him. The messenger also sunk to one knee, saying. "As a thank you to Prince Carter, for seeking out My Lady's hand."

"This is," Cadoc caught his breath. He couldn't understand why they would pay for the wedding so early. If it were him, he would pay at the time of the marriage, so the wedding would have to happen. Now that he had their profits, he could cancel the wedding without a thought. "This is the dowry for the wedding?"

"No," chuckled the messenger. "This is simply an expression of gratitude. The dowry is yet to come."

Cadoc, for an instant, was pleased. If he could not have Princess Cida, at least this woman seemed to be remarkably profitable. Who could she be to have such riches at her disposal?

Inside the castle, Carter stopped running as he reached his chamber doors. Plopping onto his luxurious bed, he tried again to read his letter.

My Dearest Prince,

I am delighted in the news my father has brought me of you. Even after hearing all he had to say of you, I find myself eager to learn more. It is with excitement that I await your word for when I may finally meet you! Until then, please accept the trinkets I offer as gratitude for your proposal.

~ Your Lady

It was a short letter, but still, Carter found it wonderful. She had accepted! All was going as planned! Even better, she seemed to have a good heart. The prince couldn't help but wonder what she was like herself. With a smile set to his lips, he made his way back to the great hall.

"Carter!" his father called out as soon as the prince was in sight. "What did the letter say?"

With a hum, the prince handed it over. "She can't wait to meet me."

After the king hurriedly read the note, he tutted, "It took her several tries to write that?"

"It took her several tries?" Carter smiled as he took it back. Determining a new mission for himself, he exclaimed. "I should write her a letter!"

"Carter, put your head on straight," snapped the king. "We still have guests you should be attending to."

"Great!" Carter grinned as he brushed past his father. Coming up to the messenger, he asked. "Tell me, how long before you return to My Lady?"

The man simply chuckled. "We will leave as soon as we receive your reply, Your Highness."

"I should like to write My Lady a letter as she has done for me."

"I'm sure she would appreciate it very much," smiled the Ponierian. "Let me know if I may be of any assistance."

"Thank you," beamed Carter. Then he fled from the man's presence a second time. The Ponierian shook his head amusingly. Oh, to be young!

Carter ran to the depths of the dungeons with ink, quills, and paper. After ordering the guards to open the door, he entered the cell of his advisor. He didn't have the power to free him after his father had imprisoned him, but Roland was the only person he knew that could help him write the perfect letter.

"What are you doing here, sire?" the advisor asked in worry.

"I'm here to write a letter," beamed the prince, "and I need you to help me!"

"Why is it you're writing a letter?" Roland questioned. Carter quickly handed him the reply he had received from his fiancé. As the advisor read, Carter strew his gear across the rocky bench of the advisor's cell. Relief flooded Roland's voice as he responded. "She accepted your proposal."

"Yes, yes," Carter replied, pulling Roland onto his knees beside him. "Now! You know how to talk to women. What should I write to her?"

"Well," the advisor thought for a moment. "Her reply showed affection, but its purpose was to show her acceptance of you. In the same way, your letter needs to have a purpose."

"Oh," Carter laughed. "I suppose I don't even have a reason to write a letter, do I?"

"Of course, you do!" Roland said harshly. "She has accepted your proposal."

"Yeah?" Carter egged the advisor to finish the thought for him.

"She asked you to respond within this letter, to do something you are already obviously supposed to do."

"She did?"

"The wedding, sire," Roland sighed. "They need to know when the wedding will be so they can prepare. That is what you must write about."

"The wedding!" Carter gasped. When did he want the wedding? It needed to be at the perfect time, a time the advisor would know. "When do you think I should have the wedding?"

"May fifth," grinned Roland.

"That was quick," Carter gulped. So, this was what Roland had been thinking of so intently these past sixty-seven days. He had used the time to plot the end of the king's reign. The advisor planned the timeframe down to the exact day!

"It is a wonderful day, don't you think? The fifth day of the fifth month. There is a certain glamour about it."

Carter looked at the guards nervously. They couldn't know what this was actually about. "You're right. It is the perfect day, but what shall I put in the letter?"

The pair worked tediously to draft the perfect response. Even after Carter had begged, Roland made the prince write the letter in his own handwriting. "Yours is so much better than mine, though. My writing looks as if a child did it."

"If she sees your true handwriting later, she wouldn't think you wrote this letter but that you told someone else to do it for you. If you want her to like you, you must put in effort where necessary."

"I still don't like it."

"She will," Roland said in reassurance. "Women love this sort of thing."

"I hope you're right," Carter said as he read his letter one last time.

My Lady,

Thank you for your acceptance of me. I wish to know more of you as well, and I hope we may have time together to bond prior to matrimony. Please make use of the pigeon I have sent to you, and let me know when you would be able to come to my courts.

By the time you have received my letter, and I have received yours, I shall be in the Golden Palace of Remette on our eastern shore. I understand that this may affect the timeframe of your travels, but I hope it will not deter you from visiting.

As for the ceremony itself, I would like for it to be held on the fifth day of this coming May. In your reply, please let me know if this date would be acceptable to you. Though my countrymen will not know who you are, I would like them to celebrate this wedding with us for I expect it to be the most blessed of occasions.

Again, I am truly pleased that you would allow me the privilege of your hand in marriage. I look forward to when I may finally see you, face to face.

Your Prince,

Carter of Remette

"It is interesting to me that your handwriting is so poor yet your signature is perfect."

Carter shrugged. "I sign my name a lot. I don't write a lot."

The advisor rebuked, "Perhaps you should write more."

"Yeah." Carter's shoulders drooped in gloom. "I'll do that."

"What you must do now is go to your father, the king. Verify with him what day the wedding should take place. It would be best to not leave him out of this ordeal any more than we already have."

"I'll go to him right now," Carter replied as he stood, taking with him all he had brought. He still did not understand Roland's determination to keep up this act. He had never been involved! What would the king do to him if he didn't plan on releasing him? "Farewell, Advisor."

"Farewell, Carter," the advisor said softly. The prince walked away with a lump in his throat. Roland never addressed him personally in public. It was always 'sire' or 'Your Majesty'. With Roland using his name like that, Carter felt that it sounded like an eternal goodbye.

After catching a servant and having them select one of the finest homing pigeons in the kingdom, the prince took his letter and his gift to the great hall. Trudging to the king's side, Carter implored of him, "I would like to talk to you about this wedding, Father."

"That would be a first," growled Cadoc. Looking to the contents his son was carrying, he let out an irritated huff. How embarrassing to have him walk around carrying that animal! He could have at least gotten a servant to do it for him!

Carter pretended not to hear the rebuke. "My Lady has asked me to provide her with a date for us to be wed, and I think the fifth of this upcoming May would be a good date to set."

"And why is that?" snapped the king.

"Well," Carter gulped, "it would give her enough time to prepare and make the journey. And since we will soon be traveling to the Golden Palace, I gave her extra time. I had also hoped she'd come early so that I could meet her before the wedding."

Cadoc thought back to the riches he had gained so far, and greed caught hold of his heart. May was not far off! "Alright, I'll allow it."

"Really? Thank you, Father!" Carter beamed as he turned and made his way to the Ponierian. Extending toward him both the letter and the birdcage, the prince proclaimed. "Please give this letter and this pigeon to My Lady when you return to her."

"Of course, Your Highness," the messenger replied as he took the offering.

"I am hoping to hold the ceremony on the fifth of this coming May. Do you believe this is enough time?"

"We will do all we can to accommodate." The man bowed. "We shall set out at first light. For now, I am a bit tired from the journey."

"Make yourselves at home. I'll have some servants show you and your convoy to your rooms."

"Thank you, Your Highness."

"Oh no, thank you," Carter grinned. "I'll be taking my leave now. See you in the morning."

The two departed from each other. Carter set out this time to find his mother. When she saw him, she embraced him yet again.

"She accepted! She has no idea how lucky she is to gain a man like you! Are you excited? Nervous?"

"Mother," Carter blushed. "I haven't actually thought about it. I'm just glad she accepted."

Zisca's grip became tight as she thought of what had almost become of her only child. "I'm glad too."

"On a positive note," the prince said as he withdrew from her, "she seems excited to meet me."

"Of course, she is," tutted the queen. "You, my son, are the greatest treasure of this entire kingdom!"

Carter grinned. "She will arrive in a few weeks."

"A few weeks!" shrieked the queen. "We must prepare! What settings will we use? Who will we invite?"

"Calm down," Carter tried to hush her. "It's all under control."

"Do you not know what goes into a wedding?" The queen dragged her son from the room by his sleeve. As she led him off to their many chores, she told him. "We must start preparations immediately!"

Greatest Treasure

ow that his wife and son had departed, along with the Ponierians going to their rooms, Cadoc was left alone. As per his usual routine, the king made his way to the castle vault. Entering, he found a greasy man already counting away at the newly acquired booty.

"My liege!" The man bowed as he saw him.

"How much do you believe we have received so far, Dorian?" replied the king.

"At least a year's worth of profit, Your Highness."

"A year's worth!" Cadoc's jaw dropped. Had the messenger not said this was nothing like what was to come? Just who was this noblewoman? Her family had to be close to the royal family of Poniere. "Is there anything you can use to figure out who this woman is?"

"I'm afraid not, my liege," the collector said nervously. "Everything is either bare material or crafted into its own design. There are no seals or distinguishing marks anywhere to be found."

"They are taking this secrecy very seriously," growled Cadoc. "This whole ordeal has been a test of my patience!"

"I'm sorry, Your Majesty."

"It has nothing to do with you," Cadoc sighed. Rubbing his eyes, the king mumbled aloud. "Why would he put me through this?"

"If I may," the collector answered in hopes of gaining Sir Roland's old position as advisor. "Prince Carter has always had tendencies to act rashly, such as this."

King Cadoc shot him a glance then left without another word. He hadn't been speaking of Carter. When his son was involved, irritating acts like these were to be expected. Of all people, why would Roland have behaved in such a way?

During the weeks of his imprisonment, the king had not been able to look the advisor in the face. It did not go unnoticed that Roland still treated him respectfully. The advisor always bowed when the king had entered the dungeons and had made no effort to plead before the king when he came to visit Carter to pry for information.

Cadoc had felt the need to discipline him for once again getting between the king and his son when a punishment was to be given. He had hoped Roland would let slip that he had not been involved in Carter's engagement as they rotted away together. At which time, he would have been released. From the reports of the castle staff that had attended to him and Carter in the dungeon, he seemed to feel no remorse for what he had done. In fact, to all who had approached him, it seemed he was actually involved in this engagement after all.

Cadoc had understood why Roland would have stepped in for Carter's sake. He didn't like that Roland was so attached to the prince that he would lie to his king, but loyalty was an admirable trait. The king only wished the advisor was as devoted to him as he was to his son. If he had actually been involved in this arrangement, why had he done so? And to act without consulting his king! Never before had he behaved in such a manner. The Roland that Cadoc knew would only bring the prospect up for speculation, allowing the king to make the final call. In a situation as fragile as this, he wouldn't have even dared to speak an opinion. Rather, he would have simply stated the facts and possible outcomes.

As the king slouched into his throne in the great hall, he called to his guards. "Bring me my advisor."

The order was carried out at once. Cadoc did not have to wait long before the clanking of chains could be heard, jingling towards him in a rhythm. Even the way the man walked was orderly! He couldn't have been involved with something so deplorable.

As his advisor entered the hall, the little that remained of Cadoc's heart was pierced. At that moment, the two seemed to be polar opposites. The king sat comfortably upon his throne of gold, dressed in a scarlet, silk tunic. His belly extended outwards to show he was well fed. His hair was well-combed underneath his glorious crown. On the other hand, Roland looked decrepit even though he had tried to make himself presentable. The advisor's clothes, which were now old and tarnished, seemed like those of a beggar. His complexion had become as pale as a ghost and the man's body was shrunken and weak from starvation. Even his hair and beard had grown untidy during his stay in the dungeons.

Regardless, Roland walked before the guards valiantly. His actions showed that he was prepared for the king's judgment of him. As he walked calmly through the great hall, Roland did not look to the king but kept his eyes on the floor. He stopped directly before the king's throne and lowered himself to one knee in respect.

Sorrow gripped Cadoc's heart. This was the Roland he knew. Strong-willed, honorable, and loyal to his king. Looking back to those who had brought him there, the king ordered, "Leave us."

The guards did so. Roland remained silent in his bowed position. After a moment in silence, the king spoke to his advisor. "It seems the prince's engagement is a success. She's no Princess Cida, but she will do."

Roland said nothing as no questions had been asked. With a sigh, Cadoc continued. "Carter is fortunate that I have allowed this to happen."

The advisor gave no response until he heard the king's next word, at which he couldn't help but give a slight cringe.

"Roland."

The pause that followed was a clear sign that the king was waiting for him to respond. With a gulp, the advisor replied, his head still pointed to the floor. "Yes, my liege?"

Cadoc asked his question softly. He hardly wanted the answer. A part of himself hoped the advisor would tell him something other than what he had heard before, even if it were a lie. "Tell me honestly, did you advise Carter to pursue this endeavor, or did you simply try to take the blame to spare him from my judgment?"

With a nervous breath, Roland began his tale. "I'm sorry, Your Majesty, I have failed you. I truly did advise Carter."

"But, why?" asked Cadoc, still caught up in disbelief. "It is so unlike you."

"I found the opportunity advantageous. I had caught word of the gathering of nobles when I went to Morer. At first, I had thought to travel there and take one of the Ponierian noblewomen myself, but I doubted any would have me with my history to that country."

"You hate Ponierians," the king stated. "Do you expect me to believe you thought to marry one? More than that, you have never even courted a woman. Am I to believe marriage is on your mind if you only show women meager displays of affection?"

"I thought only of the profits, Your Majesty."

"The profits?" Cadoc was caught off guard. That answer was plausible.

"Yes," Roland shared a truth with the king. "I've never found much use for women. To me, they are greedy, deceitful creatures. I have shown them attention when it suits me, but I have never seen any emotional reason to be married. If I were to marry, it would be for profit or advancement."

The king leaned back into his throne. Roland's story made sense. He himself had gotten married for the profits and nothing more. As he thought, his advisor continued with his lies. "Even though she would be a horrid Ponierian, I wouldn't have minded taking a wife from those nobles. You see, I know of a few that are extremely wealthy. After the marriage and my receipt of her dowry, I would simply do my best to pretend that she didn't exist."

The king's eyes widened. That was exactly what he had done with Zisca! After profit, all he needed was an heir, and the woman had even failed in providing a worthy son.

Roland continued, "Alas, no man from that country would willingly give his daughter to me."

"Why did you need these profits?" Cadoc said, abruptly stopping Roland's tale. "What were your goals?"

"I had hoped to deliver the funds to you, my liege."

"What?" King Cadoc was shocked. Why would he marry a woman just to give the profits away?

"The thought did not strike me until I returned to the castle. I could tell that you were upset with me over my brash actions those past days, and I had hoped to make it up to you. I knew of the money those peasants had denied you, yet I went against your wishes and kept them from the destruction they deserved. I thought if I could make up for your losses, you would forgive me; but it seems I ended up causing you more grief."

"I did not rebuke you for anything," the king replied. "There was nothing to forgive."

"There is now," Roland sighed. "It was in my shamefulness that I told Carter of these things. He consoled me with the fact that Princess Cida would not choose him the same way those nobles would not choose me. It was then we shared the idea to make you pleased with both of us. Carter would go to the feast in Poniere and ask if Cida had shown even the slightest interest in him. If it were found that she did not, he would take one of their noblewomen instead. He would then give the funds to you for your pleasure."

"Why did you not share these thoughts with me?"

"I realized what a mistake it was after Carter had left, but I couldn't bring myself to tell you. So, I simply prayed that he would not find a wife at all. When he returned in that drunken state with news of marriage, I knew I could hide my shame no longer."

Cadoc thought a moment. Had Carter been drunk? Was that why he had behaved so foolishly? He looked down at the man who was still bowing humbly at his feet. Then, the king did something he had sworn never to do. He decided a man's fate with his emotions. "I forgive you of these acts, Advisor."

"You do?" blurted Roland, looking up in disbelief before gaining control of himself and adding, "sire?"

The king let out a slight grin. What he wouldn't give to have a son as worthy of praise as Sir Roland. "With all of the blessings you have brought to my court, this one offense cannot be held against you, though it is a grave one. I warn you, be wary not to disappoint me in the future."

The advisor bowed low once more. "I shall do all in my power to repay you for your grace, my liege. Tell me what it is that you would have me do, and I shall see it done without hesitation."

King Cadoc's smile remained. This was the Sir Roland he found great pleasure in. This was the son he had always wanted. Cadoc knew Roland spoke the truth; the man would do anything his king asked of him. "Freshen up and dine with me. We have much to discuss about this wedding of Carter's."

"I would be honored, my liege," Roland kept his head bowed as he stood.

"Good," Cadoc affirmed. Then he called out, "Guards!"

After being released from his chains, Roland quietly made his way to his chambers. After a quick bath, he trimmed his beard to make the edges uniform. Now that his hair was cleaned, the curls were almost uncontrollable. The coils curled an inch or two from his head, but he didn't have time to trim them as well. Placing on new robes, Roland returned to the great hall. As he entered, he found that the king no longer sat atop his throne but was seated at a table with an array of food before him. The advisor clenched his jaw. No matter how hungry he felt, he needed to keep his composure.

With a bow, Roland spoke. "How may I assist you, Your Highness?"

"Come, sit, eat," commanded the king. "We can discuss as we dine."

"Thank you, my liege." Roland took to the seat the king had gestured to, sitting at his right-hand side. The advisor waited until the king had prepared a plate before he began to make one of his own.

This act of submission did not go unnoticed by the king. He knew Roland must be starving. The man had always worn tightly-fitted clothes, but now his garments hung loose on him. That in mind, Cadoc waited a while before speaking to give Roland time to eat.

The advisor did so slowly, placing appearances over his hunger. His eyes lit up as a maid poured wine into his goblet. Sixty-seven days with only water, what torture that had been! A smile appeared on the advisor's lips as he looked happily at his drink. Taking the first sip, Roland grew suspicious. This was his favorite wine! What test was his king putting him through? Peeking over to Cadoc, Roland noticed him quietly watching.

Cadoc cleared his throat before trying to make light of the situation. "Can you tell the wine, with but a taste?"

"It is of the royal vineyards near our southern-most seaport," the advisor replied, setting his goblet back on the table.

"Very good," the king nodded his head approvingly, "but I suppose it's no surprise that you recognize it. You've been drinking it since your fourteenth year!"

"It was the first wine I ever tasted," Roland gazed at the cup as he spoke. "During our first meal together, when you bestowed upon me the right to the provenance of Morer."

"'Twas your birthright, through your father," Cadoc insisted, "and you have done well with it."

"I would never have reached such success if not by your guidance, my king. There are a great many things I could have never accomplished if it weren't for you." Roland bowed his head a bit in remorse. "I will do well to remember how large of an impact you have had on my life and treat you with a greater respect."

"It is you who gives the advice now," chuckled Cadoc as he drank some of the wine from his goblet.

"Though my title is that of your advisor, it is I who is learning from my time in your court. For that opportunity, I am very grateful."

"You are welcome. I have enjoyed teaching you," the king replied solemnly. With courage, Cadoc said what he had been thinking. Something he had never dared to say. "Over these many years, I have found great pride in you, Roland."

Roland's eyes widened at the statement. Why would the king say such a thing to a man that betrayed him? He never complimented anyone! The advisor knew he needed to tread carefully. "Then I find even more shame in my actions, my liege. For it seems you had placed great trust in me, and I have failed you."

"One failure is not enough to tarnish your numerous successes. Though I must say, I believe your latest enterprise could turn out to be a success itself."

"You do?" Roland asked without thinking. Irritated with himself for losing control of his tongue for the second time that day he added, "Your Majesty?"

"Don't be misled," the king huffed. "I am not pleased, but as far as women go, this noble seems very profitable. We have yet to receive the true dowry, but the offering her men brought with them today was a year's worth of profit!"

"A year's worth," Roland muttered, "and she is bringing more?"

"That is what I have been told," Cadoc replied, "but I am anxious. Carter was not lying when he said her family wanted to keep her identity hidden from me. You must see why this concerns me."

"I do, Your Highness," Roland forced a sigh. This was his opportunity to make the king despise this woman. If he handled the situation correctly, Cadoc would place every thought into learning her secret. "It concerns me, as well. Surely she knows that our people would accept her simply because of her engagement to Prince Carter. So, she has already lied about her motive for keeping her identity secret. There must be another factor behind her decision. What it is, I do not know."

"So, you know as little of her as I?" asked the king.

"I'm afraid so. The prince has not shared any details with me."

After thinking a moment, Cadoc requested a service from his advisor. "Her messengers are to leave tomorrow. Speak with them, and try to learn all you can before they depart."

"I will do as you wish, Your Majesty," the advisor replied. He had wanted to question them himself anyhow. Carter had said the woman was to remain unknown, but Roland needed more information for his plan to succeed.

After finishing his meal with the king, Roland began his journey back to his quarters. It seemed his life had gone back to normal. How lucky he was, not to have been killed like the advisors that had come before him. It seemed odd that he had been treated in such a way, to be given praises and special treatment after what he had done. But the advisor was not one to complain. Roland would rather have forgiveness than the fate that the previous sixteen advisors had met.

"Roland?" came a call from behind him, pulling the advisor out of his thoughts. Turning, Roland saw his prince smiling widely, as well as the queen mother. When he realized who had called for him, Roland bowed in respect. Carter put a hand on his friend's shoulder and said jokingly, "I haven't seen you in ages!"

Knowing Carter would like to speak with his friend, the queen departed. After they were left alone, Roland replied, "I have been forgiven."

"Forgiven?"

"The king has reinstated me as his advisor."

"Only you!" Carter chuckled. "I don't know how you do it."

"Nor do I," Roland said as he stroked his beard. "Tomorrow, I resume my duties. As for the remainder of this evening, I must rid myself of this horrid hair!"

"It looks good," laughed Carter. "I think you should keep it. It makes you look more distinguished."

"I don't see any hair on your face! Why should mine constantly itch?"

"My beard doesn't come in fully; it degrades me and makes me feel like less of a man. You should feel blessed that you can grow a full one. I think it would be a kingly trait to have a beard."

"Shall I nurture a beard for your sake, sire?"

"Mocking me is not a very smart thing to do, Advisor."

"I was simply asking what my prince required of me," snickered Roland.

Carter let out a yawn. "I do have a request for you."

"Oh?" questioned the advisor.

"Shall we turn in? Ever since I was released, all I can think of is my bed. I bet it will feel even more wonderful now, having slept on that dreaded rock for so long."

"It just so happens; I was on my way to my quarters. I shall see you tomorrow, sire."

"Goodnight, Roland," Carter said as they both turned in the direction of their rooms. The prince completed his journey hastily, not even bothering to change before plopping onto his silk sheets. He had been right! His bed had never felt so good!

Duty Bound

The advisor did not take to his bed but instead went to his private study. Not once throughout the night did his head touch a pillow. Instead, he planned. Rummaging through chronicles of old, reviewing the maps of the Golden Palace, and studying the usual guard patterns conducted there; he grinned to himself as he proved his former theories true. What his prince had asked of him could be done. His tyrant king could be overthrown!

As streaks of first light stretched through the sky, Roland set his plans aside. He went to trim his hair but decided to leave it as Carter had recommended. With that, the advisor set out for the great hall. It seemed he was the first one to arrive there, as usual. When servants entered to prepare the hall for breakfast, Roland ordered them to set a table with food and place settings.

Roland waited a while on his feet to seat the Ponierians at his prepped table. He didn't have to wait long before he heard voices speaking in a foreign tongue. As they entered the room, he could not help but glare at them. How self-righteous those foreigners must be, to walk these halls as if they owned them.

The travelers conversed happily with one another as they entered the hall for their breakfast. All laughter stopped as their eyes set on a figure that stood in the far corner. His gaze was cold and hatred could be seen in his eyes. The man's tenseness disappeared instantly as he walked up to the group. "It is a pleasure to make your acquaintance. I can only presume you are the Ponierian travelers sent here to represent Prince Carter's fiancé."

"Yes, we are," spoke the head messenger as he outstretched a hand. He felt guilty for having misjudged the Remettian. The man had seemed discourteous when they entered but had proceeded to take the initiative of approaching them first. Perhaps his face was just set in that angry position; the Remettian king's surely seemed to be. As the stranger gripped his hand, the messenger slightly dipped his head to show respect. "My name is Mateo. It is an honor to meet another member of the king's inner court."

"There is no need for such glorification, Mateo. Please, call me Roland." The advisor could feel the man shiver in his grasp. The remainder of his convoy backed away as if they were a colony of fish. It seemed Roland hadn't lost his touch. These people were truly terrified of him. "I hope your stay has been satisfactory?"

"Indeed, we have been treated exceedingly well." The Ponierian tugged his hand from the advisor's grip. With a gulp he asked, "Is that Roland, as in?"

"Lord Roland of Morer," the advisor used his old title for their sake. No need to scare them further by mentioning his promotion. Still, they quivered at the name. "But let's not dwell on things of the past! We have such an exciting future before us, do we not?"

The group looked between themselves nervously, some whispering in their tongue. The advisor could see this task was going to be harder than expected. He needed to make them more comfortable around him. "The prince has told me of his bride. I must say she seems delightful."

"Yes, sh-she is," stuttered Mateo.

"I await the day when I shall meet her. Tell me, have they decided on a date yet? For the wedding, I mean," the advisor resorted to small talk to show his un-involvement in the affair. At the same time, he offered them the chance to answer a question. Based on their response, he would be able to judge how the conversation would go. If they were to lie about something so meaningless, he had no hope. But, if they told him the correct date, he had a chance.

Mateo answered him in a shaky voice. "T-the prince has decided to hold the ceremony on the fifth of this coming May."

The advisor gave a slight grin; Mateo had told the truth. The messenger found Roland even more intimidating with a smirk on his lips. What could the murderer be thinking? It was as Mateo judged him; the advisor asked his next question. "At least that gives her a lot of free time. May is weeks from now! Of course, in the spring, the king usually travels to the Golden Palace. I suppose the wedding will be held there, huh?"

"You are very clever," the Ponierian forced a smile.

"I suppose traveling to that palace may add a few more days to your journey."

"Well," Mateo sighed. "It might actually add weeks."

"How could that be?" Roland played along innocently.

Thinking there was little risk in disclosing the information, the messenger answered him. "My Lady's father would not want her in areas he did not know. So, rather than spend two extra days traveling in Remette, we would travel through Poniere for most of the journey. The road we took to come here leads directly from our side of the border to this castle. There is much farmland between that road and the next, which we would use to go to the Golden Palace. We will have to travel through the north of Poniere to reach it. Thus, our journey will take far longer."

Roland couldn't believe the amount of detail this man was letting go of. No wonder the Ponierians had been so easy to defeat. They were disturbingly careless. Because of his story, Roland had found out that the woman was from the northwest part of Poniere. Otherwise, she could have traveled by the main travel route of Poniere, which Roland knew ran through the center of the country. If she was going to travel on northern roads, she already had to be from the north herself. The northwest in particular, because the road the man had spoken of was to the east. The advisor joked lightly. "I suppose you will be on a bit of a tight schedule then."

"Undoubtedly! Through all of this, we will also need to arrange the dowry we will be bringing. There is so much to do," Mateo chuckled, only to stop himself. Hadn't this Remettian butchered thousands of his people? Yet, here they were, chatting as if nothing had happened. What shame his actions brought to those he had lost to this monster's brutality! "I must be going now."

"Are you heading back already?" Roland quizzed with concern in his voice. Gesturing to the preset table, he added, "At least have something to eat before you go!"

The messenger's fear grew. For the beast to have prepared such things was a bad omen in itself. He knew Roland was not as foolish as he was pretending to be. The man had been the main strategist in the last Great War! What was his goal this morning? Did he plan to kill them as he had done before? Was the food poisoned? Mateo looked at Roland nervously. Could he be trusted?

The advisor smiled at his prey happily. After a bit of hesitation, the swarm of Ponierians placed themselves at the table. When they had been seated, they grew even more nervous. There was exactly one extra plate at the table! Plopping into his chair amongst them, Roland poured himself a drink. He then passed the jug to Mateo, who was conveniently beside him. The messenger took it with shaking hands. Roland had known exactly how many Ponierians to prepare for! What could he be up to? "T-thank you!"

"You're welcome, Mateo," Roland smiled reassuringly. Unlike the frozen guests, he began to make his plate. Roland handed the dishes he had taken from to either Mateo or the man on his other side to get the food passed around. "I must say, it's nice that the wedding will be in the spring. Have you ever been to Remette in the spring?"

"No," gulped the messenger.

"It is beautiful. Let me tell you! There is no place better than Remette in the spring; and I have been to a lot of places, you know!"

"Yes, I know," Mateo said as he added a bit of pork to his plate with beads of sweat starting to appear on his brow.

"I suppose you have too, huh?" Roland nudged. "Being a messenger and all."

"Yes."

"It's nice, us sitting down together like this. Really shows that we're moving forward, doesn't it?"

"That was the goal," smiled Mateo as he carefully took his first bite of food. All others seated watched quietly to see if he would survive. When he did not choke or even cough, they too began to eat.

"The goal? I see. This marriage is some type of peace buffer, is that it? A way to establish a trustworthy bond between Remette and Poniere?"

"Is that not obvious?" The Ponierian looked at Roland, who in turn smiled wider.

"Not really," the advisor shrugged. "I mean, if she is just your average noble, it does little good. Especially if you're from the north, like you say."

Mateo became even more frightened. He had accidentally said they were from the north!

Unphased, Roland continued between bites of food, "For this marriage to establish any meaningful connection, this secret fiancé would need to come from a noble family that is extremely close to your king, Jessinias. 'Course, I suppose that might be why Prince Carter chose her, wouldn't you say?"

"That's what you're doing!" spat the messenger.

"Pardon?" Roland questioned, but he had already gotten his answer from the anger in the man's voice. Close to the king, she was indeed!

"You're just questioning me to find out about My Lady! You're not trying to be kind to us at all! You're just using us."

"I'm sorry if I came off that way." Roland's stance became gloomy as he continued. "I was just trying to hold a conversation. You all seemed hesitant to speak with me, so I tried to talk about things you were comfortable with. We can talk about whatever you'd like."

The advisor's actions seemed sincere to those of the table. One man seated across from him asked. "Do you regret it?"

"Regret what?" Roland asked shamelessly.

"What you did in the war? If you could take back what happened, would you?"

"No," Roland answered honestly. His voice became even lower than usual with the word causing those at the table to instantly grow fearful. Ruffling his hair in agitation, Roland explained himself. "When I entered the war, I was very young and foolish. Because of that, my entire first platoon was butchered in front of me. So, you see, you are not the only ones who suffered during those years. If I'm being honest, I still hold a bit of resentment to this day. To look from your perspective, you must understand that I merely did what was required of me. Had you met me on the field, would you not have tried to strike me down?"

The Ponierians looked back and forth at one another thinking they would like to strike at him right now!

After a moment of silence, Roland added, "War is war. We are called to do things that we are not proud of, but we must do such things if we are loyal to our cause. As for what I have done? I cannot take back my actions, but they have made me who I am today." Roland looked into his palms as he thought of his past. A fire lit within him as he was once again reminded of the hatred that he held within himself. "My only regret is the one I let go. If only I had stopped that one, so many more would have survived from both sides."

"Did you ever catch him, or was he gone forever?" asked another at the table.

Seeing an opportunity to take hold of the conversation, Roland gave a sorrowful smile. "I have yet to see her again."

"Ah," jested Mateo, "a young love turned sour?"

"Not love," the advisor sighed, "more of a misplaced trust."

"Who is she?" begged the men of the table.

"My White Queen," Roland replied softly as if in a daydream of her memory.

"Sounds like a love tale to me," chuckled Mateo. "What would you do, should you see this woman again?"

"Ah, well." Roland rubbed the back of his neck to give the appearance of nervousness. "For the longest time, I had hoped to find her again during the war, but as I said, I never did. Had I done so back then; I would never have let her get away from me again. But if I were to see her now, I suppose I would have to treat her with respect as we're no longer-"

"Enemies?" Mateo finished for him.

Roland cleared his throat, sipping at his drink agitatedly. Taking notice of his uneasiness, the messenger tried to make up for the pain he had caused. "Who knows, perhaps she perished in the war. This is why you could not find her."

"She survived." Roland slammed his cup back onto the table. "She is alive and well."

The Ponierians had no response to Roland's anger. He seemed heartbroken. Could that be why he had been so wrathful in the war? The brutality of a broken heart, such a tragic story. The Ponierians found themselves forgiving Roland for all he had done. People did all sorts of foul deeds when they lost love from their lives. The advisor used their pity as a fulcrum point to start his interrogations over again. "I can only hope this woman of yours is the complete opposite of her."

"Oh! Rest assured; My Lady is nothing like the woman you speak of! She is kind, generous, and selfless. All in the kingdom think highly of her!"

"She does indeed sound lovely, such a contrast it seems. The prince is a lucky man."

"Yes, I believe he is," smiled Mateo.

"I hope King Jessinias sees this as a blessing, lest we have another war on our hands." Roland took a bite of his food happily; he was back in control.

"I wouldn't worry about that. A wedding is a blessed occasion, best not tarnish it with the gloom of war."

"I didn't mean to in any way degrade My Lady!" Roland said with worry in his voice. "I just meant; King Jessinias' daughter was also set to marry Prince Carter."

"It is a delicate situation; hence My Lady's hidden identity. But even once the veil is taken away, there will be no hysteria between our people. I find peace in that hope."

"I take courage in your assertiveness." Roland did not dare pry anymore. He had gotten all he needed anyway. For the remainder of the breakfast, they chatted amongst each other calmly. The Ponierians spoke to the advisor as if he were their friend, no longer hating him for what he had done.

While they sat together, others came to the hall to eat. As Cadoc passed by them to a table prepared just for the royal family, he gave a slight smile to Roland. How much had his advisor learned already? The Ponierians seemed to have welcomed him with open arms, such a trickster that one.

Soon after, Carter rushed into the hall. He looked at his father's table, worry sprouting to his face. To the king's left side sat the queen, but on his right were two empty place settings. Where had Roland gone? He was always one of the first people awake! Why was he not at his place? The prince spun around in worry. What had his father done to him?

"Sire," came a deep call from a side table. Amidst all the traveling Ponierians, his friend stood and bowed to him.

"Roland!" Carter beamed. "For a moment, I thought you weren't here! Wait, what is that?"

The prince was pointing to a cream-filled pastry on the advisor's plate. Roland lifted the dish he had taken it from. "Here you are."

Scarfing one down, Carter let out a moan. How he had missed eating like this! Picking up another, he asked. "Do you think there might be room for me here?"

At once, the Ponierians reassembled themselves so that Carter could sit with them. He happily did so, plopping down beside his advisor. Maids brought out a golden plate for him to eat from. After thanking them, he turned to the rest of his new table and once again pointed to the pastry tray. "Does anyone else want those?"

All rejected, having filled themselves. In relief, Carter placed the tray on top of his plate. One by one, he ate all that were left. His advisor spoke to him as he ate. "We were just speaking of the brutality of this winter. It's extremely cold out there."

"I wouldn't know. I haven't been outside much lately." The prince let out a snort. The travelers looked at him quizzingly, not understanding how that was funny. In an effort to remove confusion the prince said, "It's an inside joke."

The travelers burst out in laughter, causing Carter to turn to his advisor for understanding. Roland replied with a sigh for having to explain such a weak jest. "You weren't outside, so it was an inside joke."

Carter cackled alongside the rest. "I didn't even mean to do that!"

The Ponierians enjoyed the rest of their meal with their newfound friends. Not long after, they began their journey home. All were perplexed at how kind and enjoyable the Beast of Morer had seemed. After all the pain he had caused, it appeared Sir Roland was human after all. Better yet, they would be able to bring good news to My Lady about her future husband. Nothing like his father, the prince seemed just as kind as the woman they worked for. Perhaps this marriage would be good after all.

When they were once again alone, Carter nudged his advisor's shoulder as he laughed. "Look at you, making friends. I haven't seen you smile that much since, well, ever!"

The advisor turned to him. His joyful spirit had left him, his face in its normal, uncaring setting. "How exhausting! I don't know how you people do it."

"What people?"

"Happy people. My face feels as if it has been stretched out!" The advisor rubbed his cheeks. "And they were so loud! I fear they've given me a headache."

"I thought you liked them." The prince stooped his shoulders in sorrow.

"It was supposed to seem like I cared. All I needed was a bit of information, which I now have."

"What information is that?"

"Come with me," Roland said as he brushed past the prince. He led him back to his study, setting out all he had discovered the night before. "I am now certain I can fulfill that which you asked me to do."

"What are you saying?" whispered Carter nervously.

"You shall ascend to the throne of Remette on the day you are set to be married."

The prince was thrown into shock. Roland seemed so sure. This had to be it! "How?"

"Since I am returning to the role of Advisor, I will once again oversee most of the kingdom's military operations. This includes the normal palace guard rotations, which I have documented here."

The advisor shifted some of the papers to the prince. "With the irritating number of guards in this castle, your father will pay little mind to the small measure of guards I will set to rotate the Golden Palace. He will probably be relieved to have the space and not want me to establish the same protocols there as I have here. Should he say anything, I will tell him I changed my regulations because I knew my old style had upset him. He will agree, and we will keep things the way I have documented there."

"I don't see how this helps," Carter muttered. "There are fewer guards, but the rotations are flawless. There is at least one patrol group on a floor at a time, and these rotations will cover every inch of the palace every half hour."

"I couldn't make the plan obvious by having a hole in my security," Roland shrugged. "My guard schedules do not have flaws. The only error in our guards that night will be the traitors implanted within the rotating shifts."

"Isn't that dangerous?" asked the prince. "Some of the guards are loyal to my father. What if one turns on us?"

"Not to worry." The advisor let out an evil chuckle. "I am not planning on recruiting the king's guards. I have men of my own who I will bring in for this project."

"What are you thinking, Advisor?"

Roland smiled brightly. How he had missed the thrill of war! To have a covert operation, in which he could help his true king overthrow that gruesome fake was a delightful rush. "Jasper and his crew. I am already working with them in some aspects. I know for a fact that they will be glad to aid you in the overthrowing of your father."

"I plan to enter them into the regular guard routes, and on the night of your ascension they will provide all the support we need. Our timeframe will be short; but when it comes down to it, the eradication will not take long."

"E-eradicate?" Carter blurted out. "We-we're not going to kill him!"

"What?" asked the advisor with disappointment in his voice. "I thought that's what you wanted?"

"I want to stop him! That doesn't mean we stoop to his level," Carter sighed. "We must be better than our enemies; otherwise, we become the villains."

"I understand." Roland felt a twinge of guilt. Carter was right. He was indeed a villain for thinking such things. "The plan will work regardless. We can imprison him instead if you want. We will just have to be more careful about how we handle the situation. Your father has a vast influence. Should even one movement be made incorrectly, he will be alerted, and we will be killed."

"I agree," the prince gulped. "What must I do?"

"Prepare for your wedding, of course," grinned Roland. "Make it as big of a conundrum as possible. Drive your father mad!"

"You've yet to speak to me about my wedding."

"Why would I? It's a trade deal, no more, no less. We needed money and this woman's father had it. Her existence is of little importance, wouldn't you say? You will become king before the wedding. You can always dismiss her at that time."

"I hadn't thought of that," Carter mumbled.

"If I'm being honest, there is a large chance she may never reach the palace at all."

"What? Why?" the prince gasped.

"We are going to stage a little accident for this fiancé of yours. Jasper will relieve her of this dowry and take what he gathers to pay for the armor they need to fit in with the other guards of the castle. We need to do this. Otherwise, your father will know of the purchase."

"What of My Lady?" the prince questioned. "Surely such treatment would scar her for life! She already hates Remettians enough as it is!"

"May I remind you, sire, this is a trade deal. You don't actually believe her intentions are pure, do you? You just said she hates Remettians; that includes you. Do you really want a woman like that?" With a huff, Roland ruffled his hair. "When we do this, Jasper will be careful not to harm her in any way. She will most likely panic and return home after they overtake her. If her father is insistent on having her marry you, they will return with perhaps even twice the dowry amount as an apology. You can reject her with the excuse that she refused to show up for the scheduled wedding, or you can take the money. I would choose the latter myself, but that is just my preference."

"What if she comes anyway? The day we steal from her, I mean?"

"Then you play along until you ascend the throne. You can get rid of her after that. If she isn't horrible, you could always just accept her. She technically would have paid her dowry to you, would she not?"

"So, it's up to me, whether I want her or not?" Carter gulped.

"Precisely. The only other factors I need are the date and time she will be traveling into our territory. Once I know that, I can set things up with Jasper and his men. All should go smoothly afterward. So, what do you think?" Roland bowed to his future king. "Has your advisor served you well, sire?"

"Indeed," Carter grinned. "I take great pride in you, Roland."

A shiver took hold of the advisor. That was so similar to what King Cadoc had told him yesterday. For a moment, Roland felt as if a giant stone had been laid upon his chest. What was this feeling he was having?

"I hope this works," Carter chuckled. "After what my father did over an unwanted engagement, I doubt he would hold back punishment for this."

"Not in the slightest," Roland said nervously. "Luckily, all we must wait for is this woman's response. We should have enough time to prepare after we receive it. So, try not to worry. Just act excited for her to arrive."

"That shouldn't be too hard! It's when she arrives that I'll finally get my freedom."

"You deserve it," smiled the advisor. Not once did they speak of the plan again over the following weeks. Throughout the days, Carter and Roland went about their business to prepare for the upcoming wedding. During the nights, the advisor planned. Evaluating every aspect of what was to come.

Final Preparations

In the days that meshed of both winter and springtime, the royal family arrived at their summer home. There was a reason it was called the Golden Palace. In the sunlight, its stones seemed to be made of the precious metal. The scarlet flags of Remette were exalted against the stones' bright color. The size of the palace was massive, making it all the more impressive to the eye. It was at least three times as large as the castle they had traveled from.

Roland led the travelers from atop his black steed. As he journeyed through the town, he looked from side to side to see all who had gathered. Peasants of the outer town watched as the caravan passed by. Spotting a group of ruffians that he knew all too well, the advisor gave a slight nod of his head to them. From under his hood, Jasper noticed the action. Roland wanted to talk. Tapping on a window of the tavern he had been standing in front of, Jasper kept his eyes on the advisor. Roland, in turn, smiled slightly as he carried on in his journey.

"Wha' was tha' about?" Martin asked, crunching a bite from his apple.

"Get the lads some rooms at the inn. We're sticking around here a while."

"Wha'?" Martin asked, involuntarily spitting a slobbered bit of his apple onto Jasper's face. His leader grimaced as he wiped it away. "Why're we stayin'?"

"Roland wants to speak with us."

"I get tha' he's been nice and all, but," Martin lowered his voice so the mass of guards around the king's chariots could not hear, "he don't sit well with me. I can't tell whose side he's on."

"Then I'll go alone, but I still want you to get the rooms for tonight."

"Alrigh', alrigh'. I'll go," Martin sighed as he departed from his leader. The ruffian fumed as he followed his orders. Roland made him uneasy. It felt as if he was a spy who would kill them for the glory of the king. Aware of his past actions, Martin knew that should the king order him to do so, Roland wouldn't hesitate to take their heads. It wasn't wise, working with a man like that.

After unpacking their load, most of the weary travelers in the king's caravan took time to rest. The advisor, however, made his way into the outer town. Entering the tavern Jasper had motioned to, he saw his friend waiting near the back with two cups of mead.

The tavern was a small one. Only a few tables and chairs were scattered around its interior. The bar was in the middle of the room with tables in a circle around it. It was dimly lit with a few scattered candles. The lack of light was precisely why it had been chosen as the meeting place.

As Roland approached, Jasper pushed one cup forward. "This one is yours."

"You are a great friend," Roland said as he accepted the drink. What a delightful taste after such a long day. After drinking some of the offering, the advisor turned his gaze back to Jasper. "I have a request to make of you."

"I expected as much."

"I know what it is you want and I have found a way to get it," the advisor said as if the conversation was of little importance, "but I need your help in this endeavor. It is too great a burden for one man alone. Would you and your men be willing to follow my orders one last time?"

"I'm sorry," chirped a high-pitched voice from behind the advisor. Roland turned to find a young maiden with glowing red cheeks. He couldn't help but notice the cup of mead in her hands. She must've been a serving girl in the tavern.

"May I help you?" the advisor asked, causing her cheeks to turn redder still.

"It is you," she smiled. Setting the cup in front of him, the girl gave a slight curtsey. "I'm sorry to intrude. I just thought I'd bring this to you. Compliments of the house."

The advisor looked at his second drink. She knew who he was? That was not good. No one must know that he had been there. Roland glanced back to her, still standing there nervously. He could easily make the best of the situation. With a grin, he replied. "That is very kind of you. Tell me, what is your name?"

"My name?" The girl looked as if she might faint, now that he had asked such a thing. "I-it's Lillian."

"Lillian," Roland tilted his head, playfully admiring her. "It suits you."

"Thank you!" The maiden couldn't believe her luck. He was talking to her!

"You're welcome," Roland chuckled as he got up from his chair.

Jasper took a sip of his mead and leaned back in his seat. It seemed he would have to wait.

The advisor reached out and played with a piece of the maiden's hair. "Does anyone else here know who I am, or are you simply as clever as you are gorgeous?"

Gorgeous! He had said that, right? Lillian couldn't think straight. "Nah, nope. Just me. I didn't even tell my dad."

She pointed a thumb towards a man who was glaring at them from behind the bar. Roland paid him little mind as he released the maiden's hair, instead lifting her hand to his lips. After kissing it gently, Roland spoke to her again. "May we keep this our little secret? I should love to see that beautiful face of yours again, but to do so as myself. I see no need to add the glamor of my title."

Placing her hand to his chest, Roland brought the maiden into his presence. Smiling softly down at her, he asked. "What do you say, Lillian?"

"O-okay," she blushed in return. This was one of the most highly regarded men in the country! Not to mention, he was insanely handsome! And he had kissed her hand! She would go to the grave without telling a soul if it meant having him return someday.

"Well, in that case, why don't you use my name as I have yours?" the advisor grinned at her, still yet to release her hand from his. "You can call me by it anytime you like. All I ask is that you do so quietly. I wouldn't want others to intrude on us."

"Nor would I, Roland," she whispered back. After turning the color of a beet, the maiden scurried away nervously. Her heart raced in her chest. She said his name! Lillian rubbed her hand excitedly, how charming he had been.

Roland shook his head as he sat down. What a foolish girl! So stuck on the thought of love that she would behave so irrationally over a man she just met. Typical!

"How many tavern girls have you done that to?" chuckled Jasper.

"One of my deepest regrets, my friend," Roland said, chugging the rest of his first cup. "I've done that enough times that I can hardly find a pub which is safe for me to enter!"

"Perhaps you should be more careful."

"What's life without a bit of excitement?" grinned the advisor. "Now, back to my proposal. Would you be interested in such a transaction?"

Jasper knew he was speaking of overthrowing the king. Roland was just being precautious of others in the tavern.

"Tell me what I must contribute for my share."

"I have to receive word from one other member of the project before we can get into any of that. I just wanted to see if you would be on board. Where are you staying? I am hoping to have all I need within the week. I will come to you when I'm ready."

"I wasn't planning on staying long." Jasper scratched his head. "I'll be leaving the city soon."

Roland knew the man didn't have the money to rent a room inside city limits. "That's too bad, but it's my fault you didn't get all of the information you needed today, so take this as compensation. If you were to stay, where might I find you?"

The advisor placed a bag of gold coins onto the table. Jasper looked at it hungrily and said, "An inn called The Nook."

"I hope to see you there soon," Roland smiled before finishing his second mead. "I'll be taking my leave now."

"Farewell, my friend." Jasper raised his cup. What did the advisor have in mind?

Roland, on the other hand, brewed in his plans. He and his prince used every day to its maximum potential in order to prepare for the upcoming events. A few days after Roland had spoken with Jasper, a servant raced up to Carter with a note in his hand. "Sire, it's My Lady! She has replied!"

Struck with interest, the king, queen, and the advisor gathered around to read it over the prince's shoulders.

My Dearest Prince,

I am delighted that you are eager to learn more about me, as I also hope to learn more about you. Regarding your request, I fear I will only be able to reach you a short time before the wedding. I shall set out forthwith and plan to arrive on the first of May. I hope this will grant us a little time to get to know each other.

Highest Regards,

~ Your Lady

"The first of May." Carter took up the role his advisor had given him. "We need to prepare! Send out the invitations! The wedding will be on the fifth!"

"Ugh," groaned the king as his wife scampered from his side to assist her son with his endeavors. "Is this wedding all that boy will speak of? Yet, he tells us nothing of this woman!"

"All we know is the area she comes from, and there are plenty of noble families in that region," the advisor tutted. "I suppose all we can do is wait and see."

"Is that really all you know?" Cadoc sighed. It was irritating that such facts had been kept from him.

"The only other thing is her supposed hatred towards Remettians. Her father mentioned me in particular. Carter has asked me not to tell her who I am so that she will not be alarmed. I am only to introduce myself as the court advisor."

"Do you think you might know this woman? Is that why she holds such a grudge?"

"No, my liege," Roland replied. "It is impossible for me to have met her. No noble I ever faced; man, woman, or child would have been spared from your judgement, my king. This fact unsettles me all the more. In order for her to have accepted the proposal, she must have been from a family that was protected from our efforts in the war. Ponierians are all the same, this judgement she holds over us is nothing more than tales they've heard from one another. I doubt her family felt even the slightest harm in the war."

"That's true," Cadoc stated. "She is probably just judging you for your reputation."

"They all do."

"Is it someone she knows?" the king thought aloud. "Perhaps someone she knows hates you. She could have based her suspicion off of their experience."

The king walked away as he pondered who the prince's fiancé might be. Following his king's last words, the advisor raced to his chambers. He placed a black cloak over his shoulders, preparing to leave.

Before he could depart, he found himself drawn to his nightstand. Opening a small chest that he had placed there, Roland pulled out a purple napkin which was wrapped tightly into a ball. He carried it delicately to a side table in his study. Displayed there was a chessboard with only one piece, the white queen.

Roland sat before his shrine with the parcel. Looking to his board, he sighed. "It would make sense that she would know you. What lies have you spread about me to cause her to hate me so?"

Running a hand through his hair, the advisor groaned. "Will I forever be cursed by you, my Queen?"

Roland sorrowfully placed the napkin beside his chess piece. Without glancing to the board again, he departed to meet Jasper. After explaining the plan of betrayal to him, Jasper and his entire crew joined in on the scheme. They met with Roland over the weeks leading up to the woman's arrival for updates on the progress of the plan. During that time, the advisor took the responsibility of setting up the purchase of armor from a blacksmith in Gevhart. Once everything was prepped, all they had to do was wait for the day when the prince's fiancé would arrive.

Things of the Night

On the last day of April, the advisor passed through the outer town of King Cadoc's palace like a shadow. His elegant black horse faded into the darkness around it. The only part of the animal still visible was the white stripe down its nose. Quietly making his way to the edge of the houses, the traveler stopped at his usual tavern. After tying his horse to a post, he ducked inside.

Only three people were in the pub at the time. That assured, Roland removed his hood, revealing the dark scarlet robes he wore underneath for but a moment. His dark clothing made the blue of his eyes shine in the pale light of the place.

Looming over the bar as he slid a coin to the barkeep, Roland asked for a pint of mead. After receiving a nod from the bartender, he sat at a table near the rear exit, seemingly unaware of the figure in the shadows beside him. It was not the barkeep but his daughter who brought out his pint and handed it to him. She smiled brightly as she did so. "It's been a while since you've been in! We're glad you were able to make it back!"

"I as well, Lillian. I must say your father serves the finest of mead," the advisor said in a deep, booming voice. As he finished his praise, he noticed her unhappiness with the statement. Leaning forward in his chair, he grinned up to her. "Of course, I have missed you all the more. For you are the finest of women, are you not?"

Her face flushed red as she giggled. "Oh, Roland! You're such a tease."

"You are the tease in that dress, my dear," he raised his cup in a toast to her. The girl turned into a fit of giggles as she returned to her place by her father, who did not seem as excited about the compliment. Upon his first sip of the liquid, Roland exhaled with delight. As he leaned back into his chair, the advisor brought the cup to his lips again. This time he spoke quietly, hiding his words in the shadows of his palms.

"Tomorrow, the bride of Prince Carter will arrive. I've been asked to receive her alongside the royals, so I cannot be with you when you take her en route. It is imperative that my position with the king remain stable for this to work as planned," he said with a pause as he took another sip. "I need to know you're ready. We only have one shot at this, Jasper!"

"No need to worry, Roland. My men are prepared to do what is necessary," replied the shadow in a soft voice.

"I'm simply being cautious," grumbled the advisor while taking another gulp of his mead.

"You always are."

"It is a good trait to have," he replied bitterly. "Do you remember the plan?"

"Must I repeat it again?"

"This is not a joke! If the opportunity is not taken, we risk everything!" growled Roland. The conversation had escalated, bringing unwanted attention. After surveying the room to be sure no one was listening, the advisor turned to Jasper and awaited his reply.

"The girl will be traveling through the northeastern trade route. This means she can choose from only two roads that lead to the palace, either the mountain trail or the valley grove. If we cover the mountain trail, we will be able to see her approach. Besides, that is the quickest route anyway, so she is more likely to choose it. If she goes through the valley, we will go down the side of the mountain and cut her off in the meadow."

"Perfect," exclaimed the advisor, who had been nodding his head along the whole time. "Once we have what we need, we can easily take down that tyrant!"

"I'll drink to that," chuckled Jasper as he raised his glass. The advisor raised his as well.

"To the good of the nation!"

"To the good of the nation!"

Once their glasses were empty, both men stood, nodded to each other, and departed. The advisor left the way he had come, returning towards the palace gate. Lillian watched him ride away as if in a dream. The shadow, Jasper, slipped out through the pub's back door, making his way into the night.

"Well?" asked Martin, who had been waiting for him in the alley. "Wha' did he say?"

"He won't be joining us. He is to stay with the king to welcome the prince's fiancé when she gets to the palace tomorrow."

"Wha'?" exclaimed Martin. "The lads ain't gonna be happy with this! This was his idea, and now wha'? He jus' wants us to take all the chances?"

"It's a delicate situation. Everything has to be in order for this to happen. If one thing falls out of line, we're done for. So, if the man says we are to take care of the caravan ourselves, that is what we're going to do," retaliated Jasper as he harshly pushed past Martin to mount his horse. "Unless, of course, you've changed your mind?"

"Oh, you know I'm still comin'. I'm jus' not excited, is all," said Martin. Climbing onto his horse, he joined Jasper, who was now riding away into open country.

"So, wha' we gonna tell the lads then?" Martin asked once he had caught up.

"We tell them that he is taking care of another piece of the puzzle. All they have to do is play their part, and all will be over soon."

"Don't seem too reassurin' there, Cap'n."

"You just leave them to me."

"Tha' I can do."

As they neared the fires of camp, shouting and stomping could be heard carrying its own musical rhythm.

"Ransackin' we will do, to all yer friends and you!
In the mountain pass above, and in the valley too!"

The whole crowd burst into laughter!

"To all yer friends and you," coughed the singer as he laughed again. The man seemed to have lost his shirt during his drunken concert. His sash was wrapped around his forehead instead of his waist where it belonged. Catching a glance at his incoming comrades, the singer stood and shouted. "Hey! Jasper's back! Hey, me n' the lads come up with a little tune fir ya."

"And if it wasn't angelical," retorted Jasper coldly as he dismounted, tossing his hood from his head. The light of the flames flickered against the green of his eyes. His dark brown hair was cut short other than on the top of his head, which was ruffled up from the long ride. The shadow of a beard stretched across his cheeks.

All humor died within the camp. The ruckus ceased and crickets could once again be heard as the men awaited the judgment that could clearly be seen on their leader's face. Jasper circled the fire, taking in the state of his men. The tents were barely set up. All supplies were now loosely thrown around the camp. The men themselves were in such a state that the few who were still awake were not even standing properly, if they could stand at all!

"So, is this what I am to expect every time I leave you? Tomorrow we are going to take a stride towards freedom. Yet, tonight you drink so much that you may not even wake up in the morning," he spat with utter distaste as he kicked one of the men who had already passed out.

"Sorry, sir. We got a little carried away is all," said the singer.

"Really? A little carried away? Is that what you call this, Dan?" Jasper snarled as he tore the sash off of the man's brow. Turning to the rest of the men, he declared. "We have a big day tomorrow. I suggest you all get some rest."

The men started towards their half-made quarters.

"Wait!" Jasper's shout stopped them in their tracks. "Let me finish! You will clean up this mess you've made before any of you can sleep. I don't care if it takes you all night. This type of behavior will not be tolerated!"

Painful sighs were heard throughout the camp as Jasper and Martin left them to their work. The pair walked up the mountain trail in the quiet of the night. Martin had a torch in hand, guiding the pair away from the rest of the ruffians. In the glow, his flaming red hair stood out brilliantly. The freckles across his face were easily seen against the pale of his skin. His blue eyes filled with sadness.

"Sure you weren't a bit harsh on 'em?" he asked, lighting the way for his friend.

"Did you see what they had done? Five hours, five hours! That's all we left them for, and look what they did."

"I know Jasper, I do; but we aren't military men after all. Certainly not the types who make their beds every mornin'. They was jus' havin' a bit o' fun."

"Maybe you're right. They deserve to have a little fun now and then." Jasper paused for a moment. "It's just with all that's about to happen, shouldn't they be the least bit worried?"

"Tha's prolly wha' drove 'em to drink in the first place, if I'm bein' honest," chuckled Martin. "Say, look at tha'," the man commanded while pointing toward a cluster of fires. He raced to the edge of the cliff face, peering into the darkness below. "Is tha' the queen-to-be, you think?"

"I don't know," Jasper said as he pulled a spyglass from his side, leveling it up to his eye. "It's hard to tell in this light, but it just might be! I'm seeing multiple carriages. No signs of gold yet. . . Oop!"

"Wha', wha' is it? Wha' do ya see?" Martin crouched low to the ground.

"I've got some guards here."

"Tha's a good sign, or is it?"

"Good as in it might be them; bad as in we might be outnumbered," Jasper replied, never lifting his head from the camp's outline. A flicker of light had caught his eye. Moving his spyglass, he looked closer into the darkness it had come from. He saw nothing there, but it was not long before the troops in the camp made their way to where the flicker had been.

"Interesting," he muttered.

"Wha's int'restin'?" asked Martin, who was stretching his neck out as if it could help him see farther.

"Something is going on down there. I've got a lot of movement near the north."

The guards had gathered in a half-moon around where Jasper had seen the strange light. They seemed to be looking at what had made it, but in the dark, it was hard to tell what exactly that was.

"Well, wha's goin' on?"

"Not sure. They are looking at something, but I can't tell what it is," Jasper pressed his eye harder into his spyglass. "I see it!"

"Wha'?" exclaimed Martin, who was dying with anticipation.

"They are gathering around a tent. I didn't see it before. It must be made out of dark material. I've only seen it now that the curtain is pulled back."

"Tha's it? Tha's all you've got? A tent?"

"It's more than you've got! What are you doing over there, other than making that ridiculous face?"

"Wha'?" Martin asked. He had his eyes squeezed tightly together, his nose was crinkled, and his buck teeth hung out of his open mouth in a comical way as he stretched his neck to see.

"They just got handed something from whoever is in that tent."

"Well, wha' is it?" squealed Martin, shaking Jasper impatiently.

"Just wait a minute," scolded Jasper. "They're lifting it up."

"WHA' IS IT?"

"It looks like a-" He readjusted his sights as he watched the guard pick up the object and turn to face his direction. Lifting it to his head, the guard repositioned himself until he was directly looking at Jasper through his own spyglass. "Get down!"

"Wha'?" said Martin in disappointment.

"They see us!" shouted Jasper as he drove Martin to the ground.

"Oof! Oh, come on! Wha' was tha' for?" exclaimed Martin. Jasper was too occupied with the torch, which he was now frantically trying to put out. "Oi! Are you mad?"

"Quiet! Don't you realize? If that is them, now they know someone was watching them, and they know where we are!"

"It can't be, can it?" Fear was now written across Martin's face.

With an unsure glance, Jasper turned toward the camp again to find it had gone dark. The only light available was found in the embers left at the bottom of the now doused fires. "Whoever they are, they aren't stupid."

"Why? I can't see a thing."

"That's the point, Martin," Jasper said with a sigh, clicking his spyglass shut. "Come on. We'd best head back to camp in case they are on their way here."

"They wouldn't come all the way over here jus' to kill us, would they?"

Jasper looked at his friend and asked rhetorically, "Would you go all the way over there just to steal some jewels?"

"What are we waitin' for!" Martin proclaimed, taking the lead on the path. "Let's get back to camp!"

Upon his arrival, Jasper found his team sprawled out alongside their mess. They seemed to have fallen asleep while they were cleaning. He could do nothing but chuckle. "Look at this. My best men! It seems we will need to protect them in the event of an attack. So much for safety in numbers!"

"Do you see Asher over there? Ha! He's still standin' up," said Martin, staring at a man who was leaning against his horse's saddle. Apparently, he had fallen asleep while packing his saddlebag.

Laughter rang out. "These lads can't even clean up a simple mess without fallin' over half-dead!"

"But they do make a valid point. We should get some rest. Big day tomorrow."

"I thought you said those guards was gonna come up here n' kill us?"

"No, I said they might. Tell me, would you rather go out by sitting up, being scared all night or go peacefully in your sleep?"

"I don't know tha' I could sleep now!" exclaimed Martin.

"Then you can be the lookout," smirked Jasper

"The lookout! Tha's the first man tha' gets killed!"

"Only if he doesn't do his job right," said Jasper as he entered his tent, "and while you're at it, mind picking away at this mess?"

"Oh, 'cause tha's how I wanna die!" shouted Martin at the drapes of Jasper's tent. "Cleanin'!"

The echoes of his banter seemed to cling to the night sky, but they had no effect on the sleeping men below.

10

Peculiar Heist

When the sun rose, Jasper exited his tent. The men were still in the same places they had been the night before, other than Asher, who had finally fallen to the ground.

"Hey, Martin, did you actually stay up all night?" he asked as he neared a figure who was facing the direction of the foreign camp.

"Martin?" Jasper called out again as he put his hand on the man's shoulder. The body slumped into the grass lifelessly. He let out a soft chuckle as he looked at Martin's weary face.

"So much for not being able to sleep," he said to himself as he passed by the sleeping renegade. Jasper made his way back to the edge of the cliff and studied the caravan he had seen the night before. It was more massive than he had imagined! A circle of black tents engulfed the valley just before the road split into two. Numerous chariots and carriages could be seen, as well as a plentiful number of horses to pull them. Taking out his spyglass, Jasper surveyed the camp again.

Everything in the camp was that of the highest quality. The tents were made of thin black silks. Mounted to some of the carriages were boxes. Jasper could only dream of the treasures they might have held. Gold, silver, jewels, and fine silks! His eyes grew at the sight of what he would gain later that day. The whole set-up gleamed of wealth. Even the servants were clothed in better materials than he.

It was clear which of the carriages were for the noblewoman and which were meant for her workers. Artwork etched in gold traced the outside of the main carriage. The golden hubcaps of the wheels alone were worth a fortune. What a booty to be had!

"No wonder the prince is going to marry her," Jasper muttered, shaking his head in disbelief.

Only one thing stood in his way, the guards. There were at least one hundred of them in the camp. A little under half had black armor, while the rest wore gleaming steel. All of which were currently feasting on a breakfast of bread and other pastries. Jasper smacked his lips at the sight.

Studying the way in which they stood, he grew more jealous of their stature than their food. Even when eating breakfast, they all stood in unison, a tidy formation of men ready for anything. He thought of his own camp. His men were still sleeping and scattered throughout the dump they had created the night before. With a sigh, he watched the travelers below. How could his men take on an army like that?

"Them lucky pigs!" said a voice from behind him.

"Ah, my trusty lookout. No one kill you during the night?"

"Ha ha! Very funny."

"I thought it was."

"Seriously though, jus' look at 'em, feastin' like kings!" Martin's belly growled with hunger. "I wanna eat like tha'!"

"And one day you will. It won't be long now," Jasper said, leaning back into his spyglass.

"I hope you're righ'."

"I'm always ri-" The figure of a woman caught his attention. "Looks like we've found our queen-to-be!"

"Wha' does she look like?"

As she pulled back the drapes of the tent, Jasper spoke the only thought that entered his mind, "Beautiful!"

"Wha'? Let me see," commanded Martin as he took the spyglass from his friend. Leveling the tool, he asked. "Where is she?"

"She just came out of the tent in the northern part there," replied Jasper, gesturing to the biggest tent of all.

"B-E-U-T-Y!" Martin spelled out, unaware that he was missing a letter.

"Told you!"

"Only one problem, though."

"What?" asked Jasper, not understanding how there could be anything wrong with the woman he had just seen.

"Tha's the maid."

"No!" Jasper's jaw dropped. The girl he had seen could be no less than a princess.

"Oh yeah, she's a maid," chuckled Martin as Jasper snatched the spyglass from his hands.

"She can't be!" Looking at the woman again, Jasper's heart pounded. The longer he looked at her, the more he fell in love. Her face was that of an angel. She had gracefully curled brown hair that was so dark it seemed almost black. Her deep brown eyes were filled with joy and light. Her golden skin shining in the morning sun as she walked ever so gracefully towards the guards, holding a tray in her hands. As they stacked their dishes on it, she smiled and bowed her head. Her beautiful hair fell against her face as she did so.

"Unless you know of any nobles who wash their guard's dishes," Martin snickered again.

Jasper smiled to himself as he turned back to his partner. "Even better."

"Wha'?"

"She's a maid!" Jasper's eyes sparkled with excitement.

"Yeah, I told you tha'?"

"If she isn't noble, I may just have a chance with that one!"

"Oh please. Wha' are you gonna say? I'm here to rob your mistress, but would ya like to court me after?"

"Couldn't just let me have a moment, could you?" Jasper growled, turning back towards the camp.

"Not a chance."

With a sigh, Jasper watched the woman disperse of the dishes and turn again to the guards. "Well, if it isn't her, who could it be?"

"My guess is her," Martin proclaimed as he pointed towards a woman dressed in black and scarlet colored, velvet robes near the entrance of the main tent.

"She's hideous!"

"You're jus' sayin' tha' 'cause you like the maid," chuckled Martin as he nudged Jasper's shoulder.

"No," Jasper bickered. "I'm saying that because she has her face covered."

"Alrigh', my turn," Martin stated as he took the spyglass yet again. Jasper was right. The woman was covered from head to toe. No distinguishing marks could be made of her appearance. Her face was hidden with a black veil, and her head shielded underneath her cloak. Even so, as she approached the guards bowed their heads to her. They did not eat again until a nod was given from the hidden woman. "I s'pose you're righ', but it's gotta be her. I mean, look at the guards!"

"Well, at least we've found the target. She definitely fits the description. Secretive and hiding her identity from the public."

"Poor fella."

"Who?"

"The prince," sighed Martin. "I mean, this whole time I've wondered 'bout this secret weddin' deal he's got going on. I know that he needed some money, but why would a foreigner be willin' to pay a prince to take their daughter? You'd think it'd be the other way 'round. Lookin' at her, I think I know. Ever seen a pretty lass who'd cover from head to toe like tha'? She's got to be an eyesore!"

"That's an awful thing to say," laughed Jasper.

"I'm bein' serious!"

"I know, that's what makes it so funny!" They laughed together at the prospect.

About an hour later, the travelers were almost finished packing up their camp. The only tent left to demolish was the noblewoman's. She had returned to it shortly after speaking with her guards that morning. Seeing their prey's progress, Martin and Jasper returned to their own camp and shook the sleeping men back into consciousness.

"Come on, lads. Rise and shine!" shouted Martin, whose efforts were merely met with groans and grumbles.

"You heard the man! Get prepared! Who knows when the caravan will make its move?" demanded Jasper in retaliation to their sluggishness.

"What makes you so sure they will be coming this way anytime soon?" asked one of the sleepy thieves.

"Take a look for yourself," said Jasper leading him up the path to the cliffside by the hair on his head.

"Ow, ow, oh!"

"Wait, what is it?" asked Dan as he rushed to the edge, the rest of the band following him.

"By golly, that's a lot of people," said another.

"A lot of guards."

"Looks like they are already on the move."

"Wha'?" questioned Martin, whose sight had been blocked by the rest of the men. They had only just started on the final tent moments ago!

"It's true, the caravan is on the move," said Jasper. "There are so many people, by the time they get the last tent loaded up, it will be that carriage's turn to leave."

The caravan moved like the army it was. Each person had a role, no one moving out of step from another. Guards accompanied each of the carriages while others on horseback flanked them. Soon, no trace of the caravan was left in the valley they had camped in.

As they moved, there was an obvious separation between the carriages of the woman and those of her servants. The first half of the caravan held itself a few strides away from the rest. The front carriages had gold delicately patterned around the outside to bring glory to the woman who owned them. The ruffians concluded that if there was gold etched on the outside, then the rest of her treasure must be kept within.

The thieves watched in excitement as the travelers set out on their course, eagerly awaiting their chance to strike. Which road would they take? How much gold would they collect? Would they put up much of a fight? The anxiousness of the men was almost uncontainable. The closer they approached, the more it grew.

In Jasper's crew, there were fourteen men, himself included. When they made the mistake of counting the guards in the first half of the convoy, they grew weary. Knights adorning black armor guarded the main section of the caravan. There were fourteen guards on horseback around the carriages, not to mention the guards on the carriages themselves! Four rode in the front of the caravan, four in the back. In addition, one rider was placed to each side of the carriages within the first half of the convoy. There were four more guards on each of the three main carriages themselves. Two sat in the front, one on each side of the driver, and two stood on the back ledge. The total counted was twenty-six, which outnumbered the thieves by twelve.

The middle carriage held the woman, which left the remaining two for her treasures. And with carriages of that size, the treasures within had to be beyond imagination! The profits seemed worth the risk to Jasper and his men, but their time-frame had been shortened. The men would have to take down the first half of the convoy within a few minutes in order to escape before the second half arrived. If the remainder of the guards were to reach them in time, there would be no way to defeat their forces.

"When should we attack, Cap'n?" begged one of the miscreants.

"Nearly time, they are almost at the split," replied Jasper. "Once they choose a direction, we take 'em down."

"I hope they choose the mountain path. I'd hate to run all the way down to the meadow," sighed Martin.

"You could use the exercise," laughed Jasper in an effort to lighten the spirits of his group. He watched the caravan turn to the right, heading into the shadows of the trees. "And it seems you'll have it. Let's move out!"

Groans came in response to the order as the band of men thrust themselves off the mountain top, running down a hidden path at full force. Each held a longbow in hand and carried a sword on their hip. They had to reach the meadow before the caravan!

As they neared, the sound of hooves could be heard trampling through the forest. The men quickly took their stations in the meadow. Hiding behind trees and boulders, they disappeared into the atmosphere just before the caravan reached the clearing.

Seeing the heads of horses push through the shrubby path, Jasper made his declaration. "Halt! We mean you no harm. If you do not raise arms against us, we will let you leave this place in peace. If you resist, you will feel our wrath!"

The caravan kept moving, raising their weapons and shouting out something in a language Jasper and his men did not know.

"Well, seems we've got ourselves a bit o' a language barrier," stated Martin from behind his tree.

"I said halt!" shouted Jasper again as he aimed an arrow at the ground in front of the travelers. His men followed suit, shooting near the feet of the horses.

More jumbled words came from the small army as the carriage guards pulled out their bows, aiming at the trees in retaliation.

"Seems they're not quite gettin' the message," joked Martin.

"Perhaps we make them understand," retorted Jasper as he planted an arrow in one of the guard's shoulders. The man fell from his horse on impact, grunting in agony as he landed.

Another more feminine voice shouted out in the foreign language. *"Enough! There is nothing here worth dying over! Put away your weapons and dismount. The thieves will not harm us if we cooperate."*

"My Lady?"

"Do as I say! All will be over soon."

"Of course, My Lady," replied one of her guards as he dismounted his horse. *"You heard her, sheathe your weapons and dismount!"*

"Wha' are they doin'?" asked Martin suspiciously.

"What they are told," replied Jasper. "Ok! Good! Now, I want all of you on your knees and away from the carriages!"

The woman's voice rang out again, seemingly translating the message. The men followed the order, all the riders dismounting. The drivers and carriage guards left their posts and kneeled on the ground next to the carriages. Furthermore, six hidden guards emerged from within both the front and back carriages.

Each section of men gathered evenly in groups according to their positions in the caravan. The four riders of the front and back kneeled two by two. The men covering the outside carriages kneeled with the two guards on each side of the driver, the six interior guards, and the two side riders behind them.

The guards of the middle carriage, however, would not yield. The two riders assigned to this carriage stood on each side of the doorway. In unison, they turned the handles to open the doors for the woman. The four remaining men stood behind them, guarding them and the treasure they were about to reveal. The noblewoman's driver was busying himself with the horses, trying to tie all of them down so they wouldn't get away as the commotion went on.

Jasper and his men made their way out from their hiding place behind the trees, laughing at the thought of this army giving up so easily to their small group. Upon their arrival to the scene, the woman stepped out of her carriage. She walked towards Jasper, as he seemed to be the leader.

When she walked, her guards followed her. As she stopped in front of Jasper, they kneeled behind her. After his task was complete, her driver also scurried behind the guards and kneeled. It was then the woman spoke in a soft, clear tone. "I have done my best to accommodate your wishes. Even I would kneel before you, but this dress makes the task seemingly impossible."

Her deep blue eyes set on those of Jasper's. Her stare made him feel uncomfortable. Somehow her grace made him feel ashamed at the thought of her kneeling to him. In person, she shone with beauty. Even though she had hidden herself with layers of clothing, her outline was exquisite to the eye. Her clothing looked surreal in the midst of the forest. She was meant for a greater place than this.

As she waited for a reply, she studied the thief. He seemed unsure of himself. Odd really, seeing as how he had just defeated an army. Even then, he did not seem as phased by the idea of a fight as much as he was by her approach. Meaning he had some sort of military background. But if that were true, why would he have attacked a noble? He obviously wasn't of nobility himself. She could tell by the mud-stained clothing he wore. Nothing out of the ordinary. His brown hair looked as if it had never been brushed. The stubble on his chin showed his lack of shaving. The only clean thing about him being his green eyes, which had now been averted.

"I'm sorry for the intrusion, my lady. I would not ask a woman, especially one of your title, to kneel before me. You may do as you please. My men and I will be gone in a moment. We only want to see what you have in your carriages," responded Jasper, his eyes set to the ground. In utter disbelief, his men slowly went to the carriages to look inside, trying to understand what had just happened with their leader. He was always so daring and confident, but the woman had tamed him with just a few words.

"I may do as I please?" she questioned. The woman leaned down to catch his gaze, but he again turned his head from her.

"Y-yes, my lady."

Touching his chin, she lifted his head and forced him to look at her. Jasper was struck by her eyes, like endless pools of water. They were the only part of her face he could distinguish, the rest hidden under the shadows of her cloak and veil. Even so, he could see her power within them.

"What is your name?" she asked him quizzingly.

"I, uh," he stuttered, not wanting to reveal his name. She looked at him more intently, never ceasing in her efforts to learn the secret.

"Oi!" shouted Martin angrily. "There's nothin' here!"

"What?" said Jasper as the woman released his chin from her fingers. He looked at his men, all of which were nodding in the agreement that there were no treasures, empty hands raised in the air. "It must be with the rest of the caravan."

Just then, Jasper realized he didn't hear the sound of any more horses which meant that the second half of the caravan must have taken the mountain pass. He looked back to the woman in spite, her head now tilted to the ground the way his had been.

"You were just a distraction! The real woman and her caravan are probably halfway to the palace by now!" he screamed at her, disbelieving how he could have ever mistaken her for a noble. What a treacherous woman she was! Now, because of her little schemes, he and all of his men might perish!

"B-but, wha' are we gonna do?" asked Martin, fear in his eyes. "We needed this. You said we needed this!"

"I know what I said."

"We're all gonna die, aren't we?"

"We'll figure something out," Jasper consoled, his voice laced with a mixture of anger and fear. "You and your people may be on your way. You're of no use to us now."

His response shocked her. Even in defeat, the man had kept his word not to harm them. How honorable for a thief.

"They are finished with their search," she said to her guards in their tongue. *"Take your positions. We leave for the palace forthwith. Oh, and Joseph, could you switch roles with Andre? He should sit down and tend to that wound."*

At her command, the men got up from the ground and headed to their positions. One from the first carriage traded places with the injured rider, who in turn was helped into his seat by his comrades.

Meanwhile, Jasper's men were whispering amongst themselves. "We're just going to let them go? They cheated us. Shouldn't they be punished?"

"We said we wouldn't hurt them if they cooperated, and they have. So, technically, they've earned the right to leave," Jasper responded to them.

With all of the men in their positions, the woman looked back upon the group of thieves. Seeing the terror on their faces, she felt pity for them. Calling from inside her carriage, she said, "Gentlemen."

The men looked from side to side before realizing that she was addressing them. "You have proven yourselves to be honorable, even as thieves. What you tried to do here today seems not to be of greed but necessity. Even once you realized you had nothing to gain, you kept your word to me. You have allowed me to continue on my journey. For that, I feel you deserve a great deal of praise. Hopefully, this will suffice."

She tossed her purse to Jasper. When he had caught it, the caravan went on its way; leaving the thieves behind.

"What a smart lass, keepin' her purse under her cloak! I didn't even think o' tha'," chuckled Martin. "And wha' a large purse it is! Open it. Wha's inside?"

Jasper tugged at the cords of the purse in astonishment. So, was she a noble after all? Why would she send all of her riches a different way? Taking such a chance could have gotten her killed! There was something he was missing, but what could it be?

Martin shrieked as he saw what they had gained. "Would you look at all tha' gold! You could buy a castle with tha'!"

"Let's hope so," said Jasper, still puzzled as he closed the bag.

11

The Arrival

That same morning, preparations for the woman's arrival were being made at the palace of King Cadoc. Platters of the most delicate dishes were set out for her pleasure. All of the guards were adorned in brilliantly polished armor. All the peasants of the area had gathered in the courtyard in hopes of seeing the prince's secret fiancé. In the prince's room, however, different preparations were being discussed.

"They know she is coming today, right?" asked Prince Carter as Roland entered his bedchamber. Carter's hair was severely disheveled from a long night of worry. His bed was a rumpled mess and its scarlet and golden blankets were strewn across the floor. Piles of different outfits were tossed across the place. The prince himself was curled into a tight ball on one of the couches in his quarters, looking desperately out the window. He must never have found the right outfit because he was wearing only his white undershirt and trousers.

"Yes, sire. I spoke with Jasper just last night. Everything is prepared," replied Sir Roland, who was wearing a tightly-fitted scarlet dress shirt and black trousers. His boots came high on his calf. Around his shoulders was a cloak bearing the brave dragon symbol of Remette.

"Thinking of this makes me nervous. We only have one chance, you know. If they injure her in any way, I don't know what the king will do!" Carter rambled on, his eyes never lifting from the window as he watched fearfully for the arrival of his fate.

"Your father will not be able to harm them, so long as he doesn't know who they are," reassured the advisor. "Do not be so worried. They will attack the caravan soon; that much is certain. After that, the rest of the plan will easily fall into place."

"But let's just say they don't take it down. Let's say they miss it and she comes here. Or, or let's say they do ransack her, but she comes here anyway. Then I'll have to marry her and take care of her! I'm definitely not ready for that. She'll probably cry for days on end about her encounter. Oh no! I can't do it! I can't!"

"Carter, get it together," snapped Roland as he shook the prince back to sanity. "You won't need to marry her! We will have everything in order by the wedding day. Upon your ascent to the throne, you can dismiss her from your court."

"I don't know. The deal was I marry her." The young prince nibbled at his fingertips. "Getting her mixed in with all this doesn't seem fair."

"That was your decision!"

"I know it was, but I don't know what I was thinking! Well, I know what I was thinking; I just don't know why I thought it!"

"You're babbling now."

"I know," said the prince with temper in his voice. After a long silence, he spoke again. "I feel I have to marry her. It would be the honorable thing to do. In truth, I suppose that I am more worried that she won't want to marry me."

"The woman has already shown that she wants to marry you, sire. There is no need to worry about that. Perhaps, you'll like her once you get to know her as well."

"You're right as always, Roland. I'm just nervous."

"There is no need to be nervous. Should you ever feel that way, just remember that what is to happen is for the benefit of the country."

"Well said," came a booming voice which echoed off of the stone walls. Carter jumped to his feet, Roland simultaneously spinning to face the entrance of the chamber.

"My king," the advisor called out.

"Hello, Father," Carter shivered. How much had he heard?

"Roland has great advice for you, my son. A man's first duty should be to his kingdom. This marriage is your way of serving your country," the king stated. "Besides, I thought you were excited to meet this woman? Haven't you been spouting on about her these past few months?"

"Yes, Father. I am excited. I'm just nervous to see if she is as wonderful as I have been led to believe!" Carter forced a smile. He actually hadn't thought to consider her personality. She had simply been the best offer on the table, the only offer actually.

The king huffed in disappointment at his son, "It doesn't matter what her qualities are. The engagement is set and final. The thought of her wealth should be more than enough to seal this deal. Not to mention, you say her beauty is beyond compare."

"Well, I haven't actually met her. That is just what her father said to me." After a brief pause Carter continued in a quiet voice, his eyes adverted to the floor. "I don't know if it is her wealth that should be important to me. I actually feel quite guilty, knowing that was the reason that I chose her."

"You're right," Cadoc nodded. "Her wealth isn't important; it's what you can do with it once you have it! I'm sure the reason for your decision did not go unnoticed, but she accepted you regardless. Now, listen carefully to me, son. You have arranged this wedding without my consent. You will not humiliate me further by canceling it."

"He will not fail you in this, Your Majesty. He is just a bit nervous, that's all. When it counts, I'm certain he will complete the task without hesitation," interjected Roland with a reassuring smile.

"You should spend more time with Sir Roland here and get your priorities straight," said the king, patting Roland's shoulder as he passed by.

Cadoc grimaced at the mess that was his son's room. He stepped over a pile of clothes to reach the window. After a moment, he said,

"This will be a major change for us, having this woman come here. Best not to mess it up."

"Trust me, Father, no one knows the importance more than I."

"That is because you will not share with us," his father growled, never looking at him. "I am trusting you, Carter. You made a bold choice by taking this woman without my consent. I only hope you don't get cold feet."

The young prince gulped under the pressure of his plans. The prince and his mother were no more than prisoners to the castle, along with everyone else in the kingdom. Carter had no power in the eyes of the people. He was just a flashy pawn the king liked to push around for looks. He couldn't help but wonder, would he really be able to overcome his father?

Marrying this woman was just the beginning. She was the first step towards him becoming king. As for the disposal of his father, the feat was seemingly impossible. Not only did the king have a firm hold over the kingdom's funds, but he also had mercenaries at his disposal. Men who enjoyed hurting others no matter who it was they were called to torture or destroy.

Prince Carter's plans made his stomach turn. This was treason of the highest degree! If he were to fail, the king would not hold back on the punishment. Not only on the prince, but on his mother as well. As his father liked to say, 'The best torture is making a man watch as those he loves are ripped from him.' The prince couldn't bear the thought of what would happen to his dear mother. She was one of the only people throughout his life who could give him a sense of calm amidst the storms of tragedy he'd faced.

"Carter! Are you listening to me?"

"What?"

"Honestly, I don't know what you feel you can accomplish living in daydreams instead of reality. Focus!"

"Of course, Father. What is it you were saying?"

"I was saying you need to know how to greet her when she arrives," snapped the king. "Present yourself like a prince. Certainly not with glassed over eyes!"

"Right. Yes. When she gets here." Carter's eyes widened as he fell back into his chair. "When she gets here!"

"As I said, he's just a bit nervous, my liege," chuckled Roland, who was trying to lighten the situation.

"What is there to be nervous about?" roared the king. "When I married your mother, we met at the ceremony! You have been granted a week to get to know this girl first!"

"It's four days! I can't love someone in four days!" cried the prince. "What if I hate her. What if she hates me!"

"It doesn't matter!" Cadoc spat in growing irritation.

"Perhaps if you got your mind off of it for a while," advised Roland in an effort to change the subject.

"I agree," said the king while looking around the pilfered room. "Just focus on getting dressed. Roland, you can keep a lookout for the caravan, can you not?"

"Of course, my liege," he replied with a bow. The advisor smiled with the knowledge that it wouldn't make it on time anyway. With that, the king left the room.

"Roland."

"Yes, Carter," said the advisor softly as he gazed out the window.

"What should I say?"

"If I were you, I'd try to make it dignified," Roland thought out loud, "Perhaps you could say, 'Greetings, my lady, welcome to Remette. I hope you will find it to be as beautiful of a land as I have found you to be as beautiful a woman.'"

The prince laughed. "Isn't that a bit corny?"

"In my experience, women are easily smitten by ridiculous praises such as that. You want her to like you, do you not?"

"Of course."

"Then everything you say to this woman should be a hidden compliment."

"Do you think that'll really work?" The prince picked at his fingers, much to the displeasure of his advisor.

"Definitely! Another thing to remember is always to look your best and to showcase your strengths. Some of the main things women look for in a spouse are stability and integrity."

"I thought you weren't ready for marriage? You sound more prepared than I do!"

"No, sire. I'm not ready for such a commitment. Making a woman love you is just the first step. Marriage consists of keeping her happy. I haven't quite developed my skills in that area yet."

"Oh Roland, you make me laugh," chuckled the prince as he stood. "I suppose I should get ready!"

Anxiously awaiting the arrival of the kingdom's new princess, the prince filtered through his dispersed clothing. Carter decided he may as well dress for comfort as the flashier of his outfits were too itchy. In the end, he adorned a bright green shirt and some brown trousers. He placed a ceremonial sword with a hilt that was encased in rubies and diamonds on his belt. Setting a golden crown on his head, he went to the window.

Was she actually going to get there? Would the ambush scare her away? He sighed and closed his eyes. This was almost too stressful. He had too much to worry about without dealing with a wedding as well!

"Feeling better, I see," said the king as he entered the prince's quarters again. As he arrived, Roland bowed and exited, leaving the father and son alone.

"Yes, Father, but I'm still a bit nervous," Carter replied, helplessly fighting to clip on his cloak. Cadoc thought for a moment to order his son to wear traditional robes of scarlet, but it was too late for that now.

"Don't be," said the king in a cold tone. "I know you'll make me proud."

"I hope so," said the prince with a nervous gulp, looking down at his feet. He didn't believe there was anything in the world he could do to make that bitter man proud. He couldn't help but wonder if his father would continue with his usual punishments even after the woman came. They would be even worse, should she not arrive.

"Remember to greet her honorably when she arrives."

"Yes, Father."

"What will you say?" Cadoc asked. He turned around in a huff when no reply was given. Surprisingly, his son was proudly extending a hand.

"Greetings, my lady, welcome to Remette. I hope you will find it to be as beautiful of a land as I have found you to be as beautiful a woman," smiled the prince, copying what his advisor had told him earlier.

"Roland come up with that for you?" the king asked, already knowing the answer.

"Actually, he did."

"It's perfect."

"I hope so," said the prince, his face once again wrought with nervousness. His eyes widened with fear as he heard trumpets sounding. At the same moment, a frantic looking Roland burst into his bedroom.

"She's here!" shouted the advisor.

"Splendid. Come along, Carter. Let's greet her," replied the king without a shred of excitement in his voice.

Prince Carter gave a worried look to Sir Roland as he passed by him. He could tell the same thoughts were running through his advisor's head. How could she be here already? If the caravan had even made it through, they should have at least been late! Did Jasper and his men miss the convoy? Did the Ponierians kill them all? Did the foreigners learn of the prince's plans?

Panic! That is all the poor prince felt as he grudgingly made his way to the courtyard. His mother and father walked before him to greet his fiancé. Carter tried to act excited, but he was filled with emptiness and sorrow. A massive weight seemed to be pressing on his stomach. The plan had failed. Now, yet again, he was the king's pawn. He was marrying a woman whom he had never met before, and the arrangement would only serve to further benefit the king. He shuddered at the thought. What if he didn't love her? How could he marry her, knowing he could never love her?

Carter looked up at his parents. Both seemed practically delighted to be meeting this woman together, but the young prince knew the truth. The couple hated one another. They had married under similar conditions. Queen Zisca's father had been the most profitable noble in the realm. Shortly after achieving rights to her fortune, Cadoc killed the prince's grandfather. He then proceeded to take Zisca's inheritance and used it to provide for his war effort against the old king. Though Carter didn't plan on anything as drastic as killing his fiancé's family, it still seemed wrong to have lied about his true intentions. Not once had the prince considered his fiancé in a loving way. Her only place in his life was to provide him with funds. Perhaps he was more like his father than he had realized.

Turning to his advisor for comfort, he found hope. The man's face was set ahead, continuing on towards their fate. Knowing the secrets that the advisor held, the prince knew he must be afraid. However, Roland, his dear friend Roland, never faltered. He always did what needed to be done. The thought made the prince's heart lighten as he patted his friend on the back.

"You are my rock," Carter said. "What could I have ever accomplished without you?"

"Everything you have accomplished, you have done so by yourself, sire," replied Roland with a sense of reassuring courage, "and one day, you will rule this land."

"Thank you, my friend."

"It's time," said Roland as they neared the palace door. The prince's parents waited hand in hand to emerge.

"That it is," replied the prince, gesturing for his servants to open the door ahead of them. "That it is."

The crowd cheered as the royal family emerged in red and gold apparel, except for the prince who stood apart from them all. The king and queen moved to the right of the palace door, holding to one another as they waited for the arrival of the prince's fiancé.

Taking his position to the left of the palace door, stood the king's advisor. The women in the crowd moved to Roland's side of the court in an effort to get close to him, as he was well known for his pleasant looks.

Last to emerge was Prince Carter, his crown cresting his brow. The crowd that had gathered watched him with intense gazes that made him gulp under the pressure he was facing.

Not much time had passed before the first riders in the procession came into view. Ponierian servants were tossing ribbons and flower petals along the road as the carriages made their way to the palace's door. During their approach, the servants leapt and danced while elegantly showering the people of the crowd with riches. As they did so, the crowd cheered praises to them in the truest happiness they had felt in years!

Everything about the caravan was impressive from the knights dressed in gleaming armor with purple capes to the servants wearing elegant clothing of blue and green as they danced with their treasures before the royal family. Even the size of the group was impressive! The line of carriages seemed to be never-ending, much to the despair of the prince who found it harder to stand with every passing moment.

The royal household waited patiently by the castle doors as the events unfolded. Guards of the palace were spread all along the grounds, making the might of the king and his family stand out by their great numbers and flashy attire. The Remettian servants were dressed in high-quality robes which were specially made for the event. Likewise, those in the crowd had been provided with clothing that made them more appealing in the eyes of the foreigners. All this was done in order that the royals would be seen at their best by the prince's fiancé. No matter her title, a message was to be sent back with those who had escorted her to her new home. Remette was a powerful and great nation. Even without a marriage of unity between the kingdoms of Remette and Poniere, the house of King Cadoc would remain forever. That was the message the king grinned about as the Ponierian soldiers could be seen darting their eyes between the king's guards.

The prince started to make his way towards the stairs, smiling anxiously with his hands behind his back. To his fiancé it would seem that he was eager, but in reality, he was squeezing the blood out of his hands due to fear. Behind him were his parents. His father scowled what he thought was a smile at the travelers. The queen was frantically clapping her hands with excitement. Sir Roland quietly overlooked the scene, showing little emotion from the shadows where he stood behind the royal family.

Finally, the carriages came to a stop and silence overtook the crowd. The prince re-adjusted his robes while setting a course towards the carriage door. Before he could make it to his destination, the door burst open; catching him in midstride.

His eyes grew wide as he heard a high-pitched squeal which was followed by a small girl who jumped from the carriage. She twirled on her heel as she took in the sights around her. She wore a dark purple dress with silver threads etched into the material and a thin purple covering over her face. The colors she wore brought out her dark tan and raven black hair which draped over her shoulders. Her brown eyes were wide with excitement.

"Oh, wow!" she exclaimed through a thick accent, never ceasing in her turning. "Your palace is so pretty!"

Fear wrenched at the prince. What was this girl, eight years old? He turned to his parents, who looked just as shocked as he did. His mother had her hands frozen in mid-clap. His father shook his head with anger in his eyes. Carter looked back to the girl in front of him. Why was the girl so young? He had been told she was near his age! Was this some kind of degrading joke from that Ponierian? It would make sense that they might do such a thing to humiliate their former enemy. The prince shook himself; this is why he should never make decisions alone. If only Roland had gone with him to meet the Ponierians, then he would have never done something so foolish.

Remembering that he was expected to greet the newcomer, the prince turned back to the little girl. She was now pointing at the gargoyles and speaking in a foreign language to a giant man dressed in all black, most likely her personal guard. He was covered from head to toe, like a faceless shadow. The man made Carter nervous. He was huge! Especially for a Ponierian.

"Greetings, my lady, welcome to Remette," said the prince, who could not bring himself to finish the rehearsed line.

"Hello!" shouted the little girl. Carter went silent, his face red as he had no idea what to say.

"I was just telling Frank how much I love your castle! On my way over I was dreaming of what it might be like, but it is so much prettier in person! My sister is going to love it here! She'll be arriving soon." The girl gave a quick curtsey. "I'm Miriam, by the way."

"Y-your sister?" Carter stuttered, sweat rolling down his face.

"Well, yeah," Miriam giggled. "Daddy said you wouldn't know I was coming. He also said to tell you he hoped you wouldn't mind it."

Carter shook his head to show the girl that her presence didn't bother him. She paid his plight little mind as she mumbled to herself, "He actually told me that he thought you would be happy I was here, 'cause I was the only one who wanted to be!"

Carter was struck. His fiancé didn't want to be there? Perhaps this was just a trade deal to her as well. What could he do? If she hated him, should he dismiss her? He looked back to his father, who had never ceased in his scowling. The prince could only hope that he would be able to change the woman's mind about him.

"I wonder where Sissy is," Miriam pouted. "I figured she'd be here before me. I mean, she left before I did. Frank said she took the long way, so maybe that's why she's late."

Carter's mind was boggled. What could he do to make his fiancé like him? He doubted that a simple greeting would be able to swoon a woman who hated him. He would need to ask Roland. One thing that brought the prince ease was the fact that his fiancé's carriage was late. Perhaps Jasper and his men had intercepted her carriages after all. Collecting himself, the prince said, "You must have had a long journey. Why don't I show you inside?"

Miriam squealed in delight and started towards the castle. As she did so, she spoke in a different tongue to her bodyguard, presumably Frank, who turned and relayed the message to the servants. Upon the girl's instructions, the workers started unloading their plentiful riches and carrying them to the castle. The mounds of gold seemed uncountable; bringing a slight smile to the king's ever-scowling face. The rest of the kingdom waited quietly, still unsure of what was happening.

The little girl, Miriam, started scampering back and forth through the halls admiring all of the paintings and helping herself to the dishes of food on the tables. She seemed unaware of the stains the pastries left as she shoved them under her veil. Not for a moment did she stop exclaiming her excitement loudly to her bodyguard.

After following the girl into the castle, the prince said to her, "Is it alright if I have my advisor show you around? I ought to go back outside and wait for your sister."

Sir Roland looked at the prince with a mixture of anger, dread, and fear written on his face. Carter looked back at him, smiling a good luck smile. It was slightly comical to see Roland with such a face. The prince thought back as he watched terror take hold of his advisor. Was this the only time he had seen Roland afraid? Who would have thought the advisor's bane would be this small, happy child.

Miriam gasped aloud and raced past the prince to the advisor, who she had just noticed for the first time. Looking at Roland with adoration she squealed, "You have such pretty hair! People where I come from don't normally have golden hair like that! It's so curly and bouncy too! Can I touch it? Can I?"

Roland gave Carter a disgruntled look, but the prince seemed too out of sorts to care. Knowing there was little else he could do, the advisor knelt down on one knee to appease the requests of the soon-to-be member of the royal family. "As you wish, my lady."

"Yay!" The girl patted his head in utter joy. Once she had ruffled his curls, she went back to her fast-paced exploration of the castle. This left her guard and Roland with no choice but to chase after her as she called out. "I want to see the rest of the castle! I'm just so excited!"

The prince shook his head in amusement, but soon returned to worrying while he wondered what the girl's sister would be like. Some of his nervousness had gone away. If the younger one was so joyous, perhaps the elder would be nice as well. Carter could only hope she was kind enough to give him a chance, although it seemed that she had already made up her mind about him. Of course, he couldn't blame her for not wanting to be there. His thoughts were interrupted by the sound of trumpets.

"She's here," Carter said to himself. After a deep breath, he walked back outside.

Her chariots were fewer but more elegant in design. Their gold overlays were easily worth as much as the riches the servants had brought in earlier. Carter stood tall, trying to hide the terror which had overcome him. The prince became frozen where he stood, his heart like a stone in his chest.

Since he seemed unable to escort her, the lady's guards took the initiative. They climbed down from their posts on her carriage and prepared for her to emerge. A stepping stool and carpet were laid out for her. Once this task was done, they grasped the handles of the carriage doors and turned them simultaneously. The prince's heart pounded as they opened the door. Extending their hands for support, the guards helped to escort the woman as she gracefully stepped out onto the ground.

All was quiet as the mysterious woman captivated the attention of all those present. The commoners looked back and forth between her and the prince as they waited for him to introduce himself to her. In the silence, her guards left their stations and gathered behind her like an army. Each section of the caravan stood ready in a similar pattern to the one they had taken in the woods.

When Carter had finally found his strength, he made his way towards her. At first, her figure was hidden from sight, but as the prince approached, the woman withdrew her cloak. To the king's disgrace, Prince Carter stumbled while traveling down the stairs. Barely recovering his balance, Carter looked up at the woman and was struck with awe.

Now that her cloak was removed, her outline could be better seen. She had on a scarlet colored, velvet dress with a beautiful pattern sown in black. The pattern was outlined with thread that looked like pure gold. She wore a necklace and matching earrings of diamonds and rubies, all of which were placed in an elegant golden setting. The colors she wore brought out her skin's pale glow, making her raven black hair even more radiant. A matching black veil hid the bottom of her face from view, leaving her eyes as the only portion of her face visible. The prince took little notice to her veil, as he was entranced by brilliant blue eyes. Within moments, he felt himself becoming lost in them.

A disgruntled cough came from his father, pulling the prince back to sanity. Carter lifted himself to his full height to address her. Once again, he tried to use the greeting Roland had provided to him, but was distracted when he realized how petite she was. Her head only came to the top of his chest! As she gazed up at him, he felt himself being drawn to her more and more. She was, indeed, precious. "Wel-... Gree-... H-hi."

She giggled in amusement before speaking. Unlike her sister, she did not seem to have an accent. "It is wonderful to meet you, dear prince."

Her voice was soft and calming as she curtsied to him gracefully. "I have heard so many things about you and your kingdom. Now that I have met you, I see they had it all wrong."

The prince was terrified. He had ruined everything! His mouth dropped open by the harshness of her statement. As he seemed unable to come up with an appropriate reaction, an involuntary groan escaped from him.

"You are far more perfect than they had described," she added. He could see a hint of her smile through the thin cloth she used to cover her face. Her cheeks rose with happiness, and her eyes grew even brighter now that they were filled with joy.

Gasps were heard throughout the courtyard. Even the queen let out one of them. Her words melted the prince instantly. What a wonderful woman! Carter still said nothing. It seemed impossible for him to do anything but smile.

"I hope you find the gifts I have brought for you to be of your liking," she continued as he did nothing but stare. "My father shines his blessing through the dowry offered to you and your family."

The king and queen made their way down while their son stood like a pillar between the guest and the door. The people in the crowd watched quietly as he looked at her.

"Yes," grunted King Cadoc on his son's behalf. "We are very pleased to welcome you here. I hope you will enjoy your time in our courts."

"I already am." She curtseyed to him and the queen. "It is an honor to meet both of you."

"Oh!" the queen gasped happily. "Why don't you come inside! I'd love to get to know you!"

Her husband glared at her for her overexcitement.

"I would like that ver-" The woman's reply was cut short by a loud screech.

"Sissy!" cried Miriam as she ran out of the palace door to meet her sister; her guard and Roland were still chasing after her. "Sissy! You have got to see their palace! It's so beautiful!"

The woman turned her head slightly and looked down at her panting sister. Miriam was covered in stains and crumbs from the snacks she had found. It would seem she had also fallen during her adventures, as the hem of her dress was torn. The elder sister looked upon the younger in disappointment. One scolding glance from the older sibling sufficed to bring the younger back in order.

The effects of Miriam's misbehavior were easily observed by the ragged state of her caretakers. The man they had charged Miriam with looked out of sorts. It was obvious that he hadn't had much practice with children her age. The woman couldn't help but take in his looks: curly golden hair, pale skin, and blue eyes. There would be no mistaking who he was as she whispered under her breath, "Black Knight."

What had these Remettians been thinking, placing her sister into the care of such a beast? Was it some type of hidden disrespect? She could only imagine how frightening it must have been to her poor Miriam.

Meanwhile, Carter could not help but continue staring at his elegant future bride; unsure if she was real or an illusion. He watched as she cared for her little sister. She would be a good mother, caring so much for her sister like that. But what was she whispering about a black knight for? Maybe it was a nickname for her sister's caretaker.

"You mustn't behave so rashly, darling," the woman said while fixing her sister's ruffled hair. She simultaneously shot the guard, Frank, a nervous glance. The man nodded in response to the silent exchange, and then returned closely to the little girl's side.

Miriam composed herself and looked down at the ground, tracing a cobblestone with her toe. "It really is nice here though."

"I'm sure it is," cooed the woman softly as she turned back to the prince and elegantly extended her hand. "Perhaps you would like to show me?"

"Uh, y-yeah," the prince stammered, placing her hand onto his arm. What delicate hands she had, he thought to himself as he led her inside. Following the betrothed were Miriam and Frank. Beyond that, Carter's parents walked closely together, conversing about their son's future. In the back was a frazzled Sir Roland, who was not used to the amount of energy found in children.

As the prince led his lady throughout the castle, she studied him. He was indeed a handsome man with his deep brown eyes that she could always catch staring at her. He had a clean-shaven face which showed his dimples as he smiled. His brown hair was well combed. Not to mention his physique! She smiled slightly to herself as she held to his thick, strong arms. Perhaps this arrangement would not be so bad. His palace was impressive also, filled with wonderous treasures of wealth and art. It was bright and seemed full of happiness, but only time would tell if her new home would bring her joy or misery.

Misery. She clung to the word in her mind as they traveled around the palace. How could she feel anything else? She may never see her family again, and for what? Some absurd deal that her father made? 'It is a noble way to serve your country,' he had said to her. What is so noble about being sold to the highest bidder?

The facade of a happy marriage within the royal family of Remette hadn't ended well in Prince Carter's history, or rather, his country's history. She was well aware of how he had gotten that crown on his head. His family was full of betrayers. He may be nice to gaze at, but he was by no means the lovesick puppy he was pretending to be. She was probably just fooling herself.

As the battle went on in her soul, the woman unknowingly let out a soft sigh. Carter felt a twinge of sadness in his heart. She seemed troubled. Was she not having a good time?

"So, what do you think of the palace?" the prince asked her, nervousness written across his face. "D-do you like it?"

"It seems wonderful," she replied quietly as she questioned to herself whether she could ever be happy there.

The distance of her words dropped the prince's heart to his stomach. She hated him! He had known she would. What to do, what to do?

"Uh, are you hungry?" he asked, sheepishly stealing an apple from a nearby plate and raising it up for her. As he did so, he remembered she was wearing a veil over her mouth. She dipped her head and took his offering. Holding the fruit in both hands, she stared down at it as they walked. Without her hand, Carter's arm grew cold. His chest became empty when he realized she was avoiding him whilst twirling the fruit in her fingers.

"My Lady," he said with a gulp. His face brazen red after realizing she was indeed his lady.

"Yes, my liege," she asked, never lifting her head.

"Di-did you have a good trip on your way here?" the prince asked, now flustered as she had called him 'my liege'.

"Yes, it was overall quite pleasant," she replied softly. "It was wonderful to see all of the new landscapes. My home is so much different than yours."

"Oh, I don't know," said Carter, trying to cheer her up. "I remember when I visited your land. It was beautiful! I promise you, My Lady, there are more similarities between the two than you might think."

She looked at him with surprise. "You came to Poniere?"

"But of course," the prince replied while bravely taking the apple from her and placing it on a nearby table. "I had gone to meet with some of the Ponierian nobles. It was at that party that I met your father. It was also that night that he told me how wonderful you were. How he thought we might be good for one another."

"He did?" shrieked Miriam, which made Carter jump slightly. He had forgotten she was there! "That's so sweet! You know, Daddy talked about things like that all the time at home. All these men he had met, and that they might be good for Sissy to-"

The woman turned and raised a finger to her sister. "Now, you know better than to interrupt people when they are speaking," she said nervously. Staring intently into the girl's eyes she continued, "Remember what we talked about?"

"Yes, Sissy."

"What did you talk about?" asked Carter sadly. She had received other offers? The prince looked at the beautiful woman before him. Obviously, she would have! His fiancé turned back to him and smiled softly, her face red.

"We had discussed that she needed to behave herself if she were to come with me on this trip. By the cake stains on her clothes, I doubt she was up to much good while I was away."

"I was good, Sissy. Honest!"

"I know you were," said the woman, holding her sister's hand. She looked at the prince again. "You were saying?"

"Ah. . . I met with your father during the party of Ponierian nobles." Carter paused for a minute, trying to find the best way to tell the story. He would need to prove she had made the right choice by picking him above her other suitors. "He happened to be sitting beside me at the banqueting table. He told me many stories about your land, and I began to love it as much as my own. As well as the people there. Such a wonderful culture you come from, My Lady."

A smile stretched across the woman's face as the prince rambled on about his journey. Now that Carter had begun to tell the tale, his nervousness went away. His fiancé compared him to the Remettian flag, which bore a proud dragon upon it. The prince seemed noble, intelligent, and powerful in her eyes. He was a strong suitor and a seemingly perfect choice for a spouse. By her past experiences, she had feared he would be brash and evil like the Remettian soldiers that ripped apart her homeland. Thankfully, her father had judged his character well. He truly seemed to be a good man at heart.

"Anyway, it was as we dined together that he told me of his eldest daughter."

"What did he say?" Miriam squealed in excitement from the woman's side.

"Well," Carter crouched down, looking the little girl in the eyes as he restated what he had heard from the woman's father, "he told me of her exquisite beauty. Not just that, but also of her cleverness. A woman so intelligent, she knew more about his lands than her father himself!"

Miriam giggled, but her sister's face turned a deeper shade of red.

"I couldn't help myself," Carter continued on with his story. Turning back to his fiancé he said, "I had to know more of this woman he had spoken of. A true wonder she must be, I thought. And the more I learned of you, the more I had wanted to meet you. I hadn't believed him when your father said you were too pure for the sight of a man. Seeing you, I must admit he was right!"

The queen gasped aloud. It was so endearing to see her son this happy. The king grumpily nodded his head. The boy had finally started to make a positive impression. As for Roland, he watched in somewhat of a shocked state as the man who had no chance of swooning a woman effectively did so. What had happened to his nervous prince, he wondered?

"From what your father had spoken of you, I knew you were the best woman I could ever dream of meeting. It was to my delight that your father bestowed his blessing upon us to be wed. An even greater pleasure still, when I heard of your acceptance of me."

The two girls looked at Carter quietly, both entranced by his tale. It was Miriam who spoke first. "Were you really that excited?"

"Yes," Carter chuckled nervously. Why wasn't his fiancé saying anything? He had just made a heartfelt declaration. "I was nervous for quite some time before I heard back from your sister."

"Why were you so nervous?" Miriam quizzed again. Carter found himself with nothing else to say. How was he supposed to admit he knew his fiancé hated him and everyone present?

Her elder sisters' eyes grew wide for a moment as she read the prince's expression. She covered for her sister's behavior with a light rephrasing of the prince's words. "I think he meant excited, sweetheart."

"But, why would he be excited if he didn't even know he was getting married?" Miriam asked honestly. The prince's fiancé's cheeks were as deep red as her dress, now that she found herself unable to stop her sister from embarrassing her.

Carter found relief in Miriam's last question. With a deep breath, the prince replied. "It was because of something your father told me."

The woman let out a slight gasp. Beside her, Miriam began to glow once again with happiness. "Something Daddy said? What did he say?"

"He said, 'To whomever she will choose to wed, will be to whom I shall give her.' Then he paused for so long I thought he was never going to speak again. But when he finally did, he said, 'As I ponder who may one day care for her, I can think of none I find more worthy than you. So, if you wish it be done, let it be so.' And so it was."

The prince smiled softly to his fiancé at the completion of his tale, gently taking up her hands once again. He could hardly understand why he felt so happy to hold those petite hands of hers.

His fiancé smiled up at him. She really must lose the grudge she held against this prince and his people. He had done no wrong against her. He seemed as kind as her father had described. She needed to be more open-minded. Perhaps not all Remettians were bad after all.

Thus far, he had been nothing but kind. Perhaps these things he was saying were indeed truths. Did he admire her? He had said so. What a testimony that had been! Perhaps she had even been wrong about him wanting no more than her father's riches like the other suitors. He seemed sweet.

The advisor watched the lovers walk away, hand in hand. Impossible! That very morning, Carter had no idea how to introduce himself, let alone provide a heartfelt testimony!

"Roland," came a gruff whisper from the king, who had also remained behind. "Can I see you for a moment?"

"Of course, my liege," the advisor replied solemnly. "How may I be of service?"

"Let's start by getting away from all of this romanticizing," King Cadoc said, pointing his thumb angrily towards his overjoyed son.

"I would like nothing more," nodded Roland in agreement.

12

Questions of Attraction

The two ventured down the hall to a small room where their conversation was sheltered. It was a tight fit, a small space that made Roland begin to worry. The king normally never went in a room smaller than four times this size. What could this be about?

"You're probably wondering why I asked you here," spoke Cadoc.

"I simply wonder how I can be of assistance," Roland said calmly. He had mastered talking with the king. Sometimes he would even catch himself accidentally slipping into this cold creature outside of Cadoc's presence. He hated the man he had been made into; nonetheless, it was the man he needed to be.

"I'm here to inquire of the lady."

"Prince Carter's bride?"

"That's right."

"What is it you wish to know?" Roland asked. She had only just arrived; he hadn't gathered any additional information for the king yet. He had been too preoccupied with the child she had brought with her. More so, the advisor hadn't been able to stop thinking of Jasper and what might have become of him.

"I haven't gotten to speak with her yet, but it seems Carter and his mother took an instant liking to her. Then again, they are both tender people, so their judgments don't account for much. What was your impression of her? Carter will marry her either way. I just wonder how friendly she truly is."

Roland didn't know what to say. He didn't trust her; she had just arrived. Not to mention her devious Ponierian nature. On top of which, she seemed to have evaded his trap, showing herself to be a cunning woman. The advisor didn't want to think of the possibility of her having a connection to his White Queen. He would rather the secrets of his past would remain just that, secrets. But to tell the king these things would be suicide! He would just have to enjoy the fact that Cadoc did not seem to trust her either. That portion of the plan had remained intact.

"She seems like quite the woman, but truthfully, I have made no judgment of her."

"Really?"

"I am afraid so. She seems distant to me, but perhaps that is because of her identity secrecy. Another factor could be her stress from this new place and her upcoming wedding. We know she is uncomfortable around Remettians, that might also add to her behavior. In the end, time will tell all. Once the wedding ceremony is over and her veil is removed, the truth will be revealed to us."

"As clever as always, Roland," said the king. "But you know me. I hate patience."

"If you seek alternate options, you could try to get to know the woman during the days before the wedding. From what you learn, you could make a judgment."

"I might just do that," thought Cadoc. "Alright, one last question for today."

"Yes?"

"Do you know what happened to the woman's convoy?"

The advisor's heart pounded in his chest, but he forced his features to show not even a flicker of interest. "Something happened to the caravan? I hadn't heard of anything. Would you like me to look into it?"

"Yes, I would. It seemed when she arrived, one of her men was injured. He was shot in the shoulder, and the wound was fresh. The court physician is attending to him as we speak."

"I apologize, my liege! I hadn't heard!" Roland was shocked. Evidence. There was evidence of an attack this whole time, and he had been stuck in the haze of the woman's arrival. Could the shot be traced back to Jasper? To himself? "I will look into it straight away and report to you as soon as I find anything."

"I'm counting on it," the king patted his shoulder as he drew past. The touch of the king made Roland feel cold. Not much longer now and he would never need to bother himself with the man again. It wasn't until he finished this thought that Roland's chest became heavy. What was this re-occurring feeling? The advisor let out a sigh. Just hold out a few more days. The uprising is coming.

A few minutes after the king departed, Roland exited the room, letting out another sigh as he shut the door. Changing back into character, he lifted his head to meet the eyes of the prince's fiancé. She had come out of a bedroom close by, which her servants were now lugging her possessions into. The prince must have gone to fulfil daily duties while letting the woman unpack her belongings.

The woman looked him up and down with suspicion. Instead of addressing him, the woman quickly nodded her head in recognition. She then turned to go to the great hall. Roland looked about to find anyone else in the hallway, but he found no one. They must have all been preoccupied with unpacking.

"My Lady," he called out as he ran to catch up with her. "Why are you walking here all alone?"

"It seems my time alone will come to an end, thanks to you." Her cold tone sent chills up his spine. The advisor could hear a tint of nervousness in her words, though she had tried to hide it. He couldn't blame her for her judgment. There was no mistaking how suspicious he must have looked sneaking out of a broom closet. Nevertheless, Roland started his interrogation without hesitation.

"I was informed one of your guards was injured during travel. I want you to know that I am here to help in any way that I can.

If you could tell me what happened, I will search for the one responsible."

"I don't think it is worth any concern. It was just a simple accident in the woods. Andre is recovering well, so there is nothing more to do with it."

Roland was shocked by her response. She even knew the guard by name? What kind of noble was this? He didn't even know the names of all of Jasper's men, and they were working as a team! "Accident, you say? I was told it was more of a battle wound."

"Who told you that?" she scoffed.

"Rumors, I suppose," said Roland, irritated that she had switched the conversation to question him.

"Well, one shouldn't believe everything they hear," she paused and then smirked slightly. "Just a bit of advice."

Roland cleared his throat in indignation. He was the advisor! Had she really just given him advice? This woman had a spine on her! Then again, as the future queen, she could have his head in an instant. "My Lady, I didn't mean to intrude."

"I'm sure you didn't," she sighed. With a pause, she spoke again. "How about I make you a deal?"

"A deal?" Roland asked, intrigued.

"Yes. For every question you ask me, I get to ask you one."

"Oh! I didn't mean to seem like an interrogator!"

"No offense has been taken; I assure you. I know you are the court advisor," she explained. "It is your job to know everything about everyone in this country. Because you know basically nothing about me, I must seem like an anomaly. I can only assume it is an irritation to you."

You have no idea, thought Roland to himself as he replied, "You are no irritation, My Lady."

"So, you aren't interested in my proposal?"

"Is that your first question?" smirked Roland, who was proud of his intellect.

"If that was yours, it seems we both got our answer. My turn again." She paused as she thought of her first question while Roland kicked himself for being bested by her again.

"I don't feel that the prince and I have really gotten to know each other yet. How would you advise I approach him? I don't wish to marry a stranger, and my time seems to be running out."

Roland had been sure she would ask him what he had been up to in the cupboard, but her question seemed so innocent, as if she truly cared for Carter. Preparing himself to be the advisor, Roland answered. "The prince has loved every second he has had with you. I assure you that whatever you ask of him, he will grant to you. If you wish for a moment alone, he would be happy to comply."

"Well, that truly was the answer of an advisor. Whatever you think is best will work out wonderfully!" she laughed in mockery.

"A nasty habit, I suppose; nonetheless, it is now my turn," Roland chuckled, the woman nodding her head in response. "What happened to your guard?"

"He was shot."

"Well, I knew that!"

"It seems we are even once again. You didn't give me a good answer; I didn't give you one. My turn! What is it that Carter is looking for in a wife? This is a very important arrangement; I'm hoping to do my best in supporting him."

Determined to answer well enough for her to give up details, Roland began. "Honestly, Prince Carter hasn't said much of what he was hoping for. He mostly talked about the things he was worried about going wrong. You see, his parents had an arranged marriage."

The advisor paused. He couldn't speak ill of the king and queen! "He dreams to make his mother proud by not only supporting the country fairly but also providing a good life to his wife, you. From what I have witnessed since your arrival, you are even more perfect than he had envisioned, My Lady."

"I'm glad I set a good impression," she sighed.

"Are you unhappy, My Lady?" Oh! He had wasted his question! And for what, some woman's feelings? Why must he always get so involved?

"That is a hard question," she said as she looked at the floor. "I am happy to be welcomed here. I mean, I want to be happy. Truthfully, I spent most of my trip here thinking of my family. It seems silly, but every time I get close to the prince, he just reminds me of my father. Perhaps it's my emotions getting to me. I just worry I will never see my father or the rest of my family again, and I feel awful for how I've been treating my sister. I feel less connected to her here. As if I'm pushing her away so that losing her won't be as hard later."

Obviously, the woman had been holding back on her feelings for a while now. Roland sighed as he comforted her. "It is normal for one to feel this way when they are faced with a great change. Over time, you will become accustomed to this new life of yours. On top of which, if you wanted, I'm sure the prince would take you to visit your family from time to time."

Wiping at her cheek, the woman asked. "You know him quite well, don't you?"

"Yes, we have known each other our entire lives," answered Roland. "When I was young, I would be brought to the palace while my father fought alongside the rest of the king's army. During my stays, Carter and I would spend time together riding, practicing our swordsmanship, and the like. In any spare moment we could be found running amuck and pranking the staff."

"A trickster, huh? Good to know."

"That he is, but a good-hearted one."

"Obviously," she laughed as they approached the door to the great hall. "Well, I suppose I owe you a question. I thought you would have taken this opportunity to gain my name."

"I have been instructed that your identity is to remain a secret. Though, I could say likewise for you, My Lady. You did not ask my name either."

"That would be a misuse of my question," she smiled slightly. "Goodbye, Advisor."

"Goodbye, My Lady," Roland smiled a true smile as she walked away, a rare occurrence some would say.

Her last statement had puzzled him. Did she know who he was? She had acted so at ease. If she had known, she wouldn't have acted like that.

Inside the hall, Prince Carter got up from his chair to greet his bride. "Did you get all of your unpacking done?"

"It has been taken care of," she smiled at him. All eyes in the hall were on the two, making Carter grow anxious.

"Did you want to? Could we?" the prince paused as he tried to make himself speak. "How about we take a walk?"

"I was just about to ask you the same thing." The woman's cheeks rose into a smile again as she wrapped her arm in his. With a nervous laugh, Carter patted her hand with his free one. Then, the two walked off to spend the rest of the day together.

As they walked, Prince Carter's mind was split between the happiness he felt by being with her and the fear of what she thought of him. He didn't want her to think his silence meant he didn't like her. On the contrary, her glory left him at a loss for words.

The prince knew his fiancé didn't care for Remettians. The thing he worried over most was that she was scared of him. Perhaps she was truly terrified, but was hiding it at her father's order? It wouldn't be much different from how he dealt with his father. Somehow, he would have to prove to this woman that he truly cared for her and would never dare hurt her.

"I have been hoping to get you alone for a minute," said the woman, trying to break the silence. "I feel I don't know you very well, and I was thinking..."

The prince's eyes widened. What did she want? Was she canceling the wedding? He knew! He knew he should have spent the day with her instead of sending her off to unpack alone! How was he supposed to prove he cared, when he pushed her away when she first arrived?

"Maybe we could get to know each other better if we didn't have to worry about public impressions or anything. That way we can focus on getting to know one another, rather than the roles we uphold."

"Oh," Carter breathed a sigh of relief. "Yes, that sounds good."

"Great!" The woman looked ahead again. After a minute of silence, she spoke. "So, what do you want to talk about?"

"Ah! Right," Carter pondered a moment. During his thoughts, he looked at her, becoming lost in her beauty again.

"Prince?"

"Velvet," he blurted, blinking quickly to release his eyes from her.

"Velvet?" she asked, puzzled.

"You're wearing velvet. This scarlet-colored velvet, I mean. Is it your favorite color, maybe?" Carter rambled on, his cheeks turning the color as he asked.

"Oh," she blushed at the thought of him staring. "In my country, velvet clothing symbolizes that you are a person of secrecy. I thought it appropriate for the time, seeing as how my identity is to remain a secret until after the wedding."

"Huh," Carter thought of Roland. He was always wearing velvet. Wasn't it funny that he was indeed one of the most secretive people in the country? He wiped the thought from his mind, drawing his bride closer to his side. "Well, My Lady, I think you look wonderful in it!"

She grinned. "Thank you!"

He smiled nervously, bobbing his head up and down in praise to himself for landing the compliment. He stopped only when the woman spoke again. "The scarlet color was simply chosen to show my excitement for this wedding, but I do believe I like it. The color itself holds meaning. It could represent courage or importance. You see, to my people, the color of clothing is a way to represent the wearer."

"Interesting. What does mine say?"

The woman blushed. "Uh, well. The bright green usually resembles joy or prosperity. Which, in your case, could represent the royal wealth of your family."

"Why do I feel like there is more to this," laughed Carter.

"It could also mean fertility or rebirth. I just feel so silly. I thought you might have worn it to demonstrate your excitement for the wedding as well. As if it was your way of showing you wanted us to be reborn as one in union, or maybe even... Apparently, I took it the wrong way." The woman turned her head away from him in embarrassment.

What had he done? Carter had no idea that she would take so much notice of what he was wearing! He had picked the shirt out because it was comfortable. Somehow, he had to make up for the mistake.

"I didn't know that it meant so much to you," he said, softly pulling her close to him again. "I'll tell you truthfully; I am excited about this wedding."

"Are you?" She turned to look at him again. Staring at her eyes, the prince gulped. She was breathtaking.

"I am. Wh-what about you?"

"I am too." After a brief pause the woman sighed, "I suppose I'm just nervous."

"Me too," sighed Carter in return. "This is a delicate arrangement. I mean that as between you and I, not your father."

The woman smiled at his concern. "You worry about us?"

"If I'm honest, yes. I find marriage to be sacred. You see, my mother and father came together on similar terms. I am just nervous that, I mean, I worry I won't be able to make you truly happy."

The woman stopped and faced the prince. "I don't know you very well yet, but from what I have seen, you are a good man. I always knew that I would be married in this way, but I am glad that I am to be wed to a man like you."

"Really? Well, that's-" smiled Carter, his speech giving out on him again. Maybe she did like him after all.

After they walked for a moment in awkward silence, the woman spoke again. "How has your day been going?"

"Good, good, real good," replied Carter, who returned to his head bobbing.

"Good," the woman giggled at his lightheartedness.

"Uh," the prince blurted as he scratched his head. He tried fervently to think of something to say. "I haven't seen you eat yet today."

"Do you fear I eat like a cow?" the woman tried to lighten the mood.

"What? No!" exclaimed the prince, ashamed of what he had said.

"I'm kidding," the woman laughed. "I haven't eaten because this veil is a nuisance, but if you wish it, I will eat for you."

"No! I didn't! You don't have to!"

Since they were still inside the palace, the woman pulled two small cakes from a nearby table. She handed one to the prince and lowered her head to bite the other. Her movements were so delicate that the prince didn't believe she had taken a bite until she brought the remainder of the cake back from underneath the veil. He could see the tops of her cheeks moving ever so slightly as she chewed.

The corners of her eyes crinkled into a smile as she simply said. "Alright, your turn. We'll call this the chew test."

"Chew test," Carter scoffed as he took a bite of his own. Lifting his remaining cake so that his fiancé could see his completion of the task, he chewed happily. The cake was delicious! Gulping, he said. "Happy?"

"Delighted," she laughed, wiping a bit of cake gently from the corner of his mouth. The feeling of her soft finger tracing his lip made his smile grow even wider. He leaned towards her inadvertently, causing his fiancé to giggle again. "I think I got it."

"What? Oh, right," coughed the prince. What was he doing?

"Anything else you would like to know about me?"

"Well, you can eat, I'll give you that," joked Carter, popping the rest of his cake into his mouth. "The real question is, how much?"

The woman's eyes widened at the statement. Letting out a sharp laugh, she blushed and turned away. "A good bit."

"Oh?"

His response received a false sneer from his betrothed. The woman's playfulness was met with laughter as he took her hand back onto his arm. His fiancé carried on the conversation as they walked. "Alright, you know how I eat. I want to know if you do something amusing. Oh, I know! Do you snore?"

"What?" asked Carter, not believing that she had just asked the question.

"My father snores so loudly that he sometimes wakes everyone on his floor during the night," she giggled, bending over in happiness at the thought.

"Ha! Well, I, uh," the prince winced as he lied. "I don't snore."

"Well, that sounded quite convincing," his fiancé laughed.

"Okay, I may have a light snore."

"A light snore?"

"It's not a bad snore. It's nice."

"Oh, okay. A nice snore," the woman laughed happily.

Carter chuckled also. "Wow! First floor already? How about you lead the way, My Lady! We'll see how well that tour paid off."

"Hmm," she thought for a moment. "You showed me the castle, but I've never seen your stables. Would you mind taking me there?"

"Stables? I guess so," Carter shrugged at the thought. Most nobles would never enter a stable. Instead, they would have servants prepare horses for them. What a wonderful woman, he thought, willing to get her hands dirty.

While they were admiring the horses and gear, the prince's fiancé studied the inside of the building. The design was amazing!

Everything in this palace was made to catch your eye. As she looked around, her eyes stopped on a majestic black horse. She reached her hand out, the steed bringing its nose to her in response.

"Do you like that one?" asked the prince. "That's the Advisor's horse. I think he calls it Hymir."

"Is it? I suppose it reminds me of mine," the woman responded. "He's over here, by the way."

She walked to an adjacent pen, extending her hand once more. At the sight of her, the horse turned to face her. It was also a dark beauty, a brown color instead of the black of Sir Roland's. It grabbed at her palm with its lips, searching for a snack.

"He seems to like you."

"Dargent has always loved his mommy, haven't you, dear?" she said happily as she handed him the remaining part of her cake. With the treat in his mouth, the horse bobbed his head up and down as he chewed the unfamiliar substance. The creature's excitement caused the couple to laugh.

"He really likes that, doesn't he?"

"You would not believe the things this horse eats!"

"Doesn't seem to hurt him. He looks magnificent!"

"He is," the woman said as she stroked her steed. "Which one is yours?"

Carter walked over to a gray horse with a black mane and tail. "This one's mine."

"What a beauty! What's his name?"

"Uh," the prince shrugged.

"He doesn't have a name?"

"It's not like I spend a lot of time with him! I barely leave the palace, and usually, when I do, I just take a carriage."

"Oh," the woman pouted as she unlocked the gray horse's stall. "This poor dear. Nobody loves you, do they? But I do. Yes, I do. I love you!"

Carter chuckled, following her in. She was treating his horse as if it were a child! Once they were inside, he locked the stall door so the creature couldn't make a run for it. "I treat him well."

"Oh really," she scoffed, picking up a brush. "Have you ever brushed him?"

"Well, no. But in my defense, it's not exactly my place."

"I tend to my dearest as often as I can. I feel it helps create a better bond between horse and rider." Carter's fiancé handed him the brush, picking up another for herself. "You don't have to help me if you don't want to, but I intend to give him a proper brushing!"

Carter was taken aback as the woman started stroking the steed softly. She did not seem like she would stop anytime soon. He looked at the tool she had handed him. His fiancé seemed to know what she was doing. The prince himself felt a little embarrassed that he had never brushed a horse before. With a slight sigh, he tried his hand at it.

He could feel the horse's skin twitching as he brushed it. A few strokes in, Carter felt something was near his shoulder. Turning slowly, he met the eye of his horse.

"Oh, hello," he said as he patted its nose.

"I think he remembers you. What do you think of this man, huh? Is he good like you?" she asked the horse as if it could respond.

"He's a lot bigger than I remember," Carter told her earnestly.

"He is a big one," she giggled. "Perhaps one day you might take me for a ride?"

"A ride? Of course!"

"Wonderful! Now keep on brushing! We have a lot to do!"

The two spent a long time grooming the prince's horse. To onlookers, the sight was unbelievable. Both of them had on priceless attire laced with gold and jewels, yet they groomed the steed relentlessly.

Some servants passed by and offered to help, but Carter simply told them to bring some grain and an apple for a treat. A delight it seemed to the horse as he ate his snack. When they were finally finished with their work, the prince and his bride stepped back to admire the horse once again.

"He looks splendid," the woman exclaimed.

"He does, doesn't he?" smiled Prince Carter. "You know, I think I've found a name for him."

"Oh? And what would that be?"

"How about Lage? Since he and I are on better terms, I feel he is more of my companion than anything."

"Lage. I like it, very masculine."

"Then Lage it is!"

Smiling, Carter's fiancé drew closer to him. "Perhaps we should go back now? It's starting to get dark."

"Ah," the prince replied. He didn't want to leave yet. They were having such a good time. "I suppose you're right."

With a curtsey, the woman turned to the castle's courtyard. It took every ounce of the prince's courage to stop her. "My Lady!"

"Yes?" she asked, facing him again. Taking a gulp, Carter approached her.

"This may seem crazy, seeing as how we just met," he looked into her eyes, "but I feel I have come to care for you."

"And I, you," the lady replied. Carter could see the corners of her eyes crinkling as she smiled at him.

"I don't mean to sound too bold, but I," the prince stopped with panic in his heart.

"Yes?"

"Could I," he sighed, "escort you back?"

"I don't see why not," said the woman, extending her hand. Carter yelled at himself within his mind. Was he such a coward to not even ask her this? He was the future king! The least he could do was show a bit of courage!

"A-actually," stuttered Carter, "that's not what I wanted."

"Oh," replied the woman in disappointment as she drew her hand back to her side. "Then what did you want?"

"I hoped I might," he gulped again, "embrace you."

Silence. That's all Carter heard for the next few seconds. In his head, it seemed like hours. The woman gazed around the stables, checking to see if anyone else was there. Was she going to confront him? Whatever she said, he probably deserved it. This was too soon! What had he done?

"I suppose that would be alright," she responded softly. Her cheeks were stained bright red as she said it.

Carter's eyes widened with disbelief. She was allowing him to hug her! At first, he felt joy in his heart, only to have it soon overtaken with nervousness. He had never hugged a woman before, other than his mother, but that was different . . .wasn't it?

"Ah, okay," the prince blurted nervously. He lifted his arms to embrace her, moving them about as he tried to find where to hold her. Should he go over her arms? Under them? Maybe one arm in, one arm out?

Seeing his inner struggle, his fiancé stepped forward. She wrapped her arms around his waist. Her head leaned against him, which only came to his upper chest. The prince draped his arms over her shoulders and pulled her closer to him. All of his movements were careful, for he was taken aback by her petite frame. As he drew nearer, his nose was filled with the scent of her hair. It was a mixture of meadows and seashore. What a wonderful woman, he thought as he clung to the moment.

The Count of the Day

After Carter's bride left to go to sleep, his advisor pulled him aside to inform him of the progress of the plan. Roland's curls looked unkempt as they spiraled uncontrollably from his head, a sure sign of stressful thinking. The prince, however, was humming endlessly in happiness.

"Did she tell you anything about her journey?" Roland questioned dutifully. "One of her men was injured, but I don't know enough about the situation to know how the injury took place. Did she say she was apprehended? Is that why there were no treasures in her caravan?"

"She hadn't mentioned anything to me of a heist," replied the prince, still in a dream. "She said it was a wonderful trip."

"Sire," said Roland, interrupting Carter's daydreams. "You do realize what this means, don't you?"

"Oh!" The thought hit him. "They didn't get anything!"

"Exactly! Without that money, our plan has little to no chance of success!"

"That's no good," Carter chewed at his fingertips nervously.

"No," replied Sir Roland. "No, it is not."

"You must go to Jasper at once!" shrieked the prince. "We need to know if he was able to collect anything."

"You want me to go tonight?" asked Roland in shock. "Wouldn't that seem suspicious, especially if the girl had been attacked? It would be better if we stuck to the plan."

"We must know what is happening! Please, go and see what Jasper collected. We need to know if we even still have a plan,"

144

Carter ordered. If they didn't have the funds they needed, their entire operation had ended before it started. "I will go check on My Lady!"

"You just saw her!" Roland growled in irritation.

"Yes, but I didn't realize she was in shock! I must go and comfort her," announced Carter as he dreamed of holding her again.

"You hardly know her!" Roland spat, taken aback by the prince's sudden feelings.

"I know her enough," Carter retorted. "We had a lovely time today in the stables."

"Is that where you were?" Roland paused in shock after realizing what Carter had said. "You? You never go to the stables!"

"Well, she does, and now so do I. I think I will go at least once a week, if not more, to spend time with Lage."

"Who's Lage?" Roland was baffled. Where was the prince's head? Had he forgotten what they were in the middle of?

"He's my horse."

"What, you name your horses now?"

"That isn't a very nice tone, you know," chuckled Carter. "Haven't you named your horse?"

"There is no reason to bring Hymir into this."

"See, exactly! What's the problem?"

"The problem is that you have lost sight of what is important here, or have you already forgotten our plan?"

"I remember the plan, Roland."

"Oh, really? Because the last time I checked, whether the plan fails or succeeds, there is still a major chance that this marriage of yours is history!"

"You never know, perhaps she will love me for who I am. She is such a caring woman. I'm sure she will understand."

"Tsk," spat Roland. "There is only one good thing I've found about this woman."

Carter looked up in hope. "What?"

"She seems as distracting to your father as she is to you."

"F-father," Carter's cheeks turned red.

"Not like that," Roland laughed. "He seems to remain interested in her history. We don't know enough about her. He actually asked me to look into her again after she arrived today."

"And did you?" Carter inquired.

"Minorly, but I got nothing from it. She is a locked box, that one. Just as before, we will use her as a distraction to the king. While he is too focused on her, we can work in the background. That much has continued to go as planned. I'll give you that."

"I don't want her getting into this!" Carter placed his hands on Roland's shoulders. He looked him in the eyes as he spoke to be sure the point got across. "It's far too dangerous, and I can't have her hurt."

"No harm will come to her, I promise you. For now, let's forget this woman and focus on the mission."

"Alright. If you go see Jasper now, I'll wait for you to get back with the update."

"Very well," sighed Sir Roland. "I'll leave right away."

With that, the advisor crept down the palace hallways to the stables, clinging to the shadows. To every passing guard or servant, Roland would freeze in order to remain hidden from sight. Quietly, he saddled his black stallion, which shook its head side to side in preparation for the ride to come.

Before departure, Sir Roland took one last glance around the palace courtyard to ensure the coast was clear. Then, he sped off into the night, unaware of the fact that a nervous bride had seen him from her room's balcony.

The behavior she had seen was interesting, to say the least. The sun had already set. Where could the king's advisor be going at this time of night? She shrugged the image away. The man was a noble, was he not? His manor must be near the castle, and he was simply journeying there to sleep in his own bed for the night. Why must she always overthink these things? She let out a sigh as she turned back to her room.

Meanwhile, Sir Roland's pace never lightened. His horse's breaths grew heavy as he bulleted past the palace city's outline, through the meadow, and into the clefts of the mountains. Reaching the camping place of the thieves, he hurriedly dismounted. The group of men looked at him in horror, as if he were a thing of their nightmares. To any who didn't know him, he might seem as such.

"Well," he ordered. "How did your little endeavor go? Not as well as we had hoped, I assume, by the amount of riches that were delivered to the king this morning!"

"Roland," responded Jasper. "Please, the lads here have had a long day."

"So, you got nothing!"

"I wouldn't call it nothin'," interjected Martin. "Show 'im the purse you got from tha' lady."

With a long sigh, Jasper held out the woman's purse. "The girl played us. They had caught eye of us the night before and took the longer route to draw us in. The half of the caravan with the gold took the mountain path in order to get by us while we were ransacking a group of empty carriages. I can't believe we fell for it. I genuinely thought the woman we met was noble. She had played the part so well."

Roland huffed in disappointment. "You got one thing right."

"What?"

"The woman you met was noble," he replied. "She must've taken the long route to secure her sister."

"Her sister," muttered Jasper, thinking of the beautiful maid. "So, it was her sister who is going to marry the prince? Could they have disguised her to keep her safe?"

"No," Roland laughed. "Her sister is but eight years old!"

"Oh," thought Jasper. "What is it we should do now?"

Roland jingled the bag of coins in his hands. "Well, it's no fortune, but it is a good start. I should have enough stored at my manor to make up for our losses."

"I am sorry, my friend."

"Don't be," replied Roland, grasping Jasper's shoulder. "Make your way to my manor, and I will meet you there tomorrow with enough funds to finalize this endeavor."

"Tomorrow it is," Jasper said, "but how will you get there without the king noticing?"

Roland smiled. "I have a plan for that."

"Do tell."

"The prince's fiancé is new to this country," the advisor began his story, "so she will probably be interested in seeing it. We'll make a little journey to my manor tomorrow, where she can see the locals. Women love to be worshipped; you know. While she is preoccupied with the groveling people, I will make my way from the manor and deliver the rest of the gold to you in the local tavern."

"It is a good plan," chuckled Jasper, "only one hiccup."

"What's that?"

"This woman, she isn't like the rest. She knew we would be in the meadow this morning, had the whole thing mapped out. She told her guards to put away their arms when they doubled us in number because she knew we wouldn't get anything. The only reason we did is because she wanted us to."

"What do you mean, she wanted you to?"

"As they were leaving, she tossed us the purse," Jasper said, head hung down in shame. "We wouldn't have gotten a thing if it weren't for her pity."

Roland couldn't believe his ears. Why would the woman have done that? "So, she beat you, but then gave you her money anyway?"

"I know how it sounds, but it's the truth!"

"I believe you," replied Roland, who honestly didn't. "Not that it matters. The woman will no longer be involved with our plan. Her part is done, and I doubt we'll be troubled by her again."

"I hope you're right," Jasper said quietly, still in turmoil over his encounter with her. "Well lads, we best be off."

Roland returned the bag of gold to Jasper, giving a nod of encouragement. With that, the group of miscreants took to their horses. As they rode away, shouts and screams came from them. In the dust of the aftermath, stood Sir Roland all alone. In truth, he had always preferred it that way.

Ever since his father died, he had been alone. Too wrapped up in the responsibilities of his manor to go about meeting people. His only outside contacts were those of the royal family. During the last war, where he had been forced to work alongside others, he had met Jasper. The man had been one of his best soldiers, following him into any and every battle they had encountered. Once they returned to their soils, Roland and Jasper were supposed to part ways. Roland to his manor, and Jasper to his own. When they reached Jasper's home, they found it under the hand of another man. The king had lost it in one of his gambles while Jasper fought in the war.

As a testament to his friend, Sir Roland had opened his home up to him. When Roland was summoned to become the king's advisor, he left his estate's welfare to Jasper. The town's people flourished under Jasper's care, but deep down the man could not help but want his own home back. Over time, he put together a band of renegades from around the area. He ended up leaving nobility behind, becoming an outcast who battled against the king's evil followers.

Roland had taken a different route to destroy the king's forces. Instead of taking out the messengers, he would strike quickly, cutting off the head of the beast. For so many years he had worked for this treacherous king, and now that his grand plan was unfolding, it wasn't going as smoothly as he had hoped. Roland let out a sigh. If only it would work. He held lightly to his turning stomach; his stress must have been getting to him. With that he started back toward the king's palace, leaving behind the now empty camp.

Upon his arrival, the advisor went straight to the prince's room. He grimaced at the loud snoring he had to endure during his approach. Shaking Carter awake, Roland whispered. "Wake up! I have news!"

"Gnn-uh, Wha-what?"

"Jasper and his men only collected a meager two hundred and fifty pounds."

"Two hun-," yawned the prince, wiping the sleep from his eyes. "That's it?"

"Yes, sire."

"That's not enough!"

"I understand that," scowled Roland, "but I can get more. I need you to organize a tour for your bride tomorrow."

"Oh, I forgot. I'm getting married," said the prince, falling back into his pillow. "What should I say to her?"

"That you wish to show her a part of the kingdom she will one day rule over."

"And where is it exactly that I'll be taking her?"

"To my manor. While we are there, I will give Jasper the rest of what he needs to complete his task."

"Alright," Carter yawned again. "When are we leaving?"

"As soon as possible."

The prince snuggled into his pillow. "Then I'll be needing some rest now."

"Of course, I was just about to retire."

"Sure you were," scoffed the prince. "Off to your room to analyze the situation over and over and ov-"

A pillow landed against the prince's face, stopping his repetitions. He grabbed it to throw back, but Roland was already at his room's door. "Goodnight, sire."

Too tired to argue, the prince laid back down, falling asleep as soon as his face touched the pillow.

14

An Ill-Favored Trip

Waking up with her sister curled around her, the woman arose slowly from her bed. Poor Miriam had gotten frightened during the night and had crept into her older sister's room for comfort. The woman sighed as she dressed in an elegant scarlet outfit. Placing a golden necklace around her neck, she called out to her sister. *"Miriam, darling, it's time to get up."*

"Ugh," the girl groaned. *"Get up?"*

"Yes, we've got a big day ahead," replied the woman, placing a scarlet veil over her mouth.

"Oh!" Miriam squealed, remembering where she was. *"It's time to talk to the new family again!"*

"I'm glad you're so excited," scoffed her older sister. *"Now, run along and get dressed!"*

"Okay!" yelped Miriam as she ran out of her sister's door. The woman let out a laugh. Would that girl ever calm down?

After Miriam had dressed, the two made their way to the great hall, faces covered. Both left their hair down, falling over their shoulders. The woman had strands of gold weaved through hers. Miriam had silver spiraled instead. The colors drew out the darkness of their dresses. The gold with scarlet, the silver with a deep purple.

When the prince saw his bride approaching, he smiled nervously. That morning, he had chosen to wear his country's colors to keep from another mistaken sign due to his apparel. A golden dragon was etched into the shoulder of his dress-coat. On each button, a dragon's head extended. His crown today was thinner than the day before. To the woman, it seemed like a halo hovering over his figure.

The king and queen nodded their heads in acknowledgment, both also in Remettian colors. Sir Roland the Advisor stood behind the lot, choosing to adorn a black silk shirt. As the woman entered, he looked at her but never really showed her any notice.

The sight of him puzzled her. How was he back already? The sun had only been out an hour. Had he even gone home last night? Realizing she was staring, she turned to the prince. "Good morning, Prince Carter."

Her formalities made the prince blush. Instantly forgetting his jealousy from when she had been entranced with Roland, he spoke to her. "Good morning," he paused, remembering to keep her identity a secret. "What is it I should call you?"

"What is it you wish to call me," she replied, playfully tilting her head to one side.

Another blush. "I hm-hmm."

She stopped his efforts. "Perhaps I should come up with a new name for you as well."

Gazing into her eyes, the prince could do nothing but smile. "You have a pet name for me?"

"But of course," she giggled. "Maybe we should start again? Yeah? Good morning, dear."

The prince grinned ear-to-ear. He found himself unable to create a sentence, a repetitious symptom of the woman's presence. He had wanted to tell her something, hadn't he? It must not have been important. But then again, what could be more important than her? She liked him, that much she had made clear! Who knows why she had been looking at Roland before? It didn't matter. It was then the thought hit him, Roland!

"My darling lady," the prince replied nervously. "Would you like to meet my country? See the people? I mean, meet the people of my country?"

"I would love to," she smiled.

"Wonderful! We will leave as soon as you're finished eating," Carter stammered, pointing to the set tables of food.

"Wait . . . today?"

"I'd hate to be on short notice, but the thought just came to my mind," the prince smiled nervously. It felt wrong to lie to her, but it was the only way, wasn't it? What if she saw through him? What would she think if she found him to be lying?

"It's alright. Do you have any idea where we will be going?"

"Oh! Well, the advisor hasn't always been in these courts, you know. His manor isn't far from here, not to mention it is one of the greatest provenances in this entire country!" Carter smiled wider, hoping she would go along with his schemes.

"Your advisor's manor." With a sense of uncertainty in the fact that the prince had come up with this idea on his own, she raised the question. "How far is it from here?"

"It is but a quarter of a day's ride from here," replied the prince, his jealousy returning. Why was she so interested in Roland? Was she taken by him like the other women of the country? "We will be back before sundown."

"How exciting," exclaimed Miriam. "I've always wanted to see a manor!"

"Is something wrong?" interjected Roland, who had just appeared behind Carter's shoulder. His presence made the woman jump slightly.

"No, no! It's just so sudden. You both took me by surprise. We would love to go," she replied, grasping her sister's hand.

"I'll have my men draw up a carriage," said the prince half-heartedly, turning from her and Roland.

"I hope you have a good time, My Lady," Roland spoke again, stepping closer to her. As she became more unstable, he evaluated her response to nothing more than a harmless threat. "I will be personally escorting you and the prince to ensure nothing happens along the way."

"How thoughtful," she replied, moving her sister behind her. As if on cue, the bodyguard took the girl's other hand and led her to the safety of the pastry table.

"Prince," the woman called out. "Could we take some of my men as well? I'd love to let them stretch their legs a bit."

"Bring along whomever you would like," he responded gleefully.

The woman smiled at the prince. Roland realized that she was doing all she could to ignore him.

"Might we also take my carriage?" she said.

"I never thought of it," blurted the prince. "Would you like me to have it prepared for you?"

"I would like to take it, for good measure."

"Of course, anything for you," he replied.

She bowed her head in respect before dragging her sister back into the hall. Her behavior made Roland curious. When she had walked in, she seemed so shocked to see him there. Then, when he tried to speak to her, she drew away from him. She had even hidden her sister behind her! The last time they had spoken, it had not ended that badly, had it? She seemed petrified to be in his presence. What had he done to deserve such treatment?

Perhaps her misfortune had finally caught up to her. When she was told they were traveling, she wanted her men to come along. Maybe it was just a precaution due to yesterday's robbery. Even so, why had she still not spoken up about it? He had even mentioned the possibility of hardships. Most women couldn't hold their tongues when they were afraid, yet the only fear this woman showed was towards him.

As her guard closed the doors to the hall behind the woman and her sister, Roland looked at his clothes. The advisor traced them with his hands for good measure. He had been sure to wear clothing without his sigil for the time being. There was no way she was acting like this due to his reputation. Unless she had somehow figured it out? Roland ruffled his hair in irritation. He hoped not! Moving forward, he would deal more carefully with her; starting with this trip.

He placed his ear against the door to hear what she was saying to her guards, but it was all in a foreign language. The advisor let out a sigh. He hated not knowing things, and this woman was nothing more than a collection of the unknown. Leaving his eavesdropping behind, he reconvened with Prince Carter, who was anxiously waiting in the courtyard to spend the day with his princess. The prince was leaning against the side of a darkly-stained, wooden carriage.

"You seem cheery, sire," Roland said coldly.

"You don't," scoffed Carter. "Shocker."

"Very funny."

"What is there not to be cheery about? I mean, everything is coming together again. Why worry?"

"Because of how easily it became unraveled the first time," the advisor snapped. "Who's to say something like that won't happen again? You never know when something will go wrong."

The prince's heart sank. "Oh, yeah. I guess I see what you're saying there. Is that what you were so upset about?"

"I'm not upset, merely concerned, Your Highness," Roland slumped onto the carriage beside his friend.

"Are you sure?" Carter asked with sorrow in his voice. "Every time you get stressed, you always mess your hair up like that."

He pointed to the top of Roland's head, where his curly hair was no longer orderly but went about wildly from his earlier ruffling.

"Oh!" Roland patted down his curls, trying to make himself presentable again. "I was just thinking about today, I suppose. You didn't tell that woman who I am, did you?"

"No, why?" Carter said with a lump in his throat. Roland had ruffled his hair over her? He had never ruffled his hair over a woman before, other than his White Queen.

"It's just, she seemed quite nervous around me today, and I thought we had agreed that my influence with her people would be a setback leading up to your wedding. With the way she has been acting, I can't help but wonder if she has learned who I am."

She had been acting nervous around Roland? Why would she do that? Wait! What was it she had said when she arrived? Carter's eyes widened as he repeated. "Black Knight."

"Excuse me?" Roland snapped.

"That's what she said when she first arrived. I thought she was talking about her bodyguard, but you don't think?"

The advisor's face twisted into fury. "She said that?"

"Y-yes," Carter gulped. Was he about to marry Roland's White Queen, the most treacherous woman in all of the lands? His advisor had told of her evil, but never the name. Was his fiancé not as wonderful as she seemed?

"I was afraid of this," Roland said quietly.

The prince's heart raced in his chest. "Does that mean?"

"Not to worry, sire," the advisor sighed. "It is not the same woman."

"But she called you!"

"I understand that. I knew if this woman was as worthwhile as she was made out to be, she would have a connection to... her."

"What should I do?" Carter begged his advisor. "Is my woman as evil as yours?"

Roland looked at his nervous prince. He couldn't have him thinking about this all day. "I do not believe this woman of yours is evil. It's best to put this behind you and focus on her positive attributes. I think you'll come to find that she is a remarkable woman."

The prince felt a bit hurt. Never in his life had Roland uttered such a phrase as 'a remarkable woman'. "Do you like her?"

"I suppose so," the advisor shrugged, not understanding the damages he was inflicting. "I haven't spoken with her much yet."

"Yet?" Carter gulped. "Do you plan to... swoon her?"

"What?" Roland looked at his prince in shock. "No! I would never dare to look at her with such intentions! I think she is a good woman for you, sire."

The prince thought for a moment. He knew Roland would never betray him so much as to steal his love from him, but what if it was his fiancé that was untrue? Since the two had only just met, her heart could easily fall to another man. Between him and the advisor, Carter saw no challenge. Even with his past, Roland was a far better man than he. The prince could only hope his fiancé did not come to admire his advisor rather than himself.

"You should just enjoy your time with your fiancé," said Roland, trying to make up for the recent intensity. "I'll take care of everything else."

"Alright," replied Carter, with bitterness in his voice.

"Are you sure you aren't the one who is stressed, sire?" the advisor asked. "You've been acting rather abrupt this morning."

"I'm fine," sighed the prince. He couldn't tell Roland that he was worried about his fiancé riding off into the sunset with his best friend!

"You don't seem fine," Roland stated coldly as looked about to ensure no guards were around to hear the conversation.

Carter broke. He could never keep anything from him. "Didn't you see her staring at you this morning? You were staring right back! And her gaze didn't seem to be one of nervousness. It was closer to infatuation! I felt like a third wheel, and I'm marrying her!"

"You're worried about that?" laughed Roland. "I assure you; she has no interest in me. The woman would sooner try to kill me than kiss me!"

"I find that hard to believe. She doesn't seem like one for bloodshed, you know," scoffed Prince Carter.

"Perhaps not, but I have an uneasy feeling with her. She doesn't trust me, and frankly, I don't trust her fully either. If the woman has any feelings for me at all, I doubt they would amount to more than fear."

"Well, perhaps if you didn't sulk around behind everyone, you wouldn't appear so threatening," chuckled Carter, whose mind was now at ease.

"Are you giving me advice now?" joked Sir Roland, hitting the prince playfully in the chest.

"Oh! I'll have your head for that one!"

"I'm shaking," smirked Roland as the prince's hand flew past him in an effort to retaliate. With a swift move, Roland took out the young prince's footing, sending him tumbling face first to the ground. Carter let out a grunt as he raised himself back to his feet.

"One day, I'll get you, you know."

"That would be the day," the advisor chuckled.

"So now you're happy," scoffed the prince. "Now that you've beaten me, again! Honestly, I don't see how you still get pleasure from it."

"Every man has his faults."

"Yours being your competitive nature."

"It is better than most faults!"

"Yeah, okay!"

The boys became men when they saw the outline of the kingdom's newest princess. Behind the woman stood fifty of her personal guard, ten in gleaming steel and the other forty wearing brazen black metal. All of the guards wore a purple cloak, yet there were no distinguishing markings on them to signify the title of the woman they served. Those in steel held to the reins of their horses in one hand and clutched a longbow in the other. The remaining forty were prepared to follow the woman and her sister by foot. When they reached the carriage of the prince, the ten steel guards mounted their horses, taking to the back of the line.

"Prince," the woman smiled as she approached. "Is this the carriage we will be taking?"

"Mhmm," Carter hummed, opening his carriage door for her. "Do you like it?"

The outside had been engraved but bare. Beautiful, yet not exquisite. When she entered the carriage, she found its seats lined with silks and dazzlingly sculpted gold plating coated the walls. It was indeed a testament to the king's wealth. "It is quite beautiful."

"Woah! Sissy! This carriage is amazing. Everything they have is so gold! Even dad doesn't have a carriage like this! Ours are pretty, but, wow!"

"I'm glad you like it," chuckled the prince, who sat across from them. He had chosen to ride in that carriage with hopes to impress his fiancé. He grinned with satisfaction in his victory.

Sir Roland followed, sitting beside him. The last man in was Frank, the bodyguard. He sat directly across from Roland; his shrouded face frozen towards him. The woman sat between Frank and Miriam, who had trampled over her for the window seat.

"I feel awful that you can't see outside," continued Carter. "Would you like to switch me places?"

"Oh no, I'm alright," the woman responded nervously. Carter let out a breath of relief. He could only imagine how easily she would fall for Roland if they sat next to one another for so long a ride. He already had her simply trembling.

"Then perhaps, you would rather trade with me?" asked Roland out of politeness.

"I am perfectly fine where I am, thank you," she said sharply. Miriam turned towards her sister, hearing that tone before.

"You okay, Sissy?" she asked in their tongue. The woman looked first at her sister, then up at the men who were now staring with incomprehension.

With a smile, she replied. "It isn't polite to speak in a way in which our hosts cannot follow the conversation."

"Sorry," said Miriam apologetically. "You okay?"

"Yes, darling," she said, pulling her sister into a hug. "I'm just tired."

Roland felt pride; the little girl had noticed she was nervous. It seemed she wasn't as good of an actress as she thought. Meanwhile, the prince became the victim to even more jealousy. What he wouldn't give for a hug from his bride, to have her call him darling.

Then again, would he ever be good enough? His mother's arranged marriage didn't end so well. His greatest desire was to have a good marriage, where this woman would truly care for him. So far, she seemed interested, but only time would unveil the truth.

Dry conversation kept the group of travelers going for a while, but by the time they finally reached Sir Roland's manor they had taken to silence. When they entered the village, the people came from their homes and bowed their heads in reverence to the prince. All of them seemed happy to see the advisor, to the woman's surprise. He was welcomed with platters of meat and cheese. Once they greeted their master, the serfs moved onward to show care to the prince and his fiancé.

The advisor's head attendant provided the tour of the premises. It was indeed an impressive manor, thought the woman. The fact that was more impressive to her was that the man of the manor had disappeared almost as soon as they arrived. She couldn't blame him. She was also growing bored of the show and tell session.

Most places went through the history of their town and the people who grew up there, but this tour was strange. There were no stories of old, no emblems to resemble the power of the man who looked after the place. They hadn't even told her the name of the town! They simply referred to it as the advisor's. How arrogant did a man have to be to make his people use his title instead of the name of their town?

After a while, her head was drawn to the window, where she saw something quite peculiar. Slipping away from the group, she went to take a closer look.

Meanwhile, meeting again in the back of a pub were Jasper and Sir Roland.

"Do you have it?" whispered Jasper from the shadows.

"As promised."

"Thank you, my friend," he replied. "I truly am sorry I wasn't able to get more."

"You and your men are willing to put your blood into this," stated Roland, handing over a massive bag of coins. "What will the loss of a little gold do to me?"

"You are a true patriot."

"Enough," Roland pushed the compliment away. "Now, for phase two."

"Hey," said Jasper, turning to a nearby window. "I thought you said ole Queeny would be taken care of?"

"What are you talking about? I have her stuck in a tour."

"You sure about that?" asked Jasper sarcastically, never lifting his gaze from the window.

Roland leapt from his seat. Peering out, he saw the woman standing in the road in front of the pub. Her attention was fixed on a greasy man with a scar running down his left cheek who was continually beating an older lady. The advisor's heart raced in his chest as he recognized the faces of both the old woman and her torturer. The advisor watched in awe as the prince's fiancé flicked her hair and drudged ever closer to the scene.

"Yeah, that's her. Bold as ever," continued Jasper as he took another swallow of his mead. "Eh! Where are you going?"

"Just stay here!"

Roland burst through the door to try and stop the fiend. He couldn't be seen with Jasper, or else the woman would put two and two together, but neither could he let this behavior continue. Catching his breath, he called out. "Dorian, please! Don't you think that's enough? Just let her go!"

"You ain't paid to be my advisor," slighted the greasy foe as he turned to face Roland, holding the old woman by the hair of her head.

Roland walked closer. The prince's fiancé had moved to the shadows of an alley behind him. He could feel her gaze, watching how he handled the situation. Evaluating his every move.

"Belinda, it'll be okay. It's going to be fine, alright?" he reassured his caretaker, hand outstretched. The old woman did her best to nod in response. Why were they doing this to her? "Please, Dor-"

"Give it up, Sir Roland," said the man, drawing out the sir in a mocking way. "Keep this up, and you'll be next."

Roland stopped in his tracks, beaten by the imbecile simply because he could not overpower the king's authority. With a wicked smile, Dorian turned back to the woman he was beating. Someone brushed past Roland, taking on the challenge. As the evil man raised his hand again, it was stopped by that of the prince's fiancé.

"He may not be paid to be your advisor, but his point is accurate all the same. You've done enough." Her voice was no longer soft as it had been, but ice cold in a way that sent chills up the spines of those present.

In fury, the man threw the barely conscious Belinda down to the ground; using his now free hand to strike a blow at the prince's fiancé. She managed to block the punch, following through by ramming her knee into his chest, which sent him falling backward over the limp body.

What was she doing? Roland knew he had to do something; this woman was going to get herself killed! The prince's fiancé turned slightly, looking into Roland's eyes. He saw no fear there.

"Well?" she ordered. "Get this woman out of here!"

Pouncing on the opportunity, Roland rushed forward and dragged Belinda to safety. When the scarred man stood to face the woman again, he drew out his dagger menacingly.

"Who do you think you are, missy?"

"The question is, sir, who is it you think you are?" said the woman, copying the drawn-out sir he had used before.

Roland was frozen. This woman was not afraid. Why was she not afraid?

"I am Dorian! One of the king's top collectors," laughed the man as his crew came in behind him. Seven men grouping together to take on one unarmed woman, yet she stood unfazed. "That there garbage is forty pounds overdue to the king. I was making an example of her when-"

"Let me stop you there." The woman held up her hand. "You say you beat her because she owes forty pounds?"

"Y-yes," Dorian was having trouble understanding the woman's hold on him. He couldn't decide how to approach her anymore. She was dressed like a noble, but even they feared him.

"What if I were to pay you twice as much? Would you leave her be?"

The suggestion angered him. How dare she try and barter with him! It would impact his image with those he saw over, to relinquish to a woman. "No!"

"What can I do then, if you act on nothing but your putrid manner? Don't you know that an unreasonable man has no hope of reaching anything but an unreasonable end?"

"What did you just say to me?"

"I should have known you wouldn't be able to keep up. Too many big words for you, my dear?"

"Why you!" He charged at her with his dagger. With a simple dodge she whisked around him, taking out the side of his left knee. He buckled under the pain. Seizing her moment, she tore the blade from his hand, stepping back towards Roland. The woman twirled the weapon in her fingers as she got used to its weight.

Her enemy growled as he stood up again. His men didn't know what they should do, so they simply stood, awaiting orders. Dorian focused his gaze towards the woman again. She balanced the knife in her hand, watching him to see what he would do next.

"Now, you listen to me!" he screamed, unwittingly drawing the attention of the woman's guards. "You and your little band of pigs here will do what I say, or you will be punished!"

Standing tall, the woman flicked her wrist. The small action sent the dagger into one of Dorian's men's inner thighs who had stepped forward to get her. The man screamed in agony. Once the shock had settled, the head collector again turned to face her. She hadn't moved, still standing boldly, awaiting his next strike. Meanwhile, her archers positioned themselves around her. Too focused on his anger against the woman, Dorian charged at her without realizing the danger of his actions.

"Oh, you're gonna pay for that!" he yelled out, quickly swatting his hand at her. The woman managed to back away in time, the tips of his fingers hardly brushing across her cheek. Still, the blow was enough to make her stagger backwards. As she stumbled, all fifty of her archers took aim in formation, all sights divided between the seven men. She let out a cold chuckle as she gently adjusted her veil, which had almost been ripped from her face by the impact of Dorian's strike.

"Better hope this doesn't bruise," she said in a deadly calm, "or you'll be the ruination of my wedding day."

Dorian's heart stopped. Had he just attacked the prince's fiancé? The king would have his head!

"Now, you listen to me," she continued coldly, realigning herself to his eyes, "You and your little band of pigs here will do exactly what I say, or you will be punished."

Dorian gulped, his humiliation at a maximum.

"Be a good boy and follow the example of your friend over there," the future queen said, pointing at the man she had stabbed in the leg who was now sitting on the ground in agony. "Kneel."

Grudgingly, Dorian and all of his crew kneeled on the ground before her. She turned back to Sir Roland, who had yet to overcome his shock. His mouth was wide with disbelief. The archers lowered their bows at the woman's instruction and one man scurried over with a med-pack.

"You're Belinda, right?" she asked the poor woman as the guard started treating her wounds.

"Y-y"

"There's no need to talk. You should rest. These men are going to take care of you. Now, as for that measly debt."

The woman tore her purse from her belt, throwing it at Dorian. Never did the collector dare to stop kneeling, lest he be killed.

"I hereby declare Belinda debt-free," she exclaimed with a snap of her fingers, "along with everyone else who lives in this town!"

The people cheered as the woman's soldiers followed her instructive snap and lifted the seats of her carriage, carrying out bag upon bag of gold! They laid them all in a mountain in front of the collector. Inside the bar, Jasper slapped Martin across the back.

"Ow!"

"You didn't find that?"

"Well, who puts money under their seats? 'Onestly!"

The ruckus had drawn the prince and the rest of the travelers from inside the manor, all gathering to witness the spectacle. Carter swapped a gaze with his friend, trying to understand the situation. All he found were a pair of wide eyes and a dropped jaw. Seeing her betrothed, the woman made her way to him.

The people flocked after her, singing. "Praise be to the prince and his bride!"

Once she reached him, she took his arm and stood by him lovingly. The people grew even louder. From the background, Dorian and his men drew dark gazes of hate against her. Miriam came to her side and hugged her sister for the delight of the people.

"What's going on?" Carter asked his bride.

"That man over there was here to collect debts, so I thought it might help me win the favor of the people to cancel them. Hopefully, that will suffice," she said in a soft voice, nodding towards the enormous stack of money.

"That ought to do it," he smiled to her. "Thanks for coming today."

"We wouldn't miss it," the woman replied, holding her sister tight. "Not for anything."

Finding strength in his legs, Roland returned to his place in the pub and lifted his drink once again. There was something definitely not right with that woman. No noblewoman did things like that. They were accessories, nothing more. Unbelievable!

"I told you, she isn't like the rest," Jasper chuckled at his friend's shocked expression.

"She's not normal," Roland shook himself, placing his empty cup on the table just in time to receive another. "Now, as for phase two."

"We will leave as soon as they head back to the manor. Don't need her catching sight of us here."

"If you leave now, you may be able to return before nightfall," Roland smiled to himself. They were back on schedule. "I will meet you at the tavern just after sunset. Have everything ready and I'll get you inside."

"Alright. See you there, my friend," Jasper finished his last gulp of mead.

Roland left his crew behind and made his way back to the prince and the woman, all the while thinking of what had happened. Was this woman some kind of hidden mercenary? No. If she were, Carter would have been dead long before now. Still, something about her actions made him uneasy. They were precise. Everything was put in place down to the last second where her archers took over. Her riling of Dorian was planned in order to both get her backup's attention and to degrade him before the public. This woman was cunning indeed. Something of her reminded him of himself. How strange. He couldn't help but wonder for a moment who she might be.

"I hope you enjoyed the tour," Roland said to the group as he approached.

"We did! You have such a wonderful place!" Miriam rang out.

"I'm glad you liked it," he said to her, then he whispered to Carter. "We can head back now."

"It was great," the young prince exclaimed, "but we should head back now. What do you think, dear?"

"Yes, that is alright with me," the woman smiled at him. With pride, he led the way back to the caravan which would take them home. They sat in a similar arrangement to that morning. Only this time, Miriam sat in the middle to let her sister have an outside view. As she stared at the trees they passed by, the woman drifted into deep thought.

It had been a strange tour for sure. All of the people were so entranced with the thought of Sir Roland, but no one ever seemed willing to share why he was worthy of such praise. They must still live with the daydream that he was their deliverer during the war.

How different he was now. As that poor woman was beaten, the man shrunk. He showed no signs of worthiness for the praise he had received. There was nothing more she could find in him than cowardice and deceit.

"My dear?" Carter asked, drawing her back to reality.

"Yes?"

"I was wondering what you would like to do for the rest of the day. We will get back earlier than expected, so there will be time to do something else. If you would like?"

"Well, I have had such a pleasurable time so far! Why don't you decide again?"

Her response shocked Sir Roland, remembering her defeat of Dorian. She calls that pleasurable? The prince smiled, still having no idea of the encounter.

"Hmm," thought Carter. "It would be easier to decide if I knew a few of your hobbies, my dear."

"I enjoy reading, dancing," she paused and smiled at him, "and spending my time with you!"

The prince blushed in response. Roland, on the other hand, rolled his eyes in disbelief that the prince had fallen for such a line.

"And she likes singing! You should hear her sing! My Sissy is-" Miriam stopped due to the evil glare she received from her sister.

"I would be more interested in what you like to do, Prince," said the woman, trying to get the conversation back on track.

"Oh, I don't know," started Carter. "I suppose I enjoy jousting, melee, and other types of sparring."

"Melee? My sister!"

"Has always been interested in watching the sport!" finished the woman, again looking down at her sister. "Perhaps I could watch you spar today?"

"Would you really want to?"

"Of course," she smiled at the prince while trying to ignore the glare Roland was giving her from beside him. To the advisor, it would seem she had done more than just watch the sport as a pastime.

Arms for War

$\mathcal{A}$s the prince and his fiancé made their way back to the palace, Jasper and his men headed south, never ceasing in their efforts until they made it to the town of Gevhart. Jasper pulled on his old army cloak that bore the king's seal before stepping inside the town's blacksmith shop. The rest of his men busied themselves with a cart, preparing it to take back to the palace.

The smell of smoke filled Jasper's nose as he entered the molten building. Around him were weapons of various natures, all crafted skillfully by their maker. Orious, the blacksmith, was known throughout the three kingdoms. His craftsmanship was beyond compare. King Cadoc had been kind to him to keep his allegiance. It was beneficial to have a skilled weapons-maker at your disposal.

"Hey Ore," Jasper called out over the clanging noises. The king's guards had given him the nickname Ore due to the amount of iron ore they delivered to him in order to make the king's weapons.

"Just a minute," replied a voice from within the smoke as the clanging continued.

SPLOOSH!

"Be right there," Orious reaffirmed as he walked out of the smoke. In his hand was a blade that was still steaming after its recent water dousing. He was a small man, but stout. Not a hair was on the man's head. His skin was stained by the smoke and oil he worked with. "How can I help you, sir?"

"I am here to collect the new shipment of armor for the king's men," Jasper said boldly.

"Right. Should have known with that tunic and all," muttered Orious as he walked back into his smokey home. "Do you plan on going to the palace soon?"

"Yes, my men and I mean to make it back to the palace by this evening. We must take our positions before guests start arriving."

"That makes sense," replied the blacksmith as a loud clatter came from within the smoke. "Oh, dear!"

What was he doing? Jasper thought to himself. The man should have known they'd be coming. Roland would have worked it all out by now. Had the king found out about their plan and this was a set up? Why else would the blacksmith stall like this? Looking back to the doorway, Jasper slowly crept towards the light of safety.

"Ah, there it is!"

Jasper let out a slight gulp. Was he getting a weapon?

"Sir Roland sent you lads, didn't he?" came a question from within the smoking weaponry.

"Yes, he did," Jasper replied timidly. "We are to report to him when we get to the palace this evening."

"Could you give him this for me?" Orious asked, appearing before Jasper. The traitor flinched as he expected a blade to follow the remark. He looked down to find a small box in the blacksmith's outstretched hand. It was beautifully crafted in dark cedarwood and sealed with a scarlet ribbon.

"A box?" Jasper asked.

"Yes. It's actually for Prince Carter. He wanted it delivered to him before his wedding. Such a blessing, you guys coming today. I doubt I would have gotten it to him on time. You can take it to Roland, right? He is always by the prince, so he could deliver it for me."

"Uh, sure," Jasper shrugged, gently lifting the delicate box.

"Great!" the blacksmith said as he pulled out a brilliant red bag. "You can keep it in here for now, but don't open it! It's for the prince alone."

"Alright," Jasper said, taking the bag and carefully placing the treasure inside. "So, about that shipment?"

"You bet, come around back!"

Jasper turned and went to his horse. Placing the prince's treasure in his saddlebag, he said to his crew, "Take the cart around back. I'll be right there."

"Fourteen suits of armor for all the king's glory!" shouted the blacksmith as he admired his work. "What do you think?"

"They will do nicely," grinned Jasper as he handed him the money he had gotten from Roland and the woman. "Hopefully, this will cover the expense."

"More than enough, thank you!"

"For the box as well?" Jasper was puzzled because what they had only covered the cost of the armor.

"No, no. That was done for the prince as a favor. No charge."

"The prince will be very grateful," Jasper replied.

"I hope it lives up to expectation. You gent's want help loading these?" Orious carried on as he started moving pieces of armor onto the cart, keeping each set together. Once all was loaded, the men started their journey back to the king's palace.

Meanwhile, as soon as the prince arrived at the palace, knights were prepared for him to spar against. The woman and her sister stood to the side, watching the fights as the men trained for battle. It was indeed, gruesome. The men didn't hold back malice for their fellow soldiers. It was a blessing they were using wooden swords. If they had been metal blades, bones would have broken or been sawn through; rather than the inescapable bruising they were experiencing now. Out of all, the prince was superior. With his skills, he easily took out the opponents he faced. The woman became obviously impressed as she watched him.

The advisor didn't join in the fighting. He instead stood watching alongside the woman and her companions, an occurrence she did not seem impressed by. As Roland loomed over her and her sister, the prince's fiancé became nervous. It wasn't long before she suggested Miriam go with her bodyguard to see the horses. The little girl shrieked with excitement. She had never been one for malice. Without even answering her sister, she bolted away from the fields towards the castle. Once they were alone, Sir Roland turned to the woman to discuss what she had done earlier that day.

"With your bravery, you should be out on those fields," the advisor said softly, nodding his head to the ongoing fights.

"It is not my place," the woman responded simply, stepping away from him.

"It seemed to be earlier," he scoffed.

"It wouldn't have been if the situation had been dealt with properly," she snapped in return, her chin held high in irritation.

The comment stung. She thought him useless, cowardly even. If there was one thing Roland was not, it was a coward. She probably thought less of him as he stood to the side while the melee took place before him. What worse would she think of him, by the things his White Queen might have told her.

With a sigh, he tried to explain himself. "My Lady, I wanted to help Belinda, I truly did. But you see, Dorian's rank is higher than mine within the royal household, so I could not challenge his actions. I am an advisor, but I cannot demand people follow my instructions. Such action could be taken as treason."

"Belinda," she said, never turning her head from the battles before them. "You seem to care for her."

"Yes," replied Roland. After a long pause he realized the woman was waiting on details, so he explained. "She raised me when I was young. My mother died when I was six years old and my father was a busy man, so he brought in Belinda to look after me. When I was fourteen, he also passed, leaving just Belinda, George, and I in that manor."

She stated innocently. "George was the man who gave us the tour."

"That's right."

"I see, and you cannot interfere with the business of this Dorian because he is higher than you in rank?"

"Right again, My Lady," Roland answered, wondering how she had turned the conversation to him instead of herself.

"How is it that the king's advisor has a lower standing than a collector?"

Roland cleared his throat. This was high-level information, but then again, she was a member of the royal household now. "He is closer to the king than I, having held his position longer."

"How long have you been the king's advisor?"

"Three years," he replied solemnly. "Not long after the last Great War."

She turned to face him; the blue of her eyes alight with suspicion. "You fought in the war?"

"I did, My Lady," Roland said nervously, concerned about her reaction. It seemed she hadn't figured out who he was after all. So why had she been acting so strangely towards him?

She turned again to the fights. "Then I suppose what I did today didn't seem like much. There is no need to call it bravery, Advisor. We all know there are others far braver than I. Men like your Lord of Morer, for example."

"You speak words of honor for him, yet you carry bitterness in your voice, My Lady."

"I suppose I am a bit bitter, but we all have those from the war we find it hard to forgive," she replied, never looking to him. "Wouldn't you say, Advisor?"

Roland knew she was taunting him. For a moment, he had believed she didn't know who he was, but now the answer was clear.

"That is the effect of war," Roland replied, his anger soaking his words without his consent. If Carter's fiancé had hated him before, she would surely hate him now. "Even when you win the war itself, you do not win every battle. It is the battles lost to your enemy which develop your hatred for them. In my experience, such hatred never leaves you. As I am sure you are aware."

"Why would you think that, Advisor," she said, looking once again to him. Her eyes pierced Roland with their coldness. She had used his title repeatedly to relay how little she cared for it. It was as if she was rebuking him for his efforts to hide his identity. Such a hypocrite, this woman. What had he done to deserve such animosity towards him?

"I suppose it disgusted you the moment you saw me, My Lady, being that I am Lord Roland of Morer. The man upon whom you have placed so much hate," the advisor stated in a deep tone as cold as her gaze had been. "I can further assume you have no intention of forgiving me for whatever it is you are holding against me."

Taking a step away from him, she stated. "I don't appreciate that tone, Advisor."

"I apologize," Roland growled. "I didn't realize I had made you feel uncomfortable, but I must ask. What is it I have done to make you hate me so much?"

"Watch out," she warned, looking between him and the battles beside them. To Roland, it seemed she was hoping for the prince to come and save her from him.

"I don't mean to bother," he snapped, "but it amazes me that you would hold such a grudge against me when we have never even met before!"

"I said, watch out!" the woman gasped, grabbing his robe and pulling him towards her. Their faces just inches from each other. Her eyes became wide as she looked at him, her cheeks flushed red with embarrassment. How unladylike! He would have fallen into her had he not caught his balance by slamming his hand onto the pole above her head. The other landing on her waist as he fell. Realizing how this may look, the advisor's cheeks also grew a bright scarlet. Hearing a thud behind him, Sir Roland spun around, the woman releasing her grip on him.

The thud had been the impact of a now broken spear. Its head was stuck in the wall behind where Sir Roland had just stood. How humiliating. He should have seen that coming. The woman had even warned him! The woman! She had saved him, just as she had saved Belinda before. Could he do nothing right? To need a woman to attend to everything in his life. His cheeks flushed to an even darker red.

"Princess!" screamed Carter. "I am so sorry! If you had been harmed, I don't know what I would have done!"

"No need to worry, dear prince. Sir Roland pushed me out of the way. All is well," she smiled at him, then turned to Roland. "I do apologize for tarnishing your robes. You took me by surprise."

"It was nothing," said Roland, brushing at the wrinkles her grip had left. She had covered for him! Letting him get the glory when she saved his life! There was something definitely going on with this woman. The advisor's irritation grew.

The prince became even more jealous. Roland had saved his fiancé from his own foolishness. How could she ever love a man as foolish as he? He gazed at Roland, whose cheeks were still bright red. Did Roland care for her as well? With a sigh, Carter took up the woman's hand. "I think that is enough excitement for one day. Shall we move on to something else?"

"Alright, what is it you would like to do?" the woman asked. What more was there? It was getting dark already.

"Well, I-" Carter stopped. "Mother?"

In the distance, three figures could be seen running towards them; Miriam, Frank the bodyguard, and Queen Zisca. The queen's face was filled with delight as she chased after the little girl. Miriam was dashing back and forth to catch fireflies. It was the happiest the prince had seen his mother in years. He let out a small laugh. Her efforts were hilarious. She flopped back and forth like a dying fish as she tried to run.

The woman giggled beside him as her sister pulled at the queen's hand to help her on their way. The queen's eyes opened wide, as did her mouth when she and the little girl toppled over one another in the grass. Both remained where they had landed, cackling uncontrollably as the prince's group approached.

"Mother," laughed the prince, "are you alright?"

"Oh, yes! Miriam and I were just playing with the horses when she said you had her sister watching you and your men practice with your swords," she huffed out of breath. "So, we came here to rescue her! Then, we saw the fireflies."

"I wish we had something to put them in," pouted Miriam as she looked at the glowing lights around her.

"We can go inside and get you something to keep them in for now," smiled the woman at her sister. "We had just finished with the melee training anyway."

"Have you?" The queen looked at her son. Carter lowered his head, remembering the accident. With a smile, she turned to the woman. "Perhaps you and I could get to know each other. It's a bit late today, but I would love to do something together tomorrow! It's not every day my son gets married, now is it?"

"Well?" The woman looked at Carter to find out what to do next. He smiled, giving a nod in approval. "I would love to!"

"Wonderful! Now, Miriam and I are going to get a jar for these fireflies, but tomorrow morning it'll just be the three of us!" The queen took the girl's hand as they joyfully ran back the way they came.

"I don't think I've ever seen my mother this happy," chuckled Carter. "She truly adores you!"

"Do you think so?" giggled the woman.

"Definitely," smiled Carter softly. "So, catching fireflies. Is that how we will end the day?"

She smiled back at him. "Would you really do that?"

"Of course! I used to smear these things on my face like warpaint!"

"Ew!" she laughed. "That's disgusting!"

"Hey! You just wait," the prince leaned over her playfully. "Once I catch one, maybe I'll give you some warpaint!"

The woman let out a playful scream as she ran towards the safety of the castle. The prince took off after her, leaving the advisor behind to watch as the two chased around like children. The woman shrieked again as the prince neared her, both laughing joyfully together. They seemed fitting for one another, both light-hearted souls.

Still, there was something off about this woman. She was a completely different person in the advisor's presence. Thus far, he had been unable to distinguish who she truly was. Was she as happy and charismatic as she was behaving now, or was that an act to cover the bitter coldness he had grown accustomed to when in her presence?

Carter seemed to enjoy her; that was all that mattered. It lifted the advisor's spirits to see his prince at ease. Whatever her past, Roland would accept her so long as she could make Prince Carter happy. That, she seemed to do effectively. The advisor would have never imagined that the future rulers would be chasing insects like commoners. Hopefully, the king wouldn't hear of this.

As laughter rang out, Roland felt cold. He shook his head at them and made his way to the castle. How long had it been since he played like that? In truth, he envied their happiness. For so long, he had been empty. He could only wonder what it might be like to experience such an innocent joy as that, whether it be real or not.

In the Dark of the Night

After changing into his black, velvet cloak, the advisor took off the ceremonial short sword he had been carrying, replacing it with a longsword. Having the weapon with him made him feel more at ease. With a blade such as this at his side, there was no way he would encounter trouble during his mission that night.

Just as the night before, he crept past servants and guards until he reached the stables. Once inside, he quietly made his way to Hymir. First, he put on the horse's bridle. As he put the saddle on the horse's back, he froze. Slowly turning to see if someone was there, he looked intently at his surroundings. He was alone.

Giving up on his search, Roland turned back to his work, tightening the straps on his saddle and mounting. As he started forward, he flicked his hood over his head to shelter his face from view. It was as if his horse knew they were trying to be stealthy. Hymir quietly entered into the night. However, they were not as stealthy as the shadow that followed in their wake. A figure who, like Roland, was dressed in all black.

The feeling of eyes on his back never left the advisor throughout his journey. When he had first surveyed the room, he had seen no one, but his instincts told him otherwise. Those instincts had never failed him before. He reached his hand into his travel pack, pretending to look for something as he quickly scanned the path behind him. He was right! A figure on horseback was following at a distance, keeping to the shadows.

Trusting his gut, Sir Roland rode through town, passing the tavern where Jasper was waiting for him. The hooded man knocked at the window to call to him as he passed by their meeting point. Roland nodded his head slightly to show he knew what he was doing. He then turned down the back alley where Jasper's men were waiting. They parted as he rode past them. Understanding what he was doing, they climbed the walls of nearby buildings and waited for the follower to come through the ambush point. To their dismay, no one came.

After a few minutes, Roland reemerged from his hiding place in the dark alley to make his way back to the pub. There didn't seem to be any more horses out front than before. Perhaps he had been wrong about his tail. Shrugging, he went inside. With a smile from the barkeeper's daughter, his drink was brought out to him.

"How are you this fine night?" she smiled at him. Roland twirled to see the room, no unfamiliar faces. All was well.

"I'm wonderful, thank you," he grinned back. Content with his privacy, he sat down in his usual spot near the back. Lillian pouted behind the bar because he hadn't spoken to her longer.

Leaning over to Jasper, the advisor whispered, "How was the trip?"

"We have everything we need for orientation. I was able to purchase all of the armor meant for the next band of the king's guards. I can use it to get my crew into the castle. We will be able to regulate into the late shift, no questions asked."

"How has their training been coming along?" asked Roland.

"It's alright," shrugged Jasper. "They'll fit in with the new scrubs easily enough."

"Good. You can follow me back in tonight. Do you have it with you?"

"Yes, it's just around the corner."

"Perfect, now all we-" Roland froze mid-sentence as he found a body in the room he hadn't seen before. How did he miss that? The advisor's eyes grew wide as he shifted in his chair. He leaned toward the table and whispered to Jasper. "We've been compromised."

"What?"

Roland turned to face him. "Over my right shoulder, you'll see someone sitting in the back corner. He looks too far away to hear what we are saying, but it's suspicious all the same. Tell me, does he look familiar?"

Jasper looked past his comrade into the dark corner across from them. He whispered. "I don't see anything."

"Neither did I. Look closer."

Reluctantly Jasper did so, trying not to seem like he was staring as he surveyed the distant corner. Again, he saw no one, but something did catch his eye. A chair was missing from the far table. All of the tables in the pub were surrounded by four chairs, but this table only had three. It was as he was recounting that he caught the sight of a body amidst the shadows. The only reason he saw it was because of a slight movement it had made due to his persistent glare.

"Woah," Jasper gasped as he faced Roland. "I didn't even see tha' guy! But I'll tell you one thin', he ain't from around here!"

Roland briefly found amusement in Jasper's speech. Normally the man tried to avoid such disoriented speech as not finishing his words, holding true to his noble birthright. Apparently, he had been hanging around Martin a little too long. Now that he was shaken, it seemed to be pouring out of him.

"That's what I suspected, but I can't see him very well. I believe that is the rider who was following me earlier. How did they know I would come here? It must've been when I signaled you as I passed by. Did you see him come in while I was away?"

"No," Jasper said in what he thought was a whisper, "but I had gone out back for a second to tell Martin what was happening. Maybe he slipped in then."

"One thing is for certain. We need to reconvene. Meet me at the camp. I'll be there as soon as I can. Take alternate routes, stick to the shadows."

"What about you? He followed you here, didn't he? What if he goes after you?"

"That's the idea."

"What are you, insane? I've never met an assassin before, but I'm pretty sure that man is one. You leave, you're dead!"

"Perhaps, but if we stay here, we're both dead. So, wouldn't you rather take the chance?"

After a short pause, Jasper answered. "I'll take Dreibund Alley!"

"There's a man." Roland hit Jasper's shoulder for encouragement as he walked out the front. Chugging the rest of his mead for courage, Jasper slipped out the back door. The shadow departed through a nearby window, slipping into the night.

Roland threw himself onto Hymir and set off at a quickened pace trying to lure the adversary towards him. At first, he traveled down only cobbled roads to leave behind a noisy trail. After a few minutes, he switched to dirt paths. All the while, the advisor was filled with immense fear because he did not hear the approach of another rider. If it was an assassin, as Jasper had proclaimed, he could be walking straight into a trap. With that in mind, he stopped for a while, hiding in the shadows of a small alley. Once he felt that it was safe, Roland set out for the renegade's camp, free of any followers.

Meanwhile, when Jasper reached his crew, he told them to stash the armor they had brought so that they could travel faster towards the camp. He felt it would be better for them to get it on the way back to the palace. The armor's weight would only slow them down, should they take it to camp and return with it later. Best to travel quickly now, so they had a higher chance of survival.

Martin took the conversation a little too lightly. "Wha' do you mean, survival? You think me n' the lads'll catch a cold?"

All of the men laughed loudly at the statement, bringing the fear inside of Jasper to its maximum. He hadn't felt this way since the last war! The thought of being prey to another man was a feeling he had wished never to have again. Then he realized, one man! That's all it was! He and his men, fourteen in all, could easily take down one man, could they not?

With a sigh of relief, he said to them. "You're right. I was overthinking thi-"

He was stopped by a shout from Martin. "Look out!"

Jasper was pulled towards his men as they all backed away from the darkness of the alleyway.

"C-C-Cap'n! Wha' is tha'?" Martin continued with an outstretched finger pointing into the night where a figure could be seen crouching in the dark.

Reeling around, sword in hand, Jasper stated calmly. "Why, it's a dead man."

His followers cackled in response, drawing their swords also; but the figure did not move. Instead, it crouched quietly in the darkness.

"Have you really followed me from the pub? That was a mistake if you ask me. I mean, think about it," Jasper paused to add a dramatic flair to the situation. "If you had taken me earlier, it would have been one highly skilled fighter against one regular man. Those are pretty simple odds."

Raising his arms to welcome his group to the fight, he continued. "But one skilled fighter against fourteen armed men, not so much."

Martin and the rest of the group charged forward, running past their leader to take down the intruder. Only then did the shadow draw out its weapon. Jasper's men swung their swords back and forth like fiends, trying to strike the opponent. Dodging their simpleminded jousts, the shadow defeated the first three of the men simultaneously.

After it had evaded their first attack, it targeted the backs of their necks and their temples. With short, harsh blows, the men were knocked out cold. In response, the rest of the crew staggered backward for a moment. Then again, they still had the upper hand in numbers, so they slowly re-approached their opponent.

As they came closer, the assailant ran a few paces to the left. Jumping onto a cart to gain inertia, their attacker traveled across the side of a building. Flicking back around, it kicked a man on the temple, causing him to drift into unconsciousness. During the fall, the shadow twisted off of its victim, driving the butt of its sword into the throat of another. The man fell to his knees, struggling to breathe. The shadow, however, landed softly on its feet. It then lifted its gaze cunningly upon the remaining men.

"So, you were able to take out five men," Jasper retaliated. "There are still nine more of us! Do you really think you can take us all?"

Not saying a word, the figure shimmied skillfully into the light. No real description could be given for the creature in front of them. It wore all black. Its face was covered in cloth, so not even its eyes could be seen. The size of the man could not be measured either, by how he had positioned himself. Jasper thought the sword looked somewhat familiar, but in this stressful moment the place he had seen it before did not come to him. It was much thinner than the hunting and double-edged swords in the area. From what Jasper could see, it was made of an elegant black metal, and the hilt was engraved with astounding craftsmanship of silver. The fuller of the sword was also laced in silver. It reflected the moonlight since it had not yet been touched by blood. Most swords' cross guards were thick and dull, but this weapon was beautifully shaped in a wispy design that completely covered the assassin's hands.

Looking down at his own sword, Jasper said. "Nice piece. I just hope I don't damage it as I send you to your death!"

"Yeah!" shouted a member of the crew. "What do you think you can do with just one sword anyhow? We got ten times that many over here!"

Jasper sighed out of embarrassment. Where did Martin get these men?

The assassin flipped his sword into a downward vertical position, the hilt at his eye line, the tip pointed to the ground. His hands clutched the hilt, right over left. Looking over the hilt at his prey, the attacker pulled the sword apart, the one becoming two. In one swift motion, the swords were at his sides. To further impress the onlookers, he proceeded to flip the two swords in his hands, bringing them back and forth in a motion that made it seem as if they were passing through one another.

"Now you've done it," exclaimed Jasper as the dark figure approached him. His men gathered around him, huddling together for their best chance of surviving the fight. The shadow said nothing, simply looking at them.

The quiet of the night sent chills up Jasper's spine. The longer the attacker waited, the more his fear grew. He could see Martin's limp frame in the shadows behind the monster, along with the other four who were defeated. Hopefully, they were alright! Where was Roland when you needed him?

Growing bored of his prey's predominant cowardice, the assailant flicked his swords together in a short pattern. A loud smack came from behind Jasper's crew. Another man down. "There are two of them!"

"No," Jasper gulped as he turned back to his original enemy. Beside him stood a partner, both with dual swords ready for battle. "There are four."

Jasper could see his whole crew shivering in fear. The four figures quietly moved towards them in response. All of their movements were light, as if they floated above the ground. Even in their approach, the shadows showed flawless technique. They shifted their swords around themselves in a delicate pattern. As they encircled the thieves, their blades weaved between them to create a fence-like structure. Jasper and his men became locked inside of it with no means of escape.

The ruffians were left dumbfounded. If these assassins wanted them dead, they would have been already. They had just assumed the attackers were there to kill them, but the shadows had hardly used their swords yet!

"What do you want?" Jasper asked, fear in his voice. The head figure pointed at him with a sword in response.

"Me? Y-you, want me? Why?" Jasper questioned. Again, the man just gave a simple gesture of the sword. Flicking it as if to tell Jasper to remove the hood he had been wearing the entire evening.

"We ain't givin' you nothin'!" bantered one of his miscreants. A nod came from the assassin Jasper had been addressing. Another behind the unfortunate man of Jasper's crew slashed his sword quickly forward. A blood-curdling cry went out as the crewmember fell to his knees, a massive wound running along the top of his right arm.

While Jasper and his men were distracted, three of the four assassins lunged towards them. The attackers took the group apart, one member at a time. Soon only Jasper was left standing, the rest now forced into kneeling positions if left conscious. With a swift kick to the chest, the head assailant thrust Jasper against a nearby building's wall. He gasped for breath as he dropped his sword.

"Ugh," he moaned. "Wha-what do you want?"

Still, no words came from the attacker. With one sword pressed against Jasper's throat, he sliced through the hood's material with the other. The cold metal brushing across Jasper's head made him hold his breath out of fear. When the deed was done, his hood fell to his shoulders in two pieces. His face became exposed to the light of the torch to his left. The figure leaned in closer to get a better look. Upon recognition, he pressed his sword against Jasper slightly harder, leaving a gash on his neck. He spoke a single word. The coldness of his voice made Jasper fear for his life. "Ladrón."

Afterward, the assassin dropped his catch, the other three following suit. Jasper clutched to his wound as he watched the mysterious soldiers walk over the bodies that littered the alley. He seemed so defeated there on his knees with his men sprawled unconscious before him, his foes walking away care-free without a scratch.

Hopping over the last of the bodies, the four men clicked their swords in unison. It was a different pattern than before; this one a bit more elegant than the call for aid had been. In response, four horses came from the shadows across the street. The dark figures clasped their swords together, sheathing them back onto their sides before mounting their steeds. Looking one last time at their disabled prey, they trotted away towards the palace gate.

Jasper sat in awe, replaying the fight over and over in his head as his crew slowly came back to life. All of that effort just to see his face? Once they had, the men just left. What had been the point? The attackers must have known Roland. Why else would they follow him? Maybe they were trying to find out who he was meeting? It couldn't be that big of a deal. Could it? They wouldn't even have recognized him because he was a nobody now. No land, no title, no value. He let out a sigh at the thought. Deep down, he had a dark feeling that he was actually recognized by the attacker that had ripped his hood. Whatever he had called Jasper was not something good.

"Everything alright, Cap'n?" asked Martin, who was now bandaging up the man who had been cut.

"Yeah," Jasper got up. "We should head to camp. I'm sure Roland is already there."

Once all of the men were back on their feet, they packed up their gear. They also took the guard uniforms, now that the assailants were gone. All moved slowly, still sore from the recent attack. In reality, it was astounding that they had even woken up due to how late it was!

When they finally reached the camp, Roland leapt up. "Where have you been? I've had to sit here!" He stopped after seeing the state they were in. "What happened to you?"

Jasper jumped down from his horse and replied angrily, "Oh, you know. While you bravely led the creep from the tavern away, we got attacked by him and three others in the alley!"

"What?" exclaimed Roland. Though now it did make sense that he couldn't hear an approach when he was riding away. He hadn't been followed after all.

"Yeah! So, the next time you get one of your brilliant ideas, how about we think it over a little better, huh?" Jasper brought his hand to his neck again, reliving his pain. "They attacked us a while after you'd gone, but it isn't like they were after anything. I don't know. The whole encounter was a bit odd."

"Wait, you're saying that four men took down all of you?" Roland ruffled his hair in disbelief. These were the men that he was supposed to rely on to gain freedom? "Did you at least land a hit?"

"Not a one."

"How reassuring," Roland traced his bottom lip in thought. "Walk me through what happened."

"Well, I met up with the crew and the man from the tavern was behind me. He took out five of us within a couple of minutes. Then three more showed up and wiped the rest of us out! In the end, the man from the pub cut off my hood and looked me dead in the eye. After that, they called for their horses and rode off."

"Where did they go?"

"To the palace," Jasper replied.

"Must be someone we know then. Did you get a good look?"

"Not really. They were dressed in all black and kept their faces covered, and they wore baggy clothes so we couldn't see their figure."

"How tall were they?"

"Don't know that, either. They were always slouching."

"Well, that's not helpful," Roland pouted. "Anything else you can think of?"

"They had strange swords, really thin. They were made out of this black metal. The best thing about them was that they came apart."

"The sword came apart?"

"Yeah, they just pulled at the hilt, and the swords split in two. True works of art if you ask me."

"Hmm," Roland thought. "Dual swords, dressed in all black. That sounds like Frank!"

"Who?"

"He's the woman's bodyguard. He was at the manor when they visited, remember? The freakishly large man who was always by the prince's fiancé and her little sister."

"Oh yeah, the big, burly guy. It couldn't have been him," responded Jasper. "They were dressed similarly, but I don't think any of the men from tonight were as bulky as he is. Plus, when the assassin saw my face, I was sure he recognized me!"

"But they are similar?"

"No doubt," Jasper nodded. "When one of the men in the alley talked, it was in a foreign language. Quite like those Ponierians."

"Then they must work for-" Roland stopped. "Get dressed. We're going to the palace!"

"What? Now?"

"Do it!"

Jasper and his men suited up in their new armor as quickly as possible. Clambering onto their horses, they sped back to the palace. When they arrived, Roland nodded to a servant who was making his way to them. The nighttime stable boy bowed and proceeded to relieve the men of their horses, promising to brush them properly before the morning. Jasper's men chuckled at the treatment they were getting. They felt like royalty!

Passing through the stables, Roland heard the sound of sighing. He and his crew followed the sound to four black steeds, all penned next to each other. They were trying to calm down from a recent ride. Instinctively, Roland entered the first stall and stroked the creature kindly.

"What are you doing?" Jasper called after him.

"This horse has been ridden recently." The advisor pulled at the horse's halter, bringing it up to Jasper. The steed jerked its head up and down, unused to Roland. The man patted it in response. "It's alright. We just want to have a look at you. So, is this the rider's horse?"

"I don't know," Jasper sighed. "It was a dark horse, but I couldn't be sure if it was this one."

"Go fetch me that stable boy," Roland demanded, stroking the steed while he examined it. It had definitely been ridden that night.

Upon the return of the stable boy, Roland came out of the stall saying, "Tell me, whose horse is this?"

"I-I'm afraid I don't know, sir," the boy lowered his head to look at the floor.

"Did you prepare it this evening?"

"No, sir, it was already tacked up when I came in for my shift tonight."

"Well, it doesn't seem so prepared now. Did you clean it when it got back in?"

"How did you know it was gone?" the servant shivered, realizing he had questioned the king's advisor. "I'm sorry, sir, it is none of my business. Yes, I de-tacked it this evening."

"It's quite alright," Roland continued. "I simply assumed because you had said it was tacked up earlier that it had been ridden. Now, another question. Could you show me what you took from this horse?"

"Of course, sir. Right this way." The boy led them to a nearby tack room, pointing towards a black leather saddle with a matching bridle. Both of which had etchings of silver in them in a beautiful design. The blanket underneath was made of black wool woven thickly together for the comfort of the horse. It was one of five, the other four quite similar. The only differences between them being the varying silver designs, each man with his own pattern.

"That has to be his horse, then. The sword was all black and silver too," whispered Jasper into Roland's ear.

Roland turned to the boy. "Are you sure you don't know whose horse that is out there?"

"No, sir, they were dressed in a strange uniform."

"Did they say anything to you?"

"No, I just put the tack away. I knew where it went because I had been admiring it earlier."

"Do you remember anyone taking that horse out before?"

"No, sir. Since the travelers have arrived, it and the others have always been in the stables."

"If anyone should come for it, let me know straight away."

"Yes, sir."

In fury over his inability to find the spy, Roland made way to the castle. His men followed behind him, dressed like a pack of guards.

As they entered the castle, a real guard stopped them, addressing Roland. "Sir Roland, may I ask whom you are bringing into the palace at such a late hour?"

"I do not surmise that my actions are any of your concern, but if you must know these men are patrolling knights who have been summoned to the castle," Roland lied masterfully. "By now you must have heard that the prince's fiancé was attacked during her journey to the palace a few days ago? I have brought these men in as extras for the castle's patrol to ensure nothing else bothers her during the days leading up to the wedding."

"Oh," the guard said in a disgruntled manner. "I'm sorry, sir, I did not know."

"As I said, it's none of your concern," Roland brushed past him, leading his men inside. Their eyes were wide with astonishment. They had never seen Roland in action, though they knew he was a high ranking official. Before tonight he had always given Jasper directions, who then led the crew to do the work. Seeing him now, they not only respected him but actually felt fear due to his power.

Inside the palace walls, they were met by another servant to whom Roland gave instructions so that Jasper's men would be provided rooms. The servant led the men away, except for Jasper and the one who had been injured that night. Roland escorted the injured man to the palace physician's quarters. Even though it was late, the physician went straight to work helping the poor fellow. He also put a wrap of gauze over Jasper's neck.

After Roland and Jasper returned to the hallway, Jasper spoke. "Thanks for the patch-up, but that isn't why you brought me along, is it?"

"No," Roland whispered. "There is someone we need to see, but you're going to need to keep your helmet on."

"Alright," Jasper placed the armored helmet over his face. "So, who are we going to go see?"

"We need to get to the woman before her spies can."

"You mean the assassins! What if they are already there?"

"Then we shut them up."

"No, you don't understand! These men are good. Maybe even as good as you."

Roland chuckled. "I doubt that!"

17

The Lovely Maiden

Upon reaching the woman's door, Roland knocked harshly and called out. "My Lady!"

The person who answered was not the woman, but her handmaiden, Adelina. "May I help you?"

Seeing the serving girl again, Jasper's breath left him. She was even more beautiful now that he was close to her. He blushed a little at the thought. Roland, however, did not seem so aroused.

"I need to speak to your mistress," the advisor said in irritation. The maid seemed to pick up on his agitation as she looked at something inside the room, turning back to him nervously.

"I'm afraid she sleeps now. Can I help you?"

"Could you wake her up?" Roland begged. "I need to speak to her."

"I'm sorry. I cannot do that. Maybe you could speak with her in the morning, my lord," Adelina bowed, addressing him by his old title of Morer. Apparently, her mistress had been talking about the advisor behind his back; a notion that tested Roland's patience as the girl continued in her plight to send him away. "It is quite late."

Roland raised a finger to retaliate, only to be stopped by Jasper as he came to the girl's aid. "She's right. Just talk to her in the morning."

The advisor spun around; finger still erect as he whispered to his friend harshly. "What are you doing?"

"Well, I just mean," Jasper smiled as he gazed over Roland's shoulder at the maid. "Weren't you being a bit harsh?"

"Ugh," Roland tugged him to the other side of the hall. "We need to talk to her before anyone else does. That means now!"

"If she's asleep, nobody is talking to her. Just catch her in the morning before the assassins can meet with her."

"Fine," Roland sighed. "Can you stand guard and bring her to me when she comes out? I'm just down the hall."

"You bet. I'll stay right here," said Jasper, hoping to bond with the maid.

"Thank you, my friend." Roland returned to the woman's door where Adelina was waiting. "I'm going to leave my guard, Jasper, here to watch over your door. When she awakes, could you please let your mistress know I was looking for her?"

"Of course, my lord." The maid bowed, backing into the room. Once she was safely inside, she closed the door on the two men in the hallway.

"I don't think she likes you," Jasper chuckled.

"She hates me as does her mistress." Roland rubbed his eyes. "Carter's fiancé has had this distrust for me since she arrived. I thought I had patched things up a bit at first, but now I'm not so sure. Think about it. She sent a spy to watch me! Why would she do that?"

"I have no idea. Did you do anything to make her suspicious?"

"Are you kidding?" Roland whispered in the darkness of the hallway. "I am always in character. There is nothing to suspect!"

"Unless she saw you doing something you shouldn't have been, or perhaps it was something you said?"

"I said nothing! I did nothing! Yet, she has hated me from the start! If I said anything, she took it out of context. You know how women are."

Jasper chuckled. "You never change, my friend. Perhaps one day, you will meet a woman you find worthwhile."

"If I do, I'll let you know. Well, I'm off. Remember, don't let her leave without speaking to me."

"Don't worry. She'll never get past me!"

After Roland went to his room, Jasper got ready for a long night of standing guard. Now that the hallway was silent, Adelina lifted her ear from the door. She nodded to Carter's fiancé, who had been standing just out of the advisor's view the entire time. The two women spoke in their tongue. *"He is gone, but he left a guard outside."*

"Oh, did he now? Who is it?" My Lady walked closer to her maid so they could whisper, unheard.

"He said it was his guard, Jasper."

"That's a nice name."

"Yes, it is," Adelina blushed. He had looked rather nice.

"Something tells me his name wasn't the best part."

"What?" the maiden blushed even more. *"No! I couldn't even see his face!"*

The prince's fiancé laughed. *"You don't need to see a face to think he was handsome!"*

"What does it matter to you whom I think is handsome?"

"Oh, come on," the woman begged, grabbing the maid's arms. *"I'm to be married to a man I barely know in a day! I need some actual romance in my life."*

"It's in two days," sneered the maid, *"and I thought you said you liked him."*

"I count tomorrow as my last day to be myself. The day after, I will belong to him, greeting his subjects and all. So, technically it is one day," the woman sighed. *"And I do like him, but it is almost impossible for me to love the man. Love takes time; it takes growth. In my case, I cannot hope to achieve such a thing as love, simply prosperity, and the way to do that is through Prince Carter."*

The maiden hung her head as she was overcome by the loneliness oozing from her mistress. Adelina wanted to say something to cheer her up, but she could find no words. She may have been a maid, but it seemed her mistress was no more than a slave.

"But anyway, now you see my interest in your feelings for the gentleman outside. I will find happiness in your happiness." She paused for a moment. *"Adelina, I am truly grateful you chose to accompany me on this journey."*

"It was nothing."

"It is to me," the woman smiled. *"Even after my sister and Frank have returned home, I will still have my best friend. We have been together from the beginning, you and I. I cannot thank you enough for staying by my side, even when it will cost you your home and your life."*

"What life would I have had without you? I probably would have had to return to my family's mill. I would most likely end up marrying Tristan."

"Not the cobbler's boy!"

"Now you see why I left," the maiden giggled.

"No judgment," the woman laughed with her. *"Now, unless you wish to end up with this country's Tristan, I suggest you get to know that guard out there."*

"Alright," said the maiden, still giggling about her joke. *"How do you suppose I do that?"*

"Well, the poor dear has to stand out there all night," the woman responded with a fake sentiment in her voice. *"I'm sure he is hungry. I say you should take him something to eat."*

"I'm not going to take him something to eat. That's cliché."

"Perhaps it is, but he will accept it nonetheless. All men appreciate food, especially tired ones. I can hear him yawning from here."

"I'm not doing it."

Using the same fake sentiment, the woman turned to her maid. *"You poor dear. You must be so tired, looking after me all night. If only I would retire and let you go to sleep. It's too bad I won't sleep until that guard is fed!"*

"You truly are evil. You know that?"

"One of my many gifts," the woman skipped gleefully to a nearby table of treats. She filled a plate with a bit of pork, some small tomatoes, grapes, and an apple tartlet. *"Here you are, give him that. I'm sure he'll appreciate it."*

"I am so glad I was able to accompany you on this journey," the maiden sneered as she took the plate. The woman giggled in response as she

moved away from the door so the guard would not see her awake. She hid behind a curtain for good measure. She knew no matter the hour, as soon as she was found awake, the advisor would wish to speak with her. That man was the last person she wanted to see.

Adelina went to the door, tugging it open by the handle. Her eyes grew wide as she quickly backed away. Jasper had fallen asleep leaning against the door. When she had opened it, he came crashing inside. "Oof!"

"I am so sorry," the maiden apologized as she helped him. It was a miracle no one woke up due to the noise.

Jasper was not used to the weight of his armor, making him look like a bug stuck on its back as he wiggled to and fro. The woman held at her mouth as she tried to stay silent behind the curtain, her shoulders going up and down nonstop with laughter.

"It's alright. Is the lady awake?" Jasper's voice was soft with humiliation. His tenderness caught the attention of the maid.

"What?" she blushed, holding out the plate nervously. "Oh, no. She sleeps now. I just thought you might be hungry."

His eyes grew wide at the food. It looked like a delicacy compared to what he had become accustomed to. Remembering his role, he turned the food away. "That is alright. Thank you, but I must keep guard."

His stomach growled in retaliation, causing the maid to smile. "Your duty is to make sure that My Lady does not leave without seeing Lord Roland, right?"

"Yes," replied Jasper. "That's right."

"You could wait for her here just as well as out there. This way, you can eat." Adelina pointed to the table of food.

After another growl from his stomach, Jasper relinquished. "Maybe just some pork."

When he sat down to eat, the woman waved good night to Adelina. Jasper was too preoccupied with his meal to notice the woman sneaking into her room. Adelina turned her attention back to the guard as she asked him. "Can I get you a drink? Wine, or mead?"

"I shouldn't drink while on duty."

"I also have water?"

With a slight pause, he nodded. "Mead will be fine."

As she poured his drink, Jasper took off his helmet to eat. His face was just as handsome as the rest of him. Even in the darkness of the dimly lit room, his eyes glowed a brilliant green. Adelina had always dreamed of meeting a man with eyes like his. Most of the men of her country carried the same color brown.

To the maid's disappointment, Jasper ate and drank quickly. He didn't want the woman to come out and recognize him. Even so, he savored every bit of food that entered his mouth. What quality! The mead was by far the best he had ever tasted. Placing the helmet back on his head, he stood to leave.

"Thank you for the meal, my lady," he said, not knowing what to call her.

The maiden looked at the floor in sadness. "I am not My Lady, just Adelina."

"Adelina," Jasper thought out loud. "What a pretty name."

"Thank you," she smiled widely.

"Welcome," he said, cheeks bright red behind his helmet. "Uh, goodnight!"

Jasper charged out of the door, taking to the safety of the empty hallway. That was smooth, he thought to himself. He couldn't have just said something flirtatious like a sane person? Of course not! He had to run out of the room, and so awkwardly too! He would never get to speak to her again!

Inside, the maid cleaned up the dishes and lay down to sleep. She would kill her mistress for this! What utter humiliation! Through the night, her worries drifted away into the dark folds of rest.

"Wake up, wake up," the woman shook her into consciousness.

"What?"

"How did it go?"

"Humiliating, I think I made the poor man nervous. He had no interest in me whatsoever," she let out a sigh. *"Don't you ever make me do that again, you hear!"*

"Was it really that bad?"

"Yes!"

"Was he handsome, at least?"

"Oh, yes!"

"Description, please!"

The maid smiled as she remembered his face. *"He has brown hair, a gorgeous little beard, and the nicest green eyes I've ever seen!"*

"Aren't they the only green eyes you've ever seen?" her mistress laughed.

"Yes, but green eyes are now my favorite!"

"Well, that's good. I've seen a few people around here with them. If you and the guard don't end well, you've got some options!"

"I suppose you're right. What if he will never look at me again? I acted like a love-struck child last night."

"No need for judgment yet. We'll see if he comes to his senses," the woman sighed. *"For now, we need a way for me to get past him. It's my last day of freedom. I will not have it ruined by that advisor!"*

Quite an Interesting Talk

Roland woke early, going to Jasper. "Has she come out yet?"

"No, she must still be sleeping."

"Ugh," Roland growled. "Why can't she just come out of there? It isn't that hard of a request!"

"Give her some time, my friend. The sun isn't even up yet."

"We don't have time! I'm going to tell Carter. You just wait here, and don't let her leave!"

"Will do."

When Roland reached Carter's room, he was met by snoring once again. These two are perfect for each other; he thought in his head, sleeping the day away.

"GOOD MORNING, PRINCE," he shouted.

"Ahh, whaa!" Carter flopped around in his sheets in terror, landing on the floor in a bundle of blankets. Wriggling himself free, the prince faced his foe head-on. "You scared me half to death!"

"I'm sorry, sire," Roland grinned mischievously.

"Sure, you are." Carter rubbed his eyes. "This better be important."

"I think it is. It concerns the woman."

"What of her?"

"You should know, Jasper and his crew arrived last night. They had the gear."

"Did they happen to have anything extra with them?"

"I'm sorry. They made no mention of it."

The prince held his head. "Oh, I hope they got it! Then again, maybe Ore is bringing it here in person."

"Carter," Roland interrupted his meltdown. "My Lady sent spies to follow me last night. They attacked Jasper after we met. They saw his face."

"Wait," he paused in shock. "So, that means!"

"That means if she hears about it, she will know I am working with the man who robbed her. She might even do something about it."

"You could get killed!"

"It's worse, I'm afraid," Roland sighed. "This could destroy the entire plan."

"What do we do?"

"Honestly," he thought for a moment. "I have no idea."

"I don't understand why she would have anyone follow you." Carter pushed him jokingly, trying to raise his spirits. "You're not suspicious at all! You know, now I believe you. She hates you."

"Hatred I can deal with, but this is serious."

"Well, just talk to her about it. You'll be fine. She is a caring woman. I'm sure she won't make any rash decisions."

"You think so highly of her," Roland chided. "What would I tell her anyway? Yeah, you got me. I had my right-hand man rob you, but it didn't work anyway. So, call it even?"

"Ha! No, not that, but I know you can get through to her. You have a way with words. If that doesn't work, we could always just do it the easy way."

"Don't even say it!"

"We could let her in on it."

"That's exactly what I told you not to say! This woman can't be involved. What if she disagrees? What if she tells the king? It would be the death of us."

"You don't know that. I think if she knew the whole story, she would be on our side. She is such a wonderful woman," Prince Carter smiled to himself.

"Let's say she does agree with us, what then? We are in the middle of the uprising and someone puts a dagger to her throat. What will you do? It would be over. I'm telling you, for now, she is nothing but a loose end. It's best to keep her in the dark and then explain things to her afterward."

"Alright, I...I trust your judgment." Carter gulped at the thought of his fiancé with a dagger to her throat. Such an atrocity could never be allowed to happen.

"Good. Now, I'm going to do my best to solve this little problem. Then, I'll train up our recruits throughout the day. So, you'll have lots of time to be with your fiancé. Just try to have fun."

"Fun." Carter thought of what he was hiding, what he was planning to do. "Oh yeah, loads of fun."

Meanwhile, Jasper stood ever patiently, watching over the woman's door as his stomach began to yearn for more food. The feast he had been given during the night seemed to have lost its fill. He looked out the corner of his eye at the dish of cakes a servant had placed on a table around the corner. How badly he wanted one, but he knew if he were caught, the king would have his head. No guards or servants were allowed to eat the food of his tables, lest they face death. With a sigh he turned away, looking again at the wall in front of him. As he tried to forget his hunger, he counted the stones for the twentieth time. One, two...*GROWL*

He couldn't take it anymore! Giving in to his hunger, Jasper spun on his heel and hurried to the cake platter, shoving one into his mouth. Oh, the pleasure! Was he not in heaven? Unable to control himself, he picked up yet another and lifted it to his lips. It was then, the woman's door opened. She looked up and down the hall but saw no one as Jasper was hidden behind a wall of stone. Feeling uncertain, the woman looked cautiously around the corner of the hall to find Jasper. He was still gorging on the forbidden food of the platter.

"Mmm," hummed Jasper with another bite. The woman brought her hand to her mouth to hold in her laughter at his delighted eating. Glancing back in at Adelina, a scheme developed in her mind. With precision in her movements, she swung around the corner. She ran straight into Jasper, who was preoccupied with the cake in his hands.

"Oof," the woman exclaimed upon impact, the hit smashing Jasper's cake across his armor's breastplate. As he staggered back, the woman took his hand to help balance him, which was helpful because he was still not used to his armor.

"Oh! I am so sorry," she said, still holding to his hand. "That was entirely my fault! I didn't see you there!"

Happiness shone in her eyes as the woman spoke. Jasper stared at her in shock. Did she recognize him? Being this close to her again, he remembered her authority. He was unworthy to look at her, let alone have her hold his hand.

The woman's gaze went from his eyes to his chest as her smile grew even larger behind the veil. He followed their path with his own to find the massacre of his stolen breakfast on his chest. His heart sunk. It was obvious what he had been doing. Even if the woman spared him, any guards he passed would lock him up instantly.

"Well, that's no good," the woman giggled.

I'm doomed! Jasper thought to himself.

"Look at the mess I've made! I can't have you walking around like that, now, can I?" The prince's fiancé pulled Jasper by the hand she had been holding back towards her door. "Adelina dear, look what I've done! Can you help this poor gentleman clean up his armor?"

"Uh," began the maid.

"Thank you! I hate doing this, I really do, but I have to get going, you see?"

A glint of orneriness flashed in the woman's eyes as she left Jasper before Adelina and made her way from them. What a success! The woman thought to herself. Not only did I get rid of that shadow and his master, but I opened up an opportunity with that man for Adelina! She will be thanking me every day until the grave!

"If you would take off your armor," Adelina said quietly from inside the suite, "I will polish it for you."

Jasper's mind was reeling. Had that just happened? He was sure he would die, but here he was safe and sound. Better still, the woman of his dreams stood right in front of him.

"S-sir?" Adelina questioned, nervously trying to get his attention. I'm going to kill that traitor the next time I see her, the maiden thought to herself.

"Huh? Oh, r-right, sorry," Jasper stuttered as he began unclasping his armor. Why had that woman just let him go? Maybe she didn't know it was a crime to eat the cakes? Wait! The woman! She had to be long gone by now. Roland would kill him when he found out!

"My lady," Jasper coughed. "Do you happen to know where your mistress is going? Sir Roland was hoping to speak with her."

"Ah," she replied. "Yes, you will be happy to know; I told her that Lord Roland wanted to talk with her."

"Really?" Jasper asked. She was headed in the opposite direction of Roland's room when she ran into him. "So, is she going to speak with him this morning then?"

"I think so," Adelina said as she started to clean the armor. Jasper responded with a sigh of relief.

"She said," the maid paused, trying to pronounce it all correctly. When she spoke again, her dialect was in Remettian, a perfect recreation of her mistress' speech. "It seems I'll be having quite an interesting talk this morning. Then she left."

"Oh." Jasper's relief was cut short. She may have been talking about speaking with her spies. If she knew Roland was desperate to speak with her, it would solidify her suspicion about him. Roland had to talk to her before she talked with her spies! There was no time! "I am so sorry, my lady, would it be alright if I returned here for my armor later? You don't need to clean it; I will do that. I just have to go!"

"Of course." She bowed. "I am sure you are quite busy."

"Thank you!" He bolted out the door to chase the woman, only to be met by his worst fear. "R-Roland!"

"So, you kept her in her room. Great!" Roland walked past him gleefully. "My Lady?"

Jasper's eyes grew wide in horror, his heart racing as he could do nothing but watch his friend's dreams shatter.

"Lord Roland," shrieked Adelina as she bowed slightly to him. "How may I help you?"

"Where is your mistress?" Roland asked in confusion, as she was nowhere to be seen. His eyes came to rest on Jasper's armor laying on the table. He hadn't been wearing his helmet either. Something wasn't right.

"I am sorry, my lord! My mistress left a few minutes ago."

"What!" Roland's anger shook the room. The girl cringed before him. Jasper himself took a step back in an attempt to evade the wrath of his comrade, who charged past him into the hallway. "Do you know which way she went?"

"N-no, I am sorry, sir. I thought she was going to meet you!"

"Meet with me?" Roland asked. His voice was quiet, but he was still huffing from his rage.

"Sí! Yes! She said she would have an interesting talk this morning," the girl said, quivering in fear.

"Alright, thank you." This time, the advisor's voice had returned to its usual icy calm. To some degree, it was even more frightening than a shout. He spun on his heel and left the two behind him. The advisor searched quietly for the woman, like a bloodhound sniffing out its prey.

After a silent I'm so sorry to Adelina, Jasper followed his comrade in search of the woman. He gulped in fear once he got within swinging distance of Roland.

"I thought I told you to watch the door," Roland asked with darkness seated in his words.

"I know. I'm sorry! She caught me off guard while I was eating a cake, and I smeared it on my armor and-"

"And she had you go into her quarters, where the maid cleaned it for you. While you were distracted, she got away."

"Clever one, isn't she?" Jasper forced a half-choked chuckle. Roland stopped walking, making Jasper bring his hands up to guard himself against a blow.

"She didn't see your face, did she?" Roland asked, his voice still in a deadly tone.

"What?" cringed Jasper, who was still hiding behind his arms.

"The woman, she didn't recognize you, did she?" Roland repeated, turning to face his friend.

"No, I didn't take the helmet off until after she left."

"That's a relief, but the problem remains. If she isn't meeting me, she will meet with those spies of hers. Once she does that, we're done for!"

"I know, I'm sorry," whimpered Jasper.

"Hey! Hey guys," rang out Carter's voice as he scampered down the hallway to them. "Thank goodness I found you! I've been looking everywhere. Sheesh! You must have been walking really fast! I could have sworn I heard you by My Lady's room just a moment ago!"

Jasper slowly lowered his arms back down to his sides. It seemed he would live another day. How he had missed that happy little prince!

"Prince Carter! It's so good to see you," Jasper grinned at the man who had saved him from persecution.

"Same here! Did you talk to My Lady?" Carter snapped his fingers as he jumped to a different thought, "Oh, oh! I've got something important I need from you! Did the blacksmith give you anything for me? It should be quite small."

"He gave me some kind of box, but he told me not to open it. I don't know what it is."

"That's it! That's it!" Carter clutched Jasper's shoulders as he started jumping up and down in excitement. "Where is it? Do you have it on you?"

"No, sorry."

"Take me to where it is! I need that, please!"

Roland shook his head as he walked away from the two. They may have forgotten, but he was still on a mission. He needed to find this woman quickly. The further he walked, the more nervous he became. My Lady may already be meeting with her sources. Sir Roland clenched his jaw in determination. He had to find her before that happened!

As he was lost in thought, a pair of arms reached out and dragged the advisor into a dimly lit storage closet. On instinct, he drew a dagger from his side, bringing it to his attacker's belly. He barely stopped what he was doing in time. In the last instant, he recognized who it was that had dragged him in there, who was now holding him against a wall.

"My Lady," he gasped as he sheathed the weapon that he had almost killed her with.

"I know why you wanted to speak with me so urgently," her voice was calm and dark. Her fury laced every word she spoke to him. "Don't try to pretend. You've been letting me know every second since I arrived. All your questions, the little hints. I understood all of it!"

"My Lady, I really needed to speak with you," Roland tried to respond to her accusations. It seemed she had already met with the spies.

"Why? Have you not taken enough from me? That little robbery in the woods. That was you, wasn't it?" She pushed him harder into the wall, an action he could have easily freed himself from. The advisor simply thought it was better to let her feel she was in control.

Roland looked into her fierce eyes as he replied. "Ah."

"I know that you've been leaving the palace every night since I arrived to meet with your little crooks. I know you're up to something. At first, I thought you might have needed the money to fund the repressed. Now, I'm not so sure! Perhaps you've returned to your old ways, Lord Roland of Morer!" Still pressing him to the wall, she sneered. "So, tell me. What is it you're after?"

"My Lady, I-" Roland paused. She could not know the truth! "I deeply regret what I've done to you, but you must understand, I do only as I am told."

"What do you mean?"

"What I mean is," Roland lied cleverly. "When the prince returned from the middle kingdom betrothed to a random noblewoman, such as yourself, of whom he would give no details, the king began to worry."

Her grip released as she bought the lie. Roland felt a sense of relief. If there was one thing you could count on in a woman, it was her sense of unworthiness.

Roland took the initiative. "King Cadoc had always hoped Carter would be betrothed to Princess Cida of Poniere as a way to unite the kingdoms. I'm sure you know of the tale. The king raised his son with that knowledge in his head. So, when the news of this engagement reached him, he became unhappy."

She thought for a moment. "But, what of your crooks?"

"Them? They are mine, of course. I will not deny it. You remember the group of collectors you met in Morer? Well, the men you met in the woods are my version of that. Only instead of collecting payments, they collect information for me."

"Why would the king ask you to steal from me, no matter my title?"

"It was meant to be a jostle in your journey. Since Carter made this deal with your father, the king could not stop it. Especially since we don't know who either you or your father are. The way we planned it, you would either give up on the engagement and return home, or you would arrive and Carter would reject you due to your weakened state. However, that's not how it ended. Thankfully, when you got here, the king saw your potential. That is when he asked me to start showing interest in your hardships."

"As another test?"

"Yes," Roland completed the lie happily. "In fact, I believe he will also be talking with you personally soon as a final test, but you must promise me you will not tell him that I have informed you of this endeavor. He will have my head if he knows I have told you his judgment of you."

"Don't worry," the woman sighed. "He has a right to his thoughts. I won't tell Carter either. The prince chose me, so it shouldn't matter who here rejects me. Perhaps one day, I will make it up to them."

Roland couldn't believe what he was hearing. What a gullible girl.

"I'm sorry I was harsh before," she said. "I should have known it was for the king. I suppose I just got riled due to what I have heard of you. The Evil Lord of Terror! Ahhh!" The woman swung her arms about as she laughed. "Not so terrible after all, huh?"

With that, she left the room. Roland was stuck on the nickname she had called him. Evil Lord of Terror? Is that really what they called him? She was so calm about it, as if it were a normal thing to call someone! The whole middle kingdom must call him that! What of the northerners, did they hate him too?

Let Training Commence

His mind wrought with despair; Roland wandered hopelessly to the practice fields. Oh, look at the Evil Lord of Terror! First thing in the morning, guess what he's going to do? Train! Who knows, maybe he'll spice it up today, switch from regular dummies to human targets. Nothing's good enough for him unless he gets to spill blood!

"How irritating!" Roland muttered to himself as he lobbed off the head of a dummy with his sword. Was this monster really who he was? He had told himself it was just an act, but you can't act all the time. Not this long.

"Woah! Would ya look at tha' boys! Tha's our teacher for the day. One swing and the head goes flyin'. You sure are the Beast of Morer!" laughed Martin as he approached with the group of ruffians.

"Beast of Morer," Roland mumbled to himself. Is that all he was? A terrifying beast that parents told their children about at night? That's not what he wished to be.

He thought back to his childhood. When he and Prince Carter played side by side people thought they were mirrors of one another. Both at ease, pure in all that they did. How had Carter remained so pure? The man was a light to all, without defect. But here was his reflection: damaged, crushed, and crumbled. He was no more than a dark shadow living behind the light of the man who was his best friend.

The only hope Roland had to cling to was the thought of shedding this dark cover once the king had been overcome. On that day, he would no longer be seen as evil! He would walk in the light by the side of the true king. He and Carter would rise together, making this kingdom into the land they had both dreamed of their entire lives.

"Alright," Roland called to the men as he came out of his thoughts. "All you worthless bundles of steel! Unless you want to end up like that doll, pay attention to everything I say to you. We will start with some drills. Then, when you're ready, we'll move on to something a bit more fun."

"Drills? Oh, come on! It's not like we was just given our first sword this morning! Let's start the real stuff!" one of the men shouted out in retaliation.

"So, you think you're ready?"

"Yeah!" he shouted again.

Martin hit the blabbering suit of armor over his head. "Shut your flappin' lips, Dan! You got no idea what you're gettin' us into!"

"Look," Roland sighed. "My time is quite valuable. Instead of wasting it by bickering with one another, why not choose what you would like to do. It would give you a strategical advantage to learn new fighting techniques from the drills before the next phase of training, but if you would like to start 'the real stuff' as Dan so eloquently put it, I will instead suggest changes to your current fighting styles as we move forward. I'll give you a moment to decide."

There was a long pause as the men tried to understand what the advisor had just told them. After a brief whispered discussion between them all, the men turned back to face Roland. Martin scratched his head nervously; it would seem he lost the discussion.

"Have you decided?" the advisor asked.

"Yeah," exclaimed an excited Dan. "We wanna do the real stuff!"

"Very well," Roland said as he walked into the center of the training field, Jasper's men following him. When he turned back to them, he spoke. "Everyone pair up with another member of your group."

The men did so, choosing the people they were closest to and happily making six groups of two.

"Now, take some of the training swords and prepare," Sir Roland said with boredom in his voice. Whoops of excitement came from the men in response.

"We're gonna knock those other teams senseless!" chuckled Dan to his partner, who laughed in response. The pair almost ran into Roland, who had appeared behind them as they cackled endlessly together.

"That would be difficult, seeing as the first task is simply to overcome the man you have been paired with," the advisor said coldly with a devious smile. "Best of luck."

"Wait. What?" Dan stood flabbergasted. "No way!"

"All teams, you and your partners are now enemies. When I give the word, you are to attack. Do not cease until one of you surrenders to the other. As you fight, I will examine your stance, strategic patterns, and other aspects of your technique that may make you vulnerable. I will address you on anything that may make you weaker and provide tips on strengthening your position during the fight. I'll advise you to learn as much as you can; not only of yourself, but also of your comrades. Their weaknesses could either lead to your downfall or your ascension."

The men fell into quiet distress. Had he not earlier said this would be fun? What could be fun about this? Taking note of their silence, Roland continued. "We will go through this portion of training one team at a time. Since he was so eager, Dan's team will go first. The rest of you decide the order in which you would like to proceed."

With that, everyone but Roland, Dan, and his teammate, Mathias, left the fighting grounds. The two friends faced each other as Roland coldly said, "Begin."

Dan struck first, swinging his sword harshly at Mathias' right side. He blocked it easily, but the shock from the attack was written across his face. The other men cheered from behind the fence; however, Roland did not seem impressed. "You're losing too much force with a blow like that. It's all going into extension. This is a close-range attack. Shorten your movements or you'll be left wide open."

"I know what I'm doing," growled Dan with anger as he used the move again. This time Mathias was prepared. He ducked down to dodge the swing and tackled Dan around his unguarded stomach.

The two stood up again to continue their fight, Dan rubbing his midriff in pain.

"Told you," Roland sighed, unamused.

"Yeah, well, he wouldn't have thought of it if you hadn't said anything," Dan shouted as he pointed his wooden weapon at Mathias.

"Stop whining and pay attention," the advisor stated uncaringly.

"I a-" Mathias' sword caught Dan in his side, knocking the air from his lungs. Another band of cheers rang out from the sidelines.

"That was good, but not quite as strong as it could be. You're only using the strength of your arms. If you position your body right, you'll get over tenfold more power in your strike." Roland began his next lesson, positioning Mathias' arms and legs as Dan crawled back up onto his feet. Grimacing in pain as he lifted the wooden sword again, Dan turned with conviction to defeat his old partner.

"Right about there," the advisor said from behind his new student as he backed out of the way. Mathias struck from the angle in which Roland had placed him, knocking a now dazed Dan to the ground once more. The force of the hit was so strong that the sound of it echoed around the training ground. A large dent was left in Dan's armor that ran across his chest. Had it been a real blade, he would have been sawn in two.

There were no cheers from the onlookers this time. They all stared in disbelief at the sight before them. Even Mathias himself stood with wide eyes as he looked at the hilt in his hands, the rest of the sword having been splintered upon impact. How had so much power been achieved so easily?

Roland being the only one unaffected, said softly. "It would seem we have our first victor."

The advisor patted Mathias' shoulder as he walked past him to Dan. He looked down at the man with disappointment. "And our first flop."

He lifted his eyes to the onlookers whose mouths were still hanging open in disbelief. "So, have you decided who's next?"

The vicious training cycle lasted half of the day, the last set of fighters being Martin and his partner Gad. The two squared up as Roland nodded. "Begin."

Gad lunged at Martin, who knocked the blow aside, stepping around his assailant easily. Roland shot him a glance but instead addressed Gad. "Your footing caused you to be off balance, taking away from your strike. This, in turn, made you vulnerable to Martin's counter-attack. Be more vigilant of your surroundings; otherwise, you'll die before you can land a blow."

"Y-yes, sir."

Gad ran at Martin again, looking back and forth from his feet to his sword. Martin blocked his strike, then went for one of his own. His movements were slow, allowing Gad the opportunity to take his sword from him. After disarming him, the young man looked at his partner with excitement in his eyes.

"I surrender," stated Martin with his hands in the air.

Roland scowled from behind them. "Martin, can I see you for a minute?"

"You bet!"

The two walked away from the others as Roland leaned in and asked. "What was that about? You threw that fight."

"I don't know wha' you mean," Martin said innocently.

"You lost on purpose. Why? Do you think it's a good thing to give that boy a false sense of self?"

"I just wanted him to have good teammates, is all, and look how proud he is, beatin' his ol' caretaker."

"You're almost the same age as him. Why would you show him such favoritism?" sighed Roland as he tried to get his point across.

"I've looked after him since his dad died in the war. You could say the lad is like my little brother."

"Do you think what you did was a good idea? If you really care, show that boy his inferiorities. Otherwise, someone with a real sword might do it for you." Roland turned back to the group. "Alright, take your places."

Each of them went to their new group. One joined the victors, and one went to the flops.

"Now, all victors," Roland stopped mid-sentence as he saw Jasper and Carter approaching the grounds. Jasper seemed to have gotten his armor back from My Lady's maiden, as he wore it proudly. "Where have you two been?"

"Oh! We went and got My Lady's present! I almost couldn't wait. I almost peeked myself, didn't I?"

"Yes, sire," chuckled Jasper.

"I wanted to give it to her now, but mother hasn't yielded her yet today. Going through all of the queenly duties, tea parties, all that girl stuff. I mean, I saw her, but I didn't even get to talk to her yet today. She was beautiful, though," Carter hummed to himself.

"Well, I got to talk to her," Roland grumbled, crossing his arms at the thought of her.

"Oh? How did it go?"

"All has been taken care of."

Martin whispered to Dan in the flop group. "Look at his face! I bet tha' woman's the one who got 'im huffin' this mornin'!"

Laughter rang out amongst the thieves, which Carter joined in on even though he didn't hear the joke. All happiness evaporated as the cool stare of the advisor set out against the group.

"We were just about to move on to the next set of training. Would you two care to join in?" Roland asked Carter and Jasper.

"I'd love to!" shouted Carter. "What are we doing?"

"We just got finished with one-on-one battles. Next is a game between the victors and flops. Which group would you prefer to be in?"

"I'll go with the flops," Carter cheered in excitement.

"Oh, sire. I can go with the flops if you'd like," Jasper chimed in, showing his reverence to his prince. He had hoped Carter would go with those of higher standard.

"Are you kidding?" laughed the prince as he skipped past Roland. "Flops for life!"

"They are on the right, sire," Roland smirked, having been infected by the happiness of the prince.

"Alright!" Carter laughed as he picked up a wooden sword. "What are your names, teammates? I'm Carter, by the way. I haven't seen you before! Other than you, Marty! How have you been? It's been ages!"

"I've been well, sire. Thank you!" Martin said, making his speech as clear as possible since he was addressing royalty.

Roland shook his head as he began his next game. "Alright, there are seven people in each group. Within each of your groups, make two teams. One with three members, and one with four."

Grudgingly, the trainees did as they were instructed. The victors went to where they were assigned by Jasper, who had automatically been given the place of authority. He sent four of his best men away, keeping only two to fight by his side. He would later realize how much growth he had missed by not watching over the morning's training.

In the group of flops, things were not decided so easily. At first, all the men wanted Carter to choose. He shrugged off the offer, saying he didn't know enough about them to decide. Together the men created two teams which they thought would work best together. Carter simply went where he was told, the ruffians shaking in fear to tell him.

"Have we made our teams?" Roland asked.

"Yes, sir," chimed the groups.

"The two groups of three, form one big group. The groups of four, do the same."

"But we would be outnumbered," stated one of the men from the flop's group of three.

"Doesn't matter," shrugged Roland. "Have you no faith in your team?"

"He's right. We have to depend on each other, whether we are six or eight," said Jasper to his group of six. The men found reassurance in him. The group of eight may have Prince Carter, but theirs had their leader, Jasper.

"Each team be sure to choose a leader," Roland instructed.

The group of six chose Jasper. The group of eight was taken over by one of the victors, whose name was Wilton. Being a victor, he established himself above the flops.

"Now, face each other as teams and work together against your enemy," Roland said as he leaned into the railing at the outskirts of the ring, watching the progress of the fight.

Some of the men made the mistake of hesitating, leading to the almost instant annihilation of half of Jasper's team. Carter laughed hysterically as he bashed his foes. The rest of Jasper's group came together for a defensive action as the remainder of Carter's team ran at them.

"All flops," Roland yelled out, "overthrow your leaders and the rest of the victors!"

"That's what I'm talking about!" Carter screamed in excitement as he turned from Jasper's team to his own leader, Wilton. Jasper only had one flop left on his team, which he knocked down as soon as betrayal flashed in the man's eyes. He and his men then waited to see the outcome of the other team's fight.

Wilton and the rest of the victors grouped together to face their flop teammates. Carter turned to Martin gleefully as he said. "Four of them, four of us. Each man gets his own. I'll take the guy all the way to the left. After that, it's up to you and your crew."

"Wha'?" Martin asked to thin air as he heard a loud crack from the opposing team. He turned his head to see one of Wilton's men unconscious on the ground, the happy prince skipping past them to sit with his advisor.

"Alrigh', I s'pose it's up to me now. Lads! Take the stragglers. I'll take down Wilton."

"I could take Wilton," cried out Dan.

"No, let Martin have 'im. You take the guy on the right, I'll take the one on the left," said Benjamin, the final flop of the crew.

"Go!" Martin and his team launched simultaneously at their enemy. Taking them out in one smooth streak.

"Well done! So, the remaining teams are that of Jasper and Martin. We can continue as groups, or you can leave it up to the two team leaders alone. Which will you choose?" Roland asked them.

"What about our group?" questioned Gad from beside Jasper. "We have one less person."

"You may pick another person from the arena to add to your team if you choose to do the group activity."

A few minutes later, the two teams came to Roland, who was messing around with the leftover wooden swords and shields.

"We have made our decision," Jasper said.

"Which is?"

"We would like to face off as teams, and my group would like to bring on Wilton as our fourth member," replied Jasper.

"Alright. Take positions," Roland said with a sigh of discontentment. "The next challenge will be a fight between the two groups. The winning team will be the only one to partake of the final challenge."

The eight men faced each other, separating between the opponents they hoped to defeat; Carter against Jasper, Martin against Gad, Dan against Mathias, and Benjamin against Wilton.

"Begin." The cold word set a fire within the men who eagerly charged each other, giving no mercy to their foes. Carter and Jasper fought neck and neck, both smiling from the challenge they gave to one another. Martin held nothing back as he took on Gad. He had to show him what a real battle would be like, no more games. Dan did his best to repay Mathias for his brutal victory as he swung unendingly towards him. Benjamin and Wilton weaved in and out of each other's reach to try and take advantage of the fight.

"Alright, I can't wait anymore," Roland said as he jumped into the arena in front of them, making the fighting stop all at once. He held a wooden sword in one hand, a shield in the other. He looked up at them with a smile. "I'll fight both groups."

"Form a team!" Jasper screamed as Roland took out his first two victims.

"Ho-no, Hooo-no," shrieked Martin. "There was nothin' in the books about this laddie! If I wanted to be on the bad side of the Lord of Morer, I wouldn'ta took this job!"

"Jasper, you should be sorry," Roland teased with a cruel grin as he circled his prey. The men in the stands watched intently on the battle that was about to unfold.

"W-why?" Jasper gulped. He always hated training with Roland. Every second truly felt like it was your last! Even Carter held his gaze steady against the man, no longer playing around.

"You could have had me on your team, but you went and chose him," chuckled Roland as he pointed his sword at the limp figure of Wilton. "Now you've lost every chance you had of winning this game."

"We haven't lost yet!" screamed Dan as he ran forward.

"No! Don't!" cried out Martin.

"I told you, don't extend that much," Roland said, knocking the blade from Dan's grip. The ruffian followed his sword with his eyes as it fell away from him.

"I also said, pay attention," Roland growled as he bashed the man with his shield, sending him flying like he had the sword. With a sigh, he turned again to the group of men. "Three down, five to go."

"Okay, so, let's just attack together, right?" asked Carter from the center of the group, where he had gone as a safety precaution. He had hoped that Roland would wear down a little as he picked off some of the other people, but the prince should have known that would not happen.

"Yes, on three," Jasper instructed. "One, two!"

Roland attacked, breaking through the hold of the unprepared team. He struck Gad unconscious and scattered the rest of them apart. He was surrounded, yet spoke casually. "Never let your opponent know what you're thinking or what your strategy is. Once they know that, you're no more than meat for them to slice."

"How is this for strategy, Advisor?" shouted Carter as he charged, the other three men following suit. Deflecting the first hit, Roland weaved in and out of their strikes. With his movements, he caused their swords to attack others of their team. In the end, he defeated them by their own blades, not needing to use his own.

As grunts and moans came from the fighters, Roland answered cheerily. "It wasn't bad, but I had already planned it that way."

He turned to the prince and his followers. "Two final lessons for today. First, be aware of the fight so you can't be baited to move the way your enemy wants you to. Second, have a strategy in mind so you don't end up swinging your weapon aimlessly. I've found it to be best to remember tactical maneuvers in sequence, so that they can be performed on instinct. That way, even in a quick-paced fight, you can direct the moves of the battle appropriately."

The men groaned as they got to their feet and returned their practice weapons. The advisor waited for them at the gate of the arena. "Who's hungry?"

Planning for Days to Come

"Is that it?" squeaked the Queen as they passed a white gown made of the finest silks.

"Oh, no! That's my gown for the day after. I still need to look like a bride when the commoners see me," the woman said, opening a closet that held the true dress.

"Put it on for her, put it on!" giggled Miriam.

"Yes, please," cheered the Queen, who was still adoring the design.

"Alright, Adelina," the woman called out, her handmaid coming in from the hall. "Can you help me?"

"Yes." The girl bowed.

"Oh my!" Queen Zisca stood amazed. "You're fluent?"

"Adelina," gestured the prince's fiancé with her head. It took the handmaiden a while to realize what was going on. She was thrown into shock! This foreign queen had addressed her personally!

"Ah, a bit. My Lady has helped me learn. I'm not too good, but I know some." She coughed nervously, having almost given up her lady's name.

"That is amazing!"

"Gracias." The maid bowed again and scurried to the woman's side. They departed to change her into her wedding gown. Adelina apologizing non-stop in their language for almost ruining the wedding surprise. With a little reassurance, she and the prince's fiancé returned to their spectators to show off the gown's splendor.

"Oh," gasped the queen, "you look beautiful!"

The woman spun in her golden and white gown, another testimony to her obscene wealth. The lace that covered it was so delicate, the pattern seemed to crystalize. Her long veil covering her face, draped over her shoulders, and in the back, it went down the tail of her dress.

Her sister was now lying horizontally across the bed. Miriam smiled at the sight of her sister's beauty, sitting up to better see her. "Isn't she? I hope I can be as pretty as you someday!"

"Miriam, you're already far more perfect than I will ever be," said the woman, squeezing her sisters' cheeks. The girl let out a squeal as she tickled the prince's fiancé in retaliation. As the woman made her getaway, Miriam attacked the Queen who burst into laughter from the little girl's frantic tickles.

"Alright, settle down. Let me get out of this dress first," the woman laughed.

After she had changed back to her old robes, she dashed after her sister playfully. The girl screamed happily in response. Queen Zisca laughed at their efforts. It had been so long since she had seen such innocent joy in the palace.

Meanwhile, the prince and his men were headed inside to fill their now empty bellies. As the weary fighters passed by the woman's room, they stopped for a moment, listening to the never-ending laughter that came from inside. With chuckles of their own, they continued on their way to the great hall. The prince smiled at his advisor.

"She's amazing, isn't she?" he asked about his bride. "She and my mother get along so well. She is always happy and . . . she's gorgeous. Let's not forget that!"

"I must admit she does have nice qualities," replied Roland half-heartedly.

"But?" questioned Carter.

"But," he continued, "she is hiding things from us. Not just her name, but other things that I don't fully understand yet."

"And we both know you hate that, Mr. I-Need-To-Know-Everything!"

Roland looked at him with disappointment. "I don't think this is a joking matter."

"I know, I know. I'm sorry."

Roland began. "It's just that she–"

"Prince," said the woman from behind them. It seemed her time with his mother had come to an end. Zisca and Miriam went the other way down the hall to their next adventure.

"Ah, he-hey," the young prince stuttered as he adored his bride in her elegant scarlet dress. This one seemed more form-fitting than the one she had worn yesterday. The darkness of the material offsetting with her light skin. She seemed more worthy to be in the palace than he. What a fine queen she would make! She was absolutely stunning in his kingdom's colors!

Roland grimaced as he moved aside. He knew what the woman's presence meant. Carter would lose all focus for the remainder of the day.

"Hey," giggled Carter's bride. "How has your day been?"

"It was wonderful," grinned the prince. What a wonderful woman, caring about his day.

Roland unwittingly shed a sigh from behind him. All the thieves tensed in their armor as they feared she would recognize them. To their fear she smiled innocently, taking in the state of their armor. Even the advisor seemed to have a slight stain on his pant leg. Was that all he had received from a long day of training? She let out a slight shiver before returning her attention to her betrothed.

"Mine was too," she responded. "Have you been training again today?"

"Oh! Yes," Carter exclaimed, unaware that he was covered in dirt and sweat from his fighting. "How did you know?"

"You really do enjoy that, don't you?" she questioned happily.

"I do," Carter smiled. "We were just going to the great hall to eat. Did you want to come?"

Roland's eyes opened wide. Bells went off in his head as he thought. No, no, no!

"Actually, I am a bit hungry," the woman thought aloud, but when seeing the expression on Roland's face, she rephrased. "You know, my prince, you have so many guards. Ever since I left my sister and the queen, I have been alone. I am actually starting to feel a bit insecure."

"Oh?" Carter asked, taken in by her words. "I can get you someone if you'd like."

"I'll just need one man," she said, touching his arm. "One that is a bit hungry and wouldn't mind a private picnic."

"Wha' a sly little fox, eh," whispered Martin to Jasper, who was too distracted by Adelina to care. He gave her a little wave. She smiled and looked at her feet.

"Is tha'?" Martin exclaimed at the exchange.

"Shhh!" Jasper growled at him.

"Hungry, huh?" Carter said as he thought. "I'd tell you to take one of these guys, but I fear I may grow jealous of them having a private picnic with you. If anyone was to go with you, I'd . . . oh! I get it! Shall we set off?"

"I'd love to," Carter's fiancé smiled as he took her hand onto his arm. He was a little dirty, but his joy was the purest she had ever seen. This one will do, she thought to herself.

"How was your time with Mother? I could hear the laughter as I passed by. Kind of felt left out, if I'm honest."

"Did you? Oh, we had a glorious time. Miriam started a tickle fight that she had no chance of winning. Queen Zisca and I annihilated her in the end!"

"You're telling me that my mother joined in on a tickle fight?" Carter laughed. This was the queen of all Remette they were talking about.

"Well, not in the tickle fight," the woman leaned towards him. He came closer to her in response. His bride whispered. "It ended up being an all-out pillow war!"

Prince Carter burst out laughing. "Now I really wish I had been invited!"

"Is that a challenge?" the woman drew even closer to him, tilting her head to the side playfully. Her eyes catching his heart yet again.

"Pfff, I uh-" There went the prince's words again. How did she do that? He scratched his head, trying to remember how to speak. "Ta-huh."

The woman giggled in response.

"You're too cute," she said quietly. Carter blushed due to her remark. She thought he was cute!

Roland glared at their backs the entire time they walked away. She had stolen Carter! That boy was so entranced he couldn't think straight.

"Is it jus' me, or does he have a thing for tha' lady?" Martin whispered to Jasper.

"Of course, he does! They are getting married."

"Not him, the Advisor. Look how red he got!"

"Are you kidding? He can't stand her."

"Did he tell you tha'?"

"Well," Jasper thought for a moment. A woman Roland liked? Sure, he got a lot of women, but he had never truly cared for one. "No, it can't be."

"What are you two whispering about?" asked Roland, turning to find their staring eyes. "Hurry up and get something to eat. Afterward, we go over your patrol schedules for tomorrow."

"You got it," cheered Martin, turning to Jasper. "But you have to tell me how you got to tha' maid!"

"I'll tell you over dinner."

The smell of the palace food filled the ever-hungry Martin's nose. "Is tha', is tha' pork?"

The group sat at one of the tables to the front of the hall, gorging on the food made for the king's guards. It seemed like a feast to the thieves, but the king himself would not think of touching such meager portions. This truth could be seen in the plates that had been prepared for the advisor. All food brought for him was on golden plates, unlike the wooden ones used by the guards.

Out of kindness to his crew, Roland asked the servants to take his plates back. He instead ate the food the rest of them did, treating them as equals to himself. The servants who had brought him the wrong meal fell to the ground as they humbly apologized to him. It was a reverence Roland paid no attention to.

A sense of unworthiness shrouded those who sat and ate with him. Was this not the man they trained with? They felt terrible for how they had treated him, like he was no more than them. And the prince, could they not also have treated him with more respect?

"So, Jasper, what was it you and Martin were talking about?" Roland asked, trying to break the silence.

"Ah, well."

"We was talkin' 'bout how he made a move on the lady's maid," Martin interceded.

"What?" Roland blurted in astonishment.

"Seriously!" Jasper growled at Martin for giving up the secret.

"You mean, the maid who polished your armor for you," Roland said, a cold tone in his voice. That was why he had been so easily distracted that morning.

"Yeah," Jasper gulped.

Roland could do nothing but chuckle. "What's her name?"

"Adelina," Jasper answered, wiggling uncomfortably in his seat.

"And you've made a move, as Martin put it?"

"Well, I had to go back and get my armor. When I got there, the woman was with the queen mother. So, Carter left to put her present back in his room. While he was gone, Adelina helped me put my armor on. She had taken the first part of the day to polish it for me. Anyway, before I left... I asked her to meet with me tonight."

"That is sweet," Roland smiled, only to have his face turn to astonishment. "Wait. Tonight? We have things to do!"

"I'll see her after."

Roland closed his eyes and clenched his jaw. His teammates kept being whisked away by these women. The day had started coming to an end, and they still didn't have tomorrow mapped out! One mistake, and the plan would crumble. "Alright, I hope it goes well."

"You do?" Jasper was shocked. He had been sure the advisor would at least beat him a little for doing this amid such dangerous times.

"I do, but be sure to get some rest tonight, you have had hardly any these past few days."

"Yes, sir!"

Roland got up from the table. "Meet me in my chambers for your assignments once you've finished eating."

The doors of the hall burst open behind the advisor. Roland hung his head at the sight of the man who had entered.

"You!" Dorian, the collector, snarled as he pointed his greasy finger at the advisor. "How dare you show your face around me after what you pulled in Morer yesterday!"

"I promise you, Dorian, what happened was not at my hand, but that of the new princess."

"Don't you go smooth talkin' me! I'll go to the king right now and have your title!"

"You seem upset," Roland remained patient. "Is there anything I can help you with?"

"I got something-"

"Dorian!" came a roar from the hall. "You in there?"

"Yes, my liege!"

"How went your trip to Morer? I heard Carter's fiancé gave enough payment to cover the dues of the entire town!"

"You heard of that, my liege?"

"Of course! Thanks to Roland, nothing evades my eye," the king laughed, walking into the hall. Jasper and his men cringed at the sight of their oppressor.

"Simply trying to serve you to the best of my ability, Your Highness," Roland bowed his head with a smile. The entire gesture seemed so genuine; his traitors felt they were being set up for a moment.

"Ha! If only I had more men like you," the king patted his back as he turned to speak to Dorian again. "So, how much did you collect?"

"One and a half times more than last year's total income, my liege," Dorian replied.

"Who knew my son getting married would be so profitable, eh," cackled Cadoc.

"Speaking of," Roland lowered his voice so only the king could hear. "Did you speak to the woman today? I know you were thinking about it. I only hope you found the reassurance you were looking for. I spoke with her this morning. It seemed to go well."

"Actually, no. Zisca has kept her and her sister all day, so I haven't had the chance. Now that you mention it, I should talk to her privately. To extend my hand, you understand."

"Of course, my liege. The prince is with her now. I would suggest the gardens. I believe they were having some type of picnic."

"A picnic? I tell you that boy takes so much after his mother. Always in a daydream that one. Alright, to the gardens I will go, but first, Dorian."

"Yes, my liege," bowed the greasy man.

"Take me to this booty you have collected. I would very much like to see it with my own eyes."

"Right away!"

The king turned back to his advisor. "We'll talk later. After I have a chat with the woman."

"I will be here when you need me," Roland smiled to his king.

"You always are." The king and his greasy collector left to adore the kingdoms latest treasure. Roland turned the opposite way towards his room, Jasper and his men staring blankly at the man they had just watched speak with the king. It was a face they did not recognize, yet one they saw often. A shiver took ahold of them. It was difficult to know where the man's loyalty truly lay. He had spoken to the king as he had just been talking with them.

"Alright, let's head out," Jasper said, leading his friends to follow the King's Advisor. "Roland! Wait up. We're ready now."

The man smiled at him with a different smile, this one much weaker than the one he had given the king. In his eyes, Jasper could see his true despair. The man was in pain.

"You alright?" Jasper asked him quietly.

"Definitely. I'm just glad we are finally going to get something done," Roland said as he took the lead to show the group to his quarters. He clutched to his stomach. When would this feeling go away?

"Okay, he scares me," Martin whispered to the group while nodding in the direction of the retreating advisor. Agreement came from them.

"Give it time. You'll find that man to be one of the best you'll ever meet," Jasper reassured them.

"I'm not sayin' he's not nice. I'm sayin' he's scary."

"Quiet already," Jasper snapped as they entered the advisor's quarters. They were extremely impressive. There seemed to be no end to them. The men walked first into the common room of the series. Everything was orderly within the space.

They followed Roland through a library to reach his study. Those rooms were just as impressive. When the thieves had gathered, Roland brought out maps of the palace's structure, walking the men through the patrol routes.

"We will want to be sure to control not only the floor where we will take the king but also the floors above and below. We don't want any surprises during our chat. There are regular standing guards at each of the staircase entrances as well as rotating guards on each floor. We won't need to cover the fourth floor because Cadoc won't be making it that far up."

The advisor laid three identical keys on the table in front of the ruffians. "Before you are the master keys of the palace. I am the only one who has access to these. One man from each group of guards will take a key and lock all the doors on your floor during the route. This will keep the guests in their rooms and out of the way in case a ruckus starts."

"The patrols that cover the floors operate in circling motions. That is where I have you grouped for the undertaking. Three or four of you will be placed on the rotating shift per floor. If trouble arises, your jobs will also be to strike against your fellow guardsmen and take out the standing guards to ensure we will not be disturbed."

"There is a rotation for the alarm sentinel every half hour. I have assigned Gad to that position at the time of the uprising. Your job is to keep the alarm from going off, no matter who tells you to sound it. Defend the alarm from the king's men who try to raise it. I will send a group to back you up if it gets too out of hand."

"Guards will be gathering in the great hall tomorrow at daybreak to discuss short term changes to protocol. These will last the next few days as the royal wedding is taking place. Because of extra guests staying at the castle, extra precautions will be taken. I created this new schedule, so you will be where you need to be exactly when you need to be. Do not stray from where you are assigned."

"While the rest of you take care of the guests and the guards, Jasper and Mathias will accompany Carter and I. Our group will be the one to overthrow the king." Roland gulped, his stomach hardening once again. He pushed the feeling aside as he continued. "We will attack after the palace has gone to sleep, overpowering the king in his bedroom. By the time everyone wakes up, Cadoc will be in shackles, and the new king shall be crowned."

The ruffians cheered, a cold sweat leeching from the advisor's skin. Roland looked at the purple napkin on his chessboard in the corner. What was this feeling? He sensed that something was wrong, but the plan seemed so perfect. Was he making a mistake, as he had before?

"You alrigh', mate?" Martin questioned. It was the most perplexed he had ever seen Roland in his life. The sight was a bit frightening, to say the least. This man was their leader, the only one who could pull this off.

The advisor's face stiffened into its usual unremorseful state. "The only advice I can offer is that you remember your training and act natural out there. One more day, and we will all be free men."

Excited nods came from the crowd as Roland finished. "When the sun goes down tomorrow, so does this tyrant king. Any questions?"

"No, sir!"

"Good, then you can have the night to rest for tomorrow," Roland said as he opened the door of his study to let the men back into the hall.

Around this time, the king made his way into the garden. It was an astounding place. Rows upon rows of beautiful flowers bloomed in an array of colors, cackles could be heard coming from the center of the flowers. As the king approached, he found his son and the kingdom's newest princess, just as the advisor had said he would.

"Just toss it, trust me, just toss it," laughed Carter as he crouched on his knees. The woman sat on the blanket across from him, sitting up on her side. Her hand was inside the basket of food.

"I tell you," giggled the woman, "I have terrible aim!"

"And I'm a terrible catch," the prince laughed again. "Come on! Toss it!"

With that, the woman threw a grape she had been holding, the prince chomping at it with all his might. Shock sprang across his face as he claimed his victory. "Yeah!"

The prince's bride laughed at his happiness, causing the king to grimace even more than usual.

"Carter," he snarled to get his son's attention.

"Father! What are you doing here?" Carter asked as he stood, helping the woman up as well. She brushed herself off before bowing her head to the king.

"I came to borrow your fiancé for a moment."

"What?" Carter asked. "W-why?"

"I'd just like to get to know her a bit better." Cadoc reached out his hand, the woman taking it with another bow. "You can keep Dorian if you'd like."

The greasy man scowled at the prince, who in turn let out a gulp. "N-n-no thanks!"

It was too late. The king had left with his bride. Carter hung his head. He had only just gotten her back and now she was gone again.

Unpleasurable Company

The king and Carter's fiancé walked silently for a moment. The tap of their feet on the cobble of the courtyard was the only noise to be heard. The woman did not look at him but ahead. She did not act in such a way out of fear but to show herself as one of equal footing. This gesture could have ended in punishment, but it actually made Cadoc more interested in her.

"I cannot help but wonder where it is you are from, My Lady," he said to her in his usual gravelly tone, "but I know it is the wish of your father to keep such facts from me until the wedding is over, so I will not make you tell me. It is a bold step on his part, wouldn't you say? Treating me, a foreign king, with such a hand?"

"It is indeed," she said with a sigh, "but if I am honest with you, I do not believe that the precautions he required for this arrangement were to disrespect you in any way. He holds you and your son in the highest regard. If it weren't for the allegiance between King Jessinias and yourself, the entire middle kingdom would have been swept away in the last Great War; my family included."

She continued, "No, the reason we have gone through such things is to ensure my safety. You see, I grew fearful of Remettians after the war. I hope you do not see it as a slight against you. I simply have had harsh experiences that caused me pain and worry. My father knew this when he spoke to the prince about me. More so, I believe he felt knowledge of my union with your son spreading too quickly would have endangered my well-being. I do apologize sincerely for any grievances I have caused you."

The king was taken aback. This girl spoke with the fluency and authority of a diplomat. "It's alright. I'm not angry, simply curious. I can only assume your father is of high standing in King Jessinias' court by the answer you gave just now. You surely are a clever one."

"Thank you," she smiled.

"So, on your journey here, what happened to your caravan? How is it that one of your guards was wounded?"

The woman thought back to her conversation with the advisor. It seemed the king was testing her yet again, but she had promised not to say anything about what she had learned. "I was stopped by a group of thieves."

"What?" King Cadoc stopped walking out of shock. The woman figured it was an additional effort to his routine.

"They shot one of my guards to get us to stop. I had everything valuable in the other caravan, so I simply did as they asked. When they found nothing of value, they retreated. I'm just thankful that it was only Andre who was wounded, and not more of my men. Besides, he seems to be healing well. For that, I am truly grateful."

"And you've just kept this to yourself? I would have sent troops to bring the ruffians to justice!"

Sure you would, thought the woman. "It is alright. I was unharmed. Besides, there was no need for me to bother you with something so insignificant. I'm sure you are quite busy."

"You are a member of my house!" Cadoc spat. "I promise you, whoever has done such a thing to a child of mine, whether you be by blood or bond, will be punished."

The woman could not understand his reaction. Had he not sent those thieves himself?

"But, what of Sir Roland's men?" she inquired. He couldn't harm the men he had ordered to attack her, could he?

"What men?" asked the king. "Roland has not led any men since his regiment in the last Great War."

"He-" the woman was flabbergasted.

"Enough of him, tell me more of these thieves. I will cleanse my lands of them!"

"Oh, great and glorious king!" came a shriek that interrupted their conversation. The two turned to see a blonde-haired woman bowing low to the ground in front of them. A brunette man did the same beside her.

"My sister and I have arrived to enjoy the celebration of Prince Carter's marriage. Alas, we are a bit early," said the man, never lifting his head.

"Arise," ordered Cadoc. "I will have a servant prepare rooms for you. May I present Prince Carter's bride."

The two got up and bowed again. "My lady, we are so pleased to meet our future queen. I am Sir Frederick of Luxborne, and may I introduce my sister, the Lady Faigel."

"Pleased to make your acquaintance," the woman replied, her head elsewhere. The advisor had tricked her! What an arrogant man.

"Oh, great king, we praise you! We are so pleased to see you in person," the little lord rambled on. "We have brought gifts for your court to show our excitement for your son, the prince's marriage."

Cadoc forgot about the woman and her testimony, the riches in front of him spoiling his gaze. "Let me show you inside!"

"Why, thank you, my king," smiled Lord Frederick.

The woman stayed in the yard as the pack made their way into the palace. She held to her stomach, an uneasy feeling taking over her. Fear. Fear of the animal who had tricked her so easily that morning. What a fool she had been! How could she alert the king of the snake he had been feeding, the one which would soon turn and bite at his master's heel?

He had lied about the attack. If the ruffians did not work for the king, then they must be against him. The attack was for some greater purpose! When it had happened, the woman thought they needed the funds for the poor. Thinking back to her tour of Morer, did not

Roland simply watch as a woman he cared for was beaten? The lowly must not be his purpose. What was it the man had said when they robbed the caravan? 'We need this, or we will surely die'?

This attack had been planned, created for a single purpose. If not to help the poor, then it must be to help the advisor himself. It was only to be expected of a beast like him. A position next to the king would never be enough. That small band of renegades, they were his hidden resource. The king must be warned, but how?

These people, these distractions, made it impossible for her to get him alone. This was probably the only time he had set aside for her this entire week. How could you get a man of such importance alone long enough to deliver an accusation of this magnitude? Moreover, she had no proof. Without knowing her identity, the king probably wouldn't listen unless she had something solid. The advisor's standing with him was nothing less than honorable. She would need strong evidence to raise questions about him. What of Carter? The man lived off of the words of his advisor. He would be far too easy a catch. Like an innocent lamb led to slaughter.

She let out a sigh. "What to do?"

"If it's advice you need, I've been told I am helpful in that area," came a cold chuckle from behind her.

The woman spun on her heel to face the predator with disgust written on her face. She quickly shook herself. If this fiend knew of her understanding, he wouldn't hesitate to end her. Then she would never be able to warn Carter or the king. For now, it was all about getting evidence.

"Going back out to meet your men tonight?" she asked in a shaky voice. How was he so intimidating?

"Oh no, My Lady. No more tests, I assure you," Roland gave off a fake smile. It seemed she hadn't exactly gotten over the whole 'Lord of Morer' business.

"Then, what are you doing out here?" she rebuked, spite lacing her words.

"Have I not the right to walk about this palace freely?" the advisor asked, moving towards her. The woman backed away in response. She gave a fearful gulp with the realization that she was no more than a bird caught in the cage this snake had made. In her gut, she felt the truth; this creature before her had every inch of this palace under his thumb. The king and prince were living their lives in the light of the place as this demon set snares around their feet, she herself falling into them.

"Y-yes, of course," the woman stuttered, something Roland had yet to experience.

"Are you alright, My Lady?" Roland tilted his head to the side in concern as he drew nearer still, extending his hand to her.

"I'm fine!" she blurted in a frantic effort to escape from his presence. In her struggle, she caught the hem of her gown, sending her sliding towards the ground. A gentle hand caught her arm, another at her waist, a pair of blue eyes gazing down at her.

"Are you sure about that, My Lady?"

"Uh, I-I, um," the woman gulped again. He was so close she could feel the warmth coming off of him. He was indeed threatening. To appear so gentle, yet his bloodlust was bottled up under the face he showed her. Face! She lifted her free hand to her veil to be sure it was still in place.

With a sigh, Roland lifted her up, never releasing his grip on her. "You're starting to sound more and more like Prince Carter each day, My Lady."

She said nothing, too afraid of him to respond.

"If you really want to know, I saw the prince in the garden with Dorian. Afterward, when I bumped into the king and a few new guests, I presumed that you may have been left unattended. So, I came here to find you." Roland released his grip on her, feeling strange for having held her too long. "I thought I would escort you to wherever or whomever you wished to go. Then you would not need to remain in the courtyard looking so glum. It's getting dark anyway. No need for you to be out here all alone."

"Thank you," she said carefully. "I'd like to go to my room if that's alright."

"Certainly, lead the way."

"Oh, no! Please, you lead," the woman said, backing up from him.

"Are you sure you're feeling alright?" Roland asked her softly.

"I'll feel better once I get to my chambers!" she snapped in reply.

"Of course."

The two set out on their way in silence, barely looking at one another. This is what I get for being nice, Roland yelled at himself, an awkward walk down the halls. I should have just stayed in my room!

"Here we are," Roland pointed to her door. "Have a good night, My Lady."

He felt a gust of wind as the woman rushed past him to the safety of her door. She didn't say a word to him. No thank you, nor goodbye. As she opened the way to her room, the woman called out. "Adelina!"

It was then Roland remembered, even in her room, the future queen would be unattended. Adelina was probably with Jasper at the moment. Realizing he would have to wait with the princess a bit longer, the advisor gave a weary sigh. There was no reason for a royal such as herself to be left defenseless.

"It seems she isn't here, My Lady," he said, leaning on her doorframe.

"What?" the woman gasped as she realized he hadn't left. How did he know Adelina wasn't there? Did he kill her? Why was he just standing there? What a creep!

"Well, she isn't in here, is she?" Roland gestured to the empty room.

"I suppose not," the woman mustered her courage. "I'll just have to find her!"

She started past the advisor into the hall to find her missing friend, only to have him curl around behind her, walking at the same pace. She whisked back to face him. "What are you doing?"

"I told you before. I am to take you to wherever or whomever you like. If you're going out into the night to find this girl, I will accompany you."

The woman's face flushed red behind the veil. Was this another one of his tricks? He probably planned to do something awful to her if he could get her somewhere secluded. "I-I guess I'll just stay here then."

"As you wish," the advisor turned to let her go back into her room, where she had left the door open earlier. She rushed past him the same as she had done before. This time slamming the door shut to the advisor's face, followed by various clicking noises. She was undoubtedly secure behind all of the locks she had set into place.

"Good night," Roland grumbled to himself. With a sigh, the advisor leaned against the corridor wall. It seemed he was going to have yet another long night.

Inside, the woman changed into a black cloak. There was no telling where Adelina was, but by now, Miriam would have gone to sleep. Frank would have returned to his quarters since her sister was in her room. All she had to do was get to him. Once she found Frank, she would have him get all of her men on guard. With her plan set, she unlocked the door.

Roland heard clicking once again. He shook his head at the woman's efforts and simply waited where he had been leaning against the wall. The door opened, flooding light over him from the candles in her room. She charged into the hall quickly, not even taking notice of him as she passed by; she was too set on her mission. The woman was dressed in all black, most likely a way to blend in with the shadows of the night.

"Where is it you're going now, My Lady?" Roland said with a sigh.

"Eeep!" She fell back into the wall opposite of him, her hands before her, ready to protect herself. "You-you're still here?"

"Indeed," he kicked off of the wall. "Now, is there somewhere you wanted to go?"

"No," she replied in a startled voice.

"Then are you cold or something?" The advisor pointed at her cloak.

"Oh, no," she shook her head nervously.

"What are you doing out here, My Lady?" Roland asked, losing his patience.

"Going back to my room."

Roland blocked her path. "There is no point in going back into your room if you're just going to sneak out later. Why don't you tell me where you want to go?"

"I want to go to my room!"

He rubbed his eyes as he yielded again. "Fine! In you go."

As she went inside and closed her door, he stopped it with his hand.

"W-what are you doing?"

"I don't want to stand out here all night," the advisor's words losing the softness he was trying to relay earlier. As the sun set, his anger rose.

"Then go to your room!" The prince's fiancé pushed on the door but couldn't move it against Roland's strength.

"So that you can sneak off on your own? No way!"

"I'll stay here!"

"Are you going to wait for your maid to get back, or are you just going to go to sleep?"

"I'm waiting for Adelina!"

He forced his way into her room. "Then, I'm waiting with you."

"You can't do that! I'm a lady!"

"That's precisely why I'm doing it." Roland helped himself to one of her lounge chairs, glaring at her in fury. "Leaving a lady, such as yourself, without a guard or caretaker to look after you, I will not have it."

Slowly, the woman closed the door and made her way to the chair opposite of him. She had been defeated. All that was left to do was wait.

"Still cold, My Lady?" the advisor asked in contempt. She was still wearing her cloak.

"S-sorry." She got up from her seat and removed it. After hanging her cloak on a hook, she lifted a plate of cakes from the table and asked, "Would you like something to eat?"

"No, thank you, My Lady," Roland sighed. "You are the future queen. If anything, I should be serving you."

"Ah." She set the plate back down. "Alright."

"Are you sure you're feeling okay?" Roland asked again. She had seemed on edge the whole evening.

"I feel fine."

"It's just, you've been acting rather strange this evening," Roland leaned forward, looking to her intently.

"I could say the same for you," she snarled.

"I beg your pardon?"

"Insisting to watch over me, that doesn't seem to fit you."

"Then I must say you don't know me very well, My Lady. My first obligation is to this country, which you are now a part of."

What a load of dung, the woman thought. All he really cares about is himself.

"I have taken precautions to be sure no member of the royal household is left unattended. The fact that you are not yet set into those protocols made you vulnerable this evening. No matter how unreasonable it may seem, I cannot go on knowing that one of those under my guard may be at risk. So, just in case anything unexpected were to happen, I'm going to wait with you for your maid to return."

"I'll be sure to keep a few of my guards with me at all times tomorrow," the woman gulped. So, he was in control of the entire palace! How would she ever alert the king?

"That would be wise." Roland turned his head to the balcony. "What a lovely view."

"Thank you," the woman replied cautiously as Roland got up from his chair. He leaned onto the railing of the balcony as he soaked in the night. He had missed the night air! It seemed like an eternity since he had the pleasure of sleeping under the stars.

The woman came beside him, thinking it safer to play along than making a run for it. The two peered over the city out into the wilderness beyond. Placing her hands on the railing, she took a deep breath beside the advisor. All peace she had attained was shattered a few moments later. "My Lady."

"Yes?"

"You still owe me a question," Roland said, never looking at her. His hands were clenched into fists as he said it. Whatever the question was, she felt she didn't want to answer.

"I'm not so sure about that." The prince's bride hoped the advisor would allow her to dismiss their deal. "You have been asking quite a lot of questions tonight."

"Yes, but your answers to those questions could have easily been lies." Roland clenched his jaw. She had obviously been lying about things up until now. "This question requires your complete honesty, which is why I am using the favor you owe me."

"What is it?" she gulped.

The advisor looked nervously into his hands. "What did my White Queen tell you of me that made you hate me so much?"

Hearing him say the words filled the woman with terror, but she couldn't lie. "I know what happened between you two. I know the horrible things you promised to do to her, should you ever meet her again."

Roland's shoulders sunk in response to her testimony. His face remained blank as he looked across the countryside. Stuck on the subject of the White Queen, the woman forgot all he was about to put her through. She could only see his grief. Perhaps he regretted what he had said and done.

The woman approached the advisor to comfort him. She placed her hands directly beside his on the railing of her balcony, so they almost touched, to show him that she wasn't afraid of him. She leaned slightly, so she was facing him directly as she softly spoke. "That does not mean I hate you, nor does it mean she hates you. In fact, she had hoped to make amends with you, but has thus far been too afraid to contact you."

"Too afraid to contact me?" The advisor ruffled his hair. As he looked across the fields in irritation, he spat, "She should be."

"I don't understand?" Carter's fiancé replied in worry, having only now noticed how close she was to Roland. Her hands stuck to where she had placed them unwittingly. How had she not noticed earlier; how large this man was? He could squash her in an instant!

Roland looked at her, his hatred was clearly seen. "Whatever that self-righteous woman told you about me. It is all a lie."

The woman wrenched her hands away to protect herself. He was so intimidating! The advisor continued coldly. "It was she that betrayed me. It was she who made me into this monster she has taught you to fear. I am the victim, My Lady. I hope one day you will see that."

"What are you trying to say?" the woman retaliated defensively. "That she deserves the brutality you spoke of in your letter? I have seen it, and it is something I will not forget!"

"She showed you that?" Roland's voice became soft and full of shame. He looked at his feet. "Those were the words of a young fool, no more. I'll admit that act on my part was shameful, but that doesn't outdo the evils she inflicted upon me!"

"She did nothing to you!" spat the prince's bride.

Cheerful talking could be heard in the halls. Roland knew it was Jasper and Adelina returning, but then he realized what was about to happen. If he could recognize Jasper's voice, wouldn't the woman? If the maid brought him inside again, she would definitely remember him from his face! Roland may have told her Jasper was an informant of his, but he shouldn't have been inside the palace walls. If she were to catch him here, she would know that he had been lying that morning.

"It seems your maid has returned, My Lady. I'll be leaving now." Roland hurriedly departed from his place at the balcony, killing the unpleasant conversation. He dashed into the hall, where he found Jasper hovering over his maiden.

"Well, I suppose this is good night," Jasper smiled, playing with a piece of the young woman's hair. He was ambushed by Roland before he was able to finish his farewell, who accidentally knocked the wind out of him during the retrieval.

"Your mistress is inside waiting for you," Roland said to Adelina as he dragged Jasper away. "Have a good night, my lady!"

Adelina blushed. The king's advisor had just referred to her as 'my lady'. What a dream she had been living this evening!

Her dreams fell apart as she heard a harsh whisper behind her. *"Adelina!"*

"Yes?" she asked, entering her mistress' room.

"Where have you been?" The woman hugged her so tightly she could hardly speak the answer.

"I've been with that guard, Jasper."

"The handsome one from last night?"

"Yes, and we are to meet again tomorrow!"

"I'm happy for you, but you must tell me these things. I thought you had died!"

"I'm sorry I worried you, but why was that advisor in your quarters? Were you finishing the discussion from this morning?"

"That man is nothing more than an evil crook. I want you to stay away from him. He's up to something. Once I figure it out, I'm going to get rid of him for good."

"So, you weren't finishing up your conversation from this morning?"

"No. He wouldn't leave me alone until there was someone here to care for me. The man wouldn't let me go anywhere!"

"That's so sweet!"

"Not sweet, sadistic. He is a snake!"

"You can tell me all about it. Why don't we get you to bed for now?"

Meanwhile, Jasper recovered his breath as he was dragged into Roland's quarters. He rebuked his kidnapper. "What do you think you're doing? You just ruined my date!"

An evil glare answered him. "You were only a few steps from My Lady's door. Had she come out and recognized you, neither you nor I would have seen the next dawn's light!"

"Oh." Jasper touched the side of his own face. "I suppose you're right."

"I'm always right. Now, get back to your room before you cause any more trouble." Roland said as he made his way to his bedroom. "You've gone long enough without proper rest. I'll see you in the morning, my friend."

"Good night," Jasper whispered as he left.

Morning Romanticizing

Carter slept peacefully amidst his snoring. His blanket covering only one leg, and his pillow being one of his arms. The rest of his comforters were scattered around him in a bundled mess. Stepping over a pillow lying on the floor, the advisor leaned over the prince's bed.

"CARTER!" he shouted; the young prince flailed about in an effort to get away.

"Wha-" Carter started to speak as he smacked his head on the bed's headboard. "Ow!"

"Good morning, sire," Roland said, smiling.

"Must you do this every morning?"

"You have a big day ahead. There is much to do and very little time to do it. The sun has been up for two hours now."

"Two hours? What about the guard meeting?"

"It's already over."

"I missed it?" A pile of clothing smacked the young prince in the face.

"You had better get dressed before you miss anything else."

Carter realized, for the first time, the advisor's change in style. Instead of his usual black or scarlet apparel, he wore a dark burgundy suit that bore his family crest on its chest. It had been so long since he wore his own crest, the pattern being a silver shield with two axes coming from it and a longsword down the center. Looking at the clothing he had been provided, Carter found a suit of Remettian gold colors that bore his flaming red dragon crest.

"What's with the get-ups?"

"You're joking."

Carter looked at him solemnly because he truly didn't know what was going on.

"The guests will be arriving today for the wedding tomorrow. You have to look your best."

"Has anyone gotten here yet?"

"Thankfully not this morning, but the twins from Luxborne arrived yesterday."

"Oh my," Carter grimaced. "Frederick!"

"Yes, he's here."

"I can't stand that guy!" Carter removed the shirt he was wearing to replace it with the one Roland had given him.

"Nor I, but his sister helps heal the wounds a little."

"Ha! She may be easy on the eyes, but compared to My Lady, she holds no precedence," he said with a grin. "By the way, how is My Lady? Is she already awake?"

"Yes, she is. I saw her with her sister and the bodyguard Frank early this morning, but you don't have time for that right now. We have work to do."

"But I barely got to see her yesterday!"

"Look at me, Carter," Roland said, grabbing him. "Today is not her day. Tomorrow is her day. This is you and your father's day. We have been waiting a very long time for this. Can't you just wait for her a bit longer?"

"I suppose, but won't she think I'm angry or something?" Carter pouted in his defeat.

"She'll figure it out tomorrow. Now get dressed and meet me in the great hall."

"Alright."

Roland exited Carter's room, only to find two of the woman's guards waiting for him. They were out of their armor but still stuck out in their black outfits with their swords on their sides. Roland patted his thigh. What a good idea they had.

He made his way to his room, the two men following him at a distance. How strange it was for her to stick her dogs on him. Of course, things did get a bit heated the night before. He would have to get rid of these men somehow. They were no more than nuisances to him.

Roland went to his armory, picking up a sturdy double-edged sword with his crest engraved on the pommel. It was a magnificent piece, his most trusted ally during the war. For a moment, he could do no more than admire it. How many battles did he win with this sword? With a sense of satisfaction, he placed it around his waist. He felt more like himself when he wore it.

Walking into the hall again, the advisor approached the men who were following him. "What is it you think you're doing?"

They answered in nothing but foreign rambles. How thoughtful of the prince's fiancé to send men to watch him who could not speak to him. So irritating! Roland spun on his heel to find the woman and make her get rid of her minions. He found her near the palace entrance with her sister, their bodyguard Frank, and two spare guards behind. She was hidden underneath a scarlet cloak, her sister pulling her purple hood over her head as well, as if they were headed outside.

"My Lady," Roland called out. "May I have a word?"

At first, Frank blocked his path to her, but the woman nudged him aside. "What is it?"

"I came to inquire of these men," Roland pointed to the shadows behind him.

"Ah, the one to the left is Jaquez, and to the right, Alexander."

"And what are they doing?" Roland growled.

"Watching you."

"Why?"

"Yesterday, you said that I needed to be more careful. That security was everything. I've now upped my security, and it's not like you have a personal guard, so I've lent you some of mine."

"I do not need security, My Lady."

"I would feel much better if you had it."

"Not to be rude, My Lady, but if I were to have guards on me, I'd rather they be my own. I do not know these men, so if something were to happen, I wouldn't trust them with anything."

"I suppose you're right. Very well, you may have Frank." With a gesture of her head, the giant moved to Roland's side. Her other two took their places, one on each side of the woman. Miriam giggled behind them at Roland's dumbfounded expression.

"I don't want Frank either!"

"Is one not better than two? Besides, you've known Frank for a few days now. He must be more trustworthy than these two."

"I do not need to be watched by a babysitter! Have you so little respect for me? Please, My Lady, I beg you. Take away these guards. They can't even speak to me."

"Perhaps not these two, but Frank can."

A shiver ran down Roland's spine as he turned to look at the shrouded figure. "You can?"

"Yes," came a deep growl from the mountain beside him.

"He's been helping me when I'm not sure what people say the whole time we've been here, haven't you, Frank?" giggled Miriam from behind her sister.

"What is a good babysitter for?" growled the beast again. Roland grimaced at his predicament. This bodyguard was on the verge of killing him. He could feel it.

"You're no babysitter," laughed the girl in reply.

"My Lady, I am sorry, but I will not accept any of your guards. If you want me to be guarded, for your sake, I'll have two of my men with me at all times. Will that make you feel better?"

She looked at her bodyguard, who gave a nod of approval. "That will be fine."

"Thank you," Roland said with relief as Frank took his place by the child. "I'll see you soon, My Lady."

"Goodbye," she nodded as he left. "*I certainly hope I don't see him again soon.*"

"*Do not worry. I'll position the men to be sure you will remain safe here. As for the royal family, I cannot guarantee. They will have to provide their own safety precautions. For today, I think you should enjoy your upcoming wedding. If the advisor starts to act up, I'll notify you.*"

"*Thank you, Frank,*" the woman replied. "*Miriam darling, I want you to stay close to Jaquez and Alexander for me, okay? Frank has things to do, so if you want to go do something where I'm not with you, you'll take them. Won't you?*"

"*Yes, Sissy.*"

"*Good girl! Now, is there anything you'd like to do?*"

"*Can we go see the horses?*"

The woman chuckled. How she would miss her dear sister! "*Alright, let's go see the horses.*"

Roland kicked himself as he entered the great hall. Why had he yielded like that? He barely had the forces he needed right now. To add two new guard positions would be tedious. But then again, Carter had been assigned both Jasper and Mathias.

As the advisor approached, he raised the question. "Carter?"

"Yeah?"

"My Lady has asked me to get two guards for myself at all times, but I don't want to change the schedule from where it is."

"She did?" Carter asked in sadness. He wished she would care for his safety like that.

"Yes, but I figure we will be together most of the day anyway, so would you mind sharing your two with me as well?"

"I don't mind at all. It's probably best this way anyhow." Carter shrunk a little. "She didn't tell me I needed more guards."

"If you ask her, I'm sure she'd give you twenty, sire. Honestly, it would be best to avoid such things."

"Right, yeah. Do you know where she is?"

"I left her in the entrance hall. I'm not sure where she's gotten to now."

"Well, we have some spare time, I think. Why don't we go find her?"

"Very well," Roland sighed. He had had enough of that woman.

"Prince," came a feminine shriek from the hall.

"My dear," called out Carter with a large smile which transformed into a strained grin, "-est Lady Faigel! How are you?"

A woman with perfectly curled, golden hair stood before the pack of men. She wore a light pink gown, which made her look like an elegant doll. Her blue eyes flashing behind her fan.

"I am wonderful, thank you," she said with a slight curtsey. "How are you, dear prince? Excited for the wedding, I assume?"

"Oh, the wedding," Carter began to daydream. "I am! Have you gotten to meet My Lady? She is by far the most wonder-" His speech rang short as Roland kicked his leg to silence him.

"We were just headed to find the bride now," Roland spoke up. "Perhaps you will meet her later today."

"Well, I actually saw her yesterday," said Lady Faigel as she strutted towards Roland, "but I also remember our conversation being cut short by my brother the last time I saw you."

"Oh, was it? Perhaps sometime we may start that up again. How could a man deny such a request from a woman as beautiful as yourself?" The advisor lifted her hand to his lips. Kissing it lightly, he spoke. "For now, I'm afraid duty calls."

With a giggle, Faigel blushed. "You are such a man of valor! Well, I hope to see you again soon."

"As do I, my lady," he winked as he turned to exit the hall. His three companions were left flabbergasted. He had just batted away the most beautiful and successful woman in the kingdom, and she was willing to try for him again!

"How do you do that?" Carter asked when they had traveled a bit further down the hall. "If only I could make My Lady blush like that."

"Or I, Adelina!"

"Or I, anybody," Mathias added in gloomily.

"Oh, come on. It didn't mean anything. It was just a bit of fun. All she wanted was some affection, and she got it. Now it's over."

"She is definitely looking forward to that next meeting," baited Jasper.

"Enough," chuckled Roland.

"Oh, you mighty man of valor," said the prince, fanning his face with his hand. His friends laughing together at the now disgruntled advisor.

"Adelina?" Jasper said from behind them. The whole group turned to look at the now beet-red maid. The other two maidens with her kept their pace, but Adelina was held back by the stares of Jasper's party.

The handmaidens giggled as they passed by the advisor, whispering something about him to one another. It seemed they were talking about him swooning a lady. News traveled fast with these maids, the advisor thought. He had only just seen Fae moments ago!

"H-hello." A slight smile came to Adelina's face as she traced the floor with her foot.

"What are you doing here? Where is My Lady?" Jasper asked her, no longer caring about the others of his group.

"She is with her sister. Trying to spend time before people come."

"Do you know where they are?" Carter jumped into the conversation, the maid becoming an even brighter shade of red because the prince was addressing her personally.

"I'm afraid I do not know, sire."

"That's alright. Nobody seems to," he shrugged sadly.

"We're still on for lunch, right?" Jasper got her attention again. Another blush. "Of course."

"Great. I can't wait," Jasper smiled.

"Neither can I, but I must go now." She held up the basket of supplies she was holding.

"Yeah, I understand. Take care, alright?" Jasper waved as she walked out of sight.

After she scurried away, Roland sneered, "Well, it seems you got her to blush just fine."

"Watch it!" Jasper warned.

"Oh, he got you!" Carter cackled. "This is the most fun I've had in ages! I love it when you two are together!"

The men stood around, competing against one another a few minutes before a soft call brought their time of roughhousing to an end.

"My prince," came a light coo from ahead of them. Carter looked at his bride, who was also wearing his country's golden color in a tightly fitted silk dress. Atop it, a thin, scarlet, silk cloak draped to the floor. Her hands were protected by white lace gloves that covered her to the elbow. A thin white veil draped over her mouth and a golden tiara sat on her head with inset diamonds and rubies. Her raven black hair draped over her shoulders beautifully.

"Woah," Carter gasped, taken aback yet again by his bride's beauty.

Beside her was a still blushing maiden, followed by two bodyguards. Her sister nowhere to be seen.

"I've missed you," she said softly, walking up to him. "You look so handsome today. That is definitely your color."

"Well I," he bantered. "You, you're just. Yeah."

"Adelina told me you were looking for me," the woman replied.

Roland sneered. What was she trying to do? This was a completely different woman from this morning, or last night for that matter! What was with the goody-goody act?

"Yes. I wanted to find you so that I could see you."

"Well, now you've seen me."

"May I, uh," Carter held out his arm, "take you somewhere?"

"Of course, where is it you would like to go?" his fiancé replied, giving him a hand to hold.

The nerve of that woman! Roland couldn't believe he would have to stand around all day watching those two flirt with one another. She was acting kind right now, but where was her decency before?

"Nowhere. I just want to keep you close for now. I hardly got to see you yesterday."

"I know. I hope today might be different." The woman wondered if she should tell him or wait for the evidence to show him that his advisor was evil.

"It will be," Carter smiled at her. What a wonderful woman, wanting to spend time with him.

"Actually, that may prove to be quite hard," interjected the grumpy advisor.

"I suppose you're right," Carter sighed as he remembered their earlier conversation. "I am dreadfully sorry, my dear, but there are a few things I will have to take care of throughout the day. I hope you won't mind too much."

"Do you mean welcoming guests? I had hoped we might do that together."

"Actually," he looked at the floor, "I have some people who are going to do that for us. I have to take care of a few last-minute things, but I had hoped you might enjoy the day with your sister."

"I see," sadness laced the woman's voice. "Then I must make the most of the time I am able to spend with you."

"It's not so bad. I'm sure we have plenty of time," Carter reassured her. He was a soft-hearted soul. The woman looked timidly into his eyes, making his heart flutter for a moment.

"Carter, there you are!" boomed the king's voice. "Roland, too! Perfect, I need to speak with you."

The king was dressed in robes similar to the ones that Carter was wearing. However, Cadoc also bore a scarlet cape over his shoulders, along with a magnificent crown of gold, diamonds, and rubies. He matched the woman more perfectly than anyone.

Mathias' knees shook as the king approached. He had never been so close to the man before. Thankfully, it brought him good favor. The king appreciated fright from his people. Carter held tightly to both hands of his woman hoping that his father would go away so they could have the morning together.

"How may we be of assistance?" Roland asked.

Ignoring the advisor the king turned and said, "Good morning, My Lady,"

"Good morning, my liege." She faced the king in return, Carter staying close beside her. She had them all there, but she couldn't get herself to tell the secret. What if she was wrong about her assumptions and she ruined the poor man's life over nothing?

"I must say, you look splendid," Cadoc bellowed back at her while staring at the brilliance of her outfit. "You will make a fine addition to the Royal Family of Remette."

Shock spread over those present. The king never complimented anyone! More so, he was supposed to hate this woman.

Roland couldn't help but despise her. She had not only sided with that wretched White Queen, but now she had stolen the hearts of both Carter and Cadoc. Lead filled the advisor's stomach yet again. Why did he care whom Cadoc admired? A cold sweat overtook the advisor and his hands began shaking mildly. Soon. It would be over soon.

"Why, thank you, my liege. I hope so." She bowed her head in respect.

"Do you mind if I steal my son for a bit?"

"Not at all! I'll tend to my sister. She left to visit with the queen in the gardens. Perhaps I'll meet them there. I hope you have a good day!" She bowed one last time, glancing at Carter to say goodbye, then went on her way.

"What a woman," the king muttered to himself. Carter grimaced at the thought of his father feeling the same way about her as he did. Perhaps they were not so different. "Now, you two, we need to go somewhere private."

The pack of men went to a nearby room. Jasper and Mathias remained outside as Roland locked the door behind them. "What is it, Your Highness?"

"There is a rumor spreading throughout the palace of Sir Roland's efforts to win My Lady's heart."

"What? Oh, my king! I would never!" Roland shrieked, his usual hard exterior shattered by the shock of the accusation. Carter began laughing at the premise.

"My Lady?" he laughed louder still. "Him, care for My Lady?"

"So, it is not true?"

"Father," Carter tried to speak through the laughter, "he cannot stand the woman!"

"My liege, I would never dare betray your house like that!" Roland put his hand to his chest and sank to one knee on the floor. "My first obligation is to this kingdom. I will never betray my loyalty to your family!"

"Word has spread that you were at her chambers late last night."

"What?" asked Carter in shock.

"It's true. I was there, but only to watch over her. She had no protection with her when I found her in the courtyard. She asked to be taken to her room, but not even a servant could be found when we arrived. So, I remained with her until a caretaker came."

"I should have known," cackled Cadoc. "It is so like you, with your 'everyone needs at least one guard at all times' policy. Thankfully, I've been able to shake mine off for the day. Just be sure to put an end to these rumors. It's not good for the public eye, you know."

"Believe me, my king, I will personally see to it," Roland said definitively. He had been but moments from death. Thankfully, this little rumor had solidified the king's trust in him.

"Now that that has been settled," Cadoc turned to his son, "you may go. I have some things I wish to discuss with my advisor."

"Yes, Father," Carter said as he unlocked the door and made his way to the safety of the hall. Slumping against the stone wall, he pouted.

"You wished to speak to me alone?" Roland asked of his king, his palms sweaty with guilt.

"Yes, I did," Cadoc paused. "We haven't had much time to speak to one another since this woman arrived."

"I apologize if I have neglected my duties in any way!"

"No, no," the king chuckled. "You have done well. Your efforts in the matter of this wedding do not go unnoticed. I understand how many additional tasks you've added to your workload in order for everything to be going as smoothly as it is."

"Thank you, Your Majesty." Roland bowed. "What can I help you with?"

"I've been thinking a lot about marriage lately," Cadoc looked at him with care. "You do not have any interest in this noblewoman, do you? You can tell me honestly. I know that even if you did you would not act upon it."

"I have no feelings towards that woman," Roland said in spite. Cadoc cracked a grin. It was obvious what feelings he held. He hadn't seen Roland hold that much contempt since his White Queen.

"This is pleasing to me, but as I was saying. Marriage."

"What of it? I believe everything is in order for tomorrow," the advisor said with a hollow feeling in his chest.

"It is," Cadoc sighed. "I was hoping to speak of your marriage."

"M-my marriage?" Roland was at a loss for words, something that hardly happened to him.

"You say you wish to marry for benefit, correct?"

"That is right, Your Highness." Roland's cheeks grew red. Was he about to get married?

"Have you ever seriously considered the Lady Faigel? I know you have shown her some interest in the past, but time is running out. You are both of age to be wed. Should you wait too long, she might take to other suitors. I spoke with her and her brother last night. It goes without saying; she is the best prize for a wife any nobleman in the country could choose. Should you want her, I could arrange it for you. I leave the decision to you, of course; but if it were me, I'd pick her."

"I trust your judgment, my liege," Roland said without emotion. "I have already thought of her as a potential wife, but you're right. I have never shown serious interest. I shall remedy that immediately."

Cadoc took pride in his advisor. A clever man he was, so much like himself. Patting Roland on the back, he continued his conversation. "Would you like to propose the engagement, or shall I arrange it for you?"

"I will speak with her tomorrow after the wedding," Roland forced a smile. "She might find that romantic."

"Romance is in the air, isn't it? It seems this marriage of Carter's is not as big of a curse as I had feared." While Cadoc proceeded to speak, Roland looked at his feet. A massive curse it would be, when the sun set. "Now, second order of business. It has come to my attention that Carter's fiancé was attacked on her journey here. She assured me it was of no consequence, nonetheless, I will not allow it to pass. I understand no real action can be taken until after the wedding tomorrow, but I want you to get some scouts together shortly thereafter. You must find the thieves who did this."

Roland felt a slight sense of relief. His trickery with the woman had paid off. "It will be done, my king."

"Lastly, I want to be sure everything is moving smoothly for tomorrow. People have started arriving, but I see you have them all accounted for. And Dorian on gift duty, what a great idea! He'll be able to give me the worth of every piece that goes by!"

"Not to worry, everything is in place and on schedule," Roland said, guilt weighing him down with every word.

"Good, good. I'll leave it to you then. End these foolish rumors, no more than the utterances of maids it would seem."

"Yes, my liege," Roland opened the door for him. When the king had left, the others came into the room with him.

"You're not trying to swoon My Lady, are you?" Carter asked with worry on his face.

"Of course not! How could you think that?" Roland desperately tried to fix his predicament. It was a blessing that he had not lost his head simply to rumor alone, but now he lost the trust of his dearest friend, a far worse punishment.

"Well, she's so beautiful and perfect, and I know you have a way with women. So, if you were to go after her, I'm sure you would win her heart better than I could ever hope to. How could you not love a woman as wonderful as she is?" The little prince sat on the floor in defeat.

Perhaps I got so lost in her venomous nature that I didn't see the lovely pattern in her scales, Roland spat in his mind.

"What did we miss?" Jasper asked at the strange conversation, shutting the door for privacy.

"Apparently, some maids have started spreading a rumor that I have been trying to seduce Carter's fiancé," growled Roland through his teeth.

"Oh," thought Jasper.

"Sounds like what Martin-" Mathias butted in, receiving a jab in his side from Jasper. Roland glared at him and Jasper, who had now pinned Mathias against a wall, before returning his attention to his devastated friend.

"Carter, you must know I have no interest in that woman. She is yours. I will never take her from you."

"But you must think she's pretty, right?"

"I've never looked at her in that manner, nor will I ever."

"Really?"

"Yes, really. Now, could you please focus? There is merely half a day until your ascension. You need to push this silly little foreign girl aside and get serious about what needs to happen!"

"Argh, I know!" The prince rubbed his eyes in anguish.

"Little foreign girl," Jasper muttered. "Adelina! I'm supposed to meet her at mid-day! Sorry fellas, I gotta go!" He rushed from the room, slamming the door behind him in his efforts. Roland sank to the floor beside his royal friend, sighing aloud.

"Sh-should I sit too?" asked Mathias from beside the door.

"Why do I even try," Roland groaned, rolling his eyes.

23

The Truth Unveiled

*A*fter quickly discarding his knightly apparel, Jasper made his way to the courtyard where he had said he would meet Adelina. When he arrived, he looked around in fear that she may not be there because he was late. Yet, in the light of the mid-day sun, sat the most beautiful woman he had ever seen.

She was waiting on the edge of the courtyard's water fountain, wearing a pale blue dress that made her seem as if she were of nobility. Her hair laid perfectly against her tan. Jasper looked down at his robes. He was wearing a Remettian guard's gold and red tunic. Hopefully, she liked it.

"Adelina," he called out as he ran to her side, sweat on his brow from his trials. "Sorry I'm late!"

"It's alright, I have not been here long," smiled the girl who had been waiting over half an hour by this time.

"Oh, good! At least we were both late! I'd have felt awful if you were left waiting out here by yourself!"

"I guess it worked out perfectly," she smiled again.

"So, what would you like to do? We probably don't have a lot of time now, do we?"

"My Lady is with her sister for the rest of today, so I may stay with you as long as you would like."

"Great! Then, why don't I take you for a little trip?"

"A trip?"

"Yes, I'll take you to the outer town. Have you visited it yet? It's wonderful! The outer bakery's bread is the triumph of this great city."

"I have not, but I did not bring anything to pay with."

"Please, allow me. It'll be my treat for being so late."

"How long will we be gone?"

"Maybe an hour or two," he picked up her hand. "Maybe longer. I want to show you the sights."

Adelina thought for a moment before replying. "Alright, let's go."

With a grin, Jasper led her out the inner gates and through the various shops and stores surrounding the palace. The two spent the day together, happily visiting all of the best places in the city.

Their journey lasted well into the late afternoon, Jasper cherishing the moments when he held her hand. It seemed to him that he had the true princess beside him, not the maid. When they returned to the king's inner courtyard, Jasper couldn't help but feel sorrowful that he would have to let her go.

"Adelina?" he asked of her, prolonging their return.

"Yes?" she smiled at him.

"Would you like to do this again? Perhaps tomorrow?"

"I would," the maiden grinned, stepping closer to him. "I have had quite a nice time."

"I did too. You are a woman like I've never met before," Jasper smiled, playing with a piece of her luxurious hair. How soft it felt in his hand. "You are the most precious being I have ever encountered."

The maid smiled back at him, unsure of what to say.

In the distance, the woman and her sister were lounging on the woman's balcony. They had been hiding in her room most of the day to avoid the screeching guests.

As they gazed over the golden city, Miriam shouted. *"Adelina! Sissy, look! Adelina is back!"*

The woman sat up in her chair, peering into the courtyard where her sister was pointing. She saw her maiden looking up to the outline of a muscular brunette man. It seemed Adelina was with her courter.

"Yes, I see her, but we shouldn't stare. It's rude to be involved with other people's business," the woman said, returning to her former position. The little girl beside her sunk in her chair.

"So, we had better make this quick!" squeaked the woman as she dashed inside.

"Sissy, where are you going?"

The woman rummaged around her bags for a while before asking. *"Are they still there?"*

"Yeah."

Returning to her sisters' side, the woman extended her hand to give Miriam the item she had found. *"Then, let's have a look!"*

"I met him yesterday. He seemed nice," giggled Miriam as she looked at the pair through her sister's spyglass.

"How did you meet him?"

"They were just leaving when Frank brought me in for bed. I stopped and talked with them for a bit. They seemed very happy together."

The woman snatched the spyglass from her sister's hands. *"If you've already seen him, it's my turn!"*

"Hey!"

"They've moved," the woman said, not paying attention to her sister's anger.

"They are nearer to the right wall now."

"I see them, but the shadow is hiding him. Strapping man, it would seem, though!"

"Yeah, he was really big. Not Frank big, but he looked as strong as some of Daddy's finest." Miriam leaned onto her sister's side.

"Here we go," the woman giggled. *"They're moving. Oh! He's holding her hand! A strong man indeed! Little more, little more."*

The woman jerked upright, only to place her eye to the glass once again as she double-checked herself. Still unable to understand, she asked her sister, never taking her eye from Adelina's date. *"Miriam darling, could you tell me what her courter looked like to you?"*

"I told you. He was really big. He had brown hair and such pretty, sparkly, green eyes. I don't think I'll ever forget them! He was a bit dirty too, but he said that's because he had worked for a long time. Hadn't slept well for days, I guess. He looks a lot cleaner today. He even trimmed his beard from what I saw. It looks way better!"

Could it be him? The thief from the woods? The man the advisor kept sneaking out to see had somehow snuck himself in here. Sir Roland and his tricks were becoming more and more dangerous.

Why was he here now? Why this sudden interest in Adelina? He had been at the bar when Roland went out the other night, had he not? But when he returned, this guard was placed in front of her door. How many more of those men could there be stationed throughout the castle?

"Sissy? Are you okay?"

"I'm fine. I'm simply curious." The woman looked out to the man again as he laughed with her pure maiden. What could she do to help? They were almost back. When Adelina got in, she would confirm what was going on. Then she would act.

Jasper walked his maiden to her mistress' door. Trying to be quiet so the woman would not spot him, he whispered. "Have a good evening, Addie. Can't wait until tomorrow."

"Nor I," she smiled at him. "Good night, Jasper."

Kissing the hand he held, he drew near to her. "Good night."

"Night!" squeaked Adelina while leaning against My Lady's door. With one last smile, Jasper left to return to his guard station beside the prince. The maid sighed in excitement which then turned into a gasp as she was dragged into her mistress' room.

"Agh," she gasped as she balanced herself. *"My Lady! What are you doing?"*

"Who was that?" the woman asked her with worry on her face.

"What are you talking about, Sissy? That was the man she went on a date with. We were just watching them in the courtyard."

263

"*You were what?*" the maid yelled angrily.

"*Yes, we were looking, but with good reason,*" the woman said tentatively. "*Tell me, what do you know of that man?*"

"*I can't believe you were watching me!*"

"*Adelina, tell me. What has he said of himself?*"

"*Why should I tell you?*" Adelina snapped in reply.

"*Because that man! That is the man who robbed me on my way to the palace!*"

"*No, it can't be. He–he is Prince Carter's personal guard,*" the maiden babbled.

"*He's what?*" the woman shrieked. "*I have to go! I have to go right now!*"

"*Where are you going?*"

"*To find Carter and this guard. I'm going to put an end to this once and for all!*"

"*My Lady, wait!*"

"*Take care of Miriam for me, would you?*" The woman left her maid and her sister behind. As she walked from her door, two of her guards appeared from the shadows, following her on her journey. Inside her room, Miriam did her best to console the heartbroken maid.

Carter and his advisor had gone to Roland's quarters. There, they had spent the day reviewing the plan repeatedly to ensure it played out correctly. The woman knocked on the advisor's door once she had found them. To onlookers, her actions would solidify the claims of their affair, but such thoughts bothered her little as she addressed the issue at hand.

Roland came to the door, shock on his face when he saw who stood there. Without saying a word, the woman and her guards made their way into his room. When she entered, Carter jumped up from where he had been sitting, shuffling his plans out of view.

"What are you doing here, my dear?" Why would she come to Roland's room? Maybe the rumors weren't so far-fetched. Perhaps My Lady was trying to be with Roland, but he kept her at bay because of his loyalty to the royal family.

"Yes, I'd like to know what this intrusion is all about," Roland snarled from behind her.

"Where are your guards, prince?" she answered their questions with one of her own.

"Uh, he's right here." Carter felt nervous but happy. She did want him to have guards too!

"I thought you had two?"

"Well, I do," Carter tried to explain as Roland's door opened again, Jasper coming in adorning his full guard uniform.

"Sorry fellas, that took a bit longer than expected, but well worth it, if I may say so," Jasper hummed cheerily as he walked into the deathtrap.

"You!" The woman turned to him.

Roland's heart caught in his throat. What was happening?

Jasper was frozen at the door, standing still as she casually walked within a few inches of him. His heart was beating so hard his chest hurt. On instinct, he looked down at his feet to evade her gaze.

The woman tilted her head and looked up at him, making Jasper feel as if they were back in the forest. She drew even closer, examining the face behind the helmet.

"My Lady," Roland called out, but it was too late. She had removed his helmet. With wide eyes, Jasper stared at her, still saying nothing. Behind her, her guards drew their weapons. They must have been in the caravan with her.

"Ladrón," one called out. The woman raised a hand, her men sheathing their weapons without hesitation. No one else in the room had the audacity to draw out their swords. Instead, they watched with still hearts as their lives flashed before their eyes.

"Thief," the woman repeated in a voice like ice. The ruffian gulped. That was a gaze he had hoped to forget. "It seems I now know your name, Jasper."

"My dear?" Carter called for her. This was a side of the woman he had never seen before; strong, brave, intelligent . . . and scary.

Even though she had become terrifying to him, his love for her was solidified because she had shown him her true self. A self far more beautiful to him than the shell she had been showing.

"Dear prince, I come with news," she said, returning her attention to him. Jasper was still frozen, where she had left him. Roland was also in a quiet, fearful state. "That guard is one of the men who attacked me during my journey here. I have spoken with the advisor earlier about this attack, and he assured me that it was a test set up by your father to deter me from completing this union. After having spoken with your father, the King, I have found this to be a lie."

With a quick glance around the room she continued, "I can only further assume that this man, Jasper, does not have valid credentials to be on your personal guard as he was assisted in breaking into this palace two days ago. Assisted by your advisor. I am unsure how many of the renegades who overtook me have been helped to infiltrate your staff, but I would assume the worst and say all of them. In fact, if I were to guess, that man beside you is also one of them."

She snapped her fingers, and her guards removed Mathias' helmet as she had done to Jasper. The whole company was shocked by her incredibly correct assumptions. "Indeed, he is. I fear that the advisor and these men would soon try to overtake you and your father, possibly using our wedding as a focus point to create more malleable circumstances to achieve their goals. I understand if you wish to double-check these things on your own, but I would feel much safer if they were at least placed under arrest for the time being."

What was he to do? Roland and Jasper could do nothing in this situation as they were the accused, so it was up to Carter to save them. But how? How could he save them? She knew the truth. The only thing she missed was that Carter also deserved to be on the chopping block. "Did you tell my father of this?"

"No, I came to find you for fear that you were unsafe. He had no guard this morning, yet you had these three."

The prince gave a slight smile. She was so perfect and caring. As long as she told no one else of these things, it would be alright. To just knock her out would be impossible to do quietly enough with her guards there as well. How could he strike the woman he loved? Carter realized why he had thought about what he did. To strike her down would be far more kind than what he was about to do.

"I'm glad you didn't, but honestly, I was hoping not to have this discussion," Carter replied, his voice deepened like the one used by his father. It was a harsh tone, cold, and unyielding. Never in his life had he wanted to use such a voice, but he had to do it. Roland had been right. The mission needed to come first. So, if this woman, this elegant woman, got in his way, he would crush her like any other opponent. That is what the advisor would do, what a king should do.

"Carter," Roland said with concern.

"You figured it all out, didn't you?" he continued, shivering slightly in pain as he said such evil things. The woman saw it as trembles of anger coming from him. "I'll tell you the truth, My Lady, though Roland tried to cover for me earlier. It was not my father who sent these men to attack you. It was me."

"What?" Her voice cracked as she said the word.

"You must know, when I asked your father for your hand, I never actually thought of you. I had never met you. It was a trade deal, no more, no less. I needed money; your father had money. All I had to do to take it was to take you. So, that's what I did." Carter forced himself to look at her in the eyes as he said it to make it seem more sincere, but it grew harder and harder to continue each second. She would undoubtably be left broken by the horrible things he was saying to her.

"When this wedding came about, I wasn't ready. I grew uneasy; but still, I needed the money. I came up with the heist scheme in order to give myself some leeway. I set up a little accident for you. When the men attacked and stole everything you had, I assumed that you would either finish your journey here, or you would return home devastated. In which case, I would send some presents and a letter showing my concern for your wellbeing."

Roland recognized Carter's words. They were his! When they developed the plan to free the country, he had given the same speech concerning the woman. How much those harsh words must be cutting into her.

"You would never want to come here again, and I would be free of you. If you ever actually did decide to come back, your father would most likely send twice the amount of revenue. Win, win, win. In the case, such as it happened, that you did show up at my door, I would go through with the deal and accept you."

"As for these men, they are mine. They stayed outside of the city for additional time, under my instructions. The first day they waited to see if I still wanted rid of you. If I had chosen such an option, they would have taken you in Morer, where they were stationed. Before they returned to my side, they went to collect a package for me." Carter clenched his hands as he looked at his bride. She would undoubtedly leave him now.

The woman stood quietly as the young prince shared his disgust for her, the others in the room unable to do anything but sit back and watch. She had known it was a lie. How could he have been as nice as he was pretending to be? But then again, what could she do about it?

"Please leave," she said to her guards as she waivered under her depression. They obeyed, exiting to the hall outside. Her order brought a pause to Carter's rant.

The woman collected herself before she spoke to her fiancé. "If you think this comes as a shock to me, please don't. I have always known what my purpose in life was to be. This wasn't the only offer given to my father, but he favored you above all others. I will respect his wishes as you have also agreed to do. If you choose to honor your deal, I will do my best to please you in the future. So, if it's more money you want, I can get more for you."

In a steely tone that did a fair job of covering most of the hurt in her voice, the woman continued, but a lone tear ran down her cheek without her consent. "I had heard of your family's reputation before and was aware that something like this might happen. I can only say that I am thankful you have thus far decided to accept me. I understand how impeding an arrangement such as this might feel. If you no longer want me, I will return to my father forth-with, and you may keep the bounties given to you as collateral for my unworthiness."

The young prince broke from the shame he felt. This wonderful woman! Having been crushed under such evil, she still offered him the world! She only ever hoped to please others. He walked towards her, praying he could win her back again. "You know... when you arrived here, you were so different from what I had imagined. I was taken aback by how beautiful and graceful you are. In the time we have shared, I have honestly fallen for you. The terrible things I have put you through, you deserved none of them. I simply don't want these men to also suffer because of me."

"I see," the woman said softly, now unsure of what to think.

"My Lady, I want nothing more than to accept you as you are. I only hope that you can accept me for who I am."

"I can," she said, wiping the tear away. Carter took her into his arms. Her petite body felt so delicate to the touch. He had missed holding her.

"I am so sorry," he whispered to her. Paying no attention to the others in the room, she stayed in his embrace, clinging tightly to him. Thankfulness filled her heart that even if he had agreed to marry her for the wrong reason, it now seemed he actually did care for her.

Roland and the rest of the crew quietly left them where they were. All three of the men silently praising Carter for the rescue. It had been a bit harsh, but it seemed to work out well.

Carter stroked his fiancé's back gently as he held her. The tears had seemed to stop, both slowly breathing as if they might fall asleep holding one another. Carter couldn't help but wonder if she had remained true to him after hearing of his first evil, would she also forgive him for the next? How much he hoped that she would.

"My Lady?" Carter whispered to her. She lifted her head from his chest in response. "Remember what I said about Jasper getting something for me?"

"Yes."

"Come with me. I want to show it to you."

"Alright."

The two left. She held to his arm as she had done in the past, but now she held him much tighter as she feared to let him go. When they entered the prince's quarters, the woman gazed around her. It was a lovely suite. Everything was covered in dark scarlet cloth. Wherever she looked, more weapons could be found. He hadn't been kidding when he said he liked combat sports.

"I've got it!" Carter came to her, proudly holding a small cedar chest in his hand. "It is for you, my dear. A token to show my affection for you, as well as my hope for our future together!"

The woman grasped the box with a smile on her face. Perhaps he had not been faking but had truly been this kind man all along. She smiled as she played with the bow of the package.

"But, don't open it yet."

"Why not?" she pouted.

"I want you to wait. Tomorrow, when you get wedding jitters, then open it. Then you will know that I love you!" Carter placed his hands on the woman's shoulders, looking deep into her heart with his kind, brown eyes.

The woman held to the box as if it contained her soul. Did he love her? Perhaps it was the overflowing emotions from their recent bantering, but as her heart pitter-pattered in her chest, she could only think of one thing to say. "As I love you, my dearest prince."

Carter smiled widely as his cheeks grew red. "Shall I take you back to your room now?"

"Very well," the woman sighed. "I will miss you."

"As I will you," Carter chuckled nervously, opening the door. "Come on."

The woman followed him to the hall. As Carter walked her back to her room, she took his hand, lacing her fingers through his. With her leaning into him, the prince felt a sense of happiness he had never felt before. He didn't want to leave her, but he had to get back to the group. It wouldn't be long now.

After returning his fiancé to her room, Carter made his way to the advisor's quarters. When he arrived, he was met by his friends. All of them prepared to fight alongside him as he sought to free his people from enslavement. What a blessed life he had, to have such wonderful people beside him.

"Are we ready?" he asked.

"Everything is in place," Roland said. "We head out soon."

"Good."

"And how about you? How did things end with that woman? I need you at full capacity, can't have you worrying about her."

"Oh, no! She's wonderful! I'm ready to spend the rest of my life with her. She is the perfect woman."

"Perfect? Ba-ha," Martin laughed in the background.

"What are you laughing at?" the prince asked in puzzlement. She was perfect!

"Tell me, wha' is with tha' weird veil thing she wears all the time? You gotta admit tha's kinda freaky."

"She wears it to conceal her identity from the public until after the ceremony tomorrow. Otherwise, people may target her family or even her as a last-minute effort to sway her decision to marry me. I find it endearing that she would go to such lengths to ensure her decision was not altered. Furthermore, it represents her purity to me, as I am the only one to know who she is. I am the only one found to be worthy of her."

"Yeah, I didn't get half o' tha', but it don't matter. Have you seen her face?"

"Well, no, but she is hiding her identity until we are married."

"Don't you know who she is?"

"Of course!"

"Then why wouldn't she at least let you see her face? You're the poor slob who has to marry her! So, why wouldn't she at least be decent enough to show you what you're gettin'? I'll tell you why!"

"Martin," Roland interjected. This was not helpful.

"She won't show you her face 'cause she's ugly, tha's why!"

"Quit!" Roland smacked the man over the head, but it was too late. The damage was inflicted.

"Ugly," Carter muttered to himself. "You-you're right! That's gotta be it!"

"You bet I am! Lass has messed up teeth, or a freakish mole, or somethin'!" Martin rubbed his head in victory. Got him!

"Carter, focus," Roland pleaded as the prince rolled his tongue in his mouth.

"Messed up teeth. Freakish mole. I-I have to go," he said in terror as he ran from the room.

"Look what you've done!" Roland roared to his men. "We take down the king within the hour, and he is chasing ugly women! Have I not told you how easily he becomes distracted?"

Martin howled in laughter. "Can't believe the lad would actually do it! Can you see the look on tha' woman's face when he runs in there and asks if she's ugly?"

The rest of the men joined in the laughter, all but the advisor. "All right, the games are over. To your stations!"

Disappointment sounded from them as they grudgingly went to the halls. Joining into the guard patrol routes during the shift change, the men began their mission to free the kingdom. Teams went from door to door, locking in the guests who had retired to their chambers. When questioned about this, they provided a signed order by Roland himself that stated the need for such measures.

Meanwhile, Carter arrived at My Lady's door, huffing from his recent sprint. He banged against it frantically. Adelina opened it for him, bowing as she saw who was there.

"Is My Lady here?" begged the prince.

"Is that you, Prince?" The woman came, her white veil covering her face. She was wrapped in a scarlet robe, the outlines of her white nightdress seen where the folds of her robe met. It seemed she had been preparing for bed.

Carter's cheeks grew hot. This was an indecent hour for him to barge in on her. With a gulp, he asked. "May I come in?"

"But of course," the woman granted him access. He entered, nervously twisting his hands around one another. How could he ask this without calling her ugly?

"It seems you missed me as much as I missed you," she said, her cheeks rising in a smile.

"I-I did," Carter stated, noticing the maid standing nearby. "Is your sister here?"

"No, she is in her room."

"Could you have her go away for just a moment," he nodded towards the maiden.

"Uh, sure. Adelina dear?" The maid bowed and left the room. The woman looked back to her betrothed, waiting for him to get to the point of his visit.

"My dear, of everyone here, I am the only one who knows who you are."

"Yes," she giggled. "What of it?"

"What I mean to say is, if I know you. Uh." He scratched his head in frustration. "Why do you hide yourself from me?"

The woman turned red. "What is it? Do you fear I am ugly?"

"No, no!" the prince stuttered.

"Are you sure?" She questioned, him merely gulping in response. "Rest assured, dear prince, you have nothing to fear."

She walked past him to a nearby table. She kept her back to him as she took off her veil and placed it to the side. "I will show you my face if you wish to see it. Be aware; this is as scary for me as it is for you. Perhaps even scarier, as I will be the one you find hideous."

With a deep breath, she said. "Ready?"

"Mhm," Carter whimpered as he was not ready.

"Okay," she tensed up. "No, I can't. There's too much pressure."

"Oh, come on!" Carter begged.

"Close your eyes."

"What?"

"Just close your eyes, please," she said.

Carter did as he was asked. "Okay, they're closed."

"Alright," the woman said softly. "You can open them."

Carter did so, and what he saw before him was no less than an angel. Her veil hiding the last piece of the puzzle. Making this beautiful being seem human when, in reality, she was a far more superior breed.

"You are the most beautiful woman I have ever seen," Carter said with love in his voice. She was intoxicating. He could restrain himself no longer. He approached her with one thought in his mind. As he held to her arms, he asked. "May I steal a kiss from you, my beautiful bride?"

The woman giggled, her smile making him crave her lips all the more. At first, she backed away.

"A gift for a gift, my dear!" she said, in reference to the cedar chest he had given her. Then placing her arms around his neck, she smiled at him. "This way, when you are nervous about the wedding tomorrow, you may dream of these lips of mine. Then, when you finally do get to kiss them, there will be no doubt of my love for you."

He put his hands on her waist, leaning into her. "I take it back. Why don't you open your gift now?"

"Okay!" she said happily as she evaded his lips again. She picked up her box and looked at him for reassurance, but then again, how could he not let such an angel have the gift he gave.

"Go on, open it."

She opened it with excitement, carefully pulling the ribbon from the box. As she lifted the lid, the woman let out a gasp. "Oh, Carter, it's wonderful! Could you help me put it on?"

"Gladly," he smiled, taking the box from her and lifting out a delicate bracelet. It was a simple design but preposterously beautiful. The straps were made of darkened leather. From them came an overlay of silver that seemed to twirl around itself. In the center of the bracelet stood two symbols that were hooked together. One was his mighty dragon sigil, and the other an elegant pine tree to represent her home country of Poniere.

Placing the bracelet on her wrist, he brought her hand to his chest. Pulling her close with his other, he loomed over her with a lovestruck look in his eye. "And, what of my present, My Lady."

"I told you, you may have it tomorrow," she smiled, poking his nose with her finger. He grinned for a second, entranced until he realized what she had said.

"You mean?"

"Are you saying you only let me have this so that you might steal a kiss from me," she smiled at her new bracelet.

"Uh," Carter tried to make an excuse. His efforts were spared by a harsh knock that came from the woman's front door.

"I wonder who that could be," the woman said absentmindedly.

"Isn't it obvious? The knock is as grouchy as it's master," Carter chuckled, the woman laughing with him. "I suppose that is my beckoning. I shall miss you. The morning could not come soon enough!"

She laughed, pulling him into a hug. "No, it cannot!"

Another knock came from her door, the dull thud growing in wrath. Carter knew he must go, but he did not want to!

"I would hate to leave you, dear, but I must go now." He kissed her hands. "See your beautiful face in the morning!"

"Good night," the woman giggled in glee.

Carter waved goodbye as he closed the door, the icy stare of his advisor ebbing his happiness from him, little by little. "What took you so long? We're behind schedule because of you and that woman!"

"Sorry I got carried away, but she is so beautiful! Like an angel, and she's all mine!" Carter melted yet again. Roland rolled his eyes at the proclamation, locking her door with his key. She, of all people, could not be let out!

"Shall we go see your father, my liege?"

"Yes, let's go," he hummed, still in a daze.

"Carter, please focus," his advisor sighed.

Battle of the Mind

$\mathfrak{N}$ ot long after the prince and his advisor left My Lady's room, Martin and his group of guards traveled up the hallway to her door. The ruffians locked every room, as they had been instructed. Little did they know that they had accidentally unlocked My Lady's door.

Much to their dismay, the prince's fiancé had placed two of her own men outside of her suite. The Ponierians thought it strange that these guards should lock the doors today if they had not done so in the days before. Holding out their arms, they stopped Martin on his way back to his group. The thief's heart dropped to his stomach. "There a problem, lads?"

Saying something he did not understand, the Ponierians pointed to their mistress' door. Martin held up his orders from Roland. "Look mates, advisor's orders."

"Is there a problem?" asked one of Cadoc's men from the patrol unit.

"These lads don't seem to understand tha' I have orders to lock this door."

Cadoc's guard took over the situation, commanding the Ponierians as if they were Remettian serfs. "Back away from the door! All members, guests, and foreigners are to remain in restricted zones until tomorrow morning. This does not exclude any member of the royal family."

The Ponierian guards did not react well to his undermining tone. They instead placed their hands on their swords, ready to draw if they were told to leave their mistress in her imprisonment.

"Do not threaten me!" barked the guard as he raised a hand. Besides the three thieves, all in the platoon withdrew their weapons from their sheaths at his command. In response, the Ponierians prepared to defend themselves, their swords extended before them. "Put your weapons down!"

"What is going on out here?" asked the woman as she opened her door. Martin felt a sense of dread. Had he been unlocking the doors this whole time? How did she get out? The Ponierians responded to her in their tongue. Turning to Martin and the rest of the guards, she continued. "Let me see what it is the advisor has given you."

"Ah," Martin gulped as he handed her the letter. This wasn't part of the plan! What was he supposed to do?

Reading the order carefully, the woman chuckled. "This means nothing. Are you certain the advisor gave you this with the direction of the king?"

"Yes, my lady," Martin lied. "Which is why you must return to your room and be subject to the lockdown."

"I refuse," she said, crossing her arms.

"You can't do that!" the angry guard gasped. "It is an order from the king's advisor!"

"And I am to be the king's daughter-in-law, am I not? I will do as I wish, and I do not wish to be trapped in my quarters today or any other day!"

"Listen, my lady," Martin sighed. "I'd hate to make you do somethin' you don't like, but I'm afraid we have to lock this door."

"You will do no such thing!" the angry guard snapped, now siding with his princess. "She is allowed to remain how she is."

"Thank you," smiled the prince's bride.

"'Fraid not." Martin drew his sword from his side, the others of his gang doing the same. "Of all the people who are allowed to wander about, you will not be one of them!"

"Put your weapon down!" the angry guard commanded him. What an irritating person, Martin thought.

"Get in your room, lassie!" Martin demanded as he pointed angrily towards her door.

"You can't address me like that!" she spat, her men standing between her and Martin.

"Plan B," Martin sighed. For Carter's sake, she needed to be locked out of harm's way. "Lads, let's put this hall to sleep!"

His partners chuckled to themselves as they turned on their fellow guards. Martin himself taking on the two Ponierians.

"Adelina!" the woman shrieked behind them. As her guards kept Martin preoccupied, the woman and her maiden freed themselves from the room. Around them, the hall was in an uproar. The guards were attacking one another, killing each other without cause! The women didn't know where to turn, so they did what was to be expected. *"We need to get my sister!"*

Meanwhile, Martin fought relentlessly against the Ponierian guards. They left him no choice! "I'm sorry, lads."

He thrust the blade of his sword through one of them. The other screamed out as he tried to save his friend. Pulling his sword from the belly of the first, Martin caught the blade of the second before it could harm him. The Ponierian had a curved sword, making it harder for Martin to hold his grip against it.

The guard knocked the thief's blade from his hand. In terror, Martin took up the dead man's sword. He struck fervently against his opponent, slicing open the man's throat. New weapon in hand, Martin trudged towards the battle against the king's guard. Cadoc's guards had barely been overcome by the ruffian crew when he joined in. One man left the fight, running away as he shouted. "Sound the alarm!"

"Dan, go help Gad with the alarm," Martin spat as he assumed the role of leader. "Asher, you have these guards, don't you?"

"Yes, sir," the ruffian answered, turning to his next opponent.

"Then I'm going after those women," Martin replied, clutching the key in one hand as he ran after the woman and her maiden.

Dan ran at top speed to catch the guard that had run away. By the time he finally silenced him, the damage had been done. Guests started coming out of the rooms they hadn't had a chance to lock. All eyes set on the traitorous ruffian, though no one tried to stop him as he sprinted off to the guard tower where Gad was watching over the alarm. During his journey there, he dismantled as many of his enemies as he could.

The guards went into a panic. The call to raise the alarm could be heard throughout the palace and its grounds, but the alarm did not sound. In a tower to the palace's east side, Gad stood between the guards and the alarm. It was a small room, but it remained well-lit due to oil lamps and torches that encased the walls. The room had been designed so none could evade the tower guard to raise the alarm falsely.

Huffing after his sprint, Dan took to his partner's side. Guard after guard followed him to smite the pair of traitors so that they could warn their fellows of the uprising. The two fought valiantly beside each other until a fatal blow from one of Cadoc's men struck Dan down. Gad looked at his partner, whose eyes remained open even after death. He knew he had not long for the world either.

"For the true king!" Gad yelled as he raced to the alarm bell. Picking up an oil lamp, he thrust it against the beam that held the alarm in place. Within seconds, the palace guards surrounded him. They took all of the weapons from the traitor, and forced him onto the ground. Having secured the area, the men tried to approach the now burning alarm. Before they could put the fire out, the timber gave way, and the bell fell from its perch. One clamorous ring went out as it crashed down onto the stone floor.

The guard holding Gad raised his sword to run him through. A shout from another granted the thief deliverance. "Stop! We need him alive for questioning."

The young ruffian let out a thankful sigh. As they dragged him from the room, he looked one last time to his companion. Hopefully, the others were alright.

While their traitors were trying to protect the alarm, Carter and his crew reached the king's door. Screams and shouts of treason could be heard from guards and guests alike. Throughout the hall, the wedding guests slammed harshly against their prison doors.

Every second that passed made the advisor grow more anxious. This was not going according to plan in the slightest!

From inside the king's room, shouting could be heard as he banged against his door. "Let me out! Let me out this instant! What is going on out there? Is anyone listening to me?"

"My liege," Roland called out. He would have to improvise. "Are you alright?"

"Roland," Cadoc gasped in relief. "Was it you who locked this door? Come! Let me out!"

"No, my liege, I did not lock the door," the advisor replied as he slowly unlocked it.

The king had become calm, now that he was no longer trapped. He opened the door as he said. "Then someone else must have locked it."

Roland backed away, allowing Jasper and Mathias to draw their swords against the king. The man babbled on, unknowingly. "What is going on out here?"

Cadoc's eyes grew wide at the blades that had placed themselves at his neck. The king wore nothing more than an evening robe, white hairs protruding from his flabby chest. His crown sat lopsided on his head. The miscreants couldn't help but chuckle. What an arrogant man to have worn his crown to sleep! Forcing him back into his room, they made the king sit upon the side of his bed. Cadoc's cheeks turned red with fury. "What is this?"

The advisor entered the room, leaving Carter in the hall for his safety. "It is an uprising, Cadoc."

The king's face showed nothing but shock as his advisor betrayed him. Roland had used his name specifically to degrade him. Still, Cadoc could see the pain in Roland's eyes. This seemed to be hurting the advisor as much as it hurt him. Ignoring the two men whose swords were at his throat, the king spoke to his advisor. His only hope of survival was to manipulate his advisor to join his side. "How could you do this to me?"

"Because you're evil, that's why," growled Jasper, who was at his right side.

Cadoc never lifted his eyes from Roland as he sat there. The advisor clutched to his stomach as he looked at his feet, unable to answer the question. Why did he feel such guilt?

"Roland," the king said softly. "Have I not given you everything?"

"Shut it," Jasper snapped.

Cadoc paid him no mind. "Throughout your life, have I not provided for you? Tell me, to whom else did I give such attention?"

The advisor looked up with regret in his eyes. Growing up under Cadoc's influence, Roland had not realized just how much he had gained from his king. No other time had the king personally helped a noble learn how to run their estate. He thought it was simply because he had been young at the time and needed guidance to do so properly, but Cadoc had taken it as a chance to benefit the boy he had come to care for.

When the Great War started the king tried to make provisions for Roland to remain in Morer, but the young man took it upon himself to join the army. During the Great War, Cadoc provided Roland's men with better provisions. Afterward, the king had given him one of the highest-ranking positions within the country. Cadoc wasn't a good man, but he had always been kind to his advisor.

Roland felt ripped between two sides as he replied. "No one."

His fellow traitors looked nervously at him. What was he saying? Cadoc sighed on the bed. "Then, why? Why would you do this?"

"I-" Roland's voice betrayed him; he couldn't utter a word. As his prince brushed past him into the room, he looked again to his feet in shame.

"He did it because he is loyal to me, Father," Carter began in a cold tone. "Not to you. He has not done what you wanted all these years, but what I have required of him. This should not come as much of a shock to you. You have known all along how much we despise you."

Cadoc spoke to him again, the pain in Roland's chest growing with each word. The king's voice did not sound angry but sorrowful. "Is this true, Roland? Do you despise me?"

Sweat overcame Roland's brow. He had begun to feel feverish. The advisor couldn't look at him. "We should hurry. Our timetable has shortened exponentially."

"Alright," Carter said to him. Why didn't Roland seem pleased? "Come along, Father. We are to take you to your new home in the dungeons. I have the perfect cell for you too! The one you had placed me in after my engagement."

Cadoc stayed where he was, trying one last time to regain his advisor. He could not forgive him of such an atrocity as this, but he could make Roland believe he would. Thankfully, the advisor's judgment was being weakened by the second due to the king's influence. Perhaps he held the same weakness when it came to Cadoc as he had always had for Carter. It seemed he had loved Cadoc after all. "Roland."

The advisor gulped nervously as his king spoke to him. "I have given you lands, riches, titles, and glory. Is this all you will give to me?"

Roland opened his mouth to speak, but no air filled his lungs. From another room in the king's quarters, Zisca emerged in a robe similar to the king's. "Carter?"

"Mother," the young prince blurted. She was supposed to be locked in her quarters for her safety! "Why are you in my father's room?"

The queen ignored the question as she spoke to her son. "Is it true? This overtaking of your father?"

"Yes."

She smiled brightly as she said. "Then take him quickly, and keep him from his advisor!"

"Why? Roland is on our side!"

The advisor clenched his hands into fists. He was on their side! No matter what the king had done for him, ridding his influence from the kingdom was a necessary evil.

Cadoc spoke again. "Roland, please. I would have given you my kingdom had you only asked. This...this isn't right. You must see that."

Roland looked at him sorrowfully. "I am sorry, my king."

Jasper and Mathias turned to Roland in worry. Was he going to attack them? While they were distracted, Cadoc ripped Jasper's sword from his hand. Swiftly killing Mathias, he rammed his elbow into Jasper's face during his recoil. "Not sorry enough."

Cadoc swung his sword downward at Roland, who caught the blade easily with his own. The two became interlocked within each other's grips. Thrusting his advisor into a nearby wall, the king sprinted into the hallway. Carter chased after him, drawing out his sword as he ordered. "Jasper, stay here with my mother!"

"I'm sorry, Carter," Roland said sadly as the prince passed by into the hall.

"It's alright. We just need to catch him," the prince replied as he raced after his father. Roland quietly followed behind him.

Hostile Takeover

By this time, the prince's fiancé and her handmaiden had reached Miriam's door. Behind them, they could hear Martin calling out. "Oi, ladies! Where have you gone off to?"

"Miriam darling, wake up!" the woman said in panic, shaking the handle of the door. She had been locked in!

"Sissy?" came a sleepy reply, only to turn fearful. *"Sissy! I can't open the door!"*

What could she do? She wasn't strong enough to break down the door! Then, she remembered. The guard had been holding a key in his hand! "Adelina, you stay here. I'll be right back!"

Leaving her handmaiden in the middle of the hall, Carter's fiancé took down a nearby Remettian flagpole. She twisted the scarlet flag around the metal so it would be easier to swing. Then, she hid behind a pillar with her weapon, ready to strike.

"There you are! 'Bout time you gave up," huffed her attacker. The prince's bride waited until she caught view of his head to swing her patriotic weapon. Clang! She hit him near his forehead, the man crashing backward onto the floor. Dropping her flag, she quickly took the key from his hand. The woman raced to her sister's door and hurriedly unlocked it. Picking up the girl, she ran with the key still in her grasp.

The group of women made their way to the first floor. Around them were scattered carcasses of dead palace guards. Other guards sped past without care, making for the dungeons as they spoke to one another. "This is the work of Sir Roland. It would be best to wait it out."

"Yeah," huffed another. "Never cared much for those royals anyhow."

"Better them than us," shivered another.

The woman was disgusted. They called her people weak! At least they had the courage to stand against the Beast of Morer! It would seem the battle was already won. When the palace guards learned it was Roland they faced against, they hid in the shadows. She would have to defend herself. Her chest felt empty as she looked at the bracelet on her arm. She would need to find Carter too. She couldn't let the advisor hurt him.

As she raced on to complete her mission, shouts could be heard coming from behind locked doors. The prince's fiancé went past most of them without a glance. Reaching her destination, she unlocked a door. *"Frank! I am being attacked!"*

"Oi!" came an angry scream from behind them. "Tha' hurt, lassie!"

Without a weapon, Frank made his way past the three girls. When Martin saw the giant the prince's bride had released, he stopped in his tracks. "You have got to be kiddin' me!"

All it took was one hit and Martin crashed onto the floor in a heap of metal. Frank picked up the thief's stolen sword, preparing to run him through. A frightened squeak came from Miriam as she watched. She had never experienced such a horrible thing. Seeing her sister's distress, the woman stopped him. *"Frank, just put him in your room and lock the door for now."*

The guard did so, tossing him onto the floor of his room. When the door had been locked, Frank turned back to his mistress. *"We must get you out of here before any more of these Remettians try to harm you."*

Placing her sister back onto the ground, the woman said softly. *"I cannot go. I want you to ensure that Miriam and Adelina get out safely."*

"You must go as well," Frank demanded.

"This is my home now. These people are my family. I will not leave them."

"I won't leave you," Miriam cried into her side.

"Darling, you must," the woman replied. *"I will find you soon. I promise."*

"I will remain here with you," Frank stated. *"I wish to fight this battle alongside you."*

"What of Miriam?"

"Send her with some of the other men. They can protect her as well as I can."

With a nod of agreement, the woman unlocked the door to the right of Frank's room. Two men came from it. After receiving their orders, they departed with the girl and the handmaiden. Frank and the woman did not stop as they unlocked all the doors of the Ponierian guards. Soon, the small army marched around the grounds, seeking whom they might destroy.

As far as the king was concerned, the palace was empty. The only people to be found were the dead, who still littered the grounds. All others fled for their lives. The guests whose rooms were not locked returned inside and pretended they were. What utter fools! Were there no useful people in the entire realm? Huffing with exhaustion, Cadoc saw hope in the corner of his eye. With a quick turn, he ran after his saving grace. "My Lady!"

"Your Highness!" she gasped as she saw him, leaving her place by her bodyguard. He must have been attacked himself. His blade was bloodied from the poor fool that had tried to harm him. "Are you alright? What happened?"

Cadoc smiled slightly to himself. The woman didn't know what her fiancé had tried to do. "I was attacked in my chambers!"

"Are you hurt?" the woman asked with concern as she looked him over like a mother whose child had fallen. Seeing that he was unharmed, she told him her theory. "I don't mean to sound judgmental, my liege, but I think this is the work of your advisor! Men came to my door tonight, hoping to lock me in my quarters. Their instructions signed and sealed by Sir Roland himself!"

"I believe you," Cadoc said. "It was Roland who attacked me."

"Is he dead?"

"Not yet," Cadoc gasped for air. He hadn't run like that in years! "I have been trying to find aid, but all my guards seem to be traitors."

"You may have my men," the woman replied earnestly. "I trust you will better know how we should counterattack."

"Thank you, My Lady," the king grinned. This would be easier than he thought. She trusted him completely. "How is it they are free?"

She handed him the key she had taken from Martin. "The man Sir Roland sent after me had this key to lock my door. It apparently locks and unlocks all rooms within this palace in a way which cannot be undone from inside."

"Indeed, it does," Cadoc said as he took it from her. "I have a man I believe I can trust. We should free him as well."

"Of course," she replied, looking to her feet. The woman played nervously with her bracelet, a single tear running down her face as she thought the worst. "Your Majesty?"

"Yes?"

"Have you heard from Prince Carter?" the woman asked in a shaky voice. "I know how much he adores his advisor. I fear he would have been too easy of a target for the man."

"Try not to worry," the king consoled emptily, "my son still lives."

She clutched to her chest, smiling thankfully. Cadoc rolled his eyes as he walked away. He would kill them all once he had what he needed. The king released Dorian and told him what was happening. With his new forces at hand, he was ready to strike against his enemy.

Meanwhile, Jasper tended to the queen in Cadoc's quarters. Peering from the room's balcony, he saw a terrifying sight. Adelina was preparing to enter a carriage. He couldn't let her leave! "My queen, please stay here. I'll be right back. Do not leave this room, do you understand me?"

"Yes," the queen replied. With that, Jasper raced from the room to stop Adelina from leaving him. When he was gone, Zisca quietly slipped into the hallway. She took one of Cadoc's swords with her. It was heavy, but she thought it would be the best weapon to use if someone tried to stop her from leaving. Cadoc had known she was in his room; he might come back for her.

The queen crept down the halls as she made her getaway. It was not long before she came across carcasses of palace guards. The smell of death clung to the air. Not a sound could be heard in the dark folds of the night. For a moment, she felt it safer to return to her husband's room, but in her heart, she knew she wouldn't be safe there either.

From the shadows before her, a man dressed in black approached, his sword drawn and ready to strike. With a squeak, Zisca tried her best to swing at him, but her sword had been too heavy for her. The man batted it out of her grasp without much force. He grabbed her by her arm and dragged her down the stairs to the first floor without a word. The queen screamed the entire way, trying to release herself from his grip.

From a balcony on the other side of the palace, Roland and Carter watched the Ponierian guard drag the queen away. In response to her irritating struggles, the Ponierian picked her up and strung her across his shoulder. "Roland, what do we do? That man took my mother!"

"Follow him," came the advisor's cold response. "It would seem your fiancé has sided with Cadoc."

"She wouldn't do that," Carter's voice was one of heartbreak. "She loves me."

"Then how did your father gain her guards?"

"I don't know," the prince tried to think of another possibility. "What should we do?"

"We get the queen back," Roland said, "but we need to be careful. Once we find the king, I'll act as a distraction so you can free your mother."

"What of My Lady?"

"We do not know where her allegiance lies. Leave her alone for now."

"But!"

"I will not let you get yourself killed over some woman," Roland spat. "I have already put you in enough danger, Carter. I couldn't forgive myself if you were hurt. So, do as I say, and try not to draw attention to yourself."

The prince looked at him defiantly but yielded. Seeing Carter would do as he asked, the advisor told him his plan to save the queen mother.

Zisca screamed and screamed until she was plopped in front of Cadoc. The man who carried her went past the king to the side of the woman her son was set to marry. The two spoke to one another in their tongue. Thankfully, Zisca had learned the language. *"Why did you treat her so harshly?"*

"She thought me the enemy. She kept fighting me, so I had to behave in such a way to bring her here safely."

"Leave us," Cadoc stopped their conversation. With bows, the two departed from the room Zisca was in. The queen shivered as her fears became reality. "Get up."

"Cadoc," the queen pleaded quietly, "please."

"I said get up, woman," the king snarled. Zisca had no choice but to get to her feet. Cadoc's hand wrapped around her throat, squeezing the life from her. "Did you think I would not find you? That I would not repay your betrayal?"

The queen struggled to breathe, but found it impossible. To her aid came a knock at the door. "My liege!"

"What is it, Dorian?" Cadoc growled, never releasing his wife.

"It's Sir Roland! He was spotted dashing through the palace gardens!"

Cadoc dropped Zisca, the queen coughing to regain air. Cadoc opened the door for the collector, who looked down at the broken woman. His king paid little mind as he said, "I will take these Ponierians and end him. You stay here."

"What would you have me do here, Your Highness?" the collector grinned.

The king smiled in return, whispering. "Tend to Zisca. I will lock Carter's fiancé in the room next door. Do not let anyone find her. She will be good to use as a hostage if need be."

"I would be happy to do these things for you, my king," Dorian chuckled as he drew a dagger from his side.

"Please me, and I shall make you my next advisor."

Dorian bowed as he replied. "I thank you for this opportunity."

The king set out on his mission, taking with him all of the Ponierian guards at the woman's disposal. Before he went to the gardens, he pulled his son's bride aside. "There has been a sighting of Roland. I am going there now, but I want you to remain here where it is safe. I will lock you and Zisca in these two rooms, so the advisor cannot harm you."

"I don't want to be locked away! I want to help," the woman replied.

"You have been a great help," Cadoc said, placing his hands on her shoulders, "but I cannot see you hurt, for Carter's sake."

She looked sorrowfully to the king before pulling him into a quick hug. "Be careful!"

"I will," the king replied. What a foolish girl!

Pulling away, she smiled as she stepped into her prison cell. "Find Carter for me."

"I promise you, I'll do my best," the king smiled. After locking her door, King Cadoc made his way to the palace gardens. Frank stood at his righthand side, the rest of the Ponierians behind him.

After disposing of the queen, Dorian moved on to his next task of standing guard outside of the foreign woman's room to ensure that no one came near her door. The longer he was made to watch over the woman he hated, the more he wanted to hurt her himself. Soon, his hatred overcame him. Filled with adrenaline from the murder he had just committed, he made a hasty decision. Using the key Cadoc had given him, Dorian went inside after Carter's fiancé.

Once Dorian was out of sight, Carter took the opportunity to rescue his mother. Sprinting to her door, he looked in to find her in the darkness of the room. He whispered. "Mother!"

Coming closer, he saw blood trailing from her body. The truth set in as he saw her throat sliced open. His father had murdered her for something he had done. The prince began to weep as he dropped to his knees and lifted her body into his arms. "No! Mother, no. Please."

Carter heard a woman scream from the room beside him. He knew who was in there. His fiancé. The sound of breaking furniture seemed unending, as did her cries for help. He looked down at the face of his beloved mother. Roland had told him not to help his bride, but he couldn't let her end up like his mother! He wouldn't!

Sword in hand, he quietly entered the room his fiancé was in. Before him, he saw Dorian holding the veil he had ripped from her face. Placing the dagger at her neck, the greasy man chuckled. "My, what a pretty little thing you are."

"Get off of me!" she shrieked as she pushed him, tears in her eyes.

"Don't worry, doll," The greasy man smiled as he pressed the knife-edge slightly harder into her neck, a single drop of blood trailing down his blade. "I'll take good care of you!"

"How dare you!" Carter yelled as he slammed the butt of his sword against the collector's head. The man fell to the floor instantly.

The prince's fiancé shivered in fear where she stood. Carter scooped her up as she didn't look like she could walk on her own.

He raced with her hiding her face under his chin. He could feel her tears streaming down her face. His father would pay for this!

Feeling like they were a safe distance from harm, Carter put her back on her feet. The prince inspected his betrothed to see if she was hurt. Needing comfort, the woman fell into her fiancé as she wrapped her arms tightly around him. Not once did her shivering stop as she said. "I'm glad you're okay."

Carter smiled to himself. She had undergone such a tragedy and still cared about his wellbeing. The prince held his fiancé tightly as he kissed the top of her head. "I'm glad you're okay too."

"What do we do now?" she asked.

Carter lifted her from his chest, looking her in the eyes. "I want you to go home."

"What?" She seemed like she would cry even harder at the prospect.

"It isn't safe here. I want you and your sister to return home until I get things under control. I will come for you once it is safe." Carter moved a piece of her hair from her face. "I can't have you getting hurt."

"I can't leave you here," she said with tears streaming down her face.

The prince stroked her cheek gently with his thumb, wiping the tears away. "Please, do it for me."

She held to his arms tightly. "Promise me that you will come for me."

"I promise," Carter smiled. "Now go."

Before she left, his fiancé placed her lips on his. While he held her there, Carter forgot all that was going wrong in his life. He had never been happier than at that moment. When they parted, she whispered to him softly. "I love you, Carter of Remette."

She left before he could reply, racing towards the stables to her sister. Carter watched her go. At least he had saved one of the ones he loved. Clutching to his sword, he turned the way his father had went. The king would die for the crimes he committed that day!

Reaching the stables, the woman came upon a frightening scene. Though more guards had gone to protect her sister, they seemed to be failing at doing so. Her guards fought against one of Roland's men. The guard, Jasper, had come after Adelina. Her hand flew to her lips. She needed a mask! To her left lay the corpse of one of her men. She tore the covering from across his pale, dead face.

"I'm sorry," she whispered to the corpse as she placed his mask on her face. Next, she took his weapon from his hands. She had to get Miriam and Adelina away from that man! Racing to their aid, she passed through the blockade her men had created. *"Adelina! What are you waiting for? Get in the carriage!"*

"My Lady," the maid said with tears in her eyes. *"I do not want to go."*

"What?"

"I am so sorry," Adelina bowed her head. Before them, a Ponierian guard cut Jasper's arm, making him drop his weapon. The man cried out in pain as he fell to his knees, his arm bleeding profusely.

He cared not about the pain as he looked at his fair maiden. "Addie!"

The maid began to weep as swords were placed at Jasper's neck. After securing him, the guards awaited orders for his disposal from their mistress. Miriam had crawled into the carriage and was curled into a trembling ball in the corner as she cried quietly to herself. The woman looked at Adelina. The maid was at a loss for breath over the man that had come for her.

The woman could not help but think of Carter as she looked at Adelina's face. Was this fear not her own but minutes ago? The fear of losing the one she loved? Gripping Adelina by her shoulders, she asked. *"Do you love him?"*

Adelina looked at Jasper, who had started to lose color. *"I know I only just met him, but I think I might."*

The woman motioned to the guards to lower their weapons. *"Then you may stay with him. As for Miriam and I, we are leaving."*

"Thank you!" Adelina smiled as she hugged her mistress. The guards climbed onto the carriage, preparing to get out of the wretched country of Remette.

"Adelina," the woman's voice went cold, *"should anything happen to Carter, you will tell no one who I am."*

"I won't! I would never!"

"I believe you are my friend," Carter's fiancé said as she climbed into her carriage, *"but I have seen too many friends betray one another in this place for that to give me confidence in you. I can only hope you remember the kindness I have shown, but keep in mind that if you dare betray me, I will repay what is due you."*

"I understand," the maid gulped. What had happened to her mistress to make her this wrathful? With that, the carriage set off. The maiden turned to Jasper, helping him with his wounded arm.

"Addie," he said softly with a smile. "You chose me."

"I did," the maiden replied, ripping the hem of her dress to make bandages for his cut.

The man pulled her into his embrace. "I'm glad you did. I don't know what I would do if I lost you. I love you, Addie!"

Her cheeks reddened as she smiled. "I love you too."

All the while, Roland waited near the palace gardens. It was a beautiful place. He grimaced at the Ponierian soldiers who destroyed its tranquility in their approach. He had hoped some of his men would come to his aid, but many must have perished in the fights, others taken prisoner. It seemed he would fight this battle alone.

What were there, a little over a hundred Ponierians? Some with swords, others with spears. The advisor looked on the perches above, they had archers too. Their strategic layout was different from when he fought them in the war. These were Cadoc's positionings. Perhaps this would be a good challenge. A change in strategy was always nice.

Roland turned slowly in his hiding place so no one would see him there. He had made a small fortress within the garden's center arrangement. The arrangement itself had been built with three parts. The base was made of elegant dancing statues within beautiful arrays of flowers. The tower consisted of flowers that draped over stone pillars, making a thick wall of brush. On top sat a stone statue of King Cadoc himself. It was in the middle, where Roland had set up his defenses.

He used tables from the gardener's warehouse to build a fortress behind the wall of flowers. Where there were not pillars, he laid up the tables for protection. The wooden tops working as shields from the king. He could only hope he hadn't messed up the flower arrangement too much with his work; otherwise, his surprise attack would not pan out so well.

Quietly picking up a bow he had taken from a dead guard, he aimed at the first of the archers. One by one, he took them down. They did not make a sound as he shot them through their necks, clipping both their airways and spinal cords. Next, he moved on to the men with shields at the front of the line. It would be easier to kill the rest once he had destroyed those with the best defenses. It was as the first of the shielded men dropped silently to the ground that the guards realized they did not need to search for Roland any longer. Still, they did not know where exactly the arrow had come from.

After the second man dropped dead before them, the squadron huddled together behind their partners' shields. Roland waited patiently until an unfortunate man peeked above the top of his shield. The arrow pierced through his helmet, embedding into his skull as he slumped to the side. The advisor worked quickly, releasing as many arrows as he could to kill the men who had been behind him before they could regroup, but he was in too small of a space. Cramped in his fortress, he only killed four more before they were once again hidden from him.

Cadoc's voice rang out in Ponierian, but Roland didn't know what he had said. It did not take long to figure it out. The men fanned around him in a protective circle. It was one man against a platoon! They were trapping him. He might kill some, but not all if he was caught there.

Roland gritted his teeth as he was left with no choice. Which side did he want to attack? The left had a better escape route. The advisor put the bow and arrows across his back in case he got into another good position later on. Picking up a stolen shield and his trusty sword, he burst out the left side of his fortress. The guards rushed forward now that he was in the open. Knocking down a shielded man, Roland swung his sword to behead the next. Turning his blade quickly, he slashed across the back of another.

The advisor ran for his life, leading the guards as far away from his prince as he could. He dashed through the palace kitchens, only to stop as he came up with an evil idea. Roland could hear the Ponierians chasing after him. Closer and closer they came.

The advisor made a small cut on his hand, dripping a bloody trail from the kitchen to an outside storage building. There were many rooms in the place, but he made his way to the farthest one. After his trap was set, Sir Roland wrapped his wound in a cloth and hid behind one of the rows of barrels nearest to the door. It seemed the footsteps would never end as his enemies approached. Many came into the room he was in, perhaps half of those in the small army. The others went across the hall when their partners could not find him.

Seeing his opportunity, the advisor leapt from his hiding place, swinging his sword against the wood that held up an elevated barrel. As the first fell from its place, it knocked over most of the others in the room. The Ponierians tried to come after him but were stopped by the cascade of heavy barrels. Across the hall, their fellow knights raced to kill him. Roland dropped his shield to pick up a torch.

He tossed it into the room of broken oil barrels, causing half of the troops to become trapped in flames. As they screamed in peril, the advisor hurriedly picked up his shield and raced away. Becoming too preoccupied with trying to save their friends, the Ponierian force let him escape from view.

Reaching the only exit, Roland locked the entire army inside. It did not take long before the whole building was in flames. All who had been within it perished, all but the advisor. Roland coughed as he re-entered the palace, his skin stained with smoke from his recent bloodbath.

"You're still alive?" Cadoc asked him.

Before the advisor were four more Ponierian guards. Behind them stood Frank and King Cadoc. It seemed Roland had finally met the so-called assassins. Frank must have been the fifth and final member. The advisor began to laugh. It had been so long since he had felt such adrenaline! "Did you expect me to die when you sent only one hundred men after me? Ponierians no less!"

His enemies tensed up. They might not understand what he was saying, but they knew it was about them. The king grew fearful. It hadn't yet been a quarter of an hour since he sent those men after his advisor. Had he really killed so many so quickly? Roland took his stance, stating calmly. "Shall we continue?"

"I will fight you," Frank said in a deep growl beside Cadoc, "for the honor of my brothers whom you have slain."

"There will be nothing honorable about you dying with them," Roland spat, his rage against Ponierians returning to him. The Lord of Morer took up his beastly form as he prepared to strike down his enemy. "Your people are more foolish than I remember, if you are willing to work with a man like Cadoc."

"He is your king," Frank rebuked as he passed by his four associates.

"If you attack me, I will kill you," the advisor warned.

"Like you did my men? What? Are you pretending that such evil was no more than self-defense?"

"Your judgment is clouded with your hatred for me." Roland used his shield to cover himself up to his eyes. "Your words to me are empty and without meaning."

"Perhaps actions will be more understandable," the giant snarled as he swung his blade towards Roland. The advisor caught it with his shield to test the power of his opponent's swing. It almost ripped the shield from his hand! He was a strong one indeed, but slow. What a shame, the advisor thought, such a waste of talent.

Roland lunged forward in an instant, slicing the babysitter across his belly. Frank dropped to his knees as he bled out. The advisor paid little mind as he passed by to his next victim, lobbing off the man's head. The remaining three attacked Roland in unison, hoping to win together. As they swung their swords against him, the Lord of Morer fell to his knees, shielding himself.

The action was too fast for the men to stop their blades as they traveled through the air where his chest had once been. They became impaled by their partner's swords. Before they had time to recollect their thoughts, Roland pushed up on the crisscrossed pattern of weapons above him with his shield. This forced the swords in the men to do more damage, driving the blades from their stomachs to their chests. Using the extra room he had created for himself, he ran his trusty weapon across the enemies' knees. Those who were already suffering screamed in agony as they lost control of their legs.

Roland calmly got back onto his feet. The Ponierians were no longer a threat to him. Without another glance, he brushed past them in chase of the king, who had run away after Frank was defeated. This time, Roland would not let him get away. This time, he would feel no regret as he took the tyrant's head.

It was not Roland who found the king, but Prince Carter. As the king fled, he heard the eerie call of death. "Hello, Father."

Never in his life had Cadoc heard so much venom in his son's voice. The words echoed in the darkness of the halls. He could not tell where they came from. Clutching his sword for comfort, the king shouted out. "Where are you?"

"I'm right here," came a whisper in his ear. The king swung around to face his son, but the corridor looked empty. "You have always said I was a disappointment, Father. It seems to me; I am better than you."

"Don't do anything foolish, boy," the king snarled. "I have your woman! If you kill me, she will die!"

The hall remained quiet. Soaking in the silence, the king's heart pounded in his chest. He couldn't let his son see his fear. He needed to bait him to come into the light. Chuckling, Cadoc continued. "Perhaps once I have dealt with you and Roland, I will take her for myself. With your woman, I will make myself a new heir. I can only hope this one will turn out better than my last!"

"You disgust me," Carter growled from the shadows, "but what you say is meaningless. I have already sent My Lady away. I overcame your collector and took her from him."

The king snarled. That worthless collector had failed him, just like the Ponierians! You could lean on no one but yourself! Trying again to bait the boy, he brought up the death of his mother. "Then, you have seen Zisca?"

"I have," came a cold reply. A searing pain erupted in the king's chest. Cadoc looked down to find a blade running through his torso. He had but moments. Pulling the blade from his father's body, Carter growled. "That was for her."

With the last of the king's strength, he swung around. His sword sliced across the young prince's chest at an angle. Gasping for air, Cadoc sank to the ground. Slowly, he drew one breath after another. Carter slumped onto the floor beside him. The two enemies looked at one another in silence as their life left them, their blood mixing on the floor.

Carter felt repentant as he noticed they were the same down to their lifeblood. He had turned out as evil as his father. In his heart, he felt he deserved to die for what he had done. Still, he couldn't help but think of the love he would never attain. He should have been better, for her.

"Carter," came the advisor's quiet voice, only to turn into a shout as he ran to the prince's side. "Carter!"

The wound was beyond repair. There was no hope left for his best friend. Behind Roland, Cadoc began to chuckle through bloodied teeth. "At least I can die happily, having killed the person you love most in this world."

Without another word, Roland spun to his feet and struck off the king's head. It rolled away with a look of shock spread across it. Tossing his sword down in sorrow, the advisor once again kneeled beside his dearest friend.

"I'm so sorry, my king," he apologized mournfully. "I have failed you."

"Nonsense," Carter tried to chuckle, coughing up blood in his effort.

"Careful now, just be still," Roland said softly.

"We won. Didn't we?"

"Of course. Remette is yours, as I have always wished it to be."

"Then, you didn't fail. I failed." Carter placed his hand on Roland's arm. "But that's okay. Now the people are free, thanks to you!"

"Carter, please," Roland whispered, barely able to speak.

"I have one last job for you. I have lived a full life in the time that I've been given." Carter coughed in his struggle to finish the words. "I have gained something more precious than any kingdom. Love. The love of a woman so perfect, even her lips to me are a dream. So, you promise me, Advisor. Promise me that in the days to come, you will find love as I have."

"I promise," Roland said quietly.

"Then I am at peace, having done all I ever wished to do." Carter's grip on Roland's arm tightened, only to release itself completely. Roland became empty as he looked down at his friend. The young prince's eyes had become dull, but his smile remained as true as ever.

A New Realm Emerges

After Adelina did her best to repair his arm, Jasper traveled through the bloodied halls of the palace. He had left her in the stables, promising to return when it was safe. Most of his ruffians had died during the fight. Many of Cadoc's army had remained locked in the rooms they were placed in, the rest returning to the barracks hoping that Roland would not kill them.

Jasper traveled to the second floor and entered the king's room, but Zisca was no longer there. In a panic, he raced through the halls in search of her. His heart sunk when he found her body. Jasper felt it was because he left her that the poor queen mother had lost her life. Scooping up the body sorrowfully, he continued on his way. He would tell Carter and Roland of the things he had done and hope they could forgive him.

He didn't have to go far before he found the other two royals, their blood spreading across the hallway. Between their bodies sat the advisor. Though he was the only one of the three to survive, he looked worse than the other two. Blood covered him from head to toe. Smoke stuck to his skin, showing that he had been the cause of the great fire to the west of the courtyard. He stared down at his prince with a blank look. With a gulp, Jasper called to him. "Roland?"

The man gave no reply. Jasper joined his friend, laying the queen down beside the rest of the royal family. Roland glanced at the queen, only to close his eyes as he slowly turned back to Carter. Jasper tried to console him. "I'm sorry, my friend."

The advisor raised a bloodied hand to silence him, but there was still much to do. "Roland, what are we to do now? There are still many of the king's guards downstairs. We don't know where the rest of our men are. This fight is not over yet."

"Then let's finish it." The advisor's words were hollow as he lifted the prince's body. "Wait here."

Roland carried his friend to his room, where he had attended to the prince's needs throughout his life. Laying Carter on his bed, the advisor looked upon the corpse sadly. "I will free your people, my king. If I could do nothing else for you, I will not fail at this."

With that, he left. Returning to Jasper, he took up both his sword and Cadoc's head. The pair trudged to where the cowards of Cadoc's army had hidden. Raising the dead king's head by its hair, Roland shouted at them. "Your king is dead, your allegiance nullified. Is there any man foolish enough to stand against the new order? Tell me, which of you wants to die today?"

All men lowered their weapons in submission to him. From behind the masses, rung out the voices of Asher, Wilton, and Gad. "Roland!"

After releasing those three, Roland used the key Wilton had kept to unlock the doors of the imprisoned guards one at a time. The advisor re-stated his question to each room of men. None in the palace opposed him. Near the end of the hall, the rooms were all empty. Those had been the rooms of the Ponierian guards. Martin banged on his door as he shouted. "Lemme out!"

Roland released him, Martin swinging his door open in glee. "So, we won, did we?"

"Yes," Roland said, handing him the key. "You may free the guests in the morning. Clean up the corpses before then. Place those of importance in the great hall. Pile the rest onto carts. They can be buried tomorrow."

The advisor handed the king's head to Jasper as he walked quietly back to Carter's side. He neither said nor did anything else but look at his friend's face. The longer he looked, the less he could believe the truth before him. Carter was far too pure to have an ending such as that. Even as the sun rose, his gaze never lifted and his sorrow never left him.

Martin did as he had been instructed. It took the entire night to carry out the bodies that had been left inside the palace. The fallen traitors, such as Dan, were placed in the great hall, so they could be mourned when the conundrum was over. The bodies of the king and his wife were also placed there, for Roland's sake. All of the fallen palace guards were thrown onto a cart until they could be laid out for their families to collect them in the courtyard.

Bodies of Ponierian soldiers littered the palace. The building Roland had set aflame was still burning in the morning, so they left it alone. The once beautiful palace gardens looked now like a place of horror. Their beauty and tranquility trampled down, leaving only blood and death.

As the morning brought an end to their trials, Martin went from room to room, allowing the guests to leave. The nobles shrieked at the aftermath of the battle. Even without bodies, there were stains of blood and smoke all around the palace. Everything that could have been broken, was. Not knowing what would become of them, all those who had come to witness a wedding instead waited in the courtyard for understanding. Seeing these things, Jasper went to the advisor.

"Roland," Jasper called quietly. The advisor raised his head so slightly you could hardly see the movement. "Roland, the people have gathered in the courtyard. They await a decree."

"And what decree shall I give them?" came a cold reply.

"I don't know," Jasper said softly.

"They are free people now. Let them make their own decrees," growled the advisor over his shoulder.

"Roland, please. They need guidance and you are the best person to give it to them. It is what Carter would have wanted."

"What he wanted?" The advisor flipped his chair from the speed in which he rose to his feet. Jasper cringed in fear. "Do you know what he would have wanted?"

Roland raised a bloody finger in the air. "Can you hear that?"

Nothing but silence filled the air, making Jasper even more terrified. It was a deathly silence. "I hear nothing."

"Exactly. He would have wanted wedding bells ringing from the time he awoke, to the time he fell asleep. He would have wanted to have his smiling mother helping him prepare for his wedding. He would have wanted to marry a woman fit to be queen! He would have wanted love!" Roland flipped over a table out of anger. "And now! Now, he never gets anything! What was the point?"

"The point was to save the people. They were the only ones he cared about. He cared more for their happiness than his own," Jasper said carefully. "And now, those people are lost and afraid. So, do what he can't do. Go help them."

"You're right," Roland relinquished. He turned to his friend on the bed. "I'll go make this right, just the way you wanted."

With that, he walked from the room straight to the courtyard without hesitation. As he approached, people began to mutter under their breath, taken aback by his bloody appearance. When he spoke, they became silent.

"My dear people. You may be wondering what happened last night. Why the royals are not here to greet you. I have the answer. Last night, under the direction of Prince Carter, we men you see before you overthrew the tyrant, King Cadoc." The people of the crowd looked at one another, their muttering starting again.

"Queen Zisca stood with her son during these events. With his compassionate heart, our beloved prince was willing to let his father live. However, the king did not show such compassion as he struck down both his son and the queen." Gasps came from the onlookers. Roland held up his hand to quiet them as he finished.

"The royal family has perished, our prince giving his life for your freedom from tyranny. So now I ask you, what will you do? It is time for a new order to arise. Will we be a republic? A democracy? One thing is for certain; we must all come together before another nation tries to overpower us. I'll leave you to think about it."

Roland felt good as he turned his back on the people. Just as Carter had wanted, they were free. They could make their own choices. He would not have to give any more decrees. He would go into the world and fulfill the promise he had made. He would find love, as Carter had told him to do. It was as he walked away that Roland's ideas were crushed.

"All hail King Roland! All hail King Roland! All hail King Roland!" A chant formed from behind him.

He looked at Jasper, who seemed just as shocked as he was. Finding no comfort there, he reeled around, saying to them. "The place of the king has fallen! Set up a new government by your own specifications."

The people fell to the ground before him. One from among them called out. "You who delivered us from the tyrant Cadoc! You are the new government we wish to have over us. All hail the new and glorious king!" The chanting started again. Roland backed into the palace with his hands up, trying to get them to stop. Inside, he turned to his group of men.

"What do I do?" He looked at them desperately. "I never wanted this! This was . . . it was Carter's! Not mine! I can't take this from him! I won't!"

His men looked at one another, then again to him. In unison, they placed their fists over their hearts and sunk to one knee. Adelina, who was now present, fell to the floor before him. Jasper said with pride, "They are right, my friend. No man in this world is more suited to this task than you. You will, indeed, be a great and mighty king."

Roland was shocked as his own men took on the chant from outside. Not knowing what to do, he ran back to the side of his friend. He had always known which was the right path.

"Carter?" he asked the sleeping prince. "What should I do? I don't want to betray you. I don't want this treasure of yours. But these people can't think of any other way to live their lives, except under subjugation. It's foolish, really."

He looked at the young man's pale face. A tear ran down Roland's cheek as he said softly. "Why couldn't I save you? If you were here, this whole mess wouldn't be happening. What is it you would have me do?"

You didn't fail. I failed. But that's okay. Now the people are free, thanks to you!

Roland remembered what the prince had told him before he died. He had freed the people, but now it was time to keep them free. To keep them safe from harm. Whether he did that with a sword as he had before or with a crown mattered not. He would keep his people free.

With sureness in his goals, Roland left Carter's bedside. He walked into the great hall where the other two royals were being kept. From the king's severed head, he picked up the crown of his predecessor. With the blood of his victim still on it, he placed it upon his brow. Bearing his crown, the new king stood before the masses gathered in the courtyard.

"I, King Roland of Remette, hereby declare this land free of the wrath of our treacherous former king!" The people cheered at his words. And with the statements given that day, a new era dawned for Remette.

Throughout the land, their praises rang like a song. "All hail King Roland!"

Coming Soon!

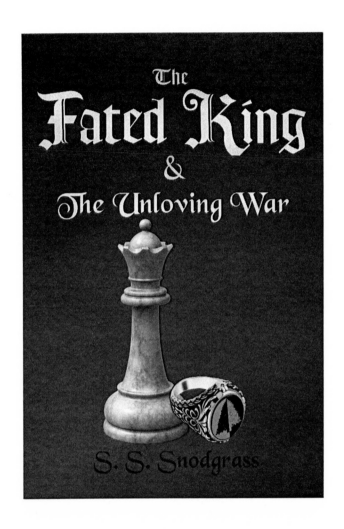

Keep up to date on all S. S. Snodgrass news by visiting www.sssnodgrass.com today! Subscribe to receive updates on all writings and releases